Amazon reviews of an earlier version of
Our Grand Adventure!
4.4 out of 5 stars!!!

"The writing is moving, engaging, and I found it to be immersive with every page. Corbett is wonderful with his narrative skills, the details he conveys throughout the text with just the needed information and not too much nor too little."

"Author Tom Corbett... depicts the past with wit, charm, and insight, weaving humor with gravitas in his unique manner."

"This book is amazing! Tom Corbett write his recollections in such a humorous and sarcastic way that it was impossible to put down."

"Great Book!! This book is full of history lessons... Corbett references the past with wonderful prose and helps the reader to understand how things were."

"The book tells the story of the author's first-hand experience of joining the peace Corps at its inception. Never thought learning about this period could be so funny, entertaining, and insightful. Truly a good read."

"(The book)... does not read like an autobiography/ memoir/ reflective/ history piece, though it has all these elements. This can be credited to Corbett's irreverent style which makes it a page turner."

"The volunteers who left home out of a to do good came home with experiences that you can't buy at a store or glean from a textbook. Tom Corbett's ability to see the humor in humorless circumstances touches off universal questions about the meaning and mystery of life."

"Anyone reading this book will come away with an understanding of the motivations, the trials, and the total transformative impact this early

Peace Corps experiment had on an idealistic group of 1960's college graduates. I thoroughly enjoyed the book."

**Amazon reader reviews of an earlier version of
A Clueless Rebel:
4.9 out of 5 stars!!!**

"Another winner from Tom Corbett. I've read several of Tom Corbett's books and I've enjoyed them all. He's a very talented author and storyteller."

"Tom Corbett is a gifted story-teller. He pours raw honesty and cleverness into his writing that both amuses and inspires you."

"An insightful and hilarious coming of age memoir set mostly in the decades after World War II."

This book has a close connection to the author's earlier work, Confessions of a Wayward Academic, where he gives insights into policymaking and welfare reform."

"Corbett does an excellent job weaving his tale in a way that both inspires and amuses, heartens and saddens."

"I found myself on an emotional roller coaster throughout the story."

"Reflective, insightful, and intimate. Experience nostalgia even if you are 46 years younger than Corbett, like me!"

"Corbett is a great storyteller who knows how to connect memories and ideas to find meaning and to make his ordinary life entertaining, relatable, and amusing."

"Never a dull moment and I found it hard to put down."

"Reading Confessions of a Clueless Rebel makes me feel I'm at a coffee shop with the author, swapping stories about life."

Reviews of the author's other works:

"Palpable Passions delivers a compelling story arc infused with historical fact that should appeal to readers…"

—Blue Ink Reviews

The book…feels like a screenplay; its dialogue is abundant and punchy, its landscapes well defined, and its characters have significant bonds. Palpable Passions uses bright, earnest characters to show that a microcosm can be as complicated as the big picture."

—Foreword Book Review

"Corbett has created a captivating novel. The book title perfectly describes the fragile thread that spirals around each individual…to create an enthralling story that anyone will love to read."

—U.S. Review of Books

"This is . . . a fully rendered tale. Those interested in the complexity of relationships…will find some rewards here."

—Blue Ink Reviews

"…Tenuous Tendrils, by Tom Corbett, is a compelling journey from exile to redemption. Like its characters, the book is quite clever and features an abundance of humor. Many heavy scenes are punctuated by conversations about the futility of war and the humanitarian failings of government also feature omniscient narrative wit that keeps the

text from being bogged down by sentiment and allows the characters' personalities to shine."

—Clarion Review

"Corbett obviously loves to tell stories. Tenuous Tendrils, by Tom Corbett, is a captivating read with engaging vignettes which paint a picture of a retired professor, his life, and the connections which bind everything together."

—Pacific Review of Books

Amazon Readers' Reviews of author's other fictional works.

"I loved how the author told each family's story back and forth chapter by chapter. The characters are so well-formed, and the accurate descriptions of life in Afghanistan really drew me in. Finished book in one day. I didn't want to put it down."

"This is truly a great read that will leave you feeling empowered and determined to make a difference in your own way HIGHLY RECOMMEND that everyone pick this up."

"It's easy to understand why this book comes so highly recommended. Palpable Passions is a powerful book. I highly recommend it to anyone who loves literary fiction."

"A penetrating look into the human soul and the fragility of relationships."

"This book was incredibly personal on so many levels. Overall, I found this to be an extremely touching and educational read."

"I personally loved this book. It was refreshing and thoughtful."

"The overall story is incredibly genuine, realistic to the time limits it covers and thoughtful. Each time I put down the book I found it moderately difficult since I wanted to know what would happen next."

"Excellent characterization and historical facts make this a compelling story as hope overcomes despair."

"Tom Corbett's "Palpable Passions" is the perfect combination of fact and fiction as it educates its readers about current events in our world today."

"In the end, we learn that no matter what this world throws in our way, our passion is what drives us to live our lives to the fullest potential. This book fascinates me because of how the author uniquely ties everything together at the end."

Selected Praise for the Author's Non-Fiction Works

"A wonderful first-person account of the ground-level of welfare reform in recent times. It was a momentous time for reform of the nation's welfare system and Corbett was in the thick of it. He relates what happened with a wry, self-deprecating of humor, but there are serious lessons to be learned…"

—Robert Moffitt, Ph.D.,
Professor of Economics, Johns Hopkins U.

"The subjects author tom Corbett tackled were both relevant and deep. [He]…is a brilliant writer [and] Confessions of an Accidental Scholar is an original book. [He]… blended the academic, professional, and personal perspectives when writing about the subject matter."

—Pacific Book Review

"Tom Corbett exposes the reader to the raw reality of confronting our most difficult social issues in this engaging, compelling, yet witty book. He brings the doing of policy alive, going beyond the dry numbers to reveal the human side of the equation."

—Dennis Dresang, Ph.D.,
Professor of Public Policy, U. of Wisconsin

"...throughout the memoir, Corbett's prose remains engaging, consistently mixing insight with the familiar jokes that one would from a close friend. A thoughtful memoir about life and politics told in a (n}... endearing style."

—Kirkus Review

"Corbett's stories from the front lines of policymaking, like All Quiet on the Western Front or The Things They Tarried, provide great insight into the way the world actually works, not what the generals or policy planners think is happening."

—Matt Stagner, Ph.D. Policy Fellow
Mathematica Policy Research, Inc.

"...the emergence of Corbett's humanistic world view...gives Ouch, Now I Remember intellectual gravitas. Corbett imparts an enormous amount of wisdom and humanity."

—Clarion Review

"...I found "Ouch. Now I Remember" to be a witty yet edifying read, riddled with some funny moments... with many of them making me laugh out loud. I enjoy his writing style, it was comforting yet

candid, like listening to a respected relative recount their own life with unabashed honesty."

—Pacific Book Review

"*The Boat Captain's Conundrum* is a winning performance."

—Forward Clarion Book Review

"*Corbett takes a topic often shrouded in numbers and dense writing and turns it into an intellectual, yet conversational memoir.*"

—U.S. Review of Books

"*Corbett's reflections, woven together with great insight and humor, transform public policy from a class that is boring and mundane to a career that can be engaging and germane.*"

—Karen Bogenschneider Ph.D.,
U. of Wisconsin

"*I enjoy his writing style, it was comfortable yet candid, like listening to a respected relative recount their own life with unabashed honesty.*"

—Pacific Book Review

"*If you truly want to understand how public policy works, read this book. Corbett's descriptions about how laws and programs are developed gives readers a real take away—genuine insight into the discipline of public policy.*"

—Mary Fairchild, Senior Fellow National
Conference of State Legislatures

Our Grand Adventure: The Trials and Triumphs of India–44
Copyright © 2022 by Tom Corbett. All rights reserved.

Additional Copies:

www.amazon.com
www.barnesandnoble.com

Published in the United States of America

ISBN softcover:
ISBN hardcover:

OUR GRAND ADVENTURE

The trials and triumphs of India-44

TOM CORBETT

*"Ask not what your country can do for you, ask
what you can do for your county."*
—John F. Kennedy

*"Failure is instructive. The person who really thinks learns
quite as much from his failures as from his successes."*
—John Dewey

"One child, one teacher, one pen, and one book can change the world."
—Mahala Yousafzai

*"Everyone has a creative potential and from the moment you can
express this creative potential, you can start changing the word."*
—Paul Coehlo

*"The greatest threat to our planet is the belief
that someone else will save it."*
—Robert Swan

Other Books By The Author

A Clueless Rebel (Revised edition, Papertown Press, 2022)[1]

Choices (Revised Edition, Papertown Press, 2022)[2]

A Wayward Academic: Reflections from the policy trenches (Revised edition, Papertown Press, 2021)[3]

Evidence-Based Policymaking: Envisioning a New Era of Theory, Research and Practice (2nd Ed.) with Karen Bogenschneider (Routledge Press, 2021)

Felicitous Fates (Papertown Press, 2021)

Confessions of an Accidental Scholar (Revised edition, Papertown Press, 2021)[4]

Ordinary Obsessions (Papertown Press, 2019)[5]

Palpable Passions (Papertown Press, 2017)

Return to the Other Side of the World with Mary Jo Clark, Michael Simmonds, Katherine Sohn, and Hayward Turrentine (Strategic Press, 2013)

---

1 Originally published as *Tenuous Tendrils* in 2016 by Xlibris Press.

2 Originally published as *Ouch, Now I Remember* in 2015 by Xlibris Press and rereleased under the current title by Hancock Press in 2018.

3 Last released as *Casual Choices* in 2019 by Hancock press.

4 Originally published as *Browsing through My Candy Store* in 2014 by Xlibris Press and rereleased under the current title by Hancock Press in 2018.

5 Originally published as *The Boat Captain's Conundrum* in 2016 by Xlibris Press and rereleased under the current title by Hancock press in 2018.

The Other Side of the World with Mary Jo Cark, Michael Simonds, and Hayward Turrentine (Strategic Press, 2011)

Evidence Based Policymaking: Insights from Policy-Minded Researchers and Research- Minded Policymakers. With Karen Bogenschneider (Routledge Press, 2010)

Policy into Action. With Mary Clare Lennon (Urban Institute Press, 2003)

DEDICATION

This work is dedicated to all those intrepid volunteers who bravely, if sometimes naively, traversed the world to do good in the early days of the Peace Corps experiment. While it is not clear how much good we all did, we gave it our best shot. A special thought goes out to Haywood "Harry" Turrentine. He was among the best of us and passed too soon. At the very least, we volunteers from India-44 left many of those whom we tried to serve with a hearty laugh or two as we set about to save mankind despite being clueless as to what we were doing. Never forget, though, that our hearts were in the right place.

I have many to thank for either inspiring this work or bringing it to fruition. First among these miscreants is Jennifer L. Noyes, who now serves as a Vice Provost at the University of Wisconsin-Madison. She encouraged this project after reading the first two edited volumes produced by the Peace Corps (PC) volunteers of India-44, an ill-starred group that trooped off to serve on the sub-continent way back in pre-historic days of the 1960s.

A second miscreant is Peter Adler of India-40, a group that already was in India when we arrived. He had the good sense to marry Carolyn Watanabe… a wonderful young woman from my Peace Corps group (India-44). Peter, a superb writer himself, expressed the strongest support for this project in anticipation of putting together a similar volume for his own group of hapless volunteers (India-40). These self-described mutts might rank as the one collection of PC volunteers who proved even more inept than us, assuming that is possible. That opinion is not shared by Peter in case you are wondering.

Finally, a word of thanks to my virtual friends on Facebook who have encouraged my literary efforts and thus motivated me to continue putting my thoughts to paper, or the computer at least. I thought Facebook rather a joke when I joined over a decade ago. Over time, however, I somehow accrued about 30,000 friends and followers before the Facebook Gestapo permanently disabled my account last year. Even Donald Trump may be reinstated after two years. The good news is that my alter ego, Jim Corbett, found 5,000 friends in just a few months. Now, if any of my aliases could only find a way to stay out of Facebook jail.

Next are the many contributors to this volume, my Peace Corps colleagues, who provided vignettes, recollections, and reflections that are found throughout. I am so grateful to those who shared their stories in writing, through emails, and in personal communications. They will not be named for reasons of privacy and based on the realistic possibility that mob hit contracts might be put out on my miserable existence. Their stories are, by turn, funny and moving and honest. While Peace Corps was still a work-in-progress in the mid-1960s, the impact our service had on us proved beyond measure and, I am happy to report, the sub-continent managed to survive our inept ministrations. I doubt we would have been what we became as full adults without having first experienced the intense crucible of both our training and our service in what was considered a most difficult Peace Corps site. In this modest work, we recall how *our grand adventure* somehow served to shape our characters and transform our lives.

I surely must thank the PC staff who trained us, both here in the States and in India. You had so little to work with. Finally, I want to thank the good people of India for putting up with us as we wandered about their country, mostly clueless, but with the best of intentions. We meant no harm and surely left you with more than a few laughs and humorous stories to share.

CONTENTS

Recalling Our Grand Adventure

This book takes us back in time, to those days when an idealistic band of youthful Americans journeyed halfway around the world in response to President John F. Kennedy's clarion call to '... *ask what you can do for your country.*' We eagerly signed up to serve in a new program called the *Peace Corps,* an initiative first spawned in those exhilarating days of Camelot when fervor and innocence trumped experience and common sense. While each of us knew our decision to volunteer for service overseas might prove challenging, we had no idea what was in store for us. As these reflections suggest, our service both pushed us as individuals and altered our subsequent lives as a collective. In these pages, I try to capture some of these transformative experiences as well as intimate possible consequences.

It goes without saying that each group of volunteers, as well as every individual, had a unique journey in India or wherever they might have served. Nothing can encompass, nor do justice, to our total experience. That caveat aside, I offer this recollection of my personal experience, along with selected memories retrieved from the aging members of India-44, as a reasonable proxy for those early Peace Corps days. In retrospect, these early years would become known as the *'wild west'* of overseas service when everything was done by trial and error. Moreover, our group served in an extraordinarily demanding Peace Corps site that was beset with many difficulties loosely measured by disease, mental health issues, behavioral problems, and perhaps the most revealing metric of all... early terminations. Nevertheless, some of us persisted in our temporary lapse of sanity, either as providers of public health services or as ersatz agricultural specialists.

Unfortunately, few of us were prepared for our roles… not by background, experience, or prior training even though the PC staff tried hard to get us ready. In hindsight, it was a situation ripe for disaster or great humor, depending on how you view the world. Despite the challenges, including outrageously poor planning, our overseas adventure managed to embrace a few of the better aspects of those coming of age during that period. It surely captured the boundless exuberance, if not hubris, which dominated the American zeitgeist in those years. More than anything else, our travails provided much at which to laugh and, on occasion, even weep over. This is no sugar-coated tale of heroic deeds and boundless success. Far from it! We were simply a bunch of smart young kids doing our best in a difficult, perhaps impossible, situation.

—

The motivation for this work might be attributed to some dubious sources, individuals who may disagree with my interpretation of history or at least their contribution to this work. Jennifer L. Noyes, a long-time university colleague of mine and now a Vice Provost at the University of Wisconsin, shoulders considerable blame for this work. Before continuing, it is important to understand one thing. Jennifer and I have traded good natured insults over the many years we had worked together. Importantly, she assures me that her title of Vice Provost has nothing to do with overseeing the vices at this world-class University, but I remain to be convinced of that.

On the other hand, it is quite true that she does not extend her praise often or lightly. Thus, her positive feedback on the two edited volumes of the India-44's Peace Corps experiences, **The Other Side of the World** and **Return to the other Side of the World**, made a deep impression on me. These two volumes, written by the volunteers themselves, recount the experiences of my India Peace Corps group in the 1960s. Frankly, I was flabbergasted by her enthusiasm and, once I realized she was not joking, became intrigued by her reaction. Damn, these were good stories.

India-44 was, surprise, the 44ᵗʰ group to be sent to the sub-continent. It was composed of two distinct initiatives that trained together but served separately. For the most part, 44-A was composed of females who would do public health work in the State of Maharashtra where Mumbai (then Bombay) is located. 44-B, on the other hand, was a collection of hapless males doing agricultural work near Udaipur, an enchanted city located in southern Rajasthan, the province bordering Pakistan in the northwest corner of the country. Thus, while 44-A and B trained together, they were assigned to separate provinces, learned different languages, and performed distinct roles. Yet, because of our long and strenuous joint training, we bonded as one. That was clear when we met in 2009 on the 40ᵗʰ anniversary of our return to the States.

Jennifer found the edited collection of reflections to be enjoyable and illuminating, even recommending them to others. She also offered an observation. While, in her opinion, the young women in 44-A performed well, the guys in 44-B were at best total screw-ups. Moreover, she thought the antics of these hopeless guys tramping around the fields of rural India while dispensing questionable technical advice would make a great sitcom. It could be a Mash-like comedy based in India and the Peace Corps as opposed to that early 1950's United Nations sponsored conflict in Korea, a so-called police action that we used to consider a real war. Strikingly, she mentioned this possibility often, as if repetition might make it so. As a man who has been married for almost a half-century, I learned early on to obey women once they make their expectations clear, which usually involves directing *'the look'* in my direction. Despite all appearances to the contrary, I am not a total idiot!

Another possible motivation for this work comes from the surprisingly positive feedback I've received for earlier releases of *A*

Clueless Rebel, my humorous memoir of growing up in the post-World War II era and *A Wayward Academic,* the witty recounting of my career as I battled welfare reform and other such contentious policy issues. The professional reviews were remarkably positive, and the Amazon reader reviews over the top. The first release of *A Clueless Rebel* earned nearly perfect accolades, 4.9 out of 5 stars, while those for *A Wayward Academic* were close behind, surprising for a book about a policy wonk and focusing on some serious social challenges. Both certainly worked as comedy but also impart some useful lessons about life. Taken together, *A Clueless Rebel, A Wayward Academic: Reflections from the policy trenches,* and *Our Grand Adventure: The trials and triumphs of India-44* capture the major themes of a clearly misspent life.

Dr. Noyes was spot on in one respect. The antics of the volunteers of India 44, particularly those clueless guys trying to be instant agricultural gurus, demand to be shared with a broader audience. The world certainly could use a few more laughs in these depressing political times. At the same time, these stories contain many insights into several notions such as commitment, compassion, and sacrifice. They shed light on that universal search for meaning among the youth of that era who were just finding their way in life. This was the 1960s after all, a decade of transition and excess, but one in which the young believed they could create a better and more just world. We might well use more of that hope, however misplaced, once again.

———

A note or two on the book itself. The vignettes and stories contained herein are grounded in some approximation of what we normally consider reality. Many of these tales, though far from all, were first put down in *The Other Side of the World* and *Return to the Other Side of the World,* two edited volumes which have been read by too few outside our circle to count, and which may now be difficult to find. Others have been retrieved from *A Clueless Rebel,* which has enjoyed a somewhat broader readership but not nearly enough to generate the kind of royalties needed to buy the yacht I covet, or even a used kayak that seems a more likely prospect. The vignettes and observations from earlier works have been substantially reworked to fit within the style and presentational framework employed in this effort. Still, many recollections are original appearing nowhere else, most gleaned from personal conversations with those I defame in these pages.

Several times I asked myself... *Is this what really happened on the subcontinent a half-century ago?* Who knows? How accurate can memories be regarding events that occurred some five plus decades in the past? In some cases, diaries, letters, and the corroboration of eyewitnesses attest to the accuracy of the shared recollections. In others, I have approximated reality by triangulating our memories where possible.

If nothing else, our chronicles serve to capture the essential spirit of our service on the subcontinent so long ago. Some details may be suspect, but the fundamentals of our experiences are true. The framework for sharing these substantive stories, however, is largely fictional. I employ an imagined dialogue among volunteers from India-44, plus cameo appearances from some volunteers from India-40, to bring our stories to life. This virtual reunion is set five decades after the original sins were committed. The inspiration for my imagined gathering emanates from several actual reunions over the past decade or so. Thus, the banter among the main characters is either grounded in reality or in my fevered imagination. Take your pick!

In the end, it is difficult for me to decide if this is a memoir or work of fiction. The specific tales shared are as authentic as I can make them. On the other hand, the humorous banter among the volunteers as they share their stories is total fiction though such a banal dialogue undoubtedly occurred during our various gatherings over the past dozen years though we guys generally behaved better when the females of 44-A were around. Women civilize men. Our interactions as presented in the subsequent pages are designed to provide a comedic framework. In my eyes, this moves the narrative along and keeps the overall tone light and, hopefully, interesting.

Since this literary vehicle used to support the shared stories is imagined, and some stories may be personal and even embarrassing, I have employed aliases for the characters in this work of literary art, except for me of course and various public figures like President Kennedy. I'm sure he won't mind, and I stopped being embarrassed by my life decades ago. All who know me realize I have no dignity or self-respect left. How could I? Most importantly, I want everyone to know I have a team of lawyers, headed by Rudy Giuliani (if he's not in prison by that time) at the ready to defend me from all slander or libel suits.

Finally, let me make one thing clear. I take many shots at Peace Corps as it was in its infancy and even poke some fun at those early volunteers who tried mightily to make the best of often impossible situations. When we served, the concept of voluntary overseas service was still in its growing phase with much to be learned and then incorporated into future program iterations.

Perhaps the biggest lesson from that era was that you cannot sweep a bunch of eager young kids off college campuses and dump them into pre-industrial villages while expecting them to perform miracles in technical arenas about which they were largely clueless. That seems obvious now, not so much then. America simply presumed a natural superiority as a nation and as a people, hubris gone amok. I would like to think that the experiences of India-44, and others like us, helped the Peace Corps concept mature and become more successful. After all, someone had to make all those initial mistakes on which real learning occurs.

No matter how difficult our service was back then, few of us regretted our time in the Corps though we have entertained occasional doubts. It changed our lives for the better while bringing us together in remarkable ways. While I remain an exception, I can assert with great confidence that the other volunteers of India-

44 have connected as brothers and sisters… a consequence of confronting shared challenges and surviving testing hardships. These bonds of collegial affection have remained over the years even though the females in our group still arm themselves with pepper spray upon my approach. However, I am happy to report that all outstanding restraining orders on me have expired, at least that is my hope. No matter, the memories of our service in India yet run deep within us and remain unforgettable, though God knows we sometimes have tried hard to do just that… forget that is!

With all that aside, let us now turn back in time to an era that seems as unimaginable and primitive to us now as the time before the internet appears to today's youth. Let us consider that moment when Camelot was thought to exist, at least in our hopes. Let us return to a time when so many of us dreamed impossible dreams and tilted at illusory windmills to make the world just a bit more compassionate and just, not only at home but around the globe. In that enduring spirit, I offer you ***Our Grand Adventure: The trials and triumphs of India-44.***

Tom Corbett
Madison, Wisconsin
March 2022

X V

Camelot Revisited

In the fall of 1960, a handsome, energetic Democratic senator from Massachusetts was engaged in a bitter and closely fought battle for the Presidency of the United States. In that moment, for those of us old enough to have experienced it, this was a contest of obvious contrasts... youth versus maturity, innovation versus stability, ethnic Catholicism versus mainstream Protestantism, energy versus solidity, and the future versus the past. The country teetered on the cusp of a transformational moment hanging betwixt the somnolent 1950s, where a gray conformity promised little more than a continuing stupor, and this new and exciting world which, while poorly defined, suggested an intoxicating future.

That unarticulated world poised over the horizon remained frustratingly out of focus. It was something better sensed emotionally than understood cognitively. One salient question defined both this moment and the Presidential contest at hand. Would the nation stay with the safe and familiar, embodied by President Eisenhower's Vice President (VP) Richard Nixon, or would it take a chance on this still unknown wild card... Massachusetts Senator John Fitzgerald Kennedy? It was anyone's guess. The struggle for our futures, as they say, was afoot. The outcome, even among the politically sophisticated, remained highly uncertain.

Senator Kennedy landed in Ann Arbor Michigan late one October night, shortly after a televised debate with his more experienced opponent. As his plane came to a stop on the tarmac, he might well have wondered what his chances were. He was gaining ground in the polls... the historic televised debates had helped the newcomer pick up ground. Still, strong reservations remained about this youthful candidate, especially around foreign policy. The 'Cold War' with the Soviet Empire was in full form. Symbolic *iron curtains* would soon be replaced by actual walls in places like Berlin, Germany. In fact, they already existed along many borders separating the Soviet Union and the so-called 'free world' countries.

In addition, fears of 'missile gaps' and falling dominoes caused many an anxious night among America's families. A political argument yet raged about *'who lost China'* to the Reds in the late 1940s. Other Americans smarted that we only managed a costly stalemate on the Korean peninsula after the Communist North wantonly attacked their brethren to the South. Growing unrest in Africa and South America seemed to offer additional opportunities for a further expansion of the Red menace. In fact, a Communist regime recently had been established only 90 miles off the shores of Florida, potentially close enough to strike sunburned vacationers in Miami Beach with little warning. *"Gee honey, it's unusually warm today,"* a fat and contented sunbather might remark as a mushroom cloud rose nearby. There was a sense among many Americans that the tide of history might not be on their side. Like today, the fabric of our Republic appeared worn and in peril.

Our national angst at the dawn of the 1960s…

Throughout the 1950s, it was feared that the Russian Bear had matched our nuclear capability, or so we thought. Most of us school-aged children practiced diving under our school desks as a way of warding off the nuclear incineration that we were assured was coming. Outside the classroom, public service announcements told us how to respond when, not if, the Russkies dropped the big one. The rules for responding differed depending on the type of signal sent. You were trained to associate distinct sound patterns with different levels of urgency, basically how fast to get your doomed fanny to the nearest shelter, if one existed and if you could recall where the darn thing was located. On the other hand, if you saw a big white flash, you were to *'drop and cover,'* a survival tactic not much better than putting your head between your knees and kissing your ass good-by. Many of us practiced that difficult maneuver weekly though it always proved rather difficult to get our lips all the way back to our derrieres.

In our childhoods, the usual fantastical monsters plaguing our nightmares had been replaced by more human-looking creatures… sinister men wearing helmets adorned with the iconic hammer and sickle of the Soviet Union. On the other hand, we were comforted by the knowledge that our own strategic bombers were constantly in the air 24-7 ready and able to strike back at our implacable enemy in case they launched a preemptive strike. It took me little time to figure out that such a vengeful response would prove of little consolation if I already had been turned into a crispy cinder. I felt bad knowing that a Russian kid of my age would now suffer a similar fate. Then again, the mantra of the day was *'better dead than Red,'* now ironic given that the Republican Party apparently wants to turn America Red these days with some supporting Russian expansionary plans in the Ukraine. Apparently, you really cannot tell the enemy without a scorecard.

Most days we feared that, when the apocalypse struck, our asses would go unloved while our derrieres would be vaporized absent any affectionate good-bye kiss. I once suggested to Suzie, who sat next to me in grade school, that we kiss each other's derrieres goodbye when the end came. That struck me as a capital idea but, for some inexplicable reason, she did not take my thoughtful offering in the spirit intended. Then again, perhaps she did. She just whacked me upside the head without saying a word.

In truth, I got a lot of those whacks and not just from Suzie. All the girls were on to me right from the get-go. How had they figured me out so quickly? I personally thought I was a prince of a young man. No matter, their early physical assaults on my body proved an excellent preparation for adulthood since, oddly enough, cheesing off members of the fairer sex would remain a lifelong skill of mine. If they ever do an autopsy on my body, they will conclude that I was tortured as a prisoner-of-war, perhaps as a POW cell mate of former Senator and Presidential candidate John McCain in Hanoi Hilton.

Getting back to my main point, always a challenge for me, the more farsighted (and affluent) of our parents erected shelters deep under their backyards. This prudent behavior was typically accompanied by intense debates on select moral conundrums. For example, should they exclude their less-paranoid neighbors, along with certain obnoxious family members, from these safe-havens when the day of Armageddon inevitably arrived. It was a classic tradeoff between self-preservation and Christian compassion. On the surface, the debate often centered on a single, rather practical issue… how long would the supply of stored liquor last?

My folks never got to these kinds of delicate debates. They always weighed the choice between security and another beer and inevitably chose the beer. Given the less than amicable character of their marriage, instant annihilation always seemed preferable to extended periods of time in a confined space either with one another or with their one issue… me. I was never deemed much of a prize by my parents, or by anyone for that matter.

As I now think on it, spiritual or moral matters did not occupy my family's time. The only time I saw my dad pray was when he was drawing to an inside straight, when he was asking God to strike his wife mute, and when he begged the Almighty to return him to that moment in time right before my conception so that this time he might remember to use that condom he had with him. My household was not the inspiration for the *Leave It to Beaver* sitcom so popular back then. In fairness, it could have been worse, and was in some of my friend's homes.

The American public clearly was nervous about the future. They kept a wary eye on international affairs and threats from overseas unless, that is, if you were from Dixie. In that case, the most ominous threat was centered close to the Mason-Dixon line with the nation's capital clearly serving as the proximate headquarters of our home-grown version of the *real* godless Communist menace… our federal government. In those days, any sense of impending angst typically proved a political plus for the Republican Party, which at that time ideologically encompassed southern yellow-dog Democrats who had not yet switched their allegiance. That would happen soon enough, right after President Johnson pushed a civil rights bill through Congress. This realignment permitted and further facilitated the hyper-polarized politics we see today.

The voting rights bill proved the final straw even though it effectively guaranteed a mature democracy some 275 years after the pledge for equal opportunity first had been articulated. The very notion of treating all people the same was a bridge too far for most conservatives and, to be honest, for many of our Founding Fathers. To them, 'all men' really meant wealthy white property owners. Contemporary conservatives promptly fled to the Republican party which, ironically enough, had been created as an anti-slavery movement. The subsequent political realignment that took place in the late 1960s did sort out some peculiar anomalies. Ancient allegiances dating back to the Civil War had created odd bedfellows but nothing stranger than diehard southern racists being shoehorned into the same party as northern liberals. Really, what did Senators Hubert Humphrey and Strom Thurmond have in common? In case you are pondering that one… absolutely nothing!

Nevertheless, Republicans had monopolized the scared-shit department and thus had a traditional advantage in grubbing up votes with this tactic. A scared voter would be a Republican voter. After all, they touted themselves as the defenders of America's national freedom and individualistic values. They did so even though it had been the Democrats who had taken us into war over the past century, purportedly to safeguard both our way of life and our sacred values.

Given this entrenched narrative, Kennedy remained worried that growing fears of the Red menace would sink him in the end, a problem for his party ever since Republican Senator Joe McCarthy of Wisconsin staked out the ultra-paranoid position that Commies were to be found everywhere, even the White House and surely in our State Department. If card carrying Reds were not in these places, then liberals and other 'fellow travelers' were seen perpetuating all kinds of mischief at the expense of our individual freedoms. These traitors likely included that neighbor who was rumored to have voted for a Democrat... a Democrat for crying out loud!

Any neighbor who wore a red blazer deserved scrutiny as a bona-fide pinko-sympathizer, and you never could really trust your pastor when he was seen contributing used clothing to the needy. After all, coddling the poor and desperate was an undeniable sign of Communist sympathies, much like those leftist priests and nuns who wanted to break up the economic oligarchies in Central and South America just to help some starving peasants. Everyone knew that Christ was only kidding when he encouraged people to help the downtrodden. After all, who would look after the profit margins of United Fruit if we started caring about starving families and children?

In those fearful days, it was indisputable that Commies were all over our government. In fact, they were everywhere. Not even our avuncular President and defender of the free world in WWII, Five-Star General Dwight David Eisenhower, was above suspicion. After all, the always sensible and fact-driven defenders of truth, the John Birch Society, told us so.

Few escaped the full-blown psychoses that were rampant in the political discourse of the day. Liberal candidate John F. Kennedy, for example, fanned the flames of our national angst by arguing that there was a dangerous missile gap between the two superpowers, the free and enslaved worlds. In 1960, JFK argued that those Reds had more warheads mounted in ballistic missiles than we had. Push a button, and they could wipe us off the face of the earth. He was later proved totally correct. There was such a gap, but it was the Russians who were way behind.

As all politicians intuitively appreciate, the truth seldom scares up votes in an election. Kennedy therefore fanned the flames of patriotic fervor by arguing that the U.S. should face down the Chinese Commies over two small islands named Quemoy and Matsu located off the coast of China. They were the focus of a dispute between Communist Chair Mao sitting on the mainland and the Chinese Nationalists on Taiwan who were headed by Chiang Kai-shek. The Democratic contender must have realized that he had gone around the bend on this one but looking tougher on the Reds than those sneaky Republicans was a paramount concern in those angst-ridden days. I dare any reader today to even find these twos dots on a map (Hint: they are near China). And no way could I now tell you which power, the Commies or the Nationalists, wound up with these two piles of useless rock. Oh, I suppose I could google it.

To further enhance our national insomnia, a group of concerned scientists had created a doomsday clock which symbolically suggested how close we were to the world's annihilation in a nuclear holocaust. The time set on this hypothetical timepiece always seemed poised to strike midnight, the hour of ultimate destruction. With each new apocalyptic headline, an every other day occurrence it seemed, the minute hand would inch closer to the doomsday moment. A nation of angst-ridden citizens continuously were found running-off to their therapists {the same guy who conveniently had a second job as the bartender at their local watering hole) as they succumbed to the grip of a full-blown cold war panic. It was an unsettling time.

Seeking a new way...

Though Kennedy played the usual political game, it appears he never felt totally comfortable with it. He understood that he needed a new twist on this old apocalyptic theme... one that might satisfy the concerns of those traditional voters who were old enough to remember a world at war, both the hot and cold versions, but which also might appeal to a restless youth. The kids of that era were growing weary of living on the precipice of a nuclear holocaust that, at a minimum, would further disrupt their non-existent sex lives. In his heart, though, this youthful candidate for the highest office in the land grew increasingly dissatisfied with the tried and true political tactic… the sure-fire vote getter of *'damning the Godless Reds'* to oblivion.

Fear and hate might well be guaranteed political winners, but such negative themes failed to long capture this youthful candidate who harbored many optimistic thoughts, at least in private. Sure, he would play the usual political game as he considered how to alter the rules. His thing was to be an innovator, a visionary, the articulator of a New Frontier. He was searching for a more upbeat message, one that might reach the young and the restless. As the campaign tightened, he struggled to find a new wrinkle in the stale old debates. There would be no winners in a nuclear holocaust. And it made for bad politics. It was hard to rally people when they were counting the days to Armageddon, perhaps even harder to get them to make a political contribution when they could enjoy their money in riotous debauchery as the end times approached.

While his opponent was quite clear in his affirmation of the *'better dead than Red'* aphorism, Kennedy struggled for a novel twist on that stark choice, one that might replace a dystopian future with one of promise and purpose. Pondering such things late that October night, he looked out over a throng of some 10,000 mostly college students who had waited patiently for his late arrival. These students already were hardened veterans of this 'Cold War' mania. They had come of age in its midst. They now wanted something new, a more positive vision for their futures. He felt a need to say something different, perhaps something that might touch the youth in a positive way and, at the same time, erase the taunts recently levied at him by his opponent.

VP Richard M. Nixon, in their last televised debate, had insisted that only the Republicans could keep America safe in a troubled world. He did so while, in a rather ironic and clever twist, suggesting that it had been the Democrats who led the country into past military conflicts. This was an assertion of the worst kind, one that inconveniently happened to be true. Behind his five o'clock shadow and cynical smirk, Nixon staked out a position that the Dems had been the traditional warmongers while the GOP offered both peace and security. It was a powerful message that the younger candidate felt compelled to counter. The question for him was how?

What could Kennedy now say that might resonate with this young and expectant crowd? It couldn't be creating more nuclear warheads or sending these anxious waiting male students off to die in another war. The costly stalemates of the last decade did little to change the geo-political stalemate. These kids surely remembered Korea and the debacle of the French trying to hold on to their colonial possession in Southeast Asia, especially Vietnam! When the French were defeated at Dien Bien Phu, some in the Eisenhower administration advocated the use of limited nuclear weapons to prop up continued Western control. Ike, as he was universally known, intimately knew war and death on an industrial scale. He would have none of that insanity though already the seeds of America's biggest indefensible military folly of the 20th century had been sown.

Yet, an unnerving sense that the West might be losing the long-term battle with the forces of authoritarianism was in the air. It was something that Kennedy would have to address. Just what could he say that might be positive, uplifting, and which did not remind all that the iconic doomsday clock was poised to strike midnight... that symbolic moment when civilization would kiss its collective ass goodbye? After all, Suzie had already eliminated, for me at least, any possible upside to that eventuality.

What he did say, possibly unscripted and which he likely assumed would soon be forgotten by the next news cycle, rippled through the gathering and into history. Though it was a theme he had been thinking about for several years, it was never clear whether Kennedy gave these words a second thought that night:

How many of you who are going to be doctors are willing to spend your days in Ghana? How many of you are willing to work in the Foreign Service and spend your life traveling around the world? On your willingness to do that—not merely to serve one year or two in the (military) service—but on your willingness to contribute part of your life to this country, I think will depend the answer whether our society can compete.

No specific reference to a Peace Corps was forthcoming, no program was initiated that night, no actual call to arms was raised. The term *Peace Corps* was not used by Kennedy until a November 2nd speech in San Francisco when he called for a revitalization of the U.S. global engagement. No, on this night he offered only a vague invocation to a generation just coming of age, a call to serve this country in some unclear yet remarkably personal way. It was merely a suggestive call to go forth and save the world, not with guns but with open hearts. It was a transformative invocation that summoned the *'better angels'* that lurked within each of us, assuming we had any such angels in the first instance.

Five decades later, in 2011, at the golden anniversary celebration of the founding of Peace Corps, a student who had waited for Kennedy that night at the airport reflected on the frisson of excitement that his words, though ambiguous, sent through her and her fellow students. She, and many of her college peers, had been electrified. Within days, and before social media transformed communication into a painless and practical process, she used the telephone and crude signs stapled on campus kiosks to reach hundreds of local students. Most who responded were looking for where and how to sign up for this new volunteer program that, in fact, did not exist. In the coming months, the Kennedy team was to receive some 25,000 inquiries about an initiative that remained a figment of his casual rhetoric. His words had sparked a flame.

A colleague of mine, now an Emeritus Professor of Political Science from the University of Wisconsin, recalls travelling around several campuses in the Badger State drumming up interest in this international volunteering concept during those early days. He confided to me just how energized he had been by the concept. Ironically, he never became a volunteer himself, a fact I have pointed out to him on many an occasion. He left that dubious honor to the more naïve members of his generational cohort like me. Still, a clear nerve had been struck among the college aged crowd. Increasingly, the newly elected President felt he had to respond in some substantive manner.

The 1960 Presidential election was decided by a razor thin margin, probably resting ultimately on questionable late arriving votes in Cook County Illinois (Chicago). When it was apparent that Kennedy would indeed be the next chief executive officer, the birth of the Peace Corps moved swiftly. In early February of 1961, the President's brother-in-law, Sargent Schriver, laid out the principles of a so-called Peace Corps in a memo to the President. Some three weeks later, on March 1, 1961, Kennedy officially created the program through an Executive Order. Later, on September 22 of that year, the President signed legislation more formally enacting a Peace Corps program. These events were remarkably swift by Washington standards, suggesting that Kennedy was savvy enough to recognize a winning idea when it wacked him upside the head, always the mark of a gifted leader.

What was this Peace Corps thing…?

An important question remained at the time. What was this Peace Corps thing other than a label suggesting it was not about war and killing? Some argued that Kennedy had been thinking about ways to reform the Foreign Service system since he first ran for the U.S. Senate a decade before running for President. As early as 1950, union icon Walter Reuther suggested the creation of a technology corps where young people might go abroad to spread American know-how and good will throughout a globe yet reeling from a devastating war. Others note that the ebullient Hubert Humphrey (Senator from Minnesota) had proposed a similar concept during the early 1950s and that Congressman Henry Reuss, who represented the Wisconsin district just across the river from the Twin Cities, had even drafted enabling legislation that went the way of most brilliant legislative ideas… nowhere. Of course, Hubert was known to talk non-stop. He probably proposed every conceivable liberal idea under the sun at one time or another.

In 1960, this volunteer concept struck the young, a group typically preoccupied with sex, sports, and occasionally even their studies, as something new and exciting, perhaps even worth a second look. Better still, it seemed directed toward them personally even though there were no age restrictions. Could this newfangled concept be translated into something that might spread good will, alleviate human problems, and realize societal potential? Seriously, how many powerful nations ever did anything like that, go abroad not to conquer but to help, unless you somehow interpreted the forced conversion of various native peoples to Christianity to be a form of benevolent spiritual assistance. That hardly seems the case since our esteemed ancestors coupled all such spiritual outreach with the murderous appropriation of tribal lands and resources along with sharing deadly diseases for which the natives had no resistance. Whole nations of indigenous peoples suddenly were doomed to extinction while those tribes that survived saw their numbers decimated by 90 percent or more. The historical record would suggest that Christian tenets ran aground when confronted with nationalistic imperatives and sovereign entitlements? You know how that goes. If we have the power, we get the goodies.

Nevertheless, Kennedy's invocation to service and personal sacrifice was out there… a flame of incendiary intensity had been ignited. This inchoate concept was to be fleshed in by such early visionaries as the indefatigable Sargent Shriver, a future Vice President candidate with George McGovern. With enthusiastic help from Lyndon Johnson, Kennedy's VP at the time, the fledgling program would remain independent both of the State Department and the 'spooks' operating out of the Central Intelligence Agency (at least we hoped as much at the time). Johnson had this notion that 'volunteers' should not be button downed Foreign service types but young men and women willing to get their hands dirty. They should focus more on cultural and technical change at the grass roots level than on any overt or covert political machinations.

These early architects envisioned a massive program where tens of thousands of youthful volunteers would export all that was good about American values, enthusiasm, and technical know-how around the world. Such gifts of American exceptionalism were to be shared through positive examples, not bought with American treasure, and certainly not exported at the point of a gun. The work would be done not in the airconditioned offices of the powerful but in the city slums and remote villages where ordinary people lived and struggled. This would happen through person to person interactions designed to transform societies from the ground up. Indeed, it was a dramatic and uplifting vision; some might say one bordering on the delusional.

A note on historical context…

What really happened in those frantic early years of change and renewed optimism? It is difficult to get any old story right. "History," as George Santayana allegedly noted, "is merely informed rumor." Yet, some of us are ancient enough to remember the 1960s, especially as we sit in one of our many doctor's offices waiting for our latest episode of gout to be checked. We recall that long-ago era of pre-history as a quasi-mythical reenactment of the magic of Camelot, a period of unbounded energy and hope touched occasionally with much confusion and upheaval that some characterized as a juvenile form of 'acting-out.' That decade represented a toxic, yet heady, mix of blind faith diluted with measurable portions of foolishness and then frustration and eventually more than a bit of rage. We were frustrated as we discovered blemishes on our national soul and resentful that efforts to correct all wrongs were proceeding glacially, if progressing at all. Our selective memories undoubtedly embellish, and sometimes distort, reality. Yet, we might not be totally misguided in arguing that this was a moment where circumstances were right for bold new ventures and big, if always not well considered, dreams.

The country had grown wealthy after WWII. First, returning soldiers flocked into colleges and universities in unprecedented numbers under the G.I. Bill. They were followed by an increasing share of the country's youth… their offspring. A brief revolution of the heart was about to burst forth. Unlike past generations, and what we see on campuses in the present day, our generational cohort born at the end of World War II did not overly obsess about making money even as their parents pursued the American dream. Hope, along with a vague commitment to make the world a little better, would displace the traditional monetary metric of success, at least for some and at least for a little while. Personal fulfillment through creating a more just and equitable world became the holy grail for many of us, the brass rings that captured our hearts. As the old saying goes, *it seemed like a good idea at the time.* Kennedy's words and actions proved perfect for the restless mood of the nation, especially a generational cohort on the cusp of working out their personal philosophies of life while staking out their own futures.

Perhaps it is not entirely coincidental that a year later, in the spring of 1962, a group of college students, many from that same University located in Ann Arbor, convened in Port Huron Michigan to think about the future and their role in it. The statement they issued at the end of their confab started as follows: *We are people of this generation, bred in at least modest comfort, housed now in universities looking uncomfortably to the world we inherit.…* These restless young people went on to call forth their peers across the nation to do something significant and substantial with their lives, to create a more perfect society. In their heartfelt words, they called for *nothing less than the spiritual enrichment of American society, not through prayers and love-ins, but by diminishing… the materialistic obsessions that obstructed individual fulfillment.*

Their collective plea for spiritual renewal and personal sacrifice was driven by dark images of an apocalypse that awaited a societal failure to do the right thing. To them, it was up to their generation to reset a nation, even a globe, that had lost its way. They must be the ones to place the advancement of the common good above any meaningless pursuit of social status and material well-being.

The final line of their organizing statement captured a sense of disillusion and doom that hung over so many of the post-war youth, those very kids who had hid under their school desks hoping that a flimsy wooden barrier might protect them from a nuclear blast. *If we appear to seek the unattainable, then let it be known that we do so to avoid the unimaginable.* This became the anthem for the Students for a Democratic Society (SDS), which evolved as the fulcrum for a leftist thrust among the young until it all blazed out in a gasp of cynical despair, desperate rage, and ultimate nihilism.

Of course, little did that small band of students appreciate that they had tapped something central to a watershed moment in history, though they may have hoped for such in the same way each generation accords themselves a special place in history. My post-World War generation considered itself a uniquely blessed cohort, at least according to our own self-aggrandizing delusions. We were born at the end of a world-wide conflagration. Surely we could make the world a better place going forward. That was obvious to us if to no one else.

Of course, we also brought to the table a host of press clippings arguing just how superior America was as a nation and as a culture. Hell, our parents had saved Western democracies and freedom around the globe, or so we were constantly reminded. America clearly had emerged as the most powerful nation and economy in the world. In the immediate post-war years, we produced half of the world's economic output with six percent of the population. America, in our view, was the final defender of all that was good and holy. We were the planet's final hope.

Was there anything we could not do once we put our minds to the task? We were, after all, that blessed generation. We were the children of Camelot.

My college graduation picture… ready to save the world.

CHAPTER 2

Culture & Context

As the 1960s dawned, the larger issues that would tear asunder our presumptions of superiority as well as the very fabric of our society were beginning to simmer. The Vietnam conflict barely registered on the American consciousness. Rage against *de jure* Apartheid in the South and *de facto* discrimination elsewhere were bubbling ever more visibly but remained just below the boiling point. It was only a matter of time before our national shame of segregation would burst into a widespread, national conflagration. Poverty and egregious inequality of opportunity were hardly a blip on our mental screens as national issues, though they too were about to explode into our collective consciences. Our awakening realization that too many citizens were being left behind despite general economic growth led to a national War-On-Poverty in 1965. Women began to articulate their dissatisfaction at being relegated to a second-class status. One could sense similar rumblings for other groups, but the character of the coming revolution had not yet become fully understood.

The final moments of innocence...

The movie, *American Graffiti*, which poignantly portrayed the ennui and uncertainty of a group of 1962 high school graduates, captured the feel of those last moments of quaint innocence quite well. At this cusp, or tipping point in history, some of us embraced a self-anointed status as the chosen ones. While we were uneasy with the challenges before us, we remained secure in our preeminent place among nations and in our special responsibility to right all those things we had found wrong in our world. At some moment, perhaps around that fateful day in 1963 when Kennedy was snatched away by an assassin's bullet, some far away deity pressed a reset button that sent society in a new direction. It was as if Kennedy's death, at least to those of us who lived through it, released a host of pent up emotions or, more likely, repressed demons.

As we well know, all soon changed in dramatic ways... music, fashion, politics, culture, and the very meaning of a purposeful life. Almost overnight, it seems in retrospect, youth from across the land were debating and arguing among themselves about what constituted the just society along with how to seek a nobler purpose in their own futures. We really didn't study, did we? I know I didn't, not much at least. Kennedy's call for self-sacrifice was swept up in these currents of a larger cultural revolution, his death presaging social convulsions that likely would have occurred even if he had survived.

Without much forethought or reservation, many of my generation embraced a full-throated agenda of issues around which to bind up their boundless energy and purpose... peace, racial and gender justice, poverty and economic opportunity, and so much more. The self-satisfied 50s were about to become the tempestuous 60s. The Port Huron group evolved into a leftist organization (SDS) which eventually became emblematic of a generation's impotence, frustration, and eventual rage. Their final variant, the Weathermen, sought purification through violence. Similarly, the early high ideals of Martin Luther King and the Student Non-Violent Coordinating Committee (SNCC) eroded into calls for Black Power and the creation of the Black Panthers. An increasing sense of existential despair drove some, perhaps many, toward nihilistic self-destruction through violent spasms of protest and desperate acts of domestic terrorism.

In contrast, some of us who came of age in this tormented era continued to seek purpose in a less dramatic fashion. We resonated more to Mahatma Gandhi and Martin Luther King and less to

Che Guevera and Stokely Carmichael. For the most part we had enjoyed rather halcyon childhoods even if out tender years did not include demonstrable affluence or privilege. Real incomes doubled in about a generation after the second-world war with every quintile of the distribution of economic goodies seeing their fortunes improve in these blessed times. A middle class boomed to the point where kids whose parents could never have considered college themselves happily skipped off to this rite-of-passage traditionally reserved for the entitled few.

While many college students continued to do what they had done since time immemorial, get drunk and pursue carnal delights, a now growing cohort of students engaged in intense and ceaseless dialogues about what constituted a new moral order while occasionally finding time to get high and pursue those elusive dreams of erotic success. After all, there had to be more to life than acquiring that suburban home and white picket fence. That traditional dream seemed boring beyond calculation. Real satisfaction and purpose had to lie elsewhere.

Remarkably, we would graduate from our citadels of higher learning without much debt and often full of misplaced confidence. Today, the young are driven into our academies of higher learning in the desperate hope of obtaining credentials that might lead to a job that will keep them off the dole... a safety net which they doubt will exist much longer if those few commanding an ever-increasing share of the national wealth have their way.

It was so different back then. In the 1960s, we tumbled out of our universities to a world bursting with anticipation and sensing wider possibilities. We had the luxury of enrolling in courses that were interesting in themselves and not essential to any future career. We sat around late into the nights thinking great thoughts or arguing about momentous issues, important to us at least. I know I did though I probably should not speak for all my Peace Corps peers. There were times I even remained sober and serious during our never-ending political and philosophical explorations of self and society.

Indeed, those were utopian days where dreams seemed possible and our reach could exceed our grasp. Today, our young look forward to declining opportunities and a world on the precipice of extinction. Most days, they debate whether they can make enough money to satisfy their student debt before global warming puts them out of their misery. We had worries, for sure, but we also had much hope and abundant opportunities. Most of all, we had alternatives to consider and choices to make. We had to decide about an unpopular war and whether we would support or oppose it. We had to decide how we might employ our energies in a world that appeared to be changing before our eyes as racial, class, gender, and cultural revolutions unfolded before us. Ultimately, we had to formulate and articulate our world view when that world often seemed frayed at the edges. In this turmoil, we might choose to chase our dreams on the other side of the world. That, in fact, is precisely what some of us did.

Who were we?

Who were these starry-eyed idealists who trooped off to save the world? And why do such a crazy thing? It is illuminating, or fun at least, to think back on those factors that shaped our decisions as young adults. We who applied for overseas service in those early years might be considered outliers. Or were we? Such life altering decisions likely emerge from the culture of our childhood and the contexts of our environments. Unfortunately, I cannot speak for us all, only myself. So, I'll let my sample of one speak for us all.

In hindsight, we who wound up in India lived in strange times back then, surely an era that would seem remarkably primitive to contemporary kids. Most of us walked to school, and back. We used public transportation to get other places though. We even had to walk across the room to change TV channels by turning a clunky knob which had this irritating habit of coming off in our hands if used too often. And get this, we called our friends on phones that were physically corded to the wall. It proved difficult to find a private space while courting Suzie or any female, no matter how futilely, if your range of movement were only a few feet. Worst of all, our communication devices had some anachronistic kind of rotary dial that was surprisingly difficult to negotiate. This resulted in numerous wrong numbers that became apparent when you expected Suzie's sweet voice and got Sam the butcher's gravelly tones instead.

Beyond that, if you can imagine, many of us were on what were called 'party' lines where you shared your connection to the outside world with other families. Idly chatting with your girlfriend, assuming you had managed to find one, was frowned upon when another family might want to conduct important business with the outside world. What if your neighbor Joe wanted to get in touch with his bookie to lay down a last-minute bet on a sure thing? Flirting with Suzie, with whom you had less that a zero chance of scoring in any case, was not considered important business, at least not when compared to Joe's sure fire tip on a horse running in the 5th at Suffolk Downs. For some reason, your mother's idle chatting with her female friends was exempt from this sacred rule. Gossip inevitably had the highest priority.

Shocking by today's standards at least, you could not employ your communication device to transmit a sexy picture of yourself to the young lady you fancied. It could not be done as a technical matter, nor was it legally permitted. No, you would have to get a real camera and imprint your Adonis-like body on film. Then, unless you had one of those fancy Polaroid things, your negative would have to be 'developed' at a local store where some pervert would check out what you had done and either turn you over to the authorities or extort money out of you for not turning you in. If you managed to make it past that hurdle, you had to hand-deliver this representation of your naked glory to the girl of your dreams, since sending it by mail risked breaking several federal postal laws. Such a violation, if you were caught, was punishable by broadcasting to the entire world that you were a depraved pervert, which everyone already knew but, until your most recent exposure, you could at least pretend was more fake news.

Let's face it! If you were a young male coming of age in the late 1950s, you were a pervert by definition. Why else would you fess up to 897 dirty thoughts in the weekly Catholic confessional and know immediately that you were lying to God Himself since the real count was at least twice that number? Prior to going into the confessional, the great internal debate for us Catholic boys was how many indecent thoughts could you admit without the priest insisting on a parental discussion regarding your suspect moral turpitude. We were told about the sanctity of the confessional, but we had our serious doubts. On the other hand, a low number of admitted impure thoughts risked inviting doubts about your honesty before God. After all, lying to the Almighty clearly was *verboten*. Such was our moral conundrum.

There was another problem. The girl of our dreams had been trained to view our fully revealed manhood with considerable reservation, if not outright disgust. In truth, no training in this matter was necessary. Her reaction was instinctive. Your family jewels were, after all, quite disgusting looking by any reasonable and objective standard. If you managed to convince Suzie to peek, she likely would knee you in those very same family jewels you had just put on display. Then she would have her father take out a restraining order on you after, of course, he also kneed you somewhere in the vicinity of what remained of your now hideous looking manhood. If anything of this once essential appendage yet remained attached, you never doubted that it would soon be separated from your body by your own parents. These were perilous times indeed for all boys. No wonder, running off to India had some attraction.

No, we were not coddled as today's entitled delinquents are. No indeed! We were being hardened for the battles of adult life. No helmets for us as we cavorted over the byways on our bikes, no car seats when we traveled as young tots, no 24/7 supervision while marauding at will on the streets and nearby playgrounds, and no one monitored our intake of carcinogens and other crap that we now know will kill us. After school we were told to get out of the house and not to come back until the streetlights were on, if then. Left to our own devices, and absent adult supervision, we played all kinds of questionable games where we pelted one another with debris and whacked each other with various weapons as we played 'war.' Winter afforded us additional weapons of choice in the form of ice-filled snowballs. It surely was survival of the fittest. Now that I think on it, just how the hell did I make it to adulthood?

A quaint and wonderful world…

Despite the risks, my 1950s world now strikes me like an era straight out of a Norman Rockwell painting, aside from these above-mentioned efforts to cripple one another. I fondly remember a variety of vendors delivering ice (for an ice box and not a fridge), coal, milk, bread, fruits and veggies, and other necessities right to our doors. Rag men would purchase unusable items of clothing for a few pennies and other artisans would wander through neighborhoods offering to sharpen your kitchen knives for another few pennies or perhaps take your picture astride a pony for four bits. Nothing was expensive since no one had much money in the first instance. Yet, we never felt poor and it seemed that things were getting better all the time. Somewhere. there is a picture of me taken by one of these wandering vendors. I am atop this small pony proudly wearing my Hopalong Cassidy cowboy hat, or perhaps the photographer provided that prop. It was taken on my childhood street, in front of my aunt and uncle's tenement who lived nearby. I looked to be about four years of age at the time, or was it fourteen?

Life on urban streets in many eastern cities back then was a kaleidoscope of interesting sights and fascinating characters now long lost to us. Those same streets today seem abandoned and forlorn. I recently visited Ames Street in Worcester Mass., where

I spent the first dozen years of my life. I was shocked at how small and cramped it was… the passage so narrow that even one-way traffic now has problems negotiating the parked cars consigned to one side of the roadway. In my tender years, it was two-way traffic with vehicles parked on both sides. The street then seemed huge, vibrant, and exciting. Hell, I am sure we would have ignored the video options of today, even if we had them back then, to enjoy what the outside world offered us. Our worlds seemed replete with endless possibilities.

Outside our family sanctuaries in the 1950s was a continuous panorama of games played by hordes of kids on our neighborhood streets. We invented forms of baseball where all you needed was a tennis ball. We would get up spontaneous football contests where I would tell Jackie to run to the Chevy and break right where I would hit him with an unerring pass. Of course, having all the athletic talent of a wounded amoeba, the ball would bounce off a parked car's windshield while Jackie abruptly stopped after slamming into the adjacent Ford. He would raise his bruised body just long enough to give me the single finger of frustration one more time before collapsing into a heap. The game would be suspended when an enraged adult emerged to take stock of the damage done to his vehicle while hurling a continuous stream of expletives in our direction.

Team sports presented a special form of humiliation for guys like me. There was a pecking order. There are pecking orders throughout life, but the early ones marked you forever. Choosing up neighborhood teams is where one's initial sense of self-esteem was elevated, diminished or, for guys like me, sent right into the crapper. Essentially, it worked like this. The better athletes were, by definition, the captains. The rest of us losers were lined up while each captain, after determining which leader would choose first, looked us over to alternately select the remaining members of their respective teams. You felt rather like a heifer at the state fair. As the pool of players dwindled and you were still not chosen, your embarrassment grew. I felt a special shame when the kid sporting a full body cast was selected before me. Those scars remain for life.

If not immersed in these athletic events, we repeatedly relived our dreams about life as cowboys and Indians or perhaps our fantasies about heading into outer space to fight alien creatures. Since my name was the same as a popular TV and book series character of the time, *Tom Corbett Space Cadet*, I was awarded special privileges when we played at who would take on the Martians and save the earth. I at least had a special claim on that role. That still did not guarantee I would be chosen. Unfortunately, none of us had ever run into an alien from outer space so that form of entertainment was never popular. Earthly monsters like Dracula had more cachet though, in truth, we had never met him either.

I felt relatively disadvantaged in my early years. We didn't have a TV, nor did we own a car. Hell, I didn't even have a bike. Diversions, fortunately, were simple and easily found. I spent endless hours roaming the streets well beyond my own turf with little concern that some pervert might abduct me. I doubt that I would be considered much of a prize even if such miscreants were lurking about. Fortunately, none ever seemed to be. Free from worry about being kidnapped for ransom or a worse fate, we typically settled on the dominant fantasy of male pre-puberty youth in the 1950s... games of war. If air-guns and cap pistols were not at the ready, then hours were spent hurling objects at each other. If we had had any throwing talent, serious injuries and trips to the emergency room would have followed. Fortunately, we were talentless.

The biggest battles among my crowd involved who would get stuck playing the Germans, or the Japanese, or the Chinese after the Korean conflict erupted. It was usually me since I was just a bit younger than the other kids in my age cohort, and significantly more innocent. My so-called friends would say I was a bit slow. Today the politically correct term would be developmentally delayed. Assigned the role of victim, I would dodge and hide as the others pelted me with missiles that, in my memory, often were large enough to send me off to my eternal reward. Of course, a heavenly reward would be mine only if I were dispatched to the next life within minutes of my last confession. I seldom went longer than that without thinking of Suzie.

My only other hope of salvation rested on making a *Perfect Act of Contrition*, all the words to which I could never recall when desperately needed. This cure-all prayer, much like indulgences sold by medieval Popes, had magical properties but it was a tricky affair. Timing was everything for a male teen filled to overflowing with testosterone and Catholic guilt. I had to say the prayer in those moments between getting conked on the noggin with a boulder hurled at me by a neighbor kid and the moment I passed on to my eternal reward. Any longer period might permit those dastardly impure thoughts of cute Suzie to despoil my chances of paradise. Thus, I faced a fleeting window of opportunity, and I mean fleeting.

My eternal fate often was pushed aside by more immediate and compelling challenges. As I pondered matters like where I ranked on the neighborhood athletic pecking order or how my side might prevail in our game of war that day, my folks would surreptitiously change the locks on our doors and slip away leaving no forwarding address. They had long realized that siring this hopeless issue of theirs was not their brightest move in life. Much to their dismay, though, I always thwarted their plans by managing to track them down. Their mistake was in never moving far enough away.

Back then, my being selected last, or nearly last, for the neighborhood teams spilled over into life generally. For example, I had difficulty believing anyone would hire me for any job when I reached adulthood. I saw myself as a talentless schmuck. It was not that there were not enticing careers to be seen. They were all about me. I've never forgotten the sight of the 'coal man' lugging leather bags of this black treasure to a chute that sent his precious cargo into the basement of a three-flat tenement building. That looked doable to me though it struck me that the labor was backbreaking. I would look upon the worker's face caked with coal dust and conclude that I might get lucky someday and find a job that paid me to get dirty. Oh, the sheer joy of that prospect. Soon enough, though, that transcendent aspiration was replaced by another singular insight that was to remain with me for the remainder of my life. Jobs like that involved real work. I was not cut out for real work, perhaps not for work of any kind. A dilemma indeed!

The thing was this. Manual labor was hard, paid crap, and thus clearly out of the question for me. It was, as they say, a nonstarter, something to be avoided at all costs. It also helped that my own father labored in a pre-OSHA factory of the time, a noisy and dirty place designed to inflict a slow death on all who entered such horror chambers of noxious and lethal fumes. While I could not imagine who would ever hire me for anything, I knew I wouldn't follow in my dad's footsteps. I do recall thinking I could always join the army or one of the services. They took anyone, or so I thought at the time.

Most of us grew up absent much luxury. In our cold water flat, the bath water had to be heated on a stove if we were not to freeze our fannies off during the weekly cleansing ritual. Nor was there central heating. My bedroom (situated the farthest from a space heater and the kitchen stove) was so cold in winter that I could see my breathe at night. Then there were the long and sharp icicles that hung from the eves of the roof. I always had this dread that one would dislodge and fall three floors straight down before impaling my skull. Seeing death everywhere, I worried a lot. As for transport, we mostly walked, even when the snow was piled waist high. In summer, I walked miles to a nine-hole golf course, paid $1 dollar, and played 27 holes of golf before lugging my clubs several miles home. Such hardships were easily managed. Others were less so.

Worst of these other challenges involved being surrounded by Catholic girls. The young girls of my generation, being raised in religious orthodoxy, and pre-birth control pill, venerated the Virgin Mary and would prefer being dipped in a vat of boiling oil as opposed to physical contact with disgusting and horny guys. That designation encompassed all of us guys as it turned out, especially me and I was on the verge of Sainthood in my own mind. Their reluctance made sense. Besides their religious scruples, we guys were just not that enticing. Why would they ever bother with us? So, it goes without saying that our lives were erotically barren to say the least.

To make matters worse, I was totally clueless. I would laugh at so-called dirty jokes even as I had no freaking idea what they meant. I now shudder at my boyhood innocence. Getting to 'second base' meant scoring a dance with a girl at the sock hop who had polished her patent leather shoes to such a shine that you possibly might see all the way up her dress to the promised land, though there was very little, in truth, to see. Yes, these were times designed to build character in young boys, and that is exactly what happened. We surely were a sad lot of pathetic characters and I may have been the ultimate inspiration in the competition for top sad sack. Things got better in the 1960s, when we all got to college, but only marginally so for me. By then, at least, I got most of the dirty jokes.

In those ancient and long-forgotten times before the internet, and thus remembered history, we interacted face-to face with our fellow students. Though now hard to imagine, this totally is true. How utterly quaint is that? We talked and argued and helped each other toward adulthood. In our day, we did not obsess about getting into the right elementary school at age three nor did we assume our lives were forfeit by getting a B in high school geometry, which was a damn good thing since I sucked the big one at all things mathematical. In fact, I wasn't very good at any course that demanded real knowledge as opposed to those where I might rely on my endless reservoir of BS. I was blessed with a copious supply of that resource along with the Celtic muse of verbal expression, blessed gifts that excused so many academic shortcomings. And consider this! We selected college courses based on whether we might learn something interesting, not on their potential contribution to a future resume or a better paying job. Learning for the sake of learning. What a quaint concept!

In our generation, perhaps some 80 percent of college students felt that finding a purposeful philosophy of life was their most critical challenge. Today, that purpose has been replaced by the goal of making a ton of money or, for more Americans each day, making enough to possibly escape poverty or homelessness. Even today, some five decades later, I occasionally run into college classmates who fondly recall that intellectual crucible within which we all developed our individual perspectives on life. Such moments were irreplaceable, especially for first-generation college students. We loved the intellectual ferment that was our undergraduate experience at Clark University in the 1960s, a school listed as among 40 across the nation that has a significant impact on the lives of those who managed to attend said institution. You must remember that those attending Harvard and Stanford were already destined for an elite position in life, college merely assured their pre-eminent status. Clark somehow enhanced your social and intellectual capital, especially for those of us showing so little promise early on.

We were dead certain that things would be different when our generation came of age. Hard to now believe in the age of a Trump dominated Republican Party and threats of a near Fascist government in DC, but we thought our generation would usher in a new egalitarian utopia. Yup, when we controlled things, all would be different. We would right the ship of state, set things straight again. After all, we saw the world with greater clarity than our foolish elders. We had better values and were not tainted by greed and narcissism. We thought of the greater good and not just ourselves. It seemed like a reasonable hypothesis at the time. Okay, perhaps we were tetched with a bit of feverish hubris and self-delusion, but it was an honest mistake. You probably can delete the word perhaps above.

The 'wild west' of Peace Corps….

Despite all, we future members of India-44 made it through to near adulthood by the early 1960s. Then, along came this scion from a wealthy and famous family to light a flame. He would push us to *"not ask what our (sic) country could do for us, but what we could do for our country."* He motivated a privileged youth, along with those decidedly less privileged like me, to think about things beyond themselves and their narrow, parochial self-interests. He especially touched us working class kids trying to cross over into the mysterious land of economic well-being and social acceptance to pause and think of others, not just of ourselves. We were encouraged to embrace the bigger issues in the world and how each of us might make a difference. Come to think on it, it was like he was inside our heads as we struggled to come of age in our high school and university cultural cocoons.

The response to a simple exhortation made during the heat of a campaign in the wee hours of the morning proved electric. Over the next few years, tens of thousands of Americans, mostly young, would apply to this Peace Corps thing, seeking an opportunity to serve overseas. Only a subset of those aspiring to be volunteers were chosen for training and many of those were deselected (asked to leave) during the strenuous preparation. Many others left on their own as the harsh reality of their decision became clearer to them. Moreover, not all those who survived the rigorous preparation and went overseas completed their tours, particularly in the more difficult placement sites such as India, a site that suffered a high early-exit rate.

In those days, many Peace Corps sites promised little more than isolation, loneliness, disease, and frustration. You could be dumped into some rural village on the other side of the world and you really were 'there,' for better or worse. In that first decade or so, volunteers were alone and pretty much clueless about our roles.

You would be expected to perform tasks in trying conditions that were well beyond your pay level which, at $75 dollars per month, included pretty much everything. Worse, there were no cell phones, no internet, no easy modes of transportation. Many locals spoke dialects you did not learn in training. As the Peace Corps ads of the time promised, it would be *the toughest job you would ever love.* The adjective 'toughest' was an understatement, at least in our case.

Still, it looked like a grand, even thrilling, adventure to us. The 1960s later were labeled by some as the *'wild west'* of the Peace Corps concept. Much was expected of the idea and of the volunteers who flocked to serve. As Richard Goodwin, a Kennedy speech writer and confidant, said in 1963 to a group of early volunteers:

Peace Corps touches on the profoundest motives of young people... that idealism, high aspirations, and ideological convictions are not inconsistent with the most practical, rigorous, and efficient of programs. [and that] every one of you will ultimately be judged— will ultimately judge himself—on the effort he has contributed to the building of a new world society.

In the first few years after enactment, the number of volunteers roughly doubled each year. By 1966, the year that a group of volunteers known as India-40 went to India and another star-crossed collection of applicants known as India-44 started their training, over 15,500 volunteers would be serving in some 46 countries while tens of thousands of American of all ages, but mostly recent college graduates, would seek to serve. Some applicants were seeking adventure, others were motivated by high ideals, still others by less noble purposes such as delaying military service, and more than a few driven to serve by the senseless death of a President who had captured their imaginations and inspired them to seek a more noble purpose in their lives.

The response was sufficiently robust that the selection process became ever more demanding. Those in charge wondered how they might capitalize on this youthful fervor by improving both the quality of volunteers and the reach of the program. The indefatigable Sargent Shriver served as Peace Corps' head man, as well as running the War-On-Poverty initiative. Shriver had dreams of sending a literal army of young Americans to the four corners of the earth. These volunteer troops would seek to save western civilization from the dark shadows of totalitarianism. This army would not carry weapons but an arsenal of hope, would inflict not death but rather the sharing of American know-how, would not engage others in conflict but embrace them as fellow human beings in the pursuit of a common humanity. Well, that's how it played out in the fantasies that circled about the planners in Washington D.C. It now makes you wonder just how this obvious Commie plot, saving the world for humanity, became such a widespread delusion among otherwise sane men and women.

Anyone who has spent any time in the real world knows full well that there are significant gaps between intention and results. Military generals plan out battles in excruciating detail only to lose control of events on the ground within minutes. Politicians launch programs with great enthusiasm only to discover that little was done to pursue original programmatic designs and even less accomplished in the end. As the old saying goes, much more is said than done. Company executives introduce new products every season with visions of untold wealth dancing in their feverish imaginations only to suffer humiliating outcomes and disappointing balance sheets. Only a quarter to one-third of small business start-ups survive for any length of time. For every Apple, Microsoft, and Amazon, the field of entrepreneurship is littered with the carcasses of failed ventures launched with considerable hope that no one can now recall. Remember the Edsel? How about the Concorde? Of course not!

By the ordinary standards of performance in the public and private spheres, the Peace Corps concept has been a remarkable success. Almost six decades later, thousands of volunteers yet travel to the corners of the world to help others create a better society. The numbers are less these days but remain significant. Almost six decades after it was launched, there are some 8,500 volunteers serving in 77 countries. By all accounts, the program initiatives today are more sensibly defined, and the volunteers better matched to what they are supposed to be doing. Lessons were learned from those early 'wild west' days that informed subsequent iterations.

Those lessons, unfortunately for the early volunteers, were founded on the harsh experiences of those who served in that first decade of the program. During that period, hubris dominated thoughtful application of common sense, along with the astoundingly naive belief that American youth were naturally superior to their peers elsewhere. It was merely assumed that we would contribute substantially to the prospects and fortunes of our local sites with the effortlessness of Gods. After all, we were the pre-eminent superpower in the world. We must be doing something right even if it were not clear exactly what that might be. It was a kind of fanciful thinking that easily led the young sheep to their symbolic slaughter.

As it turned out, there were many reasons why the cold reality on the ground might douse the hyperbolic expectations of program planners, at least in some cases. The quality of those applying to serve was never an issue, though arguably I, then and now a klutz, was the exception to that rule. How these early warriors were to be used emerged as the salient problem.

Good intentions go sideway...

The India Peace Corps programs of the mid-1960s were a classic case in point. Poor monsoons on the sub-continent had led to drought and dampened Indian crop production. The country needed to import grain to feed the population, resulting in a depletion of their hard currency reserves they could ill-afford.

To counter any possible increase in Soviet influence on the subcontinent, President Johnson promised Prime Minister Indira Gandhi relief in the form of grain supplies, a good idea, and technical help in the area of agriculture, another good idea that proved much more difficult to execute. There simply was not a handy supply of farming experts willing to bail out India's failing crop production.

This thing called the *green revolution* seemed to offer hope. New varieties of seed had been developed in Mexico with the help of Norman Borlaug and other visionary scientists. The experimental wheat seeds generated bigger yields and had other remarkable properties. For example, the shoots were shorter and resistant to being blown over and destroyed by harsh winds, a big problem in rural areas lacking barriers like trees. The attributes of these agricultural innovations promised to boost commodity production substantially, saving India from a dire present and potentially an even more ominous future. The kicker, of course, was whether local farmers could be persuaded to try new things. Age old practices would have to change, and the damn monsoons needed to return. To get things going, someone would have to work with Indian farmers on the ground to make all this a reality. Enter the Peace Corps.

Warren Wiggins, Peace Corps Deputy Director at the time, immediately suggested that Peace Corps could fulfill the technical assistance part of President Johnson's promise to PM Gandhi. There appeared to be an endless supply of young people eager to help. The annoying fact that they had no discernible or useful skills was overlooked, or at least pushed aside. It seemed a *'good idea at the time.'* In fact, no one really thought it through well enough, or at all. These were the days of endless optimism and abundant hope. A culture whose written history goes back thousands of years would be bailed out by a country eager to send over hordes of kids who had way more zeal than experience, more dedication than common sense, more energy than technical know-how. Again, what might go wrong? As it turned out, plenty!

Initially, numbers in the several thousands were bandied about. PC staff in India were appalled at the thought, how could they use them all? Fortunately, some sanity emerged, and the number of new volunteers planned was scaled back. Already, some 700 were in India, the largest PC contingent of any country in the world. That number was soon to double as indicated in an internal Peace Corps evaluation of what happened next.

In all, 700 new volunteers had been sent to India in six months…. Almost all the volunteers were generalists with a B.A. degree and no agricultural background. They were trained hurriedly and poorly. There was not enough staff in India to check out whether there were real jobs for them at each site. A bitter joke went around that the staff had placed the Volunteers with the help of a Ouija board.

Prior to this moment in time, circa 1965 or so, we who would serve in India-44 were poised to submit our Peace Corps applications. America was increasingly troubled but had not quite collapsed into its own version of chaos and conflict that we now associate with that fractious decade. The war in Viet Nam had not yet spun out of control. We still had faces bright with enthusiasm and hearts filled with noble aspirations.

Many of us submitting applications in 1965 recalled Kennedy's clarion call for personal sacrifice. His death was yet fresh in our minds and hearts. We were searching for some way to reclaim meaning from what struck us as a senseless act of insanity in Dallas. We sought to transform that pain into a movement for good, in honor of his memory. At this moment in time we were not running away from anything… not a lackluster economy or the draft. It was a special time… an era where the nation's leader yet could inspire actions for the good of humanity, not merely for divisiveness and exclusion. No doubt, most of us were seeking a noble ideal, the creation of a better world, and perhaps some form of personal redemption. Yup, it sure seemed like it would be a *grand adventure*.

A cusp…

Little did we appreciate that we were on the cusp of momentous change in the country we were leaving. When many of us made our initial decisions to apply to Peace Corps, American combat troops were just beginning to land in Vietnam in significant numbers, turning that conflict into a full-fledged U.S. dominated conflict within a year. The Voting Rights Act was enacted, resulting in a racial backlash among Americans of various hues and a fundamental political realignment that remains with us to this day. The spark of Feminism had been lit by Betty Friedan's *The Feminine Mystique*, the second of many 'rights' movements that would sweep the land. And just around the corner would be the *Summer of Love* in San Francisco and a frontal assault on conventional culture and mainstream behaviors.

The center that bound together the American experience and culture seemed on the precipice of an apocalypse about to erupt. By the middle of the 1960s, the racial justice eruption moved out of the south into the rest of the country. Anti-war protests moved off college campuses into our communities. Assassinations and bloody riots in places like Watts and Detroit scarred the face of America, to be followed by terrorist bombings and acts of general mayhem. The so-called 'police' riots at the 1968 Democratic Convention in Chicago were a case in point.

But we merry band of world savers already would be in India… hot, lonely, remote, incomprehensible India. We soon wondered if it would be the 'grand' adventure we had imagined in the beginning. At least we seemed to have escaped the mayhem back home. Good idea or not, we endured a long and harsh training to realize our dream. We saw at least half of our original contingent of trainees fall by the wayside even before making it to the sub-continent. Little did we know at the beginning that only about one-in-four of those original, starry-eyed do-gooders who had showed up on the first day of training in 1966 would be there in Delhi at the end of their tours.

Nor were we cognizant of the political goings-on and planning failures that resulted in our being snatched up into the Peace Corps net and then dropped haphazardly into rural India on unsuspecting local officials who had no idea what we were doing in their midst, and less of an idea on how to use us. Once there, however, we would struggle bravely to apply skills for which we had few comparative advantages and less than adequate preparation despite the diligent and best efforts of a superb training staff and a brutally long training regimen.

Unfortunately, it turns out that you cannot produce specialists with a few months of training if the candidates have no prior experience. This becomes even less likely when they have no avocational skills at the outset and there is so much else for them to absorb, like a new language and the skills demanded for negotiating a radically different culture. It becomes virtually an impossible task when you change program purpose mid-training, a fate suffered by the 44-B group.

In truth, we who did make it to the subcontinent felt fortunate at the start. We had survived to this point and were sworn in as official volunteers on September 22, 1967. We felt we were among the select few that had been chosen to carry out that noble vision trumpeted by the handsome and charismatic man who had defined this new frontier. We would get the opportunity to bring the best that America had to offer to a world so in need of our good will and effervescent optimism. We were the vanguard of a new era, that new frontier, a moment in the sun when America would finally realize the better angels of its soul.

Yup, it really did seem like an excellent adventure at the start. Then again, many an idea seems good until our optimistic imaginations rub up against a raw and unforgiving reality. We were to face those realities. But, as Alfred E. Newman oft said, 'why worry?'

Hey, just what could go wrong? Keep reading and you will find out.

Group shot of India 44 at the start of training (1966).

CHAPTER 3

Reconnecting

That Peace Corps gang who responded to Kennedy's call for sacrifice back in pre-historic times, India-44, convened as a group some four decades after returning from the sub-continent. This first of what would be several reunions occurred in 2009 in Oakland, California. We shared stories and camaraderie as well as checked out the wellbeing of former colleagues, many of whom had become distant memories. These gatherings proved essential to keeping the spirit of our long-ago service alive. Without such an opportunity, recollections might be lost in the mists of time or bent beyond recognition. After all, our original service was so far back that it predated the internet and cell phones and even Monday-Night football. Back in this pre-iron age era, people wrote down their thoughts in something called the cursive style, on paper no less. For readers who have no idea what I'm talking about, the cursive style was a transitional form of written communication that linked hieroglyphics to our modern-day I-pad.

The gatherings of India 44 were a kind of therapeutic cleansing of sorts, which we needed... therapy that is. Okay, I did at least. In subsequent years, we would return several times from all over the country... Connecticut, New York, Washington D.C., Alabama, Wisconsin, Montana, California, Hawaii, among other sites. Each attendee had served in either a public health program (India 44-A); or in an agricultural program in Rajasthan (India 44-B), though we all trained together in 1966-67, mostly at the University of Wisconsin- Milwaukee campus. We were a diverse lot held together mostly by a special experience that had diminished in clarity over time, largely due to the confounding and confusing detritus of full lives. That likely is what compelled our need for some form of connection, the fear that time and age would lead us to forget an experience so special, and perhaps even one another.

What unfolds in this work emerges from several of these reunions, along with writings stemming from those gatherings. Like all our reunions, and all reunions everywhere, the central focus involves the sharing of stories, the reliving of a common past, and a search for what it all meant. These are universal quests and that is what is crucial to this tale. The personal reflections and vignettes that unfold in subsequent chapters are not invented. They are as real as our memories permit, though some doubt may remain about the full authenticity of every detail. What is most critical to assert is that I have done my best to capture and present a seminal chapter in our lives… warts and all. I only take liberties in how these memories are shared.

A remarkable group…

On paper, we were touted as agricultural experts, public health professionals, or even community developers. Reality was quite different. What the villagers thought we were doing as opposed to what our titles suggested was never recorded in any systematic fashion. I strongly suspect their impressions of us might have been humorous, perhaps hilarious, and a tad perplexing. However, most of them were too polite to share their feelings with us though there were many ill-concealed smirks. I do recall the rumor in my village that I was a CIA spy since no one could believe the story about my site partner and I being Ag experts sent from America to help local farmers.

Nevertheless, now rather elderly men and women, or should one say mature senior citizens, greeted one another as each arrived for that first gathering of the clan after some four decades. We hugged, lied about how well the other person looked, and then seamlessly fell into small talk. We had seldom seen one another over the intervening years, not at all in too many cases. It mattered not. The bond that brought each back was special, beyond ordinary calculation. It was that bond forged by a common challenge, like being in a war together or surviving a rigorous professional training program. What struck many of us is that any gaps in time seemed like weeks, not years or even decades. There was little awkwardness, almost no difficulty picking up where friendships and good-natured insults had sometimes ended with those final good-byes murmured with moist eyes as the 1960s came to an end.

Looking about, one had to be impressed with what this group had accomplished in life. A disproportionate number had earned advanced degrees from the best universities in the land including Harvard, Columbia, NYU, Stanford, and Wisconsin. Their post-PC professional endeavors ranged from service in the State Department, the United Nations, the Federal Reserve to academic positions in top schools. The members of India-44 often had wondered privately whether Peace Corps all those decades ago attracted only the best and brightest. Were their selection protocols that top-notch, or was there something about that experience which sent each volunteer on a different and more lustrous life trajectory? Back in the day, we didn't feel all that special. Rather, the opposite was true. The females of 44-A felt awkward playing the role of health professionals absent, for virtually all, serious medical preparation while the males of 44-B recall stumbling about our respective villages in a rather clueless fashion. Well, I stumbled around for sure, and I can guarantee without fear of contradiction that I was totally clueless. I'll let the others speak for themselves.

What was remarkable is that all this talent and accomplishment was achieved by this modest assemblage of now ordinary-looking senior citizens that easily fit into a typical living room. We looked much like any gathering of neighbors from an age 55-plus gated community in Florida or Arizona. You know those gatherings, where grumpy old men and crotchety old women collect for cocktails and gossip around a neighborhood barbeque where lies are shared about their prowess on the golf course and where they one-up one-another about the best fish-fry deal to be found on a Friday night. I've been to those retirement gatherings which, in my view, are almost as deadly as university faculty meetings. Alright, I'll admit that nothing is worse than those interminable faculty meetings.

Beginning in 2009, we started gathering in several sites including Oakland, Milwaukee, Washington D.C., and Hawaii. No matter the location or pre-arranged agenda, the sense of sharing remained unique, personal, intense, and illuminating. That sharing emerged from common challenges faced in the blush of innocence, but which could never be easily dismissed. They were unique to our youth and the demands placed upon us. In an important way, our reunions were a way to reach back toward fading memories and relive that moment in our lives now uncertain and illusory as we approached our golden years. Sharing ancient, perhaps fading, memories is a way to appreciate long-held emotions not fully apprehended. They are venues for exploring emotional bonds even as we obscure any obvious feelings of affection behind an exchange of humorous insults. That is what good friends do… at least if they are males. You neither give nor accept any quarter. Insults to the death!

Seeking an elusive truth…

What follows is not a transcription of an actual discussion. God forbid, we are not as juvenile as suggested by the banter in the following chapters. No, the subsequent dialogue among the volunteers is an act of the imagination, my imagination. The tone therefore reflects my voice, not that of my colleagues and friends, though I tried to individualize the characters somewhat even as liberties were taken for literary purposes. At the same time, the shared vignettes and personal stories are based in fact, or whatever constitutes fact so long after reality had played itself out. While the conversation in our imaginary gathering is essential as a literary vehicle to support our recollections, the substance being shared, and the emotions being conveyed, are as real and as authentic as I can make them.

Truth inevitably is an elusive commodity. Each vignette reflects a collective process to varying degrees, much like putting together a jigsaw puzzle. You start with a memory, perhaps an image or two. Then, you slowly put the pieces together, often with separate individuals contributing parts to the whole, even suggesting where false starts had occurred, or questionable memories had been offered. Not all the stories were so erected, but a number were. That was the beauty of such collective moments. We progressed as a team or, in many cases, helped one another sharpen our memories.

Still, I must be clear that our story, as valid as our decaying memories permit, will never be the equivalent of the actual experience. During our lengthy training, Peace Corps tried hard to prepare us for the realities we would face. But we weren't… prepared that is. You must confront reality on a personal basis, particularly if what you experience has no analogue in your conventional culture. You really did have to be there to *get it.*' This is an insight I have brought with me through life. And yet, sharing our stories is the next best thing, so sit back and enjoy.

As noted in the Forward, the names employed have been altered to protect the innocent, except for this Corbett character. It is easier that way, for me at least. I don't have to worry as much about being sued for libel or slander or defamation of character, as if any of my colleagues from some five decades ago had any character remaining, good or bad. I know the guys don't, not so sure about the gals. It turns out they always avoided me to the extent possible. Clearly they were exceptionally smart from the get-go. More to the point, this is not the documented story of India-44. Rather, it is a narrative capturing some of the unique feel of what serving in a tough Peace Corps site was like in those early days. Thus, the tales that will unfold for you are equal parts farce, insights, humor, commitment, successes, failures, triumphs, sufferings, and joys.

In the interest of full disclosure, there are many stories, probably too many, of desperate males seeking companionship from those of the more mature sex. While possibly tedious, these depictions of male idiocy are spot-on and, unfortunately, cannot be ignored. After all, India was not a great place for a bunch of young guys at their sexual peaks. It was, in fact, a kind of hell. If nothing else, our romantic foibles as we desperately, and with incomprehensible ineptness, sought erotic solace from members of the fair sex is the very stuff of legends. Again, the women of India 44-A generally were way too savvy to put up with us, with me for sure. Our futile search for intimacy therefore provides essential comedic relief when compared to the harsher realities experienced in our sites. Basically, our romantic antics were fall-down hilarious for the most part. Our real work in rural India, on the other hand, had moments of hilarity but generally was sobering, often trying, and occasionally painful.

As typical for our periodic communal dialogues, we started by going around the room. Each person shared bits and pieces of their lives. It never took long to move from recent life achievements, like the benefits of our new hearing aid or titanium knee, to the past and our Peace Corps tenure in India. These dialogues had a rhythm of their own. We would start with neutral topics before slowly dipping deeper into our emotions and experiences as volunteers. It quickly became apparent that there were dimensions of our common service that had been kept in some private place for reasons that soon becomes clear.

A couple of insights quickly emerged after the end of our service. Upon our return, few outsiders could appreciate, or had much interest, in our overseas experiences. Even when others appeared captivated, these experiences proved difficult to share with outsiders. Besides, many memories remained embarrassing, even painful. They struck us as revealing too much about our young frailties. How could you describe the pressures you felt with any fidelity, or the challenges you faced? Our family and friends had no relatable experiences. That might sound like immature whining but there is an element of truth there. And so, we stopped talking about what we had done overseas, a phenomenon often seen among those returning from war.

One reality was inescapable. In many instances, we had felt like frauds. We had endured heat, disease, loneliness, and the enervating futility of not having a clear role to play. For all that, what had we contributed to our sites, if anything? In the end, we all felt as if they had taken way more from India than we had left behind. That scale never seemed balanced inside our heads. The problem was whether this perceived imbalance was our reality or merely figments of distorted memories we somehow conjured up? Was it easier to recall the bad and forget the good? That might well be the case or might the reverse better represent reality, some sugar coating of our service. Perhaps a dialogue among us could sort out such things.

Still, we could recall some successes, though effort was required at times to recollect our so-called triumphs. Community projects were built, a few local schools erected, wells dug. Some of us helped with *local* public health initiatives, delivered babies and vaccinated children, and there even were some agricultural demo plots and chicken projects that were not obvious failures. For the record, I delivered no babies, nor did I ward off the return of the Bubonic Plague. That was left to the good angels from India 44-A. My hapless peers and I in 44-B did our best to reverse the impoverished agricultural fortunes found in our sites, hopefully assisting the area out of the ravages of a recent drought. In that regard, and perhaps owing to our inflated expectations, we could never quite shake a sense of overall, perhaps comical, failure. That negative summary took shape in various jokes shared in the one-on-one interactions. Who among us males would win the prize for being the biggest doofus? There was no obvious winner in this contest though the merits of my candidacy are indisputable, in my view at least.

Eventually, the group found a common dialogue as we all settled in the virtual living room for this telling of our stories. I recall starting with the following, perhaps universal, queries. What have you been doing recently, or for the last four-plus decades? What's going on in your life now, if anything? What do you most recall about the India experience from so long ago, assuming you have any memory left? When did you begin to lie about your accomplishments so effortlessly? And the question most often directed at me personally. Just when did your body begin to fall apart so badly, followed by a reluctant inquiry into how much time I had left on God's good earth? I did worry when two nurses from 44-A reached over to take my pulse though I still think the call for the EMTs was a bit over the top.

Inevitably, someone would comment elliptically about that nagging feeling of personal failure which stalked most of us. This was the two-ton elephant in the room. It was a guilt that tended to deflate us, but which remained hard to admit and all but impossible to articulate fully, perhaps due to difficulty in finding some adequate expression for deeply held negative emotions. Namely, we tended to see ourselves as Peace Corps failures, at least relative to the high ambitions and expectations that brought us to the subcontinent in the first instance.

Was that true? If so, why did we so eagerly collect to relive those long-ago moments. No, the reality of our days as volunteers in the early days of the Peace Corps experience are more complicated than any summary judgment of success or failure. The meaning of those days needs to be teased out slowly and carefully. In this matter, there can be no rush to judgement.

So, join us as we reminisce and cogitate about our long-ago experiences. Share our struggles, our disappointments, and even our occasional triumphs. If you ever wondered what it might have been like to give two years of your life to a somewhat ill-considered impulse, this is the place to be. It is one way to embrace a vicarious thrill that few have been fortunate enough to experience, and absent all the damned inconveniences of doing it for real. Some of you might recall that night in college way back when, the night you got drunk and you and your buddies decided that Peace Corps sounded like a capital idea. Keep reading and you just might thank your lucky stars that you sobered up in time.

On the other hand, perhaps you might regret not giving it a go. If we have learned anything over our long lives, there is no shortage of poor judgment.

Group shot of 44-A in 2009.

Group shot of 44-B in 2009.

CHAPTER 4

A Touch of Shame

We gathered in the living room of a host volunteer's home. Some sat on sofas, others on random chairs, a few finding spots on the floor. The early dialogue was amiable, if directionless. We mostly chatted about what was going on in our current lives… retirements finally reached, illnesses overcome, along with notable achievements of children and even grandchildren. At some point, though, the inevitable shift occurred. We began to peer back some five decades to relive the events that had brought us together. After all, this need to better understand our past is what impelled such gatherings in the first place. If you paid close enough attention, though, there was a bit of urgency in the air. We were septuagenarians; just how many more of these gatherings might there be?

At first, the recollections were banal, even superficial. Not entirely surprising since each of us was feeling the others out, much like any acquaintances would do after a long absence. It was not long, though, before that sense of caution evaporated. Dee was the first to strike a more revealing note, one that resonated through the room in an unspoken manner. She admitted, reluctantly at first, to what she considered her personal sense of inadequacy as a volunteer. Slight of build, and quite attractive with a pleasant face framed by brown hair that fell to her shoulders, she had studied political-science at Cal-Berkeley before joining Peace Corps to do public health work outside of Bombay, now Mumbai, in the province of Maharashtra.

In halting words, Dee shared her personal judgment that she had survived India, not contributed toward it. Haltingly, she revealed more of what she considered her shame. After a while, she looked around to sense whether she had strayed to an unwanted personal space but sensed no disapproval. Once her 'secret' was admitted, further words of self-revelation poured forth more easily, eventually spreading to the others. Decades of suppressed or half-forgotten shame would bubble up in a kind of public confessional, first haltingly and then with more ease. This was not unlike the dynamic found in Alcohol Anonymous meetings. What a newcomer thinks of as a private shame and unique failure is suddenly revealed to him or her as a shared and rather common experience. There was a tiny pause as she ended her soliloquy, as if no one knew precisely how to follow up her confessional.

"Thanks Dee, your comments are a relief." I jumped in, hoping she hadn't already regretted her honesty. "I thought I was the only total screw-up among us."

"No Tom, you were not the only screw-up among us by any stretch, just the biggest one." This friendly swipe at me, the first of what would be many, came from Harry, an African American volunteer in 44-B. Harry personified a classic rags-to-riches personal story, from humble beginnings to success in life. He was raised in an impoverished sharecropper family in North Carolina before eventually rising to a high position in a national labor union. Everyone loved Harry. He was warm and loving, typically embracing others with an infectious smile or hearty laugh. I could always tell when a loving barb was coming my way, his smile would become a bit too warm. It was his tell that he was about to be mischievous.

"Hah, hah. Bite me!" I tried but realized I should have waited for the laughter to die down before fully responding. "The truth is, all of us clowns in 44-B were clueless, most of us at least. I can't speak for the women since I seldom saw you gals while we were in-country. Come to think on it, why didn't I see you gals more?"

"We hid from you." A volunteer named Janice responded without missing a beat. "It was a matter of self-preservation. I mean you guys were… how should I put it?"

"Predators!" I completed her thought.

"Exactly," she enthused, "Corbett was for sure. So, can you blame us?" She was laughing now. "Let me absolutely be clear here. It was only one of you 44-B guys that required we have pepper spray at the ready." She pointed at me in case anyone might be confused.

I thought about that for a moment before nodding my head.

"Okay, fair enough. I get that. In any case, in India I saw the other guys from my group often enough, too often. What a bunch of classic doofuses we were, maybe except for Ben here." I pointed toward a handsome, still ruggedly built man who yet looked as if he just descended from conquering some Alpine peak. "Anyone else notice that he seemed to know what he was doing… always."

"Yes," Harry enthused. "That's for sure. And Bob, I thought he was good as well."

Encouraged, I continued. "Perhaps, that made them outliers among us losers. By the way, Ben, how the hell did they let you in with the rest of us? You had skills and everything… something of substance to contribute. You weren't like the rest of us. Were you a plant, keeping tabs on just how awful the rest of us were doing?"

"Nope, nothing special about me." Ben said sheepishly. "Now that you mention it, though, I don't talk about my Peace Corps work, never have. India 44-B? Like it never happened." Several heads from the group were nodding assent as if they understood completely. "Fortunately, no one asks, no one cares."

I puzzled at Ben's comment. Had he taken an oblique shot at his peers. Ordinarily, that was my job. I was supposed to be the bad guy. "You're right, Ben. Unless you were there, no one could understand. I kind of understand our silence."

"That's it." Ben mildly enthused. "I was not embarrassed by what I did there. It was just so hard to talk about. Perhaps that's why we started these… gatherings."

Mel, a quiet and unassuming man with an ever-present smile and quick wit, pursued the topic. "So, Ben, what gives? Did you feel you got stuck with a bunch of misfits or not?"

He seemed to think on that for a moment. "No, not really. We all struggled but…" His response trailed off.

———

It hit me that we were getting too serious too early in the afternoon. Besides, he might reveal a truth, that he had been stuck serving with a bunch of hopeless misfits. Perhaps a lighter tone was needed to keep our spirits upbeat.

"Well, I thought we were misfits but, I might add, angels compared to the nimrods from India-40 here." I gazed directly at Paul, who hailed from this group of admitted derelicts that had been assigned to do community development in the rural areas outside of what is now known as Mumbai. "It is always comforting to be able to compare yourself to the truly incompetent and supremely classless. While difficult to acknowledge that there were volunteers more useless than the male misfits of India 44-B, here sit the self-labeled mutts from 40. This really was the gang that couldn't shoot straight."

"Pathetic try, Corbett!" Paul intoned as he looked toward a couple of his cohorts who had crashed the India-44 reunion. "We were the apex of Peace Corp's work on the sub-continent. Washington used us as poster-boys for what it meant to be productive and intrepid volunteers. You losers, on the other hand, defined ineptness. Oh, and I'm excluding the talented gals from your group by the way. You guys pretending to be farmers up in Rajasthan were the sorriest bunch of volunteers ever assembled. No doubt about that."

Connie, his wife and a member of 44-A, glanced at him with a bit of suspicion. "Darn good thing you didn't lump us with the guys from B. Guess I trained you well." Paul had purloined his wife, Connie, from the mostly female members of India 44 who did public health work in rural Maharashtra. He somehow conned this lovely lass into marrying him, an act of larceny for which the males of my group had yet to forgive him, nor could they understand her lapse of judgment in agreeing to wed this low-life.

"Really?" I looked at Connie with incredulity. "You consider Paul well-trained? How so?"

"I made it very clear to my now submissive spouse that we women should never be lumped with you guys." She said that with a kind of finality, her dark eyes bright with a humor she struggled to suppress. I looked at her for a moment. Just as she had been so many decades ago, her Asian features betrayed an inner lightness about her. It was an undeniably attractive quality. "It took me decades, but I've whipped him into shape. Everyone knows, men are exceedingly difficult to civilize."

"Thank you dear." Paul caught her sarcasm but accepted her comments as a compliment. He was smart enough to know that it was always good policy to agree with your wife.

I admitted to myself that the mutts from 40 might be dull-witted but they weren't flat out stupid. "Paul, I guess you are not as dumb as you look."

Then, he went and ruined my semi-sympathetic thought by gratuitously adding. "You do know that the girls begged Peace Corps to have their group relabeled India 40-A. They desperately wanted to distance themselves from you losers. And the reason they hid from you guys all the time was self-evident. You must see it, don't you?"

"No." I answered timidly and immediately realized my mistake.

"Really, no? It's just that they were so fortunate to be assigned near some true American heroes, the sexy, virile, charming, and oh-so humble men of India 40."

Several women from my group started to guffaw but I got there first. "You mean the totally freaking delusional men of India 40! What bull…" I caught myself though I realized that nicety of language was unnecessary, if not absurd. Still, I decided to clean it up for the moment. "By the way, I didn't know there was another male group in Maharashtra called India-40, the one with sexy guys who managed to do some good while there."

The exchange of insults now was in full stride.

"Corbett, as I keep telling you, our superiority is self-evident!" Paul smiled.

The females in the room now were rolling their eyes. I could guess what they were thinking… typical of roosters found preening and prancing about the barnyard. Time to reign us in.

"The real truth… none of you clowns were exactly catches." Nanette, an African American woman from Milwaukee, chimed in.

"Okay, okay! We can debate the relative sexual attractiveness of the males of 44 versus 40 later." I addressed Nanette, rather glad that she had intervened to halt the stale exchange of insults between us males. I had always liked this comely woman who had grown up in the black ghetto of Milwaukee, a very racially divided city. She emerged into adulthood with reservations about whites yet absent any lasting rancor. Best of all, she would laugh at my awful jokes with considerable enthusiasm. I loved that, surely the quickest way to any man's heart. I smiled at her. "And by the way, my dear, I have heard on the highest authority that you once stopped an entire Indian train filled with passengers by pulling the emergency stop cord. I won't even ask why."

"Wait, who told you that?" Nanette was thrown momentarily off her game.

I looked over at Connie, her site mate in India, who mouthed the words *I'm sorry* in Nanette's direction. Then I continued. "My point is that we heard in Delhi that the central government of India was going to chuck the whole lot of PC volunteers out when they saw what mischief 40 was up to. Didn't one of your guys jump naked off a building and another try to drive back to America in a bus he purloined for the trip? A well-thought out plan for sure. And didn't someone plan a village road that ran in one big circle, perhaps based on some planning done after smoking those funny cigarettes. Okay, maybe not that one! No matter, we gentlemen of 44 arrived to save the day, and just in the nick of time."

"My word," Laura exclaimed while shaking her head. "I think I need a shovel. It is getting rather thick in here. Listen to me. Here is the bottom line. None of you guys in 40 or 44 were worth a damn. Why do you think I ignored all of you?"

"In truth, most of us gals ignored you." Maureen said with equal conviction. Maureen reminded us of Ben but on the distaff side. She exuded competence and she knew what she was doing while in India. We listened when she talked.

"Maureen, when you say 'most,' are you talking about me marrying Paul." Connie looked deflated. "I had too, I had little choice. He begged me so pitifully. The man was groveling." Then she broke into an exaggerated expression of remorse.

Paul opened his mouth but only emitted one word. "I…" Then he sat mute.

"True enough," Laura ended Paul's paralysis. "Some of my sisters like Connie here took pity on you guys but it was little more than a charitable impulse. We were raised to be kind to the lame and the desperate, particularly the cognitively impaired. Just being good Christians is all. And who could possibly be more pitiable than you guys from 44?"

"What about 40?" I asked to salve our bruised group egos.

"Oh yeah, them too."

That silenced the male sparring for the moment. I looked over at Laura while noting silently that she had never lost her attractiveness after all these years. She was right on one matter. She had ignored all of us guys, including me. What was with that? Hell, I had looked a bit like John F. Kennedy in those days, if the lighting was poor and the gal suffered from early-onset cataracts. I even had that charming Boston accent, now long gone. In those years, you would mistake me for one of the Kennedy brothers, at least with your eyes shut. Besides, my Irish wit remained undiminished even in the face of perpetual disasters with the ladies. That gift had never deserted me, though many have searched for the off switch.

I recall thinking Laura quite beguiling during stateside training. Yet, she ignored me with even greater conviction than the others. Not surprising, I suppose. Being ignored by women was a peculiar strength of mine, a well-honed talent in fact. If that skill, or perhaps napping, ever made it on to the Olympic schedule, the gold medal would be mine. It remains my unique contribution to mankind, or to my fellow males. The guys, you see, find my failures with the distaff side extremely soothing to their own battered self-esteem. When they happened upon romantic failure in their own lives, they could always point to me and say silently, or loudly, *at least I'm not as pathetic as Corbett.*

Back then, my impression was that Laura looked on me as if I were totally invisible. All through high school and college, this evident invisibility to those of the female persuasion was something which I accepted. Sometimes, I would ask a fellow male if he could see me, to test whether the sad sack who looked-back at me in mirrors might be some form of illusion. Based on their positive responses, I clearly possessed a corporeal presence, such as it was. Women just didn't care. I was not worth their time or attention.

One day in training, Laura seemed to change direction and pay attention to me. Was I about to get lucky, really? Lacking any self-confidence whatsoever, I worked my way up to making a pass but with my typically glacial deliberation. Perhaps I hesitated too long. Before I could make my patented move, she returned to her studied indifference. Her temporary interest, if real, was most likely another illusion emerging from my testosterone-fueled imagination. I had such flights from reality, but only on occasion. Mostly, I knew my place at the end of the queue. Ah, female indifference, that was my comfort zone.

"Laura," I finally said, "I always thought you gals ignored us because we were a bunch of immature and obnoxious perverts."

"True enough," Maureen intervened to advance the female position, "you were disgusting." When entering PC training back in 1966, Maureen was one of the very few bringing real skills to the table. She was finishing up her nurses training which gave her an enormous advantage going overseas. While often serious of demeanor, she employed a cutting wit on occasion. "That is why we have always felt bad for Connie who got stuck with one of the 40 guys." She smiled as she looked directly at Paul. "While they were a step above the 44 guys, the difference was negligible if I'm to be honest."

"Thank you, Maureen," Connie smiled broadly. "I deserve all the sympathy I get." This Asian- looking lass had been raised in Hawaii, coming from Japanese ancestry. She was petite, with dark eyes that flashed with humor on occasion. While generally quiet, she could bring you to your knees with a quick retort. "What choice did I have? He wore me down. Besides, he struck me as being so pathetic and I was taught by my parents to be kind."

"No argument there," Mel added in his endearing way. Soft spoken, Mel always came across as a sweet fellow with a self-deprecating wit and an infectious smile. He remained the avuncular elder in any room, looking much like that quiet accountant who did the company books whom no one noticed until that day he ran off with the CEO's bombshell secretary and half of the firm's funds. "No matter how hard we guys ran after you gals, you always managed to outrun us."

"Desperation will do that for a woman, gives us all super-powers." Connie added to howls of laughter from her sisters. "Alas, they somehow failed me when it came to Paul here."

I broke in with yet another attempt at wit. "Connie, I can see why you might have given Paul the pity vote. He is hopeless, but in a nice way… like that stray dog you feel sorry for because, after all, how else would the mutt survive. I will even admit that I have come across uglier mutts than Paul here. But a mystery remains."

"What, pray tell?" Her face betrayed concern, my reputation for mischief preceded me.

"Remember that time we met by accident on a vacation trip to Goa. You and Nanette were on the same boat out of Bombay as Ralph and me." A smile crossed my face as I saw her eyes narrow in an expression of deep suspicion.

"Corbett... " she managed, but no more.

"Ah, romantic Goa, a spot so beautiful that it was a prize destination on the hippie world tour at the time. Visions of romance danced in my head, moonlit beaches, pounding surf, exotic palm trees swaying in gentle breezes, enough to suggest terrible things to a young man battling excess testosterone and zero opportunities. If I were to be totally honest, even the palm trees were looking good to me."

Paul sputtered, "Wait, are you about to say that you hit on my wife?"

"Well..." I teased.

Connie suddenly hurled a pretzel in my direction. "Corbett!" Once again, that was all she managed to get out.

"Just relax!" I laughed heartily. "This was before the two of you even hooked-up and she shot me down in 2.5 seconds flat, if that long. I think it was my 43rd straight sortie with a member of the fairer sex that ended with me crashing and burning."

"Save the tears, buster. You won't get any tears from this crowd." Laura was quite pleased with her retort.

"So awfully sad. Really, it was amazing that a stud like me could get shot down so often. A pity... all you gals missed a chance with an unparalleled lover, that's me by the way, and a brilliant and iconoclastic thinker."

Bob interjected with a hint of exasperation. "What the hell are you talking about?" Bob was a Yale scholarship student from a large, working class Catholic family. After Peace Corps, he would eventually get a business degree from the Wharton School before working in international banking in Paris. Later, he went on to a Ph.D. in economics from N.Y.U. before assuming a position with the Federal Reserve in Washington. I asked him once why he left international banking to pursue a less lucrative, but likely more important, career in federal service. He cryptically responded that his personal ethics would not permit him to remain in the private sector. He was a person with a carefully crafted moral compass. I always listened to what he had to say. "Brilliant thinker, you? When did you last have a great idea?"

"Just the other day, out of the blue, I came up with another breakthrough technological concept. It's a million-dollar idea. Damn, I have no freaking idea how I keep doing it. I intend to call it *'Clear Rear.'*

"What?" Harry laughed, knowing something absurd was coming but unable to figure it out.

"Listen to this. You attach this device to your commode. Now for the best part, it spurts a stream of water positioned so that the area of your derriere that needs cleaning will get a good wash after you poop." I heard many groans but pushed on. "No, think about it. You will save money on TP and, in places like rural India, end the worry that someone will eat some communal food with their left hand. We should market this on the sub-continent. A sure winner. Amazing, no?"

"No!" Nanette chocked she was laughing so hard. "As if they have running water in some of our villages." One thing that marked Nanette was her large personality and a laugh that brought joy everywhere. The black woman from Milwaukee added the following. "Really, is it any wonder you had so much trouble with us, with women in general?"

"Still a mystery to me. I'm such a Prince and have great ideas like *'Rear Clear'* all the time."

"I thought it was 'Clear Rear?'" Paul commented with a smirk.

"Whatever?" I retorted.

"Corbett!" Dee broke in to focus the group roasting squarely on me. "Perhaps if you didn't drool every time you ran into one of us girls, you would have done better. That was just a bit off-putting, you know."

"Hah, hah," I retorted. "it's just that you were all so sexy and we were so…"

"Horny" Mel offered.

"Not the word I was looking for, but it will do. I think I was heading toward sad, pathetic, needy, something along those lines. After all, we were stuck in India for crying out loud. It was like being surrounded once again by all those Catholic girls back in high school. I yet shudder at that memory." I made a bitter face. "I wasn't going to mention this, but Mel here has written a wonderful piece on his travails with women he met through dating services after his divorce. He was kind enough to share it with me. Alas, it's a sad story of many failures with the distaff side, an epic tale of woe and grief. My real point is this, though. He included some disasters from his early years including his PC tenure and the final party of our combined group as we were in Delhi being mustered out. I can't recall his exact words, but he went on about not wanting to go to our final shindig because of me."

"You?" Maureen was puzzled. "I don't understand."

"Corbett!" Mel groaned but I waived him off dismissively.

"Yeah he wrote something like the following, though I'm paraphrasing here. *'I despaired of having any luck with the women in our group since I would be competing for them with Tom, who was over six feet tall and had the rugged good looks of someone who could adorn the cover a romance novel.'*"

Guffaws and laughter filled the room. "Oh, I think he was writing about me, not you. He meant Tim, not Tom… just a typo." Another 44-B volunteer, Tim, had seized the moment, smiling broadly so that no one might think he was being serious. He was self-effacing by nature, a pleasant looking and genial man with soft features and an understated presence. You would never guess that, after obtaining a graduate degree from Harvard, he had spent a career working for the United Nations (UNICEF), mostly with refugees trapped in some of the worst conflicts of the last half-century. It was dangerous work as he would be caught up in the front lines of several shooting conflicts. "After all, our names are similar, and we look so much alike. Easy mistake for Mel to make."

"Admittedly, you have many charms, Tim. However, there is no doubt that Mel was talking about this specimen of pure testosterone-driven manhood here." I gestured to myself. "Besides, you ain't no six feet-one inches tall." In truth, he came extremely close.

Paul raised his hand. "I am still grinding on the fact that you hit on my future wife."

"You are?" I responded with an exasperated look. "You should be grateful, you moron. Your spouse turned down a guy who could adorn a romance novel on the off chance she might land a mutt like you. There really is no accounting for taste. It's all… inexplicable."

"No kidding," Connie sighed in an exaggerated way. "The road not taken."

"Connie," I said absent any smile, "I will be serious for a moment. I'm sure any female who fell for my so-called charms, a very small N by the way, would agree that you took the far better road in choosing this character. And Paul, you did well for yourself. I mean, you married way above your station in life. After all, you would not even be here with us today had you not purloined the 7th cutest gal from our group."

"Seventh?" Connie responded with mock outrage.

"Okay, maybe 5th, but that's the highest I can go." Then, seeing something coming in my direction, I ducked to avoid what turned out to be a large pretzel that might well have caused a serious facial disfiguration had it found the intended mark. Connie had found her weapon of choice, a tactic that would soon spread to the others. "Okay, maybe you were 3rd, but only if the lighting was bad."

"You're being too generous there, Corbett, I had her ranked 4th." Paul said and then howled in pain as his spouse elbowed him hard in the ribs.

———

I decided it was time to shift gears. "You know, I bet we fake farmers in Rajasthan did some good in our Peace Corps days, at least when we weren't chasing the ladies of 44-A. I am loath to point out, but obviously intend to, that India was importing grain in 1967, the year we arrived. Now, get this… ta-da! It was exporting grain when we finished up two years later. Of course, some attribute this reversal of fortune to the fortuitous return of the monsoon rains. However, I personally think it was all due to the good works of India 44-B. Are we agreed? After all, numbers don't lie."

"Oh my god, he is having a 1960s acid flashback." Harry again belly laughed.

Bob then spoke up. "I hate to admit it, but Corbett does have a point, not that crap about turning India into a grain exporting nation. However, we did leave a mark or two, albeit a modest one, in our villages."

I looked at Bob more closely. He and several of the male volunteers had one irritating attribute that bothered the hell out of me. They had hardly aged over the past several decades. How did they manage that? Hell, I look like a dried-up prune that's been left out in the sun for a week. They also were successes in life. I made my way through life as a fake academic, not hard after my training as a fake ag expert in India.

Tim reentered the fray. "I managed to get back to my site after many years. Amazingly, many locals remembered me, and very fondly I might add. They even recalled my contributions, such as they were, or they were kind enough to lie."

"As a farming guru?" Paul asked incredulously.

"Hell no! I dumped the fake farmer bit and found a way to help them by digging wells for new sources of water. Now that was useful."

"Sure, you and a couple of others found a way to make a difference, but you were the exceptions." Harry added with a glum expression. Of all of us in 44-B, he had the biggest heart. His dirt-poor, black sharecropper family overflowed with faith and love. He never lost that faith, nor that enveloping love from a close family. More importantly, his infectious smile and common touch never deserted him, even as he achieved professional success later in life.

"No," Tim didn't back down. "I think we all left a mark on our villages. It's just that we tend to remember the bad stuff."

"Perhaps," Paul said without conviction. "I do have this dream where I return to my village and the people hoist me up on their shoulders to carry me about while singing my praises."

I grimaced. "I have the same dream but in my mind the villagers stone me to death. My version looks a lot like the movie scene where the angry peasant mob attacks Frankenstein's monster with scythes and axes."

"Makes perfect sense to me," Paul affirmed, "perhaps because you rather resemble Frankenstein's monster. Not as handsome I fear. Sound like him too, you make the same grunts when you eat. Perhaps if you chewed your food before swallowing."

Mel interjected before I could defend myself. "One thing we did leave behind were a lot of laughs. My god, we were so pathetic that the locals couldn't help but laugh."

Tim chuckled. "I've got a good one. One day, early on, I remember asking the local boy who cooked for me to fetch some of this snack I liked. It was spicy hot but good. When I told him how much I wanted, he looked at me funny and asked for my bike. I considered that odd but thought nothing more of it. Off he went. Sometime later, I looked on with horror as he pushed the bike back over the last hill with great difficulty before descending to my tiny village. Thing was, he had piled it high with this snack... like a two-year supply. I used the wrong word to specify the amount I wanted. Even when I returned years later, they recalled the crazy American who was addicted to whatever that crap was called."

"I hate to admit it, but you guys are right. Since that so seldom happens, I must give you your due. Indeed, we were the butt of constant jokes. In Salumbar, the outpost where Ralph and I did our mischief, it quickly became clear that we knew shit about farming, excuse my language. Eventually, we figured out that we were the objects of a local controversy."

"Which was," Maureen asked.

"Why were we there? Apparently this question occupied the town banter for some weeks after our arrival. One day, a friend from the town introduced me to the local Communist leader, or so I was told. In our ensuing conversation, he revealed these two primary hypotheses on what the hell we were doing in this remote desert backwater."

"I take it no one suggested you were there to help with their crops." Janice offered.

"Not even close. One theory was that we were CIA spies but what in God's good name was there to spy on in such an out-of-the-way place. Even the local Red had doubts about that one. The favored explanation was that we were there to learn about farming so that we could return to the States and become farmers ourselves. It was all so humiliating. After all these years, I still burn with the shame of it."

Connie, now feeling some remorse at trying to blind me with well-thrown pretzels, said encouragingly. "I am sure you're exaggerating, Tom. I bet you did some great stuff, at least when you were not off harassing us females."

"Harassing? I remember things differently, more like bringing God's greatest gift to women in need. By the way, I'm that gift."

"Oh, barf bag, barf bag please." Laura squealed in disgust.

I ignored her response, looking at the ceiling as if thinking hard on some important matter. "Here's what I recall of life as a farming expert? I spent endless hours tramping around fields with a local development officer. Why was never clear. Early on, though, I do remember this farmer asking me if his soil was good for this new experimental seed we were pushing… a hybrid wheat seed that would increase yields greatly. The guys will remember this! The poor farmer could always get a decent crop, one on which he might survive, with his usual seed. Unless disaster struck, he would be assured of feeding his family for another year by doing what he had always done."

"I know where you are going." Bob shook his head slowly.

"So do I." Ben added.

"However, by saying yes to using the experimental seed, I was asking him to take a chance on something new, and very risky. This was a high payoff, but high-risk proposition. So many things could go wrong, and he could end up with nothing. And here he was relying upon a nimrod like me for advice on what to do?"

"Better to consult a Ouija board," Mell added.

"What could I do? It was too late to escape town. I leaned over and grabbed a handful of dirt, ran it through my fingers, and threw it up in the air. Then I turned to this poor schlepp and said *'yes'* as confidently as I could. In truth, I had no freaking idea. This marginal farmer thought I knew something. He was looking at me for confirmation that he was doing the right thing, but I was clueless. You guys have all been there. You know the high stakes they faced, the penalties for failure. I would go home at night and pray I had not destroyed a family that day. How pathetic was that!"

"Beyond contempt." Maureen asserted.

"No, a harmless fib." Paul suggested. "Nothing worse than the lies you told the gals in 44-A all the time."

"Not even close" I said without a hint of a smile. "Sure, I lied to the gals, but they all knew it. All females know it, and thus roundly ignore me." Suddenly, I had a terrible thought. "You all did know I was full of it, didn't you? I mean, I just assumed that women knew instinctively that all of us guys were full of shit. I would have felt terrible had you not." Then I looked at several women in the room questioningly but none of them said anything. I was taken aback by their mute response. "Really? Some of you took me seriously! That can't be right." Still no response for several moments at least.

"Well, we were young and naïve." An unidentified female voice murmured.

"Oh shit… now more guilt." Somehow, I pressed-on. "No matter, the thing is that this poor Indian farmer trusted me. When his wheat first sprouted-up through the ground, I was taken aback that it was green. This is how naïve I was. In all our training, I don't recall seeing a young wheat crop emerging from the soil. How could that be? I only recalled images of amber waves of grain from pictures. Hell, I was born and raised near Boston. There are no damn farms there. Were the sprouts supposed to be green, or was something wrong? If I had screwed up this guy's crop, his family would be in deep doo-doo. It was not like they had crop insurance or anything. We are talking basic survival here. A crop failure would be devastating. His old methods resulted in very modest yields that were pretty much guaranteed. This new stuff demanded precise and timely adherence to proper procedures, a certain depth of planting and the correct way of fertilizing as well as adhering to a strict watering schedule. So much could go wrong. The fear hanging over me was crippling. What if I was ruining his life, putting his family into jeopardy? The guilt associated with failure would have been disabling, for him and for me."

There was silence for a moment before Mel said with wry sincerity. "Well, we always could forget our troubles by getting drunk at the local bar and partying with all those wild local women."

It took a moment, since he never cracked a smile. Then, all the males in the room laughed uproariously. When the hilarity came to a slow end, I added. "Ah yes, if there was another dominant feature of our existence in Rural India besides the guilt associated with being useless, it was loneliness. Here we are, a bunch of guys at the top of our hormone-fueled game, so to speak, and where do we end up? Godforsaken India. It was pure hell."

"Oh, you guys were always complaining." Laura offered dismissively. "Was it all so bad?"

"Yes!" This came from several guys followed my more silence as everyone pondered the question.

Slowly, I responded. "So bad? In all seriousness, that's a tough question. There's no easy answer. One thing, though, we got a lot out of being there, surely more than we contributed. Yet, we were clueless, no doubt about that. That's my story and I'm sticking with it."

"No one's arguing with you, my dear man." Mel concluded.

Several of us reflecting on our excellent adventure.

CHAPTER 5

Getting There

"How did it happen? How did we all get to India in the summer of 1967," Stan asked? His blond hair now receding but his affable manner remained the same   as it had been some five decades ago. Unlike most of us big city kids, he had made his way to Peace Corps from a sparsely settled region of the nation… the big-sky country of Montana.

"Good question." Maureen added.

"It is one I've pondered many a time." Stan persisted. He had been with us only a short time in India, but it was apparent that our training and his brief tenure in country had a profound impact on his life. As the only male of our group to serve in Peace Corps as a public health volunteer *and* as a medic in Vietnam, he had a unique perspective on things.

"Ponder no more, my good friend," I responded with my usual grin, "I have the answer."

"Oh, no," Paul groaned.

"Oh, yes! No mystery at all! We got there on an Air India flight that started to fall apart somewhere over eastern Afghanistan or maybe it was Pakistan. You can thank me later, but such insights are what made me such a successful academic and university teacher."

"Surely your students sued to get their tuition money back?" Bob tried.

Stan ignored this anemic effort at banter and continued as if I had not said a word. "I can recall how it all began for me. One day, I asked one of my friends to drive me to the Post Office to pick up a Peace Corps application. Let's see, that must have been in 1965.

The reaction of my buddy was to laugh heartedly. *Are you nuts? Why are you doing that?* His reaction just spurred me on. It just sounded challenging and interesting to me. After all, who doesn't want to help other people which, in hindsight, turned out to be most of my peers to be honest? In Montana, few my age were into saving the world. I, however, had been impressed with President Kennedy and thought he was talking directly to me when he exhorted us to '... *ask what you can do for your country.'* Those words lit a fire under me, at least enough of a flame to fill out an application."

Connie laughed. "I remember my mother's response when I called home to Hawaii to inform her of my acceptance into this so-called Advanced Training Program scheduled to start in June of 1966. She thought I had lost my mind. My dad was a bit more enthusiastic, if not a touch pragmatic, with his response... *at least my tax dollars will be well spent.* Most of my peers and family were somewhat befuddled. Many asked *why?* It was a good question. Well, the best I came up with was that Kennedy was assassinated during my first year of college. I felt this need to secure his dream of a better world. He inspired and motivated me to not let that dream simply fade away. A close second reason would have to be the prospect of '*a grand adventure'* and a grand adventure it was."

Harry next spoke. "For me, I heard President Kennedy speak about this new idea he was suggesting for young people to get involved and make a positive contribution. Then, sometime during my junior year, a Peace Corps recruiter came to campus, I filled out the darn application and the rest is history. You must remember where I came from. I grew up the fifth of seven children on a rural farm in Durham County, North Carolina. We did not have running water or indoor plumbing. Neither did we own the land, nor the mules used to cultivate the land, nor the seeds for planting crops, nor the fertilizers used to raise those crops. We were tenant farmers, you probably would call us sharecroppers, and essentially survived on a fourth of everything we raised. We were dirt poor by any standard. One thing I did have in abundance was the undeniable love of two wonderful, God-fearing parents. Giving back was just a part of me. Wish I had paid more attention to the farming my dad did, so I didn't feel so useless once I got to India."

Maureen was one of the success stories of India 44 since she had necessary technical skills to bring to the table right from the beginning. She gazed at the ceiling as she began. "When I arrived at the University of San Francisco in the fall of 1963, student volunteerism was becoming an accepted part of the campus ethos. I was shy and an introvert, but I tried my best to get involved in various causes and started to change. Still, Peace Corps was almost an accident for me. I barely knew it existed until I was walking across campus one day in my junior year. Patty, the friend I was with, suggested we stop by the Peace Corps recruiting table and see what they had to say. I hadn't even realized they were on campus. To some extent, the thought of starting my nursing career outside the states had some appeal, I wasn't all that confident in my abilities despite my 3.98 GPA. We both filled out applications, I wanted to go somewhere that spoke English, at least as a second language. I got India, of all places. English was a second language there but not in the rural communities where we were likely to be sent. Initially, that frightened me. I almost turned that offer down, hoping for a better one, but feared I would not get another shot. My friend, Patty, whom I saw as the epitome of a dedicated Peace Corps volunteer, never got a chance to go anywhere. Go figure."

"Ever wonder how they chose us," someone asked?

"Absolutely!" That response came from several directions.

"If there had been any logic involved, Corbett would never have been chosen," Janice said without cracking a smile.

"Ha, ha! However, I agree. They did exercise abominable judgment in accepting me. You know, other than having this vague desire to save the world, I was directionless in college. It is true, though, that I was a classic do-gooder... working in a hospital and with disadvantaged kids for example. As I stumbled through my courses, the prospect of this Peace Corps thing loomed larger and larger in my mind, especially since I had no freaking idea what I wanted to do in life. One of my friends at the time was Neil, a graduate student at Clark University, my alma mater in case you forgot. I knew him loosely from my old neighborhood. He was a bit older than me, so we weren't close as kids but did connect at University."

"My guess would have been you had no friends as a kid," Paul snuck in. "Sorry, continue."

"As I was about to say before that uncalled assault on my character," I gave Paul my most disapproving grimace which absolutely had no effect on him whatsoever, "Neil had done a Peace Corps stint in Iran which we talked about at great length. Coincidentally, Donna Shalala, Clinton's Secretary of Health and Human Services, and former Chancellor at Wisconsin where I spent my academic career, was in his Peace Corps group. The notion captured my interest. After all, what was a psychology major with no visible skills nor any saleable talents to do as his draft board eyed him with increasing interest? I weighed two options, graduate studies or the Peace Corps. My faculty advisor at Clark suggested that I apply to the top schools for graduate work in psychology… Harvard, Yale, and Stanford."

"You!" Paul guffawed.

"I know, right. So, I thanked him politely, exited his office, and asked myself, *'What kind of funny cigarettes is he smoking?'* That plan was a non-starter for me at the time. Hell, I was a working-class kid from an ethnic ghetto who couldn't even keep his final exam schedule straight. It would take many additional years before I realized I was not quite as dumb as I looked."

"Really?" Bob smirked. "You really think you are smarter than you look?"

"Okay, I admit I'm pretty dumb, but not the worst. There are all those Republicans and, God forbid, Trump devotees out there." Agreement could be heard from around the room. "In the end, the battle over my next step in life was brief. I read about a Peace

Corps program in India in public health. Perfect, I thought. As I mentioned, I had been working 11-7 in a hospital to help pay for college. It was a job that fit with my do-gooder self-image. I always had this crazy notion about saving the world. So, I looked for jobs where I could help others, even working with those poor kids in a War-on-Poverty program for a while. More to the point, my heroic medical career afforded me great experiences emptying bed pans, giving enemas, taking temps and BPs, and otherwise keeping the crazies at bay during nocturnal full moons. Didn't this give me a heads up for this health program, or so I thought. Peace Corps might be a way to realize my long-held dream of being a contemporary Albert Schweitzer and in exotic India no less. After all, this was the home of Mahatma Gandhi, a personal hero of mine. It was, as they say, a done deal."

"So," Maureen spoke tentatively, "you were motivated by the highest ideals."

I hesitated. "I think so. At the same time, I recall being uncertain as to whether I was good enough for graduate studies, which now seems silly given that I ended up at a top research university. But I had this huge imposter syndrome back then, much like Maureen who doubted her nursing skills. I've wondered at times if I was running away from that grad studies decision, but I really was a do-gooder." No one spoke for several seconds. "Then again, I ran away from more than that." I next murmured in a lower voice, glad no one picked up on that.

"Well, I personally think most of us were idealists, full of hope and so innocent." Sherry spoke up to my relief. She was an east coaster who still had her New York twang.

"And rather delusional, don't forget delusional." Mel inserted.

I spoke up again. "I have this admittedly vague memory that there was a conflict between the Graduate Record Exam and some form of Peace Corps exam with both being given on the same day. Anyone else recall a Peace Corps exam?" I continued before anyone answered. "Doesn't matter. In my memory, I signed up for both and later decided which exam to take. I then weighed the relative merits suggested by the hypothetical life trajectory associated with each alternative… going for a doctorate, heading overseas in Peace Corps, or winding up sporting a rifle in South-east Asia. The more I reflected on things, the better India and public health looked. But perhaps that is just a convenient memory that lends some drama to the choice… the path not taken and all that. What is certain is that I did not take the GREs until I was in India."

"Where did you take them?" Bob asked. "Not Udaipur I assume."

"Oh, no, Delhi. And the room was full, lots of young Indian kids wanted to study in the States."

Bob shook his head. "That's one thing we still do well, educate the world unless the Republicans screw that up as well!"

"Anyway, I started down the Peace Corps road and soon was Milwaukee bound for training in the summer of 1966. I can't speak for the rest of you but training for me would be another turning point in my life. Just the location of the training seemed an adventure. For a Worcester boy, Wisconsin was an exotic location. You need to remember that Bostonians believed that civilization ended at route 128, the main artery that circled the city in those days. We Worcester folk were far more sophisticated. For us, civilization extended all the way to the Hudson River."

"So sophisticated," Mel, who grew up on the west coast, said sarcastically.

"Perhaps you think I jest. However, I recall the Worcester train station as a kid, in the days when people still travelled by train. A sign there actually read *'Albany NY and **the** West.'* If it had not been for my brief Catholic seminary experience outside of Chicago, I probably would have anticipated that cows would be meandering down Wisconsin city streets and indoor plumbing to be a luxury enjoyed by the wealthy few. Despite these trepidations, it was off to Milwaukee. Little did I know that I was destined to spend my adult life in the Badger State and to fall in love with Madison, the state capital."

"Yeah," Paul smirked. "you always struck me as someone who should be milking cows each morning."

"Connie, what were you thinking when you married this clown?" I asked her.

"Got me there, Tom," she said shaking her head.

"Upon arriving, I recall being told that it would not be the public health track for me despite all my experience working in a hospital. No, I was to be a chicken guru… a freaking poultry expert. I wanted to protest and point out my years of service to the sick and dying. Instead, I hid my disappointment, fear of deselection perhaps. Of course, as my fellow male volunteers know, we were soon rewarded by learning skills that would benefit us in the coming decades… like debeaking a chicken. If you need to ask what that is, you surely must be too citified."

"I was so jealous of you guys, learning all about chickens." Laura tried but could not repress a laugh. "Really, that made you guys so sexy."

"Very funny. Then, to make matters worse, all you gals were assigned to the health program I had wanted and went to a different province. For obvious reasons, this seemed a rather grim prospect, though you gals might have been somewhat relieved, at least until you found yourself stationed near the depraved mutts of India 40. I cannot imagine you wanted to be surrounded by a bunch of oversexed young males."

"Rather a step up from the depraved mutts we trained with." Janice interjected.

"When did everyone become a comedian? Again, I ask, when? I suppose you have a point, though." I struggled to regain control. "Hell, if I were a woman, I would never be without mace and pepper spray to ward off us horny little buggers. In any case, it appears gender profiling was alive and well. The boys were to be chicken farmers and the girls would be healers."

"Still, we did get to know each other in training." Harry added.

"Yes… training. That was something. I remember the physical training very well. In my mind that would involve heroic challenges such as traversing deep chasms over rushing rivers on a rope. I worried about killing myself trying to get in shape. Fortunately, it proved somewhat less exacting. We just ran around the track at the University of Wisconsin–Milwaukee, our beloved training site. Still, even that was enough to almost kill me. Drinking a lot of beer in college, while plotting the socialist revolution, failed to shape my body into a finely-honed machine. On day one, I made it halfway around the track before collapsing, my lungs screaming for mercy. I was trying to keep up with one of the 44-A gals as I recall. Can't recall her name since she never made it to India, much to my regret. I think she was from Kentucky and had done track in college. But I do remember these nice, well developed legs she had. As I collapsed to my knees desperately sucking in all available oxygen within a square mile, her sexy body receded down the track. *Well*, I thought, *if this is my last earthly image, it could be worse.*"

"Yeah, that's what saved us gals," Laura chuckled, "Corbett was too out of shape to catch us."

"Laura," I responded, "why haven't I seen you at the Comedy Club? I mean, really!"

"Hah! I'm there often. They just won't let you in." Laura smiled as she gave me the bird.

I smiled back. "Moving on, I remember our first Indian movie. Like all Bollywood productions of the era, it lasted three days, or so it seemed. Even *Gone with the Wind* mercifully ended after eighteen hours. Somewhere around the end of the second day, the male and female leads were running toward each other across an open field. *Yes, this is it*, I thought, as did the male lead. You could tell since he was drooling, just like I did whenever around the lovely women of 44-A." I ignored the sounds of protest. "But no, just as they were about to embrace, the ground between them opened and they were separated by a damn earthquake. We had 7.4 more crises to go before they were to finally connect, at which time we saw a wonderful ballet of butterflies, a somewhat pathetic proxy for the real thing. I mean, after all, this guy put his life on the line about a dozen times to get the goodies. But it was good preparation for the deprivation of 'companionship' we would experience once we got to the subcontinent."

"Bollywood movies. I wonder if they are still the same?" Someone mused aloud.

"I see some of the dance routines playing on TVs in Indian restaurants. The women are far sexier now, the way they behave on screen that is." Bob said. "They were always sexy looking to us back in the day."

"Indian women are so hot!" Harry added to general agreement among the male's present, though it was not clear that all the females supported his global assessment.

"I remember Hindi classes and culture sensitivity classes and the Tuxedo Bar. Hmm, I recall you guys told me everyone would gather at The Tuxedo bar. Then you bastards would all meet at Buddy Beaks."

"Hey, it worked every time." Bob laughed out loud.

"Nevertheless, some good memories from our training yet resonate. We were pushed to recognize our own prejudices and unexamined assumptions. I recall one of the staff asking if we ever thought about why we call part of the globe the Mideast. *East of what?* Think about that, he prompted us, and we did, likely for the first time. I remember doing very well in Hindi class and getting puffed up about that. But when we got to India and the real world, I watched the Hindi fluency of Harry soar, while I flatlined. He had graduated from a small, southern college and I thought myself intellectually superior. What bullshit that was. I've wondered what might have happened to you, Harry, had you not stumbled into Peace Corps."

"Oh my God, I have no idea," he said with some enthusiasm. "It changed my whole life."

"Changed a lot of our lives." Nanette added.

"For sure," I added in agreement. "You know, I should be fair about our training. I did absorb a lot from our poultry training. To this day, I can still distinguish a chicken from a cow, a rooster from the hen. But a lot of the Milwaukee experience remains a blur."

"What? You don't remember the seven deadly chicken diseases?" Mel smiled slyly.

"And they are, wise guy?" I continued when he failed to respond. "One thing we cannot forget was the constant fear of being sent home. It hung over us daily."

"No shit," Harry said. "They scrutinized and analyzed and tore us apart all kinds of ways. They even had us assessing one another I believe. And then, suddenly, some were gone. The choices of who stayed or not never made sense for the most part. It does make you wonder."

"I did wonder, a lot." I said as I thought about all this. "Were they spying on us? Was it something in our backgrounds that came up? That seems unlikely. I surely had an FBI file given my anti-war activities in college. I even joined SDS for a bit before they went bat-shit crazy."

"All joking aside," I asked, "do any of you think we had more going for us than those that didn't make it?"

"Not me." Mel said.

"Nor me." Maureen chimed in.

"Forget it, we can't figure out their thinking now. However, we can all agree that I was the only real talent in 44-B." I said, knowing full well the blow-back I'd get.

With that, a hail of pretzels showered down upon me. I could not duck them all. As the assault diminished in intensity, Laura spoke. "If anyone was a risk, it was you, Corbett."

I continued undeterred. "I did recognize, however, that I was immersed in another transformative experience, somewhat like my college days. I would never quite be the same when it was over even if it was almost impossible to recall details of how it all happened.

Fortunately, I got these letters I sent to my college girlfriend at the time, the closest I came to a journal. I brought some here, just in case." I opened a folder, briefly searching before taking one letter out.

"You have letters you sent to a girlfriend some... what, four-plus decades ago?" Connie said with surprise.

"Yeah, long story. Maybe later. This one was early, from the Milwaukee training."

I really don't know where to begin. The past three or four weeks have been filled with exciting experiences, not only in the sense of different or pleasing but rather in the sense of challenge and growth. That growth and challenge emanate from a basic tension which is derived, I believe, from an elementary realization of what you are and what you want to be. The people (here) have forced me (and I them) to articulate and defend some of my most basic assumptions, my most basic sacred cows.

In the articulation of that defense, there inevitably emerges a more meaningful realization of yourself and your relationships with others. It is very difficult to put into words what I feel in my heart. The one thing of which I am certain, however, is that I will not experience this program unchanged. Whether or not I ever become a Peace Corps volunteer or not seems irrelevant. The important thing is that I feel I am changing and growing, in which direction it does not matter. I would have to assign the major responsibility (for this growth) to several staff who have encouraged and inspired an atmosphere of inquiry and questioning.

I noticed the looks on the faces around me. They were reflective, searching back to now ancient memories and feelings. Despite the popularity of the program back then, the truth was that few took the plunge. Were we nobler, more committed, better than our brethren? That is hard to accept, though we clearly were a talented lot. No, something touched us back in 1965 that sent us on this *grand adventure* like nothing else did in our young lives.

Our home during training, Holton Hall at UW-M.

Language class during training.

CHAPTER 6

Getting Prepared

After a momentary silence, Mel spoke out with a serious expression. "I've been thinking."

"I just knew something suddenly smelled strange," Bob quipped.

"Very funny," Mel shot back. "But those feelings you expressed in that letter to your college girlfriend, of suddenly changing and experiencing new things. I bet most of us had that reaction. It was like growing up suddenly, maturing on steroids."

"Absolutely! It wasn't always the big things either. Even little things stuck with me."

"Like what?" Maureen asked.

"Well, like walking down the street with Connie and Nanette. A car with a several young Black men screeched to a stop and asked if this was a protest march of some kind. Seeing a white male walking with an Asian and African American female apparently stood out to them. Their surprise caused me to think about our country more closely. Like many places, Milwaukee was seething with racial unrest, some organized by an iconic Catholic priest named Father Groppi."

"Oh yeah, I so remember him." Nanette exclaimed. "He was such a force in our community, for a white Catholic priest that is.

"One quick Groppi story. I was in a contentious meeting on open housing issues, after Peace Corps when I was in grad school at UW-M. I was sitting near a man wearing a clerical collar. So, I got his attention and asked if he could identify the speaker at that moment, some official from Washington. He turned to me and said, *'he's an asshole.'* I wasn't expecting that from a priest."

"Yup, that was Groppi," Nanette belly laughed.

"Sure was," I agreed. "Milwaukee was, and unfortunately, remains a hyper-segregated city. Remember Donald, our training director?"

"Of course," came the general response.

"At some point back in the day, I recall being at his house during a period where a prominent Milwaukee judge's home was being picketed by a mostly Black group called the Commandoes. This judge belonged to a whites-only social club which, at a minimum, was bad optics."

"Was this during our training?" Someone asked me.

"When and why I would have been at his home now escapes me… most likely it happened after India when I returned to grad-school. I vividly recall what happened, though. Donald and I, along with a congressional aide who was visiting, decided that social justice required that we join the protestors. We arrived late to the march, and the kids playing at being National Guard soldiers tried to keep us away. The visiting congressional staffer, who had been most reluctant to come in the first place, now totally lost his cool and started screaming at some twenty-year-old kid sporting a rifle and looking scared shitless. The staffer went on about his constitutional rights being violated. Funny, now I can't recall if we got to join the march or not."

"There's the problem with our memories." Mel groaned. "They are like photo albums with some of the pictures lost."

"I do recall this. Though. The judge in question turned out to be the father of my future wife's best friend, though that piece of information was unknowable to me at the time. I'm not sure he was any more prejudiced than any other Irish judge at the time, but he was very stubborn. That was clear when I got to know him. He would never respond to pressure, not be pushed around. As an aside, he helped bring a major league team back to Milwaukee and almost became Commissioner of baseball, the job he really wanted. More coincidentally, I became friends with one of the leaders of the Black Commandos much later when this man married another of my spouse's best friends. It is such a small world."

"We think we are in difficult times now." Greg noted in his usual understated way. "But the unrest in the U.S. that existed as we were leaving was quite incredible. Then things really exploded after we departed." I found Greg an interesting man. He was very quiet, introspective. But you simply assumed he was a deep pool where much substance lies beneath the surface. He worked for the State Department in the Foreign Service during his professional career. He once mentioned that he had rotated out of Iran not long before the hostage takeover in the late 1970s.

Mel spoke up next. "I have no letters to girlfriends since I didn't have any… girlfriends that is. So, I kept a journal of our training. It was rough, hours and hours of language, technical stuff, cultural indoctrination, physical exercise, evaluations of all sorts. Long hours, day after day. I have something here I want to read. It'll remind you of what we endured or, if you wish, enjoyed."

June 22nd-Wednesday: First day of classes. Two in Hindi, small groups, all in the native language. Then a large seminar on comparative studies, followed by film clips in technical studies. Ms. Mathews, a public health nurse who had spent many years in India, painted a dreary picture of what we had to face. I think they wanted scare us, get some of us to drop out. Then to Physical Education. We got lockers and had our physical exams. Ran a lot, did 31 sit ups, jumped 7'4' and did 7 pull-ups. Collapsed into bed but hung in there long enough to read all about the rare diseases in the world.

June 24, Friday: Fullest day possible! Almost fell asleep in Hindi class. Had debate in comparative studies over language. Lunch! Then built a chicken coop in technical studies. More Hindi and then a Peace Corps movie titled 'The Choice I made.' Dinner, then a tremendous values seminar that blew my mind. I talked about it for over an hour with Bob and Nanette afterwards. Now we are singing folk songs again.

June 29ʰ – Wednesday: Up at 6:00 AM. Language with Ga. Lecture in Comparative Studies on communication. Managed to finish and turn in my self-evaluation form. Then murdered a chicken in poultry class. This is not what I signed up for. Swam for first time in P.E. Saw a 'Twilight Zone' episode values class and had a stimulating discussion. Helped Greg feed the chickens.

July 2ⁿᵈ – Saturday: Up at 5:00 AM, just in time for a meeting with Donald, our training director. Went to evaluations meetings before shaving. Had 3 hours of make-up language with Raki. Rather warm day. Went with Greg to a Bernstein concert. Washed my clothes after I got back and didn't get to bed until after 2:30 AM.

"My notes go on but that gives you a taste of it. As you know, this intensity continued for what seemed like forever. We had to be the best trained group of PC candidates in the history of the program and we still knew jack-shit about chickens in the end." Mel ended with a sigh.

Bob patted his lifelong friend on the shoulder. "Don't forget, they switched us from poultry to agriculture halfway through the training. That sure didn't help"

"In the end," Tim chuckled, "we wound up knowing jack-shit about chickens *and* farming."

As several joined in Tim's hilarity, a sweet and soft-spoken woman named Kay quieted us with her words. "You are wrong in a way. We learned so much, more than you can imagine." Kay had grown up in a sheltered, southern, Catholic family, eventually getting a doctorate and teaching at a small southern college. "My world was turned upside down in training. I can remember the emotional turmoil regarding teaching birth control, as we were expected to do when we got to India. The internal conflicts for me were severe, given my upbringing as a devout Catholic and all. I was supposed to be against birth control as a matter of conscience. I mentioned this to Donald, our director who was only about three or four years older than the kids he was charged with training. He seemed more mature though, and I knew he was Catholic, that he might get it. After that week we all spent in Houston during the Christmas break, he wrote me the warmest and wisest letter you can imagine, full of philosophical quotes and personal encouragement. That whole experience was amazing."

When it was clear that she had no more to say, I broke the silence with one word. "Houston!"

"What about it?" Someone asked.

"Another photo-image from the past just popped into my head… one that brings back a training memory involving an event that pushed social injustice into our faces. As Kay mentioned, we spent time in Houston during the Christmas break of 1966. They flew us all in for little more than a week of training, probably hoping to keep us engaged and motivated while we finished up our senior years in college. Wow, they spent a lot of money on us, even if they failed to turn us guys into farmers. Nevertheless, one evening a small group of us went looking for a so-called 'private' club where you could join for an hour or so to get an alcoholic drink. There were no open bars as I recall. Being from the north and hopelessly naïve at the time, I never put it together the reason for these *private* establishments. We soon found out when we ran into others from our training group. They had just been refused admittance to such a club, ostensibly because one of them was the wrong color. Here was this young black man who was committing an unforgivable sin, wanting to join his white friends for a drink in a phony 'private' club."

"That was Jamie." Kay added the name.

Stan joined in. "Yes, it was Jamie, I recall the discussion later."

"Thanks guys, I am terrible with names. That's why I wear a name tag even around my own house, so I know who I am. You're right; now I can picture him. Jamie always impressed the hell out of me. Among us know-nothing kids, he seemed older and so mature, more directed than me at least. He was one of our best trainees."

Kay said quietly "He was very committed to civil rights and he knew what he was doing.

"Sure did." Stan added. "He persuaded us naïve, white boys with him to leave quietly after the first incident at this club. He knew the score… he had been around this track before. Still, he returned with us since we liberal white kids were so outraged by this egregious violation of basic human rights, even though he knew full well it would get dicey."

"Yeah, the rest of us were idiots. Well, it was more like we had not experienced real hate before this. So, being both foolish and naïve, we went back. I'm not sure what I expected. Maybe it was just to see an example of American apartheid in action up close and personal. Or maybe I was simply crazy. After all, we were going off to save India, how insane was that? Now I see it more clearly. Jamie knew what would happen when we went back. Yet, he never wavered. I only went because I was dumber than pile of manure and even more innocent."

Doug had been sitting silently. A big man with a shock of white hair, he had risen from a modest socio-economic background to graduate from Columbia University. Part of this success was due to an outsized personality which fortunately had mellowed with time. When he spoke, even now, his words commanded attention. "I wasn't there at the club, but I could have warned you what might happen. I had been invited by another black trainee to a party in Houston, that was his hometown, along with some of his friends. We were pulled over by some uniformed cops who had him spread eagled with his hands on the car. *'What'cha doing with these colored folks, son,'* one cop asked me. We managed to get released after sweet talking the Houston gestapo about doing the Peace Corps training bit and going to India. But this encounter was an eye opener for a kid from New York. Hate back in the *'big apple'* wasn't quite so in your face. It was there, of course, but not so obvious to me at least. I could ignore it if I wanted to."

"Hmm," I murmured. "Maybe that's why Peace Corps sent us to Houston, to open our freaking eyes. No use speculating now. In order to get proof of discrimination, someone devised a plan. Some white trainees placed themselves at the front. They dutifully paid the club membership fee and went in. I recall being right next to Jamie in our group. When he was confronted by the palace guard at the entrance to this 'club,' the nominal 'membership' fee suddenly multiplied by a factor of five or something like that."

"Oh boy!" Harry uttered as if recalling experiences as a black youth growing up in the south.

"Jamie calmly pulled out the outrageous sum requested. This escapee from world-wide wrestling guarding the entrance, seeing that Jamie wasn't backing down, next snarled, *'No, for you, the fee is a million dollars.'* I cannot recall all my emotions at that moment, but I believe a mixture of fear and then rage was involved. After a few more words, the pushing and shoving started. Being rather tall, I could look through the entrance, where I saw the patrons inside gathering into a mob. Clearly, they were eager to confront us as word spread about what was going on. As legal discrimination was falling across the country, these defenders of apartheid were intent on taking a last stand by protecting their *'whites only'* turf. Our attempts to reason with them fell flat. Shockingly, they were not impressed that we represented the United States Peace Corps. According to them, the Corps was nothing more than a bunch of Commie-faggots. I believe that was the precise term employed."

"Didn't you get the memo about Peace Corps being a Commie-front organization." Mel chuckled.

"No, damn it. My membership to the John Birch Society had lapsed by this point. A lot of this is hazy now but I do have a vivid image of a trainee named Drew dropping to the ground in the entranceway. It was a dead-weight technique he learned while resisting apartheid in his native Virginia. This moved me since he was white, which challenged my own stereotype of Caucasian southerners. He clearly had put his safety, perhaps his life, on the line for social justice in the past. Damn, we had some impressive people with us who never stayed the course for one reason or another." I paused a moment to consider just how thoughtful and caring were so many of the people around me that night in Houston.

"So, what happened next," Maureen asked?"

"Right, eventually, we were pushed out to the street and surrounded by a rather large group of menacing-looking rednecks, the size of which has grown in my mind over the intervening years. The term *redneck* still strikes me as appropriate even after all this time. As I recall, their necks were bright red for sure… with venom if not rage. On the other hand, I thought their entire heads looked crimson, the color brightening given their rapidly growing desire to beat the shit out of us, if not kill us."

"Wow, I've not heard this story before." Paul had dropped his usual wit.

"For me, righteous indignation was now equally mixed with total panic. Pooping in my pants was a real possibility in the moment. At that very moment, I saw a police cruiser coming down the street. Ta, da, the cavalry to the rescue! I really am a moron. Nevertheless, I waved frantically at them to stop. When they pulled up to determine the reason for this rowdy gathering, and my obvious alarm, I pulled a Corbett back-forty stunt."

"Meaning?" Bob pushed.

"A back-forty stunt is doing something so stupid that you should be taken out to the back forty and shot, like you do with useless farm animals."

Bob looked exasperated. "No, you dillweed, what did you say to the cops?"

"Oh, that! I indignantly asserted that a violation of the civil rights act had just occurred."

"You're kidding." Harry guffawed.

"I know, right? Not the most well thought out plan at that moment. Still, it sounded loftier to me than some obsequious plea to save my silly ass."

Paul broke the ensuing silence. "So, what happened… did the cops save that ass of yours? You still appear to have it."

I laughed bitterly, thinking back on the moment. "Not quite! I mean yes, I still have it but no, Houston's finest played no role in saving it. I yet have this image of this white cop looking at me as if I had just been dropped off by the alien mother ship. All he said was '*I don't give a fuck about civil rights.*' What in God's name made me think the Houston cops would care? I'm now surprised he didn't take out his gun and shoot me. Good thing I wasn't black. To this day, I can still recall the smirk on his face as he rolled up his window and cruised on down the street leaving us to our fate. Now, I thought, we are totally dead and went back to work on that damn perfect act of contrition I first learned as a young Catholic boy. We were taught to say that prayer if we knew death was imminent."

"And yet you are still with us." Laura said, trying for lightness but not quite making it.

"True, we did make our escape and I have no freaking idea how anymore."

"I wonder if I was there." Harry, another of our Black trainees, mused. "I surely would have remembered if I was."

"Can't tell you. I had even forgotten Jamie's name, and he was a kind of hero to me. Not that you weren't, Harry."

"Nice try, Corbett."

"After we had safely made it back, we shared our near-death experience. I do remember Mack giving a spellbinding exhortation. Remember him. He was a liberal firebrand, radical even, who had attended the University of Colorado. As I recall, he was one of the few who befriended me during training. I remember his name for that reason… that he had such low standards for friends. What stays with me was his impetuous energy, always overflowing with ideas for the coming revolution. He left us not long after we got to

India. Perhaps he was asked to leave, we were never sure in many cases. I wonder where he ended up?"

"I remember Mack," Bob said. "He was wiry and restless… always ready to take on the world."

"That's him," then a specific memory made me smile. "You know, several years ago I got in touch with Don, our esteemed training director. Not surprisingly, he remained in public service. After training us, he got a Masters from Harvard in Government, served in the Wisconsin State Legislature and later headed the Wisconsin tax department among other posts. He was still involved in education issues when we had lunch in Madison at the prestigious Madison Club."

"La de da," Mel mocked.

"Stuff it," I responded, but with a smile. "Anyway, as we were thinking back on our training days, Don brought Mack's name up. Apparently, Don had brought in a speaker who had been a father figure to him when he himself had been in school. Mack, being Mack, laid into this guy, attacking him as a sellout and blah, blah. Don could laugh at it all these decades later, but he was mortified in the moment. After all, it had stuck with him after all those decades. Those were passionate times. Back to Houston, Mack tried to talk us into going back that night, but I surely had no stomach for that. I had almost gotten myself involuntarily castrated in college once, during an early anti-war march. While I was big into causes, heroism was never my thing, not when the integrity of my family jewels might be at stake. As a group, we decided to pursue a legal remedy and the next day trooped down to see the FBI or some other federal agency. We filed a complaint that I'm sure was deposited in the circular file as soon as we left."

Tim chuckled and everyone looked in his direction. "Sorry, I was just thinking how naïve we were."

"You have another embarrassing memory." Maureen inquired.

Tim sighed as he struggled with the memory. "Not sure it's embarrassing so much as reflective of how innocent we were, and idealistic. I was sure the world would be as outraged as we were. So, I called the Associated Press that very night to report this late breaking story. Whomever I was talking with there could care less. As he yawned, at least I think I heard such a sound. He told me no one would be interested. In hindsight, he probably was correct. After the freedom riders and Bull Conner in Birmingham and the Mississippi burning summer, our small kerfuffle was not earthshattering news. It was news to us, just not to the world."

Tim then added in a tentative voice, as if the memory were hard to retrieve. "I recall Frank laughing at us when we told him what had happened."

"Frank? I don't remember him." Stan inquired.

Tim added quickly. "A Black guy who had grown up in Texas. He never went overseas but we became friends in training. He couldn't believe we were so innocent. *What the hell were you thinking? This is Texas,'* he said to us as if we were a bunch of three-year old tots. Whether we knew it or not, we white kids were growing up. Playtime was over."

Maureen spoke up. "Now that we're talking about Houston and Jamie, I remember the elevator door at the hotel opening and seeing some of our group. I gave each a quick hug, including Jamie. I can still remember the hateful looks I got from the white people who saw this. I had violated a taboo... I have despised Houston ever since."

"I only recall the club incident from the discussion after," Glen added. Glen was a tall thin man who inevitably stood out in a crowd, if for nothing more than his musical talents. He had an elongated head topped with thinning blond hair. You could not miss him in a crowd with his aura suggesting that he had never got back on the bus after the stop at Woodstock. "Hey, I also had an elevator incident in Houston."

"Do tell." Laura asked him.

"The elevator stopped and a short, rotund man sporting a white goatee and carrying a cane got on. I stared at him for a few moments before curiosity got the better of me. '*I must ask, aren't you Colonel Sanders?*' He smiled back broadly and pulled from his pocket a set of coupons entitling me to one free bucket of Kentucky Fried Chicken. I guess he was building his empire one bucket at a time."

Connie interrupted at this point. "That's fascinating, Glen, but I want to go back to Corbett who once said he almost got maimed, or was it castrated, earlier in life? That sounds like a dream come true to us gals. I'm guessing it was a bunch of disappointed women pushed to violence by your sexist behavior. I can totally believe that. Oh wait, you said it was some demonstration, didn't you? Was it against the war?"

"Good catch, Connie. Yes, this was another near-death experience for me. And being attacked by a mob of outraged women would make perfect sense but it was, in fact, a more conventional demonstration. It happened in college when I joined an early anti-Vietnam war march. This was in Worcester, my hometown, where I went to college. As I recall, it was likely the first such demonstration there, surely the first of any size. Many were to follow but this still was when any anti-war protest was viewed as subversive and traitorous. The war was still popular at this point, even in liberal Massachusetts. After all, we were defending the free world from the Godless Reds. Your average Joe thought students like me had to be outright Commies."

"You always looked like a Commie to me." Harry said with a chuckle.

"Hilarious. Anyway, we were bombarded with eggs and beer cans and threats of serious bodily harm. The moment of high drama came when the line stopped moving in a circle and a bunch of bikers leered at me, one saying loudly at a volume I could not ignore, '*Let's beat the shit out of the tall one with glasses.*' I looked about without moving my head. Yup, I was the only tall one with glasses. I tried to remember that perfect *Act of Contrition*, but I was a lapsed Catholic by this point, so the words escaped me. More likely I was focusing more on not wetting my pants."

Janice looked at Connie. "Once again, we were almost spared putting up with Corbett and, once again, God did not grant our wish."

"Hey, I'm shocked as well." I smiled. "I survived but, for the life of me, cannot recall how. Some others were pummeled. I recall I was with a gal I was seeing at the time, nothing serious since she was engaged to a guy who was stuck in some other state. For some reason she liked me, don't ask why since she was smart enough to see through me. Carol was at the top of the class, later got her doctorate at Harvard and eventually became a Dean at Rutgers. I recall thinking in that moment that I had gotten her into this terrible situation, that I would have to protect her when everything went south. More likely it was she who saved my ass."

"The 60s were something else." Someone mused.

"For sure, that decade had its moments for all of us. During that first war protest, I was scared to death when I saw the hate around me. That level of bile has a special quality to it, something you do not forget easily, and which stayed with me. Later, in Houston, I witnessed that same hate. Others have noted that it took guts to go to India like we did but I never saw it that way. I can only recall people like Jamie, Frank, Drew, and Mack. I think they had guts, courage I would never have. They faced down such hate repeatedly. They had no choice."

"I agree." Harry murmured.

"Think of those Freedom Riders who went south to desegregate interstate travel on Greyhound and other carriers. I still recall the images, just black and white kids who really put their lives on the line. I saw this documentary many years ago. I cannot forget this one scene where then Attorney General Robert Kennedy's assistant, John Seigenthaler, called the young woman who was leading another group of buses into the south. Her name was… Nash, Diane Nash. By now, there was no doubt what awaited them.

Kennedy's top man pleaded with her to stop, that they could easily be killed. Seigenthaler knew what awaited the Freedom Riders. He himself had been born and raised in Tennessee. On camera, as he related that phone call, he choked up. There were tears in his eyes when he got to one part about her response to his pleas. As he told her that he could not protect them, she responded to his pleas as follows. '*Sir, you are telling me something I already know.*' Then she added, '*Every one of us completed our last will and testaments last night.*' At that point, he just stared at the interviewer for a few moments... he had nothing more to say. Those kids had real courage. I teared up as I watched it. I'm struggling now."

Compared to what they went through, our trials were nothing." Connie murmured. No one followed up her comment as all were lost in their own thoughts.

It struck me that it was time to move on. "So, two other cross-cultural experiences from training remain with me. First, we had our Waunakee, Wisconsin, farm experience. This was after we were told that India no longer needed poultry experts but agricultural experts instead. So, we now were to spend some time on a farm in the quaint town of Waunakee to learn how to be farmers. This rural paradise is located just north of Madison and touts the fact that it is the only Waunakee in the world. This must be true since it is written on a sign visible to all visitors who happen to stumble upon this rural paradise. Apparently, no one else in the world is moved to compete for that moniker and thus rudely snatch away that singular honor from this fortunate Wisconsin site. While learning to be farmers, we lived in tents and absorbed the unique ambiance of rural life."

"How hopeless." Maureen offered.

"Tell me about it! I had avoided barbaric rituals like camping out in tents all my life. That was my dad's fault."

"You are blaming your father?" Maureen asked.

"Yes, and for good reason. He always thought outdoor living was overrated. Even picnics were off limits. *If God wanted us to eat outdoors,* my dad would often pontificate, *he would not have created restaurants.* Though not a formally educated man, he evinced considerable wisdom throughout his life, which he shared generously with me… more often than I care to admit. My favorite T-shirt, which I relished when visiting national parks, was the one proclaiming, *my idea of roughing it is when room service is late.* That always evoked a chuckle from the park rangers, but I was serious."

"Your father sounds like a wise man to me." Tim nodded.

"A man of great depth. In any case, I cannot recall what I learned on that farm, other than it deepened my appreciation for being born and raised in a city. Still, I remember people being very nice to us and the farm family neighbor's coming over for a party in our honor. At the party, they sort of looked at us as if they were doing research for a Scientific American article on discovering a new, alien species. My memory is that we could see interstate 94, the primary Milwaukee to Minneapolis artery, from our tents. This farm had a sign positioned along the highway announcing Henry's Seed Farm, or something like that. Years later, after returning to the area, I thought about stopping to ask if they remembered our little group but then feared that they would. You hate to dredge up painful memories for folk. Over the next two decades, I would pass that sign and strain to see the place where I thought our tents had been pitched. Then one day, I realized the sign was gone."

"I guess we can't go back and visit, then." Greg said with feeling. "I recall that experience so well. They tried desperately to turn us into farmers in a few weeks. It was hopeless."

"You guys spent time on a farm, we women spent time with families in the inner city of Milwaukee. That was part of our cross-cultural experience. Let me tell you, I was with a family where I saw the male head physically abuse his wife. I didn't know what to do. I was so unprepared for that, torn between my concern for her and the fear I might make things worse for her. Then I worried about violating some privacy rule. In the end, I just stuffed it inside and said nothing." Her voice broke and then trailed off. "All these years and I'm still wracked with guilt."

I expressed a feeling more than a thought. "It was a time out of time, never to be recaptured."

"It was unique, even within Peace Corps." Bob offered. "This advanced training thing Peace Corps tried with us was a trial run. All in all, it was 14 months in length or so with our senior year in college thrown in the middle of it all."

Tim gave a low groan. "And then we had India. Were there any sites more challenging? I've talked to other volunteers who served in different areas of the world. They had challenges but not like us."

"Hey, I'm a hard-headed economist and I agree totally, which you can take to the bank since I'm being objective here." Bob said emphatically. "Besides, I worked in banking for a while."

"You are so right, Bob." I deadpanned. "In fact, economists are generally called blockheads because they are so hard-headed, practitioners of the dismal science because they are so…"

"Dismal… ha, ha," his expression of disdain was accompanied by the finger of disrespect.

I moved right on. "I sometimes wonder how our lives might have been different if we had stayed in the States for those two years. Think about what we missed… the race riots, the assassinations, the cresting of the anti-war movement, friends swept away to Nam, some never to return. Were we spared a lot of trauma, insulated from emotions that scarred so many?"

"Does it strike anyone else that we were between a rock and a hard place?" Mel asked no one in particular.

"Meaning?" Maureen asked.

"We were faced with two versions of Hell, one in India and one in the States. Pick your poison." Harry smiled enigmatically. "We should have known what we were getting into on the flight over there when the damn engine almost fell off. Now that was an omen."

"Oh yeah," Mel piped up. "I recall there was an article in the Times of India the next day about all these Peace Corps volunteers escaping death. That was a stretch of course but there were some scary moments."

"Just think," I added. "If we all had perished, we would have gone down in Peace Corps lore. I bet there would even be a memorial or something in front of Peace Corps headquarters saying, '*at the last moment, India was spared from these incompetent misfits when the hand of God struck down their plane.*'"

Someone threw a pretzel at me. I did not see who.

Becoming farmers… which one am I?

Here I am, looking over the Thames on the way to India.

Flying into India, the engine fails… an 'omen' perhaps?

CHAPTER 7

The Good Volunteers

I sensed I had been talking too much. While the sound of my voice is pleasant to me, that is not a widely shared view. True, the females were getting in their shots. On the other hand, unless they shared something more intimate with the group, we guys would have little ammunition with which to humble them in our ongoing game of one-upmanship... a time-honored sport among the male members of the species. More than that, I feared the females in our group might be overshadowed by their more loquacious male counterparts. I've heard the word *'mansplaining'* bantered about a lot recently, a term I rather dislike only because it is employed too liberally and in a manner designed to shut down much needed communication between the genders.

It is true, though, that men talk a lot in group settings and usually say little of note. Mostly, we testosterone-driven half of the species thrive on sparring with one another. Females, on the other hand, seldom get into these competitive put-down contests, not with each other at least and not in an obvious manner. They tend to complement one another, even if they don't mean it. Really, what's the point with that? Humiliation is so much more fun when you are not the target? Now, it's not that I go around looking for ways to embarrass others... okay, yes I do but not all the time. It is more like this is what we males are hardwired to do. Clearly, it is a holdover from those primitive tribal days when we fought one another for the opportunity to mate with the available females in the clan. Sadly, we haven't evolved all that much since our cave dwelling days. Not quite true, the women have evolved... quite a bit to be honest. We guys, alas, remain little more than barbarous, rutting stags.

It was the same when we put together a couple of edited volumes of our Peace Corps days. With some exceptions, it was rather difficult to get the women of 44-A to open-up, with some notable exceptions. In the end, we often had to use snippets incorporated from emails they sent rather than formal vignettes or submitted chapters. I'm still not totally sure why. True, women strike me as more circumspect and private while males appear more narcissistic, the roosters of any barnyard. Really, we have little to be proud about unless our public posturing is an extension of that inbred trait to mate through the display of outlandish behaviors.

You see it all the time in the animal kingdom. The male capable of making the most aggressive roars or jumping the highest had the best chance of passing his genetic gifts on to the next generation. I never could roar loudly or jump high. I can only recall being praised for a single virtue. My college girlfriend, whom you will meet later in this tome, asserted more than once that I was always brutally open and honest. That has proved unfortunate in all mating rituals since you cannot attract females with honesty. No way! In fact, just the opposite is true. Case in point! *'Does this dress make me look fat, dear?'* Early on, I was dumb enough to answer honestly… what in god's name was I thinking. In addition to many visits to the ER, this may explain why I've passed nothing on to future gene pools.

I pondered such matters as I decided whether to venture forth in a different direction. I am always pondering such weighty matters, a tendency that supports the widespread belief that I should get a real life. Then I decided, time to hear from the stronger members of India 44, the females of our illustrious assembly.

"You know, we haven't heard enough from the distaff side. I have this long-time colleague at Wisconsin. We worked closely together until my retirement and she is now some kind of Provost at the University. Oh yeah, she is a Vice Provost. That sounds like a great job… to manage all matters of vice at the university. Hmm,

I wonder how you get that kind of work? Anyway, she read the edited volume of our adventures in India and somehow, get this, concluded that we guys were a bunch of clowns while the gals did exemplar work. Go figure! Seriously, can you believe that. With suspect judgment like that, just how the hell did they give her such an important position in the University administration?"

"I can see why. She is very perceptive." Nanette asserted.

"Well, my scholarly response to her absurd conclusion was *'phooey,'* which is a technical term used exclusively among us members of the academy. I can define it for you if needed."

"A technical term?" Maureen smiled. "Exactly what type of academy accepted you as a member… the school of circus clowns?"

"All I'm saying is that it's time for you gals to open up, share some embarrassing stuff with us."

Janice, another of the delightful women from our distaff side, laughed. "Poor Tom, we women will just disappoint you once again since we were perfect, and you guys were… not so much. Are you sure you want to go there?"

"Hah!" I exclaimed with as much righteous indignation as I could muster. "Just how perfect could you gals have been."

———

Dee, who had been sitting quietly, spoke up to my relief. "I really hate to take Tom's side on this issue, any issue for that matter, but we gals were far from perfect volunteers."

"But we were better than the guys." Laura argued. "We had to be. Just think about how low they set the bar. Hell, the water buffalo in my village were more productive, more ambitious at least, and a hell of a lot cuter."

Dee persisted, however. "Okay, let me make my point before I chicken out." She then took a deep breath before plunging forward. "I so remember that it was quite a feat among Indians when they had gotten to the point of just qualifying for a University level B.A., even if you failed. So, if you failed that final requirement, you might still be noted as Mukergee Nipal, B.A. Fail, either on the door of your business or your business card just to let people know how far you had gotten in your education."

"Not sure I know where you are going?" Maureen inquired.

"It is just that I would have felt better with the designation of B.A. Fail, Public Health from a community college than B.A. Pass with honors in Political Science from Cal-Berkeley. What did a poli-sci degree prepare me to do in India? Hell, we were supposed to be health specialists. I could see the confused looks that would follow when I answered questions from villagers about my university studies. What was I doing there? Surely a hard question to answer. While it may have been true that living in America gave me a good grasp of germ theory and an understanding of basic nutrition, I was woefully unprepared to really be of help in delivering expert health care to the residents of Risod, my site in the boonies of Maharashtra for you Rajasthani guys. I so envied any real nurse doing public health. They not only had street creds but had done rotations in hospitals and benefitted from hands-on experience. You weren't likely to get nauseated at the sight of blood."

"Funny," Maureen added, "I didn't feel all that qualified even with my nursing degree and my near perfect G.P.A."

"But you were. I was so jealous of what you brought to the table. When we arrived in our village, it was considered a progressive place even if off the beaten path. We were assigned to Dr H., our public health officer. He was from a family of medical practitioners starting with his grandfather who had been an Ayurvedic physician. One of the first days after we arrived, Dr. H. called us down to the clinic to show us a patient he was treating. He told us that this young woman was dying because an untrained village midwife had screwed up during childbirth. By the time the woman was brought to the clinic it was too late. He was sending her on to the hospital in Washim. I remember thinking in that moment, *'how can this woman be dying, she looks so awake and alert?'* I had so little experience with the dying, or the sick. My image of death was one of a long decline from visible illness and the drama of a violent end. This young woman didn't fit any concept of someone who was dying. She was not moaning or groaning, yet the doctor whom I respected was telling us she was dying. It just seemed too ordinary to be real. Yet, we heard later that she had indeed died on the trip to Washim. The depths of my naïveté and ignorance hit me like a wall."

"You were not alone." Someone offered.

"Perhaps. During our training, we had heard examples of untrained village midwives killing patients by cutting umbilical cords with dirty field tools, causing sepsis or cord tetanus. Here were examples where lack of medical expertise proved deadly. I couldn't shake the fear that I would make some deadly mistake, simply from ignorance. Not long after, we were attending a local Bollywood cinema when we got called to the clinic. Two women were in labor and needed help. This was my first experience with a live birth. I had never even held a newborn before. When it was thrust into my arms, I felt inadequate and awkward, concerned that I would be a danger to this brand-new life. Then I was expected to wash it in the chill of the night outside the birthing room. What a shock it must have been to this tiny one, to go from the warmth of a mother's womb suddenly into this cold new world. In retrospect, I might have comforted myself with the thought that rural Indian women had been giving birth in less than ideal circumstances long before I arrived. We all survived, though. In that moment, I embraced the positive, magical experience of birth to counter the shocking memory of this other young woman's early demise."

"That must have been uplifting." I tried.

Dee nodded. "Perhaps uplifting, I'm not sure. It was eye-opening, however. Suddenly I was seeing life and death at a primitive level. That never would have occurred had I stayed in a hermetically sealed existence back in the States."

"Absolutely, that has to be a positive outcome from all our struggles." Harry added.

"Yes, a bit traumatic but a positive in some ways. There were a few planned successes as well. We did get to help with vaccination campaigns for example. Still, the frustrations have stayed with me. One day we were puzzled and alarmed when we followed the health worker around a medical ward which was just a room with six or eight beds of female patients. We saw her give each patient an injection with the same syringe, which she only dipped in water between patients. Did she not understand or believe in contamination or contagion? Each patient had a different condition, the consequences of sharing a contaminated needle seemed obvious."

"How could they miss that?" Maureen grimaced. "Even the guys from 44-B would have gotten that."

"The ultimate test." Bob smiled. "If we imbeciles could get it…"

Dee continued as if he hadn't spoken. "Yet, I felt helpless, so inadequate. Could I challenge her, with my background in Political Science? Where was my authority? My confidence? Yet, that frustrating event paled in comparison to the day a mother presented Kay and me with her starving baby. Her milk had dried up and she wanted to know what she could do? Where was my B.A., Fail in Public health? Never had I felt so helpless, useless and such a fraud. What in God's name was Peace Corps thinking when they sent young and inexperienced liberal arts college graduates out to villages pretending we were healthcare experts."

Sherry looked on sadly. "You weren't alone. We all faced the angst of confronting life and death situations and not having a clue."

"Even where we had a clue, we lacked confidence. Well, I lacked confidence."

"We all did to some extent. I wish I could have gone back to India after my experiences in Viet Nam as a medic." Stan said ruefully.

Dee seemed relieved at the support. "I will say one thing. I am so grateful for the experience of living in a culture so different from my own, and for the opportunity to sometimes find a common ground with people so different. That was priceless. That opportunity and those lessons came at a price, though. Personally, I felt tainted with the failure associated with trying to fulfill an undefined mission with inadequate training and qualifications. How I longed for that B.A., Fail!"

There was a long silence as each of us dwelled on our own painful memories. Then Cate spoke up. She was a tall, attractive woman with a pleasant demeanor who had grown up on the west coast. "I can remember the shock of what we first faced, the feeling of being lost, inadequate. I think, though, it got better over time or I changed. I'm not claiming the sense of inadequacy disappeared, it never did. But things improved."

"Tell us more about that, about things getting better," I encouraged her. We risked, I thought, dwelling too much on our inadequacies and insecurities. Perhaps Cate could offer something more upbeat.

"So many images flash through my mind. There was the patient with a distended abdomen in our UNICEF operating room. I had to crank up the petrol autoclave and hand our doctor a medical instrument to tap the belly. Out spewed a galvanized bucket of TB fluid. It spouted in an arc as I tried catching the fluid in a bucket. Unbelievable! It was amazing I did not lose my lunch. More amazing, I never contracted TB."

I spoke up. "Really? I wasn't as lucky. I did contract TB, apparently in India, though it didn't flare up until a decade after I had returned to the States. Still, they traced the strain back to one common in India. I still recall the day they sent me over to the University of Wisconsin hospital to see a female physician about to retire. They explained she had been around long enough to recognize the disease. The other docs had no idea what had invaded my lung and were going to cut me open thinking what they saw on my x-rays was a deadly virus like Legionnaires disease. There big fear was that I would die before they could figure out what it was. Okay, before one of you gals say it. Yes, I escaped death once again and I apologize for disappointing you one more time. Face it, we mean guys never die young. I will be around to haunt you for decades to come."

Laura threw her head back and feigned disgust, then laughed. "Once again, our hopes are dashed. Corbett keeps surviving these near-death experiences… simply to plague us with more of his self-described wit and wisdom. Why has God forsaken us?"

"Oh, heaven help us." Kay made a sign of the cross.

"I see it is open mike night at the Comedy Club. But seriously Cate, you might also have been exposed, but it never flared up."

"That's a thought but I'm not going to worry at this late date." Cate paused as if thinking on that possibility. "Well, then there was the young pregnant woman who was carried into the exam room and placed on the floor. A flock of wailing, hysterical family members surrounded her while a Shaman cut off the leg of a chicken shaking blood all over her rigid body. This holy man was in a trance-like state, chanting unintelligible words… no doubt issuing healing requests to the spirit world. Eardrum piercing bellowing could be heard in all the stillness and then they were gone. A morbid silence enveloped us. We moved her obtunded body to the exam table while protecting her protruding belly. I held my breath as I was coached to assist with the delivery of her baby. And then an epiphany. As I forced myself to breathe, I realized that I now believed in miracles. I knew I could do this. I could work in medicine. I didn't even think of fainting. I was a doer, a responder, a nurturer."

"It was then you decided to become a nurse." Maureen asked.

"Yes, I learned how to tie the umbilical cord with alcohol-soaked cotton string under the expert guidance of our experienced midwife. I learned how to wrap the tiny baby in rolls of UNICEF cotton. With no incubators in the village, we made do. Our local physician took note of my growing interest in medicine and showed me a female patient with a rigid, frozen jaw. He explained that she had lockjaw caused by *clostridium tetani*, what we think of as tetanus. My God, the images are flooding in." She looked off for a moment.

"Hmm, none of us guys decided to become farmers, what does that say?" Immediately I regretted my interruption. "Please, don't stop now. Continue!"

"Okay, here is another memory. A crippled man was trying to make his way up the dusty path to our health compound and no one was helping him. I ran out to the driveway, put my arm around his shoulder, and helped drag him to the men's side of the clinic. Then I discovered the reason he was shunned. He was a leper, someone to be ostracized."

"Like Corbett," Bob threw out to several chuckles.

"He was treated even worse than Corbett if you can believe. No one wanted to be around him."

"As I said, like Corbett," Bob repeated, now to outright laughs.

Cate silenced us with the *'look,'* a glare all men know from our married years. We obediently quieted. "They quickly isolated me in a stone room where I had to strip off my sari, which was burned immediately. I then had to scrub and redress. This motivated me to study anything I could on the topic of leprosy and its cultural ramifications. My interest eventually brought me to the Leprosy Colony outside the Sangli District, a place run by a World Christian Outreach program. I was given a tour where I met patients and staff. I gazed into saucer-sized soulful eyes that caused me to look away for fear I would see their pain, or they might see my initial fear. Yet, almost immediately, I could see their pride as they showed me their work. They grinned with a kind of peace and sense of being beyond any disfigurement. My heart liquified into tears, and I knew the meaning of the word *'charity'* for the first time."

Suddenly, Cate hesitated as if she was embarrassed by the sentimentality she was sharing.

———

It was Maureen who rescued her. "You all know that I was fortunate enough to be a nurse when I got there. But it was not like you imagined. I wasn't brimming with confidence. I was book smart but without a lot of experience. My great grades in school did little to convince me that I knew what I was doing. Like I mentioned, even signing up for Peace Corps seemed accidental, perhaps in part to get some real-life training before embarking on my stateside career, not sure about that though."

"One hell of a way to gain some experience." Sherry said.

"For sure! It was almost for nothing."

"What do you mean?" Mel asked.

"After getting to India and finally being sworn in, Cate and I almost didn't make it to our village. My career as a healer was almost over before it even began." Maureen said.

"This sounds exciting." Laura enthused.

"It is. In typical Peace Corps fashion, they simply put us on a bus that was supposed to be an eight-hour journey to our village. But it was the end of the monsoon season and several rivers were running high, so everything took longer. In the middle of the night, we finally made it to a river that was too high to drive through. After a two hour wait, a second bus showed up on the other side and these two buses shone their lights at each other to illuminate our way across the river. We had to carry our belongings across on our heads, this was not going to be easy."

"Hey, this IS exciting." Tim emphasized.

"Easy for you to say," Maureen responded. "We were not happy campers. The river was chest deep and the fast-flowing current was pushing us to the left. Huh, that's a funny detail to recall. Anyway, Cate and I were holding on to each other with the hand that was not balancing our suitcases on our heads. Good thing. About halfway across I was swept off my feet and started downriver. Cate's grip kept me from disappearing into the darkness though I did lose my favorite girl scout canteen."

"Holy shit," Mel said, "we could have lost you."

"Rest assured, Maureen, had you disappeared forever in that raging river we would have a candlelight memorial service for you at every get together." I gave another shot at lightness.

"I could well have been included in that memorial service." Cate offered with a sly grin. "There was the time that I was attacked from behind by a snake while doing my business, if you get my drift." Her smile eased as she realized the recollection was not as amusing as it sounded. "Even if it were not venomous, I'm shocked I did not expire on the spot from cardiac arrest."

"I can see where that would at least shock the shit out of you." I laughed at my own wit. "Pun definitely intended."

"That's it, someone stuff a rag in Corbett's mouth," came from somewhere in the crowd.

"However, being the gentleman that I am, I would have sucked the venom out from your… derriere."

"The rag, where is that rag?" Laura scrunched her face in disgust.

Cate continued. "Moving on, I recall when we got close to our destination, at about 5:00 AM in the morning, a day after we were supposed to arrive. We had trouble convincing people that we were really going to this nondescript village where no one seemed to be aware of our impending arrival. Peace Corps planning strikes again."

Harry groaned. "I swear. I think their screw-ups were intentional. The PC brass just wanted to weed out the weak among us."

"Didn't quite work then. Most of us hung tough." Maureen smiled as she picked up the narrative. "I must say, though, that the next two years were an amazing mix of high adventure and excruciating boredom. We engaged in all the activities of the health center including delivering babies, educating people about nutrition, starting an immunization campaign, developing a patient record system, sterilizing equipment, and dealing with diseases I had only heard about in nursing school. I recall my first delivery being a terrifying experience. A woman went into labor while the staff and Cate were away at some scheduled event and I was alone. I had brought my OB nursing textbook to India with me, thank goodness. Throughout the ordeal, I was reading one page ahead of this women's labor."

"Damn," Stan inserted, "that's how I patched up guys on the battlefield in Nam, learning on the go. You know, trial and error."

"Not for the faint of heart, is it."

"No, indeed!"

Maureen smiled. "Fortunately, I knew the Marathi words for *'breathe'* and *'push'* but what if she needed an episiotomy? When the baby's head began to push out of the birth canal, I knew the umbilical cord was wrapped around its head. Fortunately, it was loose enough so that I could get my fingers in there to slip it over the head between contractions. All of us survived and holding that newborn in my hands was one of the most moving experiences of my life. I used an expanded written version of that experience to help graduating nursing students to get over their fears when they doubt that they can handle the responsibilities."

"Okay," I said, "I surrender."

"It's about time but what are you talking about?" Dee was puzzled.

I explained. "My colleague at the University was right. The women of 44-A did amazing stuff while we guys barely survived. Hell, our great achievements were Mel and I finally getting laid and Tim not blowing his own ass off, though I'll let them tell their own stories."

Maureen grumped toward me. "Very funny, but let's be serious. We were all doing serious stuff. Don't put yourself down."

I was about to launch into a monologue on the positive merits of getting laid as well as not blowing one's own fanny off, but Paul interrupted. "Maureen is right. Don't put yourself down, guys. Let me do that. I rather enjoy it."

"Paul." I paused for effect. "Just bite me."

"Settle down, boys." Maureen issued her mandate with authority, glancing about to see if we obstreperous males were obeying. Satisfied, she continued. "They say necessity is the mother of invention and I learned to do many things that never arose in the States. For example, we needed to get calcium into some pregnant women. An IV drip was ideal but that was not always available. This was tricky business, too much calcium too quickly could cause heart issues, the required dose had to be accurate and delivered at the correct pace. So, I would sit with the patient for an hour, injecting a needle in her vein while slowly administering small increments of fluid with this syringe. Good thing I didn't have my arthritis back then, that is very taxing. We also had creative ways of keeping the newborns warm. Here in the U.S., we use heated isolettes and cribs. We had nothing like that in a village."

Oh yes," Cate added as if memories were flooding back, "It was healing on a shoestring."

"Many newborns, so tiny they would be considered low birthweight here, were placed in metal cradles that hung across the end of the mother's bed. We would wrap strips of cotton batting around their arms and legs and create little bonnets for their heads. This was critical at night when the temps in the Decca plateau might get quite chilly. You certainly became creative. We also had a strong sense that several management changes were needed. Prior to our arrival, there was no systematic record keeping. I had the most rudimentary command of written Marathi, the alphabet, but we did create a simple record keeping system so that there was information of patients who returned to the clinic. That proved very useful, as you could imagine."

"Yes," I murmured, "paperwork is a hallmark of the American healthcare system. Ever get a bill? Can anyone figure those out? I have a Ph.D. and I'm always clueless."

"Anyone surprised at that…?" Paul looked around for reactions. "Corbett, you probably got that degree at the bottom of a Cracker Jax box."

"Cracker Jax? That dates us. No matter, the few times I'm told I owe something for a medical procedure I just ignore it. My philosophy is to wait until the sheriff shows up to cart me off to the pokey. Usually turns out I don't owe a dime but who can tell? Their threats seem ominous. *If you don't pay, we'll put out a contract on your miserable existence.'* Oops, never mind my rant. I just hate the U.S. health care financing system. Please continue."

Maureen nodded. "For once, I agree with Tom. Forgive me Lord, I will do my penance for that sin later. Oh, another challenge was sterilizing things. We had a steam-under-pressure autoclave from UNICEF that no one used since it was a mystery to them. I had used autoclaves when helping in my dad's medical practice but had seen nothing like this monstrosity, a hollow cylinder about four feet high standing another foot off the ground with a hatch-like lid on the top. Unlike autoclaves in the States, there was no safety valve, so you had to constantly monitor the gauges to make sure the damn thing didn't launch or blow the place up. Then you had to wait until it totally cooled before opening or you might scald yourself. Every time I used the damn thing, I feared being killed in an explosion. I couldn't leave the room though. Someone had to stare at these damn gauges, and I was not about to put anyone else in harm's way. I felt like I was trapped with a bomb."

"Such heroism." I stood and bowed in her direction. "I'm deadly serious here. I would have baled-out at the first sign of trouble. At a minimum, I would have stuck Ralph with the dangerous crap."

She ignored me. "Cate mentioned Hanson's disease, meaning Leprosy. By this time, most episodes were treatable and non-contagious. However, the old fears remained. We encountered an elderly man with an advanced case and severe physical deformities. As my site partner mentioned earlier, there was a famous leprosaria 30 miles away where he could be helped but we had to get him there first. Conductors would not let him on any of the buses. The local 'taxi' driver would not take him, even though Cate and I offered to pay the rental out of the few Rupees we had accumulated. The clinic doctor wouldn't authorize the use of the Center's jeep until we agreed to pay for a thorough cleaning and disinfecting of the vehicle."

"Holy shit," someone murmured, "that's cold."

"Eventually we succeeded, but it was a struggle." Cate added.

"Everything was a struggle." Janice agreed.

Maureen picked up her narrative. "One of my failures, in my eyes at least, involved the immunization campaign we mounted. Although we were exposed to the principles of community development in training, we were supposed to be change agents after all, we didn't have a clue about what we were doing. They certainly didn't teach us anything about program planning and evaluation in nursing school. By accident, we did some things right, but we also made mistakes."

"Like what." Ben inquired.

"Well," she paused as if selecting the best example. "We decided we could just start immunizing kids against diphtheria, tetanus, pertussis, and polio since we had a 'captive' audience. We could sneak into the school yard, close the gates to keep the urchins from running away, and start jabbing the kids with our miracle medicines. After all, we were doing this for their own good, so who needs parental consent. We know best, we're Americans. Thus, we never told parents about any possible side effects such as mild fevers and sore arms. Parents barraged the clinic with complaints. Many parents continued to trust us, but many others did not. Those children were lost to us. Live and learn."

"Thank God you are not perfect." Harry breathed aloud. "I was beginning to feel even more incompetent than I knew I was."

"You know, in all my four years as a nursing student, I only saw one patient die. But things were so primitive there. The midwives, as dedicated as they were, had no concept of asepsis or keeping things clean and sterile. Infections and cord tetanus rates were high. One day, a family brought in a young woman with an advanced case of tetanus. You must realize that the classic feature of tetanus is the *'rictus of death,'* where muscle spasms turn the face into a hideous grin and the back is bowed into a painful position. It is horrendous and I was told to stay with her during her final agony. What bothered me most was that there was a mission hospital a couple of hours away. They might have helped but our jeep was away, and the family did not want to spend precious rupees on a journey that might not help in any case. That is how financially desperate many families were. I have never been able to put that experience behind me, why couldn't I do anything. For almost five decades now, my feelings have ranged from frustration to grief to guilt to anger."

"Maureen, there was nothing you could have done," whispered Cate, her old site mate.

"Really, don't be so hard on yourself," Janice added.

"I know." She said. "But it still hurts after all this time."

———

"You know." I added without any sign of sarcasm. "With all the challenges you faced, all of you, I should have argued to be in your program when we first got to training. Maureen, you only dealt with one death in your nursing training. I dealt with more than that as a hospital orderly. On the 11-7 shift, which I worked while in college, you saw it all. Thing is I liked helping people."

"You?" Laura seemed astonished.

"Okay, that statement stays in this room. Agreed! I have a reputation to protect. In those first days of training I was afraid to complain when switched from public health to poultry. I thought I had signed up for the health thing. I should have put up a stink. I had these visions of being the Albert Schweitzer for India at the time."

"Think about that horror," Dee said with a smirk, "Corbett being in our group. I think we all would have deselected ourselves and gone home." Laughter broke out and much nodding of heads in agreement.

"Not me." Cate piped up. "I really wanted to be there, even if I had to put up with Corbett. Did you know that my parents tried to keep me from going? They were dead set against it. I snuck out of my bedroom window at the last minute and had my boyfriend at the time drive me to the airport. If I hadn't, they would not have let me out of the house, probably would have tied me to my bed."

"No way!" someone said.

"Absolute truth."

"Didn't they chase after you?" Janice asked.

"I don't think so. Besides, age-wise, I legally was an adult so there was little they could do. However, I didn't stop worrying until the wheels were off the runway. When I think on it now, it all seems like something that happened to someone else. I always wondered whether I was motivated to go halfway around the world to seek wild adventures or by the thought of escaping the reality of what was my home. I suppose the reason doesn't matter in the end."

"I see your problem." Sherry said. "It's the classic case of *being careful what you wish for.*"

I reflected on my own situation. "My family wasn't so bad but the thought of heading off to the other side of the world seemed like a reprieve. I was also weakening on the question of marriage, which frightened the crap out of me. I know, hard for you guys to believe but I was falling hard for some gal, but it is true. Even the best of us weaken. So, I asked Peace Corps if they had anything in outer Mongolia. Alas, India was as far as they could send me. So, I grabbed it."

"Surely, you jest, your folks probably missed you though apparently some poor girl escaped a fate worse than death." Cate tried to curb my wit.

"My parents? You mean the same people that kept moving when I was out playing as a kid, then leaving no forwarding address." I said to a round of modest chuckles.

"Give it up, Corbett, you say that but no one's buying your *poor me*' act." Connie eyed me with her best look of disapproval, the one she probably used on Paul all the time.

"I suffered so as a child." I tried looking pathetic and abused but only the pathetic part came across. "What really bothers me even now is that my best whining never got me any pity sex."

"Enough with the whining." Nanette said in her most disapproving tone while shaking a fist in my direction. "Don't make me come over there."

"Okay, okay, all joking aside, I am impressed with all you women. As I admitted, my colleague back at Wisconsin was right though she is never to know of my admission about this. You gals were a credit to the corps. You helped people, for real and I do think the world of you all. You were the good volunteers. I am proud to be associated with you."

The women eyed me warily. They were not used to me being nice.

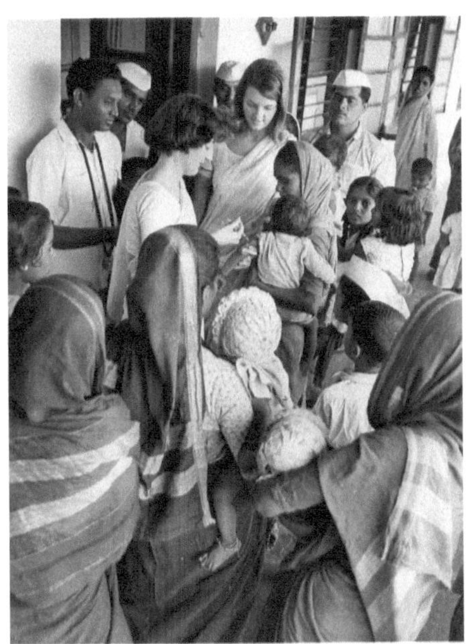

The 'good' volunteers in action, India 44-A.
[Maureen giving shot; Cate watching.]

Janice and Kay in their village, friend in background.

Those 'Other' Volunteers

It was time for the male rebuttal, if there was one. Jennifer, my UW colleague who had read early versions of the India-44 exploits, had been correct. We male volunteers who labored in Rajasthan, at least on a casual appraisal, were beyond reclamation. Then again, I tend to be tough on myself and, by extension, my male peers. What is that apocryphal Abraham Lincoln aphorism, something about *'success being the ability to go from failure to failure and never giving up.'* By that measure, we guys were successful beyond measure.

Despite my reservations, I pushed on. "Okay, my fellow 44-B volunteers, who wants to lie about some of our group's achievements."

There was silence. Finally, Mel murmured. "Our what?"

"Our successes, the things that make us proud to have served." More silence.

When it was obvious no one else was stepping up, I took the initiative. "Oh hell, I'll start. Eventually our day of reckoning arrived, as it always must. Those of us who had survived our endless training were deemed ready for prime time. By the way, who in God's name made that determination… that we were ready? We survivors of our training were the best, really?"

"Anyone feel prepared." Greg looked about the room.

No one responded. "Nevertheless, in September of 1967, after this seemingly endless period of trial by fire, we were to be dumped off in our god-forsaken new homes where we would spend the next two years. My site partner and I had been assigned to a place called Salumbar, a decent-sized town located about forty to fifty miles, or perhaps kilometers, south of Udaipur. Another volunteer would be dropped off at his site even farther south, way beyond the reach of civilization. His site was so bad and isolated that it could not be detected by modern satellite imaging. No one should have been stuck out there. Even the water buffalo had already abandoned his god-forsaken site. He lasted a few months. Too bad. Sonny was a great guy."

Harry let out a whistle. "Sonny, I so missed him when he left. I mean, he was the one other black volunteer remaining in our group. Damn Peace Corps drove him out with that placement. Your right, Tom, no one could have survived in that hellhole. I visited him once before he baled-out. His situation was hopeless."

"It was so remote; he had an overnight trip to Udaipur given the bus schedules. One day to get to us and the next morning on to the city."

"There really wasn't a level playing field in terms of assignments. Some were doable, others not." Tim added. "I know a couple of us, like me, only survived because we were able to relocate."

I nodded to him. "Got that right. But that first morning, none of us knew what lay ahead. The worldly possessions of Sonny, Ralph, and I were packed on a back of a truck along with the three of us intrepid volunteers, and off we were on that hair-raising trip down a narrow twisting road that settled out of the Aravalli Hills before reaching the bleak, desert like terrain that was to be our home. And I do mean bleak and unforgiving. We would make many trips to and from our site and Udaipur over the next two years. These sojourns took place on the local mass transit system, vehicles that surely were constructed by the guy Henry Ford forced out of business around 1909. Of course, it was always a pleasure to share one's motoring experience with locals suffering from motion sickness and fight for your seat with various species of livestock. Still, I always wondered why the goats and chickens got their seat preference before me."

"Oh god, don't remind us." Connie rolled her eyes.

"No mystery," Connie's spouse added. "The other passengers preferred the goats as opposed to being stuck next to you."

"Connie, whack Paul for me." I asked her to no avail though she did give him the *'look.'* "Anyway, the trip from Udaipur was downhill for the first half of the journey as we made our way out of the hills. Then the road wove through the bleak Rajasthani scrubland. In the decrepit modes of transportation available to us, Ralph and I oft doubted whether such ancient motoring machines would make it, or whether the duct tape would split open and the engine drop to the road. The drivers always seemed to floor it, probably because we inevitably started out behind schedule. This resulted in more ear-shattering noise though seldom any greater speed. Still, I recalled having visions of hurtling over the side of the mountain, or was it just a hill, to oblivion thousands (hundreds) of feet below. Sure enough, one day the brakes failed, and we hurtled around curves with ever increasing velocity. Everyone was screaming as I frantically fumbled for that *'perfect act of contrition'* that I had written out by now. Of course, I always had trouble locating the damn thing when needed."

"I'll teach it to you later," Kay smiled.

"Thank you, my dear," I nodded in her direction. "In that moment, I envisioned a toasty future. When I asked a priest once what I could take into my afterlife, he told me not to worry about that. The only thing I would need was a good air-conditioning unit."

"An honest priest!" Bob chuckled. "How novel."

"Yeah, with my lifestyle, everyone knew I was destined for brimstone and fire. I could always recall the first line or two of that so-called magical prayer. Maybe I might scam partial credit, like just a stretch in purgatory or something." I noticed a couple of confused looks from the non-Catholics in the room, so I pushed on "Let's just say that my prospects for getting to heaven were dim indeed. Our intrepid bus driver saved my fanny that day and, for the moment at least, and kept me from eternal damnation by ramming the bus into the side of the hill at a brief point where the elevation went up, not down."

"Damn, how close we once again came to being spared listening to Corbett's so-called wit." Paul opined. "Unlike cats with just nine, he must have at least two-dozen lives."

"Paul, be honest, you would miss me."

Paul opened his mouth, but his spouse elbowed him into silence.

"Our first trip down the road from hell, however, proved quite uneventful. Ralph, my site-mate, and I looked forward to being greeted by a group of excited locals. Surely, I thought, the arrival of the Peace Corps miracle workers would warrant some visible display of anticipation, or at least one lonely greeter. But no, the truck pulled up to a few isolated government buildings that were surrounded by . . . strike up the band… nothing. No sign of life was visible, no town, no welcoming banners, no brass band. In fact, no people at all."

"And no surprise!" Bob offered. "Your reputation must have preceded you."

I continued while multi-tasking by giving Bob the universal sign of disrespect, which he well deserved. "Okay, it was Sunday, so the empty government offices made sense. But our arrival had sparked less than zero interest. Did anyone tell them we were coming? What hit us was that everything was so desolate. The far side of the moon probably looks more inviting. The area was hard-packed dirt punctuated by small bushes and an occasional dwarf-like tree or big bush. *This looks exciting*, I thought. We said our goodbyes to Sonny, who disappeared while looking longingly toward us from the back of the truck. He had the resigned look of a condemned convict who had been told his execution time had arrived."

"So, what next," asked Dee as I stopped to reflect on that desperate look on Sonny's face that day now so long ago.

"Oh yeah. Well, Ralph guarded our worldly possessions, though who might steal them was a good question. Then again, the water buffalo looked suspicious to me. Off I went to find civilization, or at least one other human being. I mean, what if there were no humans and we had been dropped off here to die. That seemed possible in the moment. It turned out the town of Salumbar was a mile or so away just beyond the next rise in the road, depending on whether you took the short cut along a lake or followed the main highway. In any case, you could not see it from where we were to live."

Reserved Kay then cracked a joke which surprised me. "I'm sure they wanted to keep you two away from the women and children."

"*Et tu,* Kay. Damn, everyone's a stand-up comic here. Anyway, Salumbar turned out to be the major local town in that area. It still had a remnant of an old Raj palace, a reminder of its former importance. There was a bank, post office, a restaurant, several tea shops, a gas station, numerous small retail shops, and a variety of government buildings and schools. We were to be housed in the government residences located adjacent to the Community Development Office from which a variety of rural services were administered. While there were accommodations for three or four government workers on site, none of the local officials chose to live there. All preferred to live in town. Besides, the accommodations would have been cramped for staff with families. They were small and it was so freaking isolated out there."

Janice sighed. "Yes, the loneliness… that was the worst."

She had a far-away look to me. So, I went for lightness in the moment. "Then again, it is possible that rumors of our impending arrival had driven local real estate values down. All in all, the accommodations were not bad, once we swept out the scorpions, put up some screens, and the electricity arrived. We had been told that electricity was *'just now coming'* and it was, after about six months. Before bothering to install this amenity, I suspect they waited to see if we would come to our senses and flee back to America. To their dismay, and utter shock, we stayed."

"There probably was much wailing and gnashing of teeth when the local villagers realized that some of us were going to tough it out." Harry said with a grim smile.

"For sure, it seemed rough at the start. And yet, the newness of everything turned it into an adventure. Okay, it was new and exciting for a while at least, perhaps two weeks. Running water was a luxury never to be enjoyed and one relieved oneself into a hole in a small, unlit room attached to our living quarters. As you all know too well, we squatted over the hole and then cleansed ourselves with our left hand and a small container of water brought along for that purpose. When I explained our Western customs, many locals were appalled, thinking toilet paper very unhygienic. By the way, did you know the Chinese started making toilet paper in 1391, for use by the Emperor?"

Mel groaned. "Corbett, where do you come up with this crap, pun definitely intended?"

"He just makes it up," Bob added confidently.

"Scholars do not make crap up," I tried to look offended. "Just a gift, Bob, just a gift bestowed upon the enlightened few. But hitting the head, so to speak, could be an adventure at night, when tipsy, with no moon, and a forgotten torch, what we termed a flashlight in our former lives. The rest of the living quarters were adequate, a small office/living room, sleeping quarters big enough for two cots with mosquito netting, a small kitchen, and an entry way that could be used as a room I suppose. Good enough, we thought, though living by kerosene lanterns quickly grew tiring as the days shortened that fall."

"The adventure part of it doesn't last forever, does it." Greg sighed.

"True, but that was not the real problem. The physical hardships were eminently doable if we had a purpose for being there. There was the rub, as they say. We had no freaking idea what the hell we were doing. All the physical hardships were nothing compared to that, not the heat nor the things that flew about or crawled along the ground, nor the fear and reality of disease and dysentery. You adjusted to those little bumps. It was this knowledge, deep inside, that you were clueless. What were we supposed to do?"

"Nothing worse than feeling like a fraud." Mel added glumly.

"Exactly! Later in life, I would be giving talks at academic conferences, or sitting in high level policy meetings in Washington or some State Capital. I'd look about in wonder at the fact that these other people were listening to me as if I were an expert. And I suppose I did know stuff about my policy area. Still, that sense of being an imposter remained for a long, long time. Never, however, was it stronger than in India."

"You're not the only one," Dee suggested.

"I suppose, Dee, but I did not know how universal that feeling was at the time. I mean, I never felt that I might do as much harm even though my academic and policy advice later in life might impact large numbers of vulnerable people. After all, I would never meet the folks affected by these state and national policy changes, or not many at least. Those larger policy issues oddly mattered less on a visceral level. I had some sense about what I was doing by then, or at least there were others with whom to share any blame. Back in my PC site, I wallowed in uncertainty and I was, for all practical purposes, on my own. In those fields around Salumbar, I would be looking directly into the eyes of people who were on the very edge of desperation. My guesses as a crop expert just might push them over that edge. That was my Hell, and I'm sure I was not the only one. For Christ's sake, my only farming experience had been on a 10 × 5-foot garden plot in my back yard as a kid. That little experiment resulted in several scrawny radishes and a lecture from my folks about screwing up the back yard, which we didn't even own."

"At least you didn't kill anyone, which is what we gals worried about." Cate pronounced and then thought about her statement. "You didn't, right?"

"You didn't, did you?" Connie repeated the inquiry when I remained silent for a moment.

"Not to my knowledge," I said quickly. "In fact, we did have successful demonstration plots. I recall a photo of brilliant, thick waves of wheat growing next to sparser yields from local seeds. These demos were to show farmers throughout the region what was possible. That was always better than promises, like those signs you see adjacent to rural roads noting the seeds that had been used to grow such a great crop. Maybe that's only in Wisconsin."

"I don't see those in the Bay Area." Ben smiled.

"Probably not. And there were various other projects to keep us busy. We planted a local garden outside our modest abode to encourage similar efforts locally. You know… home gardens. We built a chicken coop on top of our house to encourage that cottage industry. I even convinced some of my former professors at my alma mater to get their current students to raise money we used to expand the local school library. Unlike some of you, our village didn't need a new school building. So, we contributed financially toward helping them buy more books and educational materials and thus expand their access to the outside world."

"Yes, several of us built schools, or had them built. That was something concrete we could do, no pun intended." Mel asserted confidently.

I nodded toward him. Though I kidded Mel a lot, he struck me as the kind of guy I would like to be when I grew up, assuming I would one day. He was kind and sincere and just a nice guy. Then I continued. "No question, there were some good moments. It was lovely most evenings when darkness summoned a cooler breeze off the desert. We could sit on our roof and enjoy quiet time associated with the sunsets of rural India. The pink hues of day's ending would be replaced with a canopy of stars. I remember the serenity, the almost glacial pace of life. I have never felt so connected to the world around me, nature and the stars and moon. For the only time in my life I paid attention to such things. How different from today when my smart phone connects me to an ever-changing world on a 24-7 basis."

"God, today's volunteers have it easy." Mel intoned with exasperation. "And yes, I know I sound like an old fart."

I chuckled. "Self-awareness is a blessing, but you are right. We were so freaking isolated back then, a loneliness that was corrosive if you were not strong enough. There was no internet, no cell phone, not even a regular phone with which to touch the outside world. You had to be comfortable within yourself and with the fact you might be dead for weeks before anyone would know."

"Come on, Corbett," Paul uttered incredulously. "The locals probably would have responded to the smell, then chopped you up for fertilizer."

"A contribution at last." Connie beamed.

"Ha, ha! I recall thinking as a kid that I could never live in a place with scorpions and snakes and other such creatures and now I found myself in a place with scorpions and snakes and other such creatures. Rather than go to that dark place, I uttered something innocuous. "I now have this smart phone with me that connects me to the world, instantly. I'm not sure I have to think for myself anymore, a blessing if true. Still, I can't decide if that is progress or not. Much less input from the outside world back then but more opportunity to consider what we were sensing, feeling, and doing. I wonder if all our contemporary connectivity is comparatively better than having the time to digest and interpret all that continuous input we now have. I'm thinking not."

The discussion stalled momentarily as we discussed how technology was ruining our lives until Mel took over the discussion. "One of my most painful memories came about a year into our stay. When we were up in Delhi for medical checkups, the regional PC head called me in for a private chat. Remember that Bob and I had overlapping areas. He asked me two questions. Was there enough work for two volunteers and would I accept a transfer? I said no to both. But his talk stung. Clearly, he was saying that Bob was the good volunteer and they were putting up with me… that's what I concluded at least. I walked away feeling like shit but motivated to do better."

Mel stopped there. I considered urging him to say more but, instead, turned to the one guy who seemed competent right out of the gate. We needed an upside story for the 44-B saga if, in truth, there was one to be had.

"Ben, of all us clowns, you were the one we looked up to as a technical guy, as someone who got things done. Really, you had practical skills. What I mean is that we always felt you knew what you were doing. Did you see yourself that way?"

He paused, then started slowly and thoughtfully. "Nothing like you might have imagined. It wasn't like I was a farmer or anything growing up. Like most of us, I was a city kid right out of college… Cal-Berkeley. I did, though, work with my hands a lot. Nevertheless, I struggled like the rest of you. Perhaps I just faked it better. You know, we all had challenges. If nothing else, we were always sick. Hell, if someone had a solid shit we had a celebratory party."

"Speaking on that topic," I interrupted him, "did you know that a high-tech company called Micron is developing a toilet that will analyze your poop to detect signs of disease. Yup, your commode will soon be your in-house doctor."

Everyone looked at me blankly. "What the hell does that have to do with anything?" Bob asked.

"Well, Ben was talking about pooping, I thought it was relevant. Think how far we've come since we used a *lota* and our left hand." They still looked at me blankly. "And the CEO of the company is an Indian national… Sanjay something or other."

"Fascinating," Paul murmured.

"You think so?" I was surprised at his seeming complement.

"No, not in the least. I'm just amazed at what you find interesting. Go on, Ben." With that, Paul ended my digression.

Ben continued. "Okay then! All of us lost at least 20 percent of our body weight. More crap seemed to be going out than food coming in, so to speak. Beyond that, we had taken a vow of poverty, close to it at least. And since we were not permitted to consort with the local girls, we became involuntary celibates as well. Might as well have been monks."

"You said it brother… involuntary for sure!" Mel added with emphasis.

"Moreover, we faced many dangers. No question, I will admit to feeling the same concerns as the rest of you. There were diseases, accidents, riots, and cobras. I always kept my eyes out for cobras. I recall getting on a bus one day with a highly agitated group of villagers who were yelling at the driver to get to the hospital right away. They had a woman with them who had crawled into bed with a cobra which had bitten her six times. Cobras do not have fangs per-se but many small, sharp teeth that abrade the skin so that the poison can enter the blood stream. I never found out what happened to her, but you never forgot such things. I used to walk by one bush all the time, sometimes in the dark. One day, I saw a five-foot cobra dive into a hole concealed under that bush. Not sure but it likely had been living there for quite a while."

"Okay, that would have resulted in a smelly deposit in my pants." Harry grimaced.

"Do you remember how we went everywhere on the cheapest one-speed bikes made in India, the ones always in need of repair."

"They were called Supermen bikes as I recall," Greg threw in.

"Yeah," Harry added, "because you needed to fly on your own to get anywhere."

Even the serious Ben chuckled as he picked up his narrative. "For one thing, thorns in the sand would pop the tires. We usually threw away the tires after it had over 25 patches in it. We took longer trips on those busses that always seemed to be breaking down. The seats were wooden and there might be a bolt sticking out that would rip our pants. Those busses were always packed with villagers… always. Ever see a bus that wasn't jammed? Guys would get up into the baggage racks and dangle their feet in your face. Many of the locals were not used to vehicular travel. I never met a volunteer who had not been thrown up on."

"Copy that!" Bob agreed.

"Thanks for the memories." Dee added.

Ben nodded toward Dee as if apologizing, then he continued. "You might remember that when we arrived in Udaipur. India had recently dealt with a costly armed conflict with Pakistan and a brief Chinese border incursion."

"Oh yeah," Greg interjected. "I recall one of the former volunteers who trained us saying something about the Pakistani Air Force dropping a few bombs where he had been stationed… somewhere near Jodhpur I believe."

"That got my attention at the time," I added, "though I couldn't imagine anyone wasting a bomb on Salumbar."

Ben nodded and continued. "You might recall that the State of Rajasthan had experienced several years of drought and a full-fledged famine before our arrival. There were signs of this all over. Women on famine relief work projects sat by the side of the road and broke rocks into gravel with hammers to make the road base. I saw two women working one shovel, one held the handle, the other held on nearer the flat part. Labor was cheaper than buying more shovels."

"I don't have a clear memory of any famine." Mel mused reflectively.

"I think we lucked out since the monsoons returned our first year. We missed the worst of it. It was the earlier bad years that resulted in Johnson sending agriculture help to India which, unfortunately for India's sake, included us. However, I do recall seeing emaciated farmers, with even more depleted cows, walking hundreds of miles from areas to which they had migrated in search for better pasturage during the drought. Since our job was to help them grow more food, it seemed like a great idea at the time... on paper at least."

"If only we knew what the hell we were doing." Harry sighed.

I then paused reflecting on an image from the recesses of my brain. "You know, they never seemed to complain, the villagers, no matter how desperate their situation. They might argue with one another but seldom protested so called acts of God. So freaking passive."

"That was an unfortunate product of their culture," Bob chimed in. "They saw themselves as having less efficacy in their own fates. It was all about karma and caste and being assigned to your fate which you were not to dispute. Quite different from our presumptions about life." Then he looked at Ben. "Oh, sorry Ben, please continue."

Ben picked up the thread of his recollections. "For me, like all of you, it was a challenge... everything was. Perhaps I made it look easy but..." he paused as if he didn't know where to go next. "Hell, I remember arriving in India and being told that about one volunteer a month had been tackled by a few burly staff members, sedated by a Peace Corps doctor, and escorted home. Some volunteers were reported to have committed suicide. Perhaps these were mere scare tactics, but some stories did cause nightmares. One guy purportedly jumped naked off a balcony into the U.S. Embassy swimming pool. India had a high attrition rate compared to other PC countries, so we were warned to take care of ourselves and get help if we started to struggle before something drastic happened. You didn't want to be escorted home in a straight-jacket."

I couldn't resist what I thought to be a cute quip. "Actually, I had a plan to fake it past the mental health police. I went bonkers before going to India so no one could detect any difference once I arrived in-country."

"Very funny Corbett, but this was a real issue." Harry looked serious so I repressed any further witticisms. "I think we all struggled with being tough despite having troubles coping. No one wanted to look weak so we seldom, if ever, admitted our problems to anyone… not to other volunteers and surely not to staff. Hell, staff might send you home. We had seen how others had been chopped from the program without warning. It was tough."

———

We had gotten off topic again. "Wait, Ben, you were supposed to provide us with something uplifting, a success story. Get on with that if you can."

"Uplifting? I can try," Ben said quickly. "It is true that I was lucky in my work. My village leader had spent time working with the Maharaja of Jodhpur, so he was rather wise in the ways of the world. I once asked him why he wanted a volunteer in his village, and he responded that he wanted his sons to be exposed to a person from another culture. He taught me a lot about village life. In addition, my BDO, or Block Development Officer for those in the crowd not familiar with such things, was an inspirational community leader. I had considerable support for the projects I wanted to undertake."

"Sounds like you had a good site," Maureen noted.

"I suppose I did, but it still wasn't easy. Like most of you 44-B guys, my main job was to work with the local Village Level Worker whose primary job at the time was to introduce these high-yielding varieties of wheat and corn. That first meant developing a demonstration plot or two for the next planting season. I was nervous about that. Fortunately, I had work right off the bat. There was a need to measure the water levels in all the surrounding wells. This was great for me since it helped me overcome my reticence about leaving my house and meeting the locals. I am naturally reserved, unlike Corbett."

"Lucky you!" Laura said. "No one wants to be like Corbett."

I stuck my tongue out at her but that was ignored by all.

"That first task took about a week which got me known among the farmers. I soon was seen as someone official whom they might listen to in the future. It helped them trust me."

"Yes, that was a big hurdle, getting them to trust you," Mel asserted. "So many people took advantage of those at the bottom, they were naturally suspicious and with good reason.

"Perhaps I was lucky," Ben continued. "I became a kind of consultant and jack-of-all trades, conferring with locals on such issues as electric pump design, fertilization, tree pruning, plant diseases, and insect control."

"You knew about all that stuff." Mel groaned. "You should have trained us."

A thought struck me. "Even better, Peace Corps staff should have made you a traveling consultant, circling through our sites to check out needs and help us figure out what to do."

"Maybe," Ben said warily, "but I still was terrorized about planting that first wheat crop. I had some practical skills, but I wasn't a farmer. I had little confidence in my ability to get the crop to grow, so I passed for the season. The new seed was Sonora 64, which had been developed in Mexico. When planted and properly raised, it grew like crazy. At the end of the season, however, it turned out that the gluten content, good for Mexican tortillas, did not work well for Indian chapatis. The market value was low, and many farmers lost money on the deal. It turned out that several volunteers got burned for having advocated the new seed."

"Who else remembers that? I remember many problems but not that one," Harry asked but was ignored though others seemed to be thinking about it. "Perhaps that issue was buried amidst all the other things we were struggling with at the time."

Ben raised his hand. "You know, I think it was easy to miss the value of what we were trying to do since it was hard to see the bigger picture. Face it, local agricultural practices had been relatively unchanged for hundreds of years and farmers were very, very conservative. The innovation diffusion theory in which we were trained at the time argued that a farmer would have to hear about new, even minor, agronomic practices at least nineteen times before contemplating a change in how they did things. We saw our jobs as initiating or, better still, accelerating this change in any way possible. Even if the first crop was not totally successful, the seed had been planted, so to speak, for a better way in the future."

"And if we screwed up?" Harry pondered. "Would we set back progress for the foreseeable future?"

"Most likely!" Tim concurred

"That was my worry." Greg added.

"And mine," added Hank, a 44er who had a youthful look four-plus decades after his service.

Ben was undeterred. "Sure, the early returns might be a bit disappointing, and there were environmental concerns to be dealt with, but the promise of change and new ways of doing things had been introduced. In fact, the very next year I got hold of some new triple gene wheat that promised to be a better fit for the Indian palate. This variety had been developed in India. It had short stems that did not lodge, that is fall over in strong winds. It tilled like crazy, producing twice as many heads that were twice as long. This was amazing. If we could get the stuff to grow, it would be a breakthrough."

I shook my head. "My god, Ben, you make me feel like a cretin. You knew so much compared to me."

"Pretty much compared to all of us." Harry agreed.

Maureen then added "Ben, of all the guys in 44-A, we would have taken you on our team."

"Thank you Maureen, but I was not a miracle worker. The conventional wisdom was that only a large farmer could afford to take a risk on a new crop, so I went to my village leader who seemed to be a very progressive guy and suggested that he try the new seed. He refused, saying that it would be considered disrespectful to his father to experiment with something untested."

"Oh, thank God, you're not perfect." I exhaled.

"Far from it. With that rejection, I didn't know what to do. There were dozens of other farmers, but I was not sure that I could trust them to use the new set of practices precisely, and I could not afford a failure. There was one young man in the village though. He was more of a handyman who worked on houses doing carpentry, electrical, and plumbing work. He had a high school education and always wore western clothes. While I did not consider him to be a farmer, it turned that he and his father did have a small plot of land. When I complained to him of my predicament, he jumped at the opportunity to try the new stuff though I never quite figured out his motivation. Possibly, he just wanted to show how progressive he was. In any case, he was not dependent on this crop to survive so he was ideal in a sense. I told him he would have to do exactly as I said and that I would monitor each irrigation cycle, weeding, and fertilization. He agreed and we produced a bumper crop. I can never be sure what impact on the overall village, but hundreds of years of tradition had been broken. The door was open to the future."

———

I was moved to speak. "Listening to you, Ben, all kinds of thoughts are racing through my head. I had sensed being a real failure as a farming guru. But that's probably not true. I mentioned having pictures of a demonstration plot where our high yield seed obviously produced a bumper crop adjacent to a typical yield. I recall another picture where a farmer, obviously Muslim and, from his dress, rather well off is smiling at the camera. I can't remember his name of course but it's clear he's pleased with the results and I assume this would be noticed by others. After all, that's why we did demo plots. That picture I have somewhere. I also recall a second local friend, another Muslim who owned a store in town. He liked me and we would chat frequently. He also tried the new stuff and it was a success. In my letters to my girlfriend back in Boston, either before or after she dumped me, I can recall writing some upbeat passages about what we were accomplishing. How strange."

"What do you mean strange," Bob looked puzzled? "You were an agent of change. We all were, whether we believed it or not."

"Then why did I feel like such a failure?" I dug deeper into this sense of failure. "Despite some contrary evidence, I felt like such a failure. I've never shaken that belief."

"Neither did I," Janice said as Kay nodded agreement.

"As did most of us." Mel added. "We all felt that even as we couldn't express it at the time. We looked upon Ben as a demi-god, someone to emulate."

"No…" Ben tried to say but I decided to cut off his protests of humility.

"Ben, here is my take," I inserted. "The reality of our India experience lies somewhere between our successes and what we have chosen to remember of our time there, which mostly appear to be our shortcomings. We will never get to the truth. I think, in the final analysis, our expectations ran far ahead of our abilities, or at least our performances. We were supposed to ride in on white horses and do good. In truth, we stumbled in and just tried to survive. Reality can be a harsh mistress. Perhaps we have been a bit hard on ourselves. We had such high hopes but, in the end, what really constituted success or failure? Just how would we measure it? Could we recognize it if it stared us in the face? There were no standards, no consensus on the metrics for progress?"

Bob spoke with some animation. "Exactly! It would be folly to assess our performances against standards expected in the Western world."

I jumped on his comment. "As Ben pointed out, if you broke down ways of thinking that had existed for hundreds of years, in just little ways, that was incredible progress. If you planted seeds about new ways of looking at the world, or the benefits of taking chances, even if you did not see the fruits of those lessons immediately, you had left something of yourself behind. Perhaps only a handful of locals changed while you were there. Perhaps overall yields didn't double but the very fact that a new thing had been tried with some success was big. It might not look like much to us but… it really was. The real scorecard would not be filled out until long after we were gone."

Bob spoke with reluctance. "I hate to admit this but well said, Corbett."

I remained serious for a change. "Still, one thing you mentioned rings so true to me. You had to find innovators that could afford the risk."

"Absolutely," Ben, agreed, "so much could go wrong."

I continued with my thought. "Yes! This is one reality of our plight I recall vividly. I did find farmers who would try the new stuff, they did exist. The common denominator, as I recall, was that they were not dependent on the crop to survive. Like your handyman, Ben, they had other sources of income. They spoke English or at least Hindi, not some local dialect we never understood. They were educated at some level and were among the local elite. I could not ignore the reality that being this change agent might have some adverse macro consequences."

"Meaning?" Bob asked. "I think I'm following but keep going."

"Simple enough. There already was a level of inequality between the hardscrabble farmers with their postage size plots of land and the elite farmers who had bigger plots and other sources of income. The poor ones often had many children who now were surviving to adulthood due to improvements in public health. These destitute landowners mostly spoke Mewari and probably could not read, not very well at least. They had no margin for error. They could always throw out a bunch of seed and get a yield big enough to get them through the year, if the monsoon rains came that is. What if I convinced one of them to take a chance on this new stuff? First problem is whether they would get good seed or be stuck with something that had been adulterated along the distribution chain. You recall the level of corruption we faced. Someone could dip into a bag of seed intended for the BDO, take some or all the good stuff and replace it with crap. In that case, even a scrupulous adherence to all the rules would go for naught."

"True enough, that was a problem" Greg acknowledged.

"But the bigger issue was exactly what Ben said, you needed to work with farmers who were sophisticated enough to do things right and well off enough to withstand disaster. That meant you were giving an advantage to those already ahead of the game in the local economy. I would sit at the end of the day and chew on this. After all, I was a liberal, perhaps even a leftist."

"Hell, Corbett, we all thought you were a hard-core Commie." Mel laughed.

"Sure enough." Bob chortled.

"Close enough, I guess. Bottom line, I believed in equality and a level playing field. Now, I was systematically tipping the playing field in the direction of those already successful. I would be making local inequality even worse. Some freaking agent of change. But what else could I do? We had to improve yields. The risk of failure was disastrous on both a personal and a community level. What was a clueless liberal arts graduate dumped in the middle of a semi-desert to do?"

Paul seemingly came to my rescue. "Corbett, don't beat yourself up."

"Thanks Paul, nice of you to say that." I responded, once again falling into his snare.

"It's my job to beat you up and I hate the competition." He laughed out loud.

I laughed with him, suddenly feeling lighter in spirit. "I will say one thing. I've gone on Google-Earth and looked at Salumbar, my old village. I am blown away. We were, as I mentioned, in government housing a mile out of town on the road to Udaipur. There was nothing but desert around us. We could look out across the road and see hard sand and brush, nothing fertile. I recall one day noticing that something was different. I looked out all day trying to figure out what. Then it hit me, a tree that was situated across the road, the one visible tree in the vicinity, was gone. Maybe someone needed the wood."

"Or maybe you were hallucinating."

"Not likely, but I can't discount it. The thing is, when I looked at Google-Earth today, this part of the road was full of buildings and behind them are what look like irrigation ditches and green fields. It was as if a broad oasis has sprung to life in what had been a barren, lifeless terrain. It would be nice to think, as Ben suggested, that centuries of stagnation had been disrupted during our tenure there. Perhaps we did plant small seeds of possibility that grew over time. There was nothing we could do to make society equal, that was well beyond our poor powers. We were not going to end the caste system or end all the racial and religious conflicts that beset that magnificent, if sometimes tragic, land. However, we could leave them with the notion that change and risk-taking were good things. They might not always pan out, but the hope was in the trying. Adapt or perish. That is a lesson well worth learning. Changing expectations and transforming how they looked at stuff, even at the margins, is huge. I think we might have underestimated that. Oh, I'm sure we did. Surely, we did not leave things worse off."

Stan spoke up at this point. "No, while I didn't hang in with you guys, I'm sure you did way more than you recall. As you know, I wound up in Nam so I appreciate both cultures… Peace Corps and Army Corps. No matter how screwed up our PC thing was back in the 60s, it was headed in the right direction. I listened to a radio program not that long ago. A group of Army officers were talking about how to win the war in Afghanistan. They were convinced if they could build water-sewer systems, schools, hospitals, and so on, they would win the hearts and minds of the people and, therefore, prevail."

"Well, we can say one thing for sure," I murmured.

"What's that?" Stan asked.

"Bombs sure aren't working."

—

Mel raised a hand. "Wait! Stan and Corbett may well have a point here, Stan for sure. I did leave an enduring mark on rural Rajasthan in the form of two new schools. My unanticipated, if not miraculous, contribution went something like this. I was invited to attend the Mahatma Gandhi celebration at a local school and the headmaster invited me to say a few words if I was so inclined. I knew he expected me to speak in English, but I was determined to employ my still faulty Hindi. I went on for at least a half-dozen sentences about how Gandhi's message of non-violence had inspired the whole world, not just India. The Mahatma was a big hero in America, well parts of America at least. It was brief but heartfelt."

"Were you a hit?" Paul asked?

"Initially, it was hard to tell. My presentation was greeted with a stony silence that continued even as I made my way back to my seat. Fear hit me as I contemplated the possibility that I had somehow insulted an entire nation. I could see the headmaster's face contorted as if he were trying to work through some unsolvable puzzle. Then he jumped up and announced, *'I've got it. I know what the pucka sahib was trying to say.'* Then he repeated what I had said but in grammatically correct Hindi. The appreciative audience burst into applause at my inspiring words, once they understood them that is."

"Yes," Bob smirked. "I think we can cross U.N. translator off the career option list for this character.

"No matter, over tea the Headmaster made the point that they needed a new school building which was quite apparent to anyone who bothered to look. Classes in Fatehnager then were held in a long hallway on the second floor of a large warehouse with few partitions between classes. Very noisy. The headmaster then asked if I knew about any resources or grants that might be available. I did recall hearing of such but could not dig up the details in the moment. However, I solemnly promised to check into it for him and he seemed appreciative. After some further discussion and a tour, I was ushered out into the common area where I found the entire school assembled. The headmaster took the podium and announced that *'Mr. Mel has promised to secure ten thousand Rupees for a new school building.'* At that, the crowd went wild while the teachers crowded around to shake the hand of their new hero."

"Ah, Mr. Mel, miracle worker and superhero to the next generation of scholars." I laughed.

Another member of our group, Ronald, spoke up at this point. "I so agree with Mel. This was something we could do, build schools, and help them get supplies and teach. Our real work was seasonal at best. There was time for these other things." I looked at Ronald, whose house we were using. He had been tall, dark haired, and handsome as a volunteer, but more serious than most of us. He also attended Cal-Berkeley and reminded me of Ben in many ways. I never got to know him well for some reason though he did visit Ralph and I in Salumbar. I do recall that he did these heroic bike trips across northern India that would have killed me instantly. He remained good looking, his face perhaps craggier and even more handsome than he was in his Peace Corps days. Why did I, among us males, look as if I were one step from a morgue slab.

Mel nodded. "I am thinking, *'oh shit, how did this happen, guess I better find out about this program.'* Fortunately, my memory was not faulty, such a program did exist, and the rules apparently were not onerous. Even I could navigate them. My role proved to be rather simple, to oversee the transfer of funds and see that the work was done. The actual labor was carried out by locals who made a pittance but were happy for the opportunity. I did have to serve as liaison between our village and a sponsoring group of students back in the States but that was rather a pleasure. This was surely a win-win program."

"And yet, Peace Corps never pushed this, they were even a little reluctant to have us go there as I recall." Harry said a bit gloomily. "So stupid."

"Yeah," "Bob piped up. "They were stuck in this philosophical dead end that we were to rely on our technical skills and personalities to make our contributions. Brick and mortar types of help were viewed as buying favor with the locals. Too much like charity I guess."

"More akin to rice-missionaries in the old days." I threw out.

"What?" Maureen asked.

"Sorry, that was obtuse. In the old days, religious missionaries to third-world counties often gave out rice to starving peasants when they converted to Christianity. This practice was looked down upon by their spiritual sponsors back home. Conversion was not to be bought. I think Peace Corps had a similar view. We were not to buy the affection of the locals with new school buildings or stuff that only rich Americans could afford to buy."

"Principles be damned," Mel said with conviction. "They needed this kind of help and it was something we could deliver. Otherwise, the most we had to offer was questionable advice and a few antics which provided some laughs and little else."

Bob raised his hand but gave himself away by yielding to a small laugh even before speaking. "Mel, don't sell yourself short. You provided the good people of Fatenahger with way more than a few laughs. I can't think of anything specific offhand but…"

Mel gave Bob a quick finger. "Snicker if you must. However, my reputation as a *school-wala* spread. A neighboring village approached me to see if I could help them as well, and I did."

It looked as if Bob was ready with another quip at his former brother-in-law's expense when Ben stepped in to keep us on track. "I will say one thing unequivocally, something on which we all can believe. We were the ones who benefitted from our time there. Maybe we did a little bit for our villages, but we were the winners. Our tenures on the subcontinent had the markings of a classic journey of self-discovery. Was there a reluctance to go? Trials and tribulations? Epiphanies and revelations? Failures and triumphs? A return home with a surfeit of stories, discoveries, insights, and wisdom that interested no one at all? Yes, to all that, but there was also a growth in confidence, a deeper understanding that family and an intimate social structure can provide way more happiness and satisfaction than material wealth."

"Ben is right." Mel opined.

"Yes!" Maureen joined in.

"Spot on, my friend." I added. "Though I wouldn't turn down a yacht if offered."

Ben ignored my quip. "I know I'm right, at least on this one thing. Being oneself, and moving toward a more ideal self, no matter how imperfectly, is more important than career and social status or all the other stuff people deem important. Let me add this. We returned knowing that pursuing intellectual interests, and art, and seeing the world, and enjoying adventures in nature and the challenges of conquering mountains, and service to others always trump the conventional trappings of success. These were just some of the treasures we took back with us from India."

No one said anything. No one had to.

A happy farmer with his excellent yield.

Another successful 'demo' plot.

Corbett with his garden.

CHAPTER 9

Temptations and Tribulations

Maureen spoke up with obvious sincerity. "Hmm, I'm beginning to think that you guys were not as useless as we all thought. In the old days, you sometimes struck me as little more than juvenile, oversexed males."

"Well, that's what we were." Harry smiled.

As Maureen scowled, I hastened to support my friend. "Oh Maureen, don't make the mistake of giving us too much credit. We were as bad as you thought, testosterone wise, or at least I was. No, I'm sure I can speak for all of us. The male animal clearly is a pathetic mistake of divine creation, a bad detour on the arc of evolution. Whatever negative thoughts you women harbor about us, they are spot on." As usual, I asserted my stupid opinion with unswerving conviction.

Bob smiled. "There goes Corbett, never correct but always certain."

Tim shook his head sadly. "Wait, this time he may be on to something."

"Of course I am. My friends, you ignore me at your own peril. May I remind everyone that we are mere expressions of our primitive survival instincts… behaving in ways that evolution found prudent, even necessary, eons ago."

"Wait, male perversion is prudent from an evolutionary perspective? This ought to be one of his better ones." Laura smirked.

"Absolutely!" Now that I had ventured where only the irredeemably foolish would wander, my reputation as omniscient academic and boorish blowhard had to be defended. Thus cornered,

I dived in even as reservations nibbled at the edges of my so-called intellect. "Listen, the male imperative is to spread his seed as widely as possible. Are you with me on that! The male assumes that his genetic traits are worth passing on, a bit of suspect hubris built right into us by instinct. Okay, maybe we don't assume that but a desire to spread our seed is inbred despite evidence that this might not always be good for mankind. Therefore, not to spread his seed as widely as possible simply does not make evolutionary sense. The female, on the other hand…"

"Oh my, this ought to be hysterical!" Laura literally doubled over in laughter. "Corbett is about to pontificate on female psychology."

"And physiology probably." Maureen sniffed.

"Anyone find that barf bag yet?" Connie asked with a desperate voice.

"Shush and learn, my dears." I admonished my critics. "Here's the thing. Those of the female persuasion are programmed to select out and domesticate one male since the classic pair-bond is evolutionarily prudent to raise a successful issue. The advantages of the pair-bond have become increasingly apparent as our world has become ever more complex and sophisticated. It takes a lot to produce an adult capable of contributing to the world in contemporary society. Okay, I didn't turn out well, but the principle is sound." I stopped and smiled with satisfaction only to be met with a loud round of groans. "Admittedly, the male and female imperatives are not exactly in accord with one another. We want to spread our gifts broadly while women want to nail a single mate for that pair-bond thing. The good Lord rather messed that up there, not exactly sure why. It all ends up producing miscommunication between the sexes, and a few good laughs."

"Don't blame God for your faults." Kay shook a finger at me.

"My word," Connie exhaled, "the man is delusional. So, you really think that your… imperative, or whatever you called it, is to seduce all the women you can."

"Yup, it's in the basic male makeup, you see it in the animal kingdom all the time. The dominant stag enjoys the fruits of his privileged position in the herd."

Dee laughed aloud in anticipation of her comeback. "Sure, if you want the human species to go extinct since those rutting males would continually strike out."

"And that's not true, by the way." Janice added. "There are a lot of monogamous species, the pair-bonds you mention."

"Laugh if you must, we are nature's product, or God's, however you see the world. And by the way, you gals did nothing to help us when we were on the sub-continent. Really, you could have met us halfway. What's with that anyways. No sympathy for your fellow volunteers? No appreciation for primordial male needs? No basic human empathy? No elemental Christian charity? No…"

"Charity! For you clowns." Laura cut me off mid-sentence. "Most of you were just horny bozos, perhaps still are. But go ahead, give it a try. See if you can make us feel guilt."

"How sad, not a scintilla of empathy for desperate males who were seeking simple comfort after many weeks of laboring in the desert to save the world." I looked at Laura with utter insouciance, then tried looking aggrieved as I struggled against breaking out in a laugh. "Yup, desperate is the perfect word. It's easy for you gals to make fun of us but think about our horrific situation. Here we are, at the peak of our sexuality, knowing full well that, after this, it is a slow downward trajectory in sexual performance and interest as our testosterone levels deplete with age. This should have been our moment in the erotic sun. Yet, we were stuck in a place with no sensual outlets while isolated some several hundred miles from the lovely women with whom we trained and for whom we longed. Then again, you gals never paid attention to us even during training, but at least you offered the illusion of hope. You were there, just beyond our reach. We kept thinking, maybe we'll get lucky tomorrow or next week. Now, in India, even that illusion was gone. Think about it, two years of nothing before us, not even the illusion of hope!"

"Well, Corbett, maybe if you hadn't had that drooling problem..." Nanette guffawed.

"Don't cut him any slack." Laura admonished her fellow female volunteer.

"No quarter here, I see. Tough crowd." Then, for reasons I would never comprehend, I went with honesty... never a sound policy. "To tell you the truth, I fudged that a bit. I mean, you're correct about me drooling all the time, at least when in the presence of such beauty. What I fudged was going without, how should I put it, sexual congress for the entire two years." I swept one arm up into a defensive posture in the general direction where several of the women were eying me with considerable suspicion. I anticipated an assault of pretzels which never materialized.

"Wait, you scored in India?" Mel sought a clarification. He clearly was dubious.

"Bullshit." Harry added for emphasis.

"Yes," I replied, "though it was a close-run thing. While the times were trying, they proved not to be totally hopeless, not like in high school with all those damn Catholic girls."

"Hey, I resent that," Kay protested weakly. "It's true but I still resent it."

"My apologies for pointing out the obvious about those sweet, but oh so frustrating, Catholic girls. Still, we should have gotten freaking medals for our sacrifice. After a while, death seemed like an acceptable alternative to our enforced celibacy."

"Stop with the dramatics, Corbett." Janice looked both frustrated and disgusted.

"Easy for you to say, you weren't burdened with all that testosterone. We should have gone to India at our current ages. Now, we are all pretty much beyond caring about sex. It would have been so much easier."

"Wait, you thought we women were asexual?" Laura responded. "Really?"

"Absolutely! You were hopeless." I gave no quarter. "I kept thinking then, maybe my suffering would soon mercifully end. You know, I might contract a fatal disease, or get bitten by a venomous snake, or have a terrible accident while negotiating my bicycle over some non-existent trail. The opportunities for some early demise did seem abundant."

"A lot of us were praying for that." Janice gave me a withering look.

—

"As I think on it, what probably saved our sorry asses was the fact that Ralph and I had a dedicated staff who, for some odd reason, devoted themselves to keeping us alive. My guess is that they liked getting paid. I doubt our continued existence meant all that much to them."

"My god!" one of the fine ladies from 44-A exhaled, probably happy to get off the topic of male sexual obsession. "What would we have done without our household help?" Others agreed in various ways. Apparently, the sentiment was universal.

I concurred heartily. "No freaking doubt about that. Cutchroo was our primary cook. He was a poor kid from one of the local tribes living in a nearby village and did all the grunt work necessary to keep our bodies and souls together. Rooknot was sort of our chief of staff. He had a low-level job with the government offices with which we were attached and became our go-to guy. Just think of the character Zorba, from Zorba the Greek. He never seemed to do any real work but kept us laughing."

"I loved that movie," said Hank, one of several former volunteers who now lived in the Bay Area. He was a good-looking guy with blondish hair and a thin face with good features. An attorney by profession, he never seemed to age. He still had the fresh, innocent look he had some fifty years earlier. This presented a mystery to me.

How did so many of my fellow male volunteers remain so well-preserved while I looked like a week-old piece of shit? If there is a God, and I meet Him or Her, I'm going to complain about that.

"As I recall," Mel added, "Zorba kept trying to hook up this shy Englishman with a widow."

"Yup, exactly, that was our Rooknot." I responded as I remained distracted by the fact that several of the other guys from my group still looked damn good while I looked like an early monster Dr. Frankenstein cast aside as a reject, something so moribund and disgusting looking that its mere presence would likely attract a flock of hungry vultures looking for road kill. Those guys who never aged somehow cheated though I never figured out how. I suspect they exercised or watched their diets. Such things were a bridge too far in my book. Decay and death were preferable if looking robust demanded that level of commitment and sacrifice. I shook off this disturbing reverie and continued. "Rooknot was the embodiment of the Zorba character. He inevitably had some scheme for us, and women were involved in many of them. You can probably guess what his schemes involved. Alas, we never succumbed to his entreaties. Our reputations, after all, needed to be preserved."

"Good for you." Maureen proclaimed, though she looked rather surprised and a bit suspicious.

"Bull hockey!" Harry asserted. "Who knows, maybe our reputations would have soared, they couldn't get much lower in any case. I always thought the locals looked upon us unattached males as somewhat odd."

"Perhaps that's why they kept their women locked away from us." Mel issued a low chuckle.

"Whatever!" I resumed control. "Listen, it is true our staff was always looking after our well-being. It was tough though we did get electricity after about six months of hearing that *it is just now coming.*' That helped. By the way, don't you hate that phrase, so ubiquitous in India and yet so misleading. Oh, the bus is just now coming for sure, in five minutes or five hours or five days. Just what was the definition of *'now?'*"

Sounds of agreement circled the room.

"Now, in contrast to electricity, running water was never going to happen, never even promised. That would cost money and we were not worth it. So, I remember one day I was walking over to the basin of water that we used to wash our hands. This water thing was a pain in the butt. It had to be hauled from somewhere by Cutchroo. I never did find out from where, probably did not want to know. But I think it was from a distance and then it needed to be boiled before we could drink it. We always feared that the help would have an off day and shortchange the water boiling task. Many images of dying from terminal dysentery, or worse, danced through our heads."

"You were walking to this basin of water…" Mel reminded me.

"Oh yeah, sorry. As I was putting my hands into this receptacle, I heard something splash about, an unexpected noise that caused me to jump back in alarm. As was often the case, this set off a gale of laughter among Rooknot and Cutchroo, who had come to believe we were really a couple of sad sacks but good for an occasional laugh. Watching us day after day, this conclusion was most reasonable, more like unavoidable. Surely, we had destroyed any illusions about Americans being omnipotent, or even minimally competent."

"The basin, Corbett, focus damn it." This time it was Bob.

"Oh yeah, sorry again. As our faithful staff laughed their asses off, Cutchroo casually walked over to check out what harmless critter had caused me to almost crap in my pants. But when he looked in, he let out a cry of alarm. Then he grabbed the pot and rushed out the door while muttering stuff in that local dialect of his we never came to fully comprehend. Apparently, some venomous animal was poised to strike me."

"Yeah," Ben grimaced, "we skirted disaster on a weekly basis."

"Really, how did we survive? I recall our first day in our site. I causally opened a drawer in a desk that had been left there, just checking things out. Looking up at me was a scorpion, waiving his tale and not as a greeting I feared. Oh boy, I remember thinking, this is going to be two freaking long years. After that, I never did put on a pair of shoes without checking the insides carefully, eventually relying upon flip-flops where nothing sinister could hide. I never did find out what almost killed me in that pot of water that day. However, I felt much less foolish after Cutchroo virtually crapped in his pants. He and Rooknot were not joking. Whatever it was, I had escaped a terrible fate by inches."

—

"Did you have guinea worms in your area. That's what scared the crap out of me." Harry observed.

"The guinea worm! Oh shit, that was the worst. Did you gals have those in Maharashtra?" I asked to assess how much I could embellish my story without getting caught.

"No..." came from a couple of sources.

Others simply shrugged or noted they vaguely might have heard of this scourge.

"See, you gals were in civilized areas. It was us guys who braved death every day."

"Here we go." Dee rolled her eyes.

I quickly concluded that embellishment was unnecessary, the truth was bad enough. "You scoff but listen to this. The guinea worm once had been found in stepwells throughout Asia and Europe, maybe elsewhere as well. They were eradicated with modern plumbing and sanitary water sources. But in Salumbar, my new home, the drinking water came from wells that, as I mentioned, we never actually saw but from which Cutchroo brought us our daily supply of this life-sustaining liquid. The source of our supply likely was a local community well, a stepwell. There was every reason to believe the water was teeming with all manner of things that could kill us, or at least maim us. Thus, the boiling ritual. Cutchroo was then supposed to strain the boiled water. The final step involved praying over it in the hope that we would not soon die an agonizing death. Still, we lived in abject fear in part because we did not always oversee the diligence of our staff. We never could be totally certain of escaping our worst fear." I paused for effect. but no one spoke up. "What? No one is curious about our worst fear?"

"No one is asking." Laura said drily, rolling her eyes.

"No matter, I'm going to tell you anyways."

"I was afraid of that." Laura issued with an expression that suggested she somehow had been trapped by a serial killer.

"Now listen! Aside from the usual array of deadly bacteria we contended with, the guinea worm is a cyst that thrives in these so-called stepwells, so designated since you could walk down to the water level. The cyst was small and easily ingested without knowing it, though I think we kidded ourselves that the straining of our water supply would take care of it. Eventually, this cursed thing gets lodged somewhere in your body, perhaps the lymph system. Unbeknownst to you, it hatches and begins to do its damage. After a bit, awfully bad things happen to you and you damn well know you got one or more of them."

"What do you mean by doing its damage?" Nanette asked then reconsidered. "Oh, maybe I don't want to know."

"Sure you do. An ingested cyst hatches and a worm begins to grow. Over time, it elongates down the length of your leg or arm. You first notice a pain in the affected appendage. You might think it's just a common affliction from strain or whatever. But the growing severity of your discomfort brings home the truth. Having seen others afflicted with this scourge, you realize what's coming?"

"What?" Nanette exclaimed now her interest had been captured.

"Heh, heh, your worst nightmare." I was in my element now. "Yes, at some point this lengthy worm that had been growing inside you breaks through the skin. Can you imagine seeing the head of a live worm break through your wrist or ankle! Just shoot me. The mere thought yet unnerves me. Worse, what do you do? You couldn't just pull it out. It might break off leaving most of the elongated body still inside you. An even more painful malady, an abscess I think, could develop. An infection or something equally terrible would follow. I tried not to think on the possibilities. There were many stories about potential consequences, all of them horrific."

"No need for the stories," Connie grimaced. "We can easily imagine."

"Extracting the worm had to be done with care by a specialist, an expert in these matters. Now, you could go to the local health clinic. But most of those infected were the rural poor, perhaps still a bit distrusting of government officials. Hell, some of them probably thought the British were still in charge. No, the locals often relied on traditional expertise, the dual-purpose barber and surgeon who only knew the ancient remedies. They employed those trusted techniques that had been honed to perfection over the centuries. The sign of this local miracle worker was a stick with a worm wrapped around it."

"I recall seeing those." Ben observed.

"They were ubiquitous. These skilled practitioners were trained to extract the worm very slowly and carefully by twisting the offending parasite around this stick. The skill involved was not to pull so hard as to snap the body and permit it to disappear inside the affected appendage but hard enough to extract the whole thing. I would sit up at night envisioning one of these local quacks drawing out a foot-long worm as I tottered on the verge of death by fright. The stuff of nightmares to be sure. I lived in fear of the guinea worm for two years. One of my local friends, a Muslim businessman and farmer who listened to my agricultural advice, got infected with more than one. He was out in the fields, got thirsty, and took a chance. He suffered quite a bit, and he was such a nice guy. Now, someone with my bad karma, I cannot imagine."

"Thanks, I'm going to have nightmares." Someone uttered softly as I paused for effect.

"Not so fast," Connie mused, "the thought of Corbett suffering has an upside."

I continued, discarding all defensive responses that came to mind. "You know, there is a story about the business sign of the local miracle worker who extracted the guinea worm. It was a stick with a worm wrapped around it. The dreaded guinea worm, as I suggested earlier, once was found throughout Europe in olden times. Of course, while there were so-called trained surgeons who did things like bleed you with leeches, the peasants went to the local barber if something really bothered them. Guess what, they used the same stick and worm to hawk their medical expertise. The contemporary barber poll, I have been assured on good authority, is a stylized version of the ancient stick and worm symbol."

"You are making this crap up." Paul looked incredulous.

"Me, make things up? I am once again hurt to the quick. I must admit, though, that's what my students would always say about my university classes... they were suspicious that I was making crap up. Then again, they had to listen, or pretend to since I controlled their grades. If the truth be told, I often walked into my lectures underprepared."

"No one's surprised at that but continue." This from Paul.

"This will be hard for you to believe but I was frightfully busy as an academic at a research university. In addition to the normal academic duties, I was always giving talks, traveling and consulting, and managing this research institute. There was never enough time, so I often had to wing it in the classroom. Turns out, the classes where I improvised struck me as being among my better lectures, at least according to my own delusional thinking. I had such a treasure trove of vignettes and stories from the real world whose veracity could not be checked. Unlike most of my scholarly colleagues, I spent a lot of time outside the academy in the real world. While I might embellish stuff in the classroom or in public talks, my story about the dreaded guinea worm is the absolute truth. Oddly enough, I am capable of honesty, really I am.

I can also be serious when needed. I was in too many high-level meetings to remain a lifelong doofus. Hey, you gals would believe me if I told you I would respect you in the morning, right?"

That comment was met by uproarious laughter and several versions of "NO WAY!" A few profanities were thrown in while a pretzel or two from the common snack bowl arced in my general direction. Apparently, the assembled females retained some slight degree of doubt about my integrity. Go figure!

I decided to cut my losses once again by changing topics. "At the same time as we counted on Cutchroo to save us from tainted water, we leaned on Rooknot to make life in the desert tolerable. Our failure as ag experts, the temps routinely soaring over 100 degrees, often topping 110 or 115 just before the monsoons, the isolation and loneliness, and fear of disease if not death all demanded that some solace be available and liberally employed. That is, we needed some intoxicating libation to forget our sorry plight. Rooknot, after the first few weeks of keeping us alive and, more importantly, sane eventually became concerned that he was losing his battle to keep us mentally intact.

He came up with a solution. One day, he mentioned the fact that he could get us some local brew, very welcome news indeed. I was rather shocked we never thought to ask. Though illegal, there surely would be local moonshiners eager to make a buck, or rupee that is. We never inquired what this ancient medicinal anesthetic might contain. All we knew is that he would bring liquid in unmarked bottles. The concoctions were of varying colors, usually some pastel shades like pink or orange or turquoise (whatever that is). It was cheap enough, so we knew it was not twelve-year old scotch. More likely, this local poison would rot out our stomachs if given enough opportunity. We soon had undeniable proof in support of this hypothesis."

"What do you mean?"

"Well, remember when the monsoon season hit. Everything that crawled or took to the air came to life. You could not imbibe anything without taking precautions. Let me explain for the edification of the woman of 44-A, the ones who spent their two years in the laps of luxury."

"Stuff it, Corbett," one of them said.

I pressed on despite all resistance. "You have a cup of water in front of you. Exposed to the elements, when you lifted it to your lips you would find various bugs floating on the surface, usually struggling mightily to escape this watery trap. Yuck... right! Quickly, another small survival lesson was embraced. You would cover the top of the cup, only taking the cover off as you raised the liquid to your lips to assess the contents one final time before imbibing anything. When a sip of your libation had been downed, you quickly replaced the cover."

"Okay, I remember that but what does this have to do with poisonous booze?" Harry asked.

"Simple! Ralph and I had a natural experiment going. If the liquid in the cup was water, the bugs would still be alive and trying to escape as we did that last pre-sip check. We could still see their wings flapping or legs churning. If that liquid was the local booze, we found that any insect hitting the liquid would die on contact. They would just lie there. That always made me wonder what that shit was doing to my stomach. But I never had dysentery, almost never that is, during my India stay. Not many can make that claim. So, I'm sticking with the hypothesis that this nectar of the gods was a prophylactic against succumbing to dysentery and/or death from some unnamed intestinal bug."

"Damn, we should have bottled the stuff and sold it to incoming volunteers." Mel suggested.

"The hell with them," Harry exhaled, "you should have shared some with us."

"Whatever was in it, the stuff did the trick by preventing us from going batty. Many an evening, we contemplated the expanse of an infinite sky over our isolated homestead as we drank ourselves into a blessed buzz. The trick, when we did our celestial stargazing from the roof of our government abode, was to successfully make it down the ladder to the ground at the end of the evening without breaking our skulls. Good fortune prevailed fortunately. Then, of course, came the task of ridding our bladders of any excess liquid during the night. The latrine was part of our abode but required going outside and into a separate entrance. It was merely a small room adjacent to the living quarters with a hole in the floor and no lighting. When they finally added electricity, no one thought about the crapper. So, negotiating this on nights without moonlight, especially when blessedly blitzed, was not the most easily accomplished task. The real risk to life and limb was mistakenly stepping into the potty hole, an unpleasant thought though a distinct possibility. Most nights, I took no chances. I usually said, *'what the hell'* and whizzed into the small garden we had developed just behind our place."

"What about number two?" Someone asked.

"No problem, it made great fertilizer. No wonder we had the best-looking veggies in the area."

"Gross!" One of the ladies present uttered with a look of disgust.

"Ever try anything stronger?" Paul asked. "And I'm not talking about anything to do with your disgusting latrine habits. Just trying to change topics here."

"You know, I was more of the 60s political guy than a pothead, but Rooknot was a good salesman. He never convinced us to try the local women, which demonstrates just how stupid we were, or cowardly at least. One day, though, he was most excited. He had a new plan which involved some new concoction he wanted us to try. This drink was much better than the local mystery brew according to him. He hinted that it would make us very happy!"

"Oh no," Laura groaned, "you never should have been released from the asylum."

I smiled at her. "'*Why not?*' Ralph and I said to ourselves. We trusted our faithful servant by this time and needed an escape from the daily frustrations. We took a couple of tentative sips. When it didn't put us on our asses right away, we downed quite a bit of his offering as Rooknot looked on with a huge grin. Soon, we realized that this stuff was strong, which likely explained the mischievous smile on Rooknot's face. Wow, maybe it was more than just pot since the effect was something beyond any prior experience of mine. While I had not been big into that stuff, it was the 60s after all and I was not without some sin. Sliding into oblivion, I recall thinking I was going to die. Should I try to get help? But how, I could not even move. Then, after careful consideration, I concluded that this would be a great way of buying the farm."

"Your still here, I see. We're all rather disappointed." Cate noted. "Once again, our prayers went unanswered."

I just smiled. "The next morning, I awoke and made a pledge to not try any more of that. Whatever that concoction from the day before was did not solve our main problems, like having a role to play in our sites or the lack of female companionship. That latter issue, oddly enough, brings me to my cat story."

"Oh, no," someone sighed.

———

"Ralph and I got this cat after I woke one night with a large rodent sleeping on my chest. Not sure he was sleeping… he might have been deliberating on how to tackle such a big meal. No matter, it took Ralph at least a freaking hour to scrape me off the damn ceiling. We had been setting traps each night and emptying them in the morning, always hearing the buggers scurrying around the place in the dark. That tactic was not working. There apparently was an endless supply. We needed a better approach. A cat seemed like a great solution."

"Okay," Paul asked suspiciously, "where are you going with this story. Are you going to reveal some disgusting feline fetish or some bizarre sex practice involving our furry friends?"

"God no! Get your mind out of the barnyard, you depraved letch. We guys in 44 were nothing like you perverts in 40. No, the cat was only there to get rid of those pesky rodents. I can't recall where we found him now. No matter, he did a great job until disaster struck."

"What disaster, pray tell." Someone asked while the rest of the gathering bemoaned the fact that I was being encouraged to continue.

"Just listen for a moment. It all started when a stray female cat in heat wandered toward our abode one fine day and started wailing. Billie was the name of our feline protector since it was close to the Hindi word for cat. Let me tell you, Billie literally jumped halfway up the screen door and let out this ungodly sound. I sat there watching this exhibition and pondering why human females never came wailing after me."

"Oh my god, Corbett, no mystery there." Laura doubled over with laughter.

"Anyway, Billie just hung there in the screen, caterwauling continuously. We had to let him out, he would have ripped the damn door down, or we would have after losing what remained of our limited sanity. Ralph later remarked that the only other time he saw anything so desperate and utterly pathetic and desperate was when I was around the gals from 44-A."

"Oh, you weren't that bad, Tom." Kay, our sweet woman from a large southern, Catholic family, said without much conviction. I looked at her and smiled inwardly. She struck me as innocence personified, so much like the Catholic girls of my youth who scarred me for life... those good girls who dedicated their bodies to St. Virginius of the Corporal Innocence. Even making it even to second base was an impossible dream. Despite that, I found it hard not to like Kay.

"You are sweet." I had this memory that she and I did engage in some harmless petting when our two groups had a joint meeting in India. It remained a pleasant, if uncertain, memory. Given her prudish background, however, I was dubious about its authenticity. One day, curiosity got the best of me. I emailed her asking if she recalled such an incident. Nope, nada, absolutely nothing! Perhaps that touching moment was so painful that she repressed it. More likely, I fabricated it in my feverish mind, or likely confused her with someone else beset with lower self-esteem. For a while, I debated what had happened. Had I traumatized her sufficiently so that she needed to cauterize the very image of a painful incident from her memory bank? Or, had my few positive romantic memories with the women of 44, however rare and innocent, been more illusory than substantive. Perhaps, where romance was involved, I was utterly delusional.

"Yes, Kay, he was that bad," erupted from several women in the room at the same time. This ended my inner dialogue on whether Kay and I had connected romantically at some point.

"Kay, you always were too nice for the 44-A gang. Way too nice. But back to my sad feline tale. For three days we would hear that cat wailing in the distance, followed by silence, then more cat wailing. I don't think Ralph and I got much sleep during that period, both being worried about Billie's safety and hating him for getting so lucky. We were sure that the damn cat would expire of excess exertion, but at least with a smile on his face. We did fear he might never return. But after three days, much to our relief, he dragged his sorry ass home, looking as if he had been through a war... on the losing side. Damn feline slept for a week. I really hated him after that. Not hate so much, more like an intense jealousy. His success reminded me of my plight, our plight, the hellish exile in which all of us guys in 44-B found ourselves. And here Billie was on death's door, from too much whoopie!"

"Poor things," a female voice said. "But we were all in the same boat, you know."

Mel stepped in. "No way! For women, celibacy is a choice or a preference. For us guys… it was more like slow torture."

"Spare me…" Maureen uttered with clear derision.

I cast a grateful glance in Mel's direction before resuming. I knew we all had suffered from carnal deprivation back in the days and did not want to come across as the only whiner. I decided to rescue him before the females in the room pounced on him for coming to my defense. Much as I would like to distribute their anti-male ire toward other candidates, the better angels of my nature took over. He was in trouble and I knew it…my protective instinct to aid a male brother won the moment. I was seldom so sacrificing.

—

"Changing direction, let's go back to the movie '*Zorba the Greek.*' Who could forget that unforgettable fictional character played brilliantly by Anthony Quinn? As you surely recall, Zorba was a local Greek who befriended this schmuck of a totally anal Englishman and tried to get this loser to embrace life, or merely loosen up. Rooknot, our man Friday, was Zorba and I was the clueless Englishman with Ralph not far behind. In any case, there was this great scene where a widow in the town flirts with the Englishman, whose name I forget, but the guy is too uptight to do anything. Zorba lays into this clown, telling him it is his duty to satisfy her. There is a great line, how does it go now? Oh yeah, '*there is no greater sin in God's eyes that a woman should call a man to her bed and he does not go.*' Love that scene."

Maureen scoffed. "You guys would. Don't forget that he did sleep with this poor woman and violated some local taboo. The town turned on this widow, not him, classic male chauvinism. It was an awful ending for her."

"Yeah," I winced, "I tend to forget that part. But I digress. I believe I mentioned that our man Rooknot never convinced us to sample the local feminine talent. It was not for lack of trying.

He obviously noticed that Ralph and I were behaving like our cat, that is after the arrival of his female paramour but before we let him loose to pursue his carnal dreams. We didn't exactly cling to the screen door wailing away but awfully close. Lot of unnecessary drooling for sure."

"Oh my God, spare us." Another female voice.

I tried my best to appear unimpressed by their cries of protest. "No matter! Our faithful servant was very concerned about our well-being. He started in again with his pitch to bring some women to our place. No one would know, he pleaded. In truth, we did live outside of town, in government housing where none of the real government officials wanted to live. He was probably right, perhaps we wouldn't have gotten caught. His schemes inevitably involved dead-of-night transactions, dressing the women up as guys or whatever, and always using some convoluted back way where no one could possibly see what was going on. It was all so tempting but we retained our virtue."

"Virtue? Did he say virtue." Connie was incredulous.

"Alright, alright, it was less nobility on our part and more that we could not believe that such a thing would long remain a secret. Scamming the ridiculous Americans would be a coup to be shared, right? Once out, our credibility would be shot, or so we thought. We were very concerned about our reputations, such as they were. There were stories of volunteers being kicked out of their villages for violating local taboos, like eating meat in strict Hindu areas."

"Wait," Tim laughed, "you really thought your reputations could sink any lower?"

"Good, point, didn't think that through, did I? I can still see Rooknot, his infectious grin, as he argued... *'Sahib, I can sneak them along the lake and over the hill out back, at night. No one will know.'* He was convinced he could pull it off and save us from our suffering. He was a good man. Still, we hung tough. We argued that the risk was too great though we were very tempted. He would then give us his best *'you are nuts'* look and start the argument all over again."

"So, you really never gave in?" Laura asked. "I just find that so hard to believe."

"No, it turns out Rooknot was a good judge of character."

"Not sure I follow," she followed up.

"We were nuts, totally. For some unfathomable reason, we remained virtuous and the good name of Peace Corps was spared further erosion."

"Except for the fact that the two of you were blithering incompetents," Tim added, as we all were."

"Over that," I said smugly, "we had little control. We did, however, remain without carnal knowledge of the local women, an outcome for which I am sure the local women were most grateful, even though there were some rupees to be made."

Laura gave out a short guffaw. "One thing for sure. Those poor women would have earned every paisa, and then some."

"Damn, Laura, I should have visited you, given you a chance to perform one of those corporal works of mercy Catholics always talk about."

"Hah!" She ejaculated. "You would have had no chance even if the Pope himself begged me to help you out." She arced a single pretzel in my direction.

I smiled at her, then winked. That was not my smartest move as the single missile quickly became a blizzard coming from all directions.

Our crack staff, Rooknot on left and Cutchroo on right.

CHAPTER 10

A Sense of the Place

I suddenly felt a strong need to reminisce in a more serious way. Funny, I thought, how memories at these gatherings are strung together, not in any linear fashion, but with idiosyncratic variation as if our collective focus had a mind of its own. Deeper group sharing is seldom formulaic, with a convenient beginning and middle and end. It is a crooked thread that weaves a meandering path through our hearts and minds.

I started talking, not sure where I wanted to go, beginning with the first thought that popped in my head.

"I have always liked the past, visiting famous sites, reading historical books, and the like. Earlier, I talked about how much my site reminded me of the old west except I never saw a gunfight in Salumbar. Then again, there weren't that many gunfights in the old west, despite Matt Dillon dispatching a TV bad guy on the dusty streets of Dodge every other week. Only a couple of classic mano-a-mano street duels at high noon were recorded in the wild west cattle towns. Oddly enough, the rate of gun related deaths was lower in those western cow towns than in eastern cities. Know why?"

"No, but I'm afraid you're going to educate us."

"Yes, the professor is in. Because those towns had strict gun control laws. You could not be packing within city limits. This was obviously before the NRA bought control of our government."

"I'm shocked, that WAS interesting." Dee seemed surprised. "At least he is off his romantic disasters."

"Which apparently are endless." Laura sighed.

"Glad you mentioned that. Thanks." I sounded upbeat. "To be honest, I'm at that age where I am now the perfect male. You women should be grateful."

"Oh no. I fear what's coming next." Dee rolled her eyes. "My fault, women."

"Just a quick digression. Listen, I suspect my testosterone level has diminished to about zero. Now, I can be around you women, be my witty and charming and stimulating self, and you do not have to worry about me making a pass, or even drooling like in the old days. I don't care about that crap anymore. See, the perfect man, interesting and harmless."

The women looked at me warily, but I had made my point so remained mute for a moment. "Maureen, check him for a pulse," Cate, her former site mate, suggested.

"Quiet down." I tried to take control. "I'm being serious here. Back to the real point on my mind. We were all struck by the fact that so much of what we saw in India seemed ancient and unchanging. It was the same farming technologies passed down for generations upon generations, the same rigid social hierarchy that extended back before recorded history. Yet, if you looked closer, change was in the air."

"What do you mean?" Ben asked.

Bob chuckled. "Not to worry, Ben. I'm sure he'll tell us at great length.

After wagging a finger at Bob's sarcasm, I continued. "As I mentioned earlier, our local worlds seemed poised on the cusp of change. You could especially see it in the kids, going to school and thinking about a world beyond that of their parents. Even then, India was generating more PhDs than most western nations. Now, they are a technological powerhouse, competing with other Asian powers for future global hegemony. Think about it. When you want technical support, the guy saying he is Peter from Wichita is really Patel from Bangalore."

"No shit." Paul said as form or agreement.

"However, I do recall one thing the British did not leave and that was a sense of order and the discipline of the queue. If ten Indians met at the entrance of a 500-seat movie theatre, a riot would break out even if there was no prospect of any scarcity. There would be pushing and shoving which I suppose emerged from a sense that there simply would not be enough to go around. I often felt the same about these small farmers who had far more children than they could support on their meager assets. Siring fewer children risked not having anyone to care for them in a society without a public safety net. While many more of their children were surviving and reaching adulthood, it remained hard to take that risk. India would have to make a profound, almost unthinkable leap forward if it was to absorb all the kids who would be pushed off the land in the coming decades… that Malthusian apocalypse we all worried about."

"I must admit, Corbett," Laura said, "sometimes you are interesting, even verging on being a crackpot philosopher."

"See," I beamed at Laura, "I'm now the perfect male specimen, stimulating yet sexually uninterested. I am no longer your typical male predator. And by the way, despite all my big talk, I'll bet dollars to donuts not many of you remember me hitting on you."

The women looked at one another but no one dared to speak at first. "He might be right." Laura eventually ventured. "He is the butt of our jokes but, in truth, he was harmless as I think back on it. He never bothered me at least." Some assent circled the room, but it was not universal.

"I was all bluster back then, just all talk, mostly to cover my crippling shyness and pathetic fear of being rejected." An odd silence followed as the females calculated my sincerity. They had seldom seen me even pretend seriousness, so my current mood unnerved them. "That, my dears, is quite true. I was painfully insecure. I used my witty banter to disguise the fact that I was paralyzed around you gals."

Laura, to break the silence, surprised me with words of encouragement, most likely to steer me away from a sensitive topic. "Okay, tell us more about your insights of India. We enjoy your serious thoughts, those few times you have any."

———

"As most of us know, we were always *on stage* in India. Life there was a continuing play with a set of complex characters trapped in a convoluted plot. Just consider this for a moment. In our ordinary lives, we exist in a semi-conscious state 90 percent of the time, in my case it may be 99 percent. You read your lines in life the same way you always did. Everything is repetitious. The Bard, Shakespeare that is, was right. Life is a play, and everyone has a part to play. It's as if everyone is given a script and you get your specific role down pat after a while."

"And so?" Bob prompted as if on cue.

"Aha, in India you realize at some point that everything requires thought, this freaking play is terribly hard to follow. It's all improv in your mind and no one has given you the damn script. You are immersed in a society that is an incredibly chaotic canvass of caste, color, class, religion, language, history, ethnic identity, political disposition, and on and on. You had to continuously create your lines as you went along. That is freaking hard. Maybe Robin Williams could handle it, but we were not so talented. Then, virtually every social interaction contained at least the possibility of misunderstanding and hurt feelings."

"That's so true." Maureen agreed with vigor. "I would be anxious at the beginning of each day, fearing I would make some serious *faux pas*. At the end of each day, I then would do some kind of mental review. You know, what did I do wrong today?"

"I know," Cate agreed. "I was always second-guessing myself."

"Yes, I get that though I'm not sure most of us approached things that systemically or as diligently as you two. No matter how conscious we were of the cultural strains we felt, the daily costs were there and somehow were aggregating in some inexorable fashion. Real and imagined sins piled up, even if on an unconscious level. You cannot imagine what it takes out of you to think about what you are doing and saying all the time. The ongoing effort to negotiate the labyrinths of this social web wore you down. But it was more than that. There was nowhere to go to escape the pressure. All the small, everyday scars just accreted somewhere inside, building up and up. Amazing we didn't all become alcoholics or druggies."

"I don't remember drugs being a problem in our group, but I'm sure India 40 were all potheads." Mel smirked. "And Corbett, of course, was our group bad-boy."

"Not with drugs," I protested, "other than the one-time Rooknot blew my head off. I was more of a political creature than a counter-cultural freak."

"I'll go with plain freak then." Mel chuckled aloud at his own witticism.

"All specious insults are being ignored by me. However, let it be known that I was, in truth, innocent as a babe. By the way, your name still is being recorded in my book." I tried my menacing look on Mel to no avail. "Believe me, you don't want to be *'in my book.'*"

Paul turned toward Mel who was looking on with a bemused expression. "You scared?"

"Shaking in my boots." Mel continued to chuckle.

"You mock at your own peril, my friends." I decided to return to my main theme. "The thing is this. My recollections of India are mostly disparate and unconnected images. I recall this day when I came across a discussion among the elders of a village outside of Salumbar. They were meting out justice to someone who had violated some local custom or rule. The miscreant looked miserable. I couldn't catch enough of the discussion to figure out what was wrong and wondered why this matter had not been turned over to the local authorities. Then again, trust of local officials could be tepid at best. I recall a conversation with an educated man from my town. He stressed that there might have been more justice, or at least less corruption, under the British Raj than today, meaning the 1960s. Many elders still recalled those colonial days, some of them fondly. This man argued that baksheesh, or bribery, was now omnipresent."

"What did you run across?" Kay asked.

"Oh, here's one example. Most farmers used the old buffalo driven contraptions that drew water up from their wells for irrigation. But a few of the most prosperous ones who lived nearer to town had electric-powered wells. That was great for trying the new hybrid seeds which demanded watering at precise intervals, or all could be lost. Still, there was a downside and you can well guess the problem. Those in charge of the electricity would visit the farms at the critical time and suggest that their just might be interruptions of service which would miraculously be resolved upon forking over a few rupees."

"Oh yeah." Harry moaned. 'the curse of baksheesh. I wonder if they got a handle on it by now."

"I don't recall anyone trying to shake us down, not personally. My great fear was that some so-called miracle seed that we were pushing would be adulterated further up the distribution chain. Someone would steal part of the good stuff and replace it with crap, but still sell the damaged goods at an inflated price." I paused as a thought came to me. "The only one who ever hit us up for money in our site was the town beggar. There was only one and he was a fixture. He saw Ralph and I as a source of support for sure. He had a jolly face, could have played Santa Claus if he were cleaned up. In any case, he wore the most ragged clothes imaginable that look as if they had not been washed, or replaced, since the days of the Raj. When he saw either of us, his face would light up and he'd come running. I always gave him a few coins. He was manageable, not like the endless number of destitute in any big city."

"What would have happened if you did not give him something?" Ben asked.

"Not a clue any longer, though that must have happened when I didn't have any coins on me. I can say one thing. Ralph and I never felt unsafe, no matter where we were in India. Can't say the same for the States. I came across a list of the 50 safest countries in the world and the U.S. is not on it. Vietnam is, but not us."

"Anyone surprised?" Paul asked.

When no one responded, I went on. "Oh, there was the time that we came back from a trip to find that our home sanctuary had been invaded and our belongings rifled. I don't recall anything going missing except for three American dollar bills of mine which had been ripped up. My guess is that they were looking for rupees, probably assumed the rich Americans had a hidden treasure. Flashing dollars around would tip off the local authorities as to their identity. All in all, though, the locals were nice. We could walk through the town, the villages in the near vicinity, or the fields and people were accepting of these obviously strange and clueless visitors to their land. We went to local festivals, made a few friends, and became part of the accepted landscape. I think, if we only had some legitimate contribution to make, some real reason for being there, the entire experience would have been much more upbeat. Even so, there were many positives."

"Absolutely!" Bob affirmed.

"Perhaps my greatest disappointment was letting the pressures erode my friendship with Ralph. I cannot even recall how our relationship soured but we had a rough patch or two. I suspect that was common among site partners, or at least not uncommon. But I regret that we lost touch. Maybe I would apologize but I have no idea for what. Just because I could have been a better human being I suppose."

"Don't beat yourself up. You weren't the only one to have that issue." When I looked in the direction of the speaker, I could see that they already had regretted their comment. I let her comment hang there since her former site-mate was in the room.

After an awkward pause, Mel picked up the dialogue. "Several of us tried to track Ralph down. He had been a psychologist but seemed to disappear after he retired." Mel said.

"Yes, I even sent him a copy of our first edited book of recollections, to an address in Oak Park Illinois that someone had found somewhere. Gave him plenty of contact info. The book never came back, nor did any message. I wonder if he didn't want to remember stuff. Do you think that's possible?" I mused.

"I think that very possible." Greg added. "Most of us left with unresolved emotions, with guilt, with memories we had to push down somewhere. I still feel guilty about avoiding all those self-mutilated beggars in the street."

"Hell," Harry said. "they pushed most of us over the edge. You wanted to help but the need was overwhelming. We simply were not the rich westerners they thought we were. The pressures could mount up, and then there was the loneliness, the feeling you were the biggest screw-up." He paused. "I can only imagine what those around me thought about my occasional displays of anger. I probably looked the part of the ugly American."

I cocked my head at Harry. It was difficult to see this sweet man ever losing his cool, but we all had our breaking point. "Ugly American? I thought that was my special role. I probably could have done alright as a beggar myself. There are pictures of me displaying a rather cadaverous frame, this guy with thick, black hair, and sporting cool Buddy Holly glasses... not much different than the poor souls liberated from the Nazi death camps in 1945. My poor mother, when she saw pictures taken during my tour, thought I was about to expire, and considered contacting our Congressman. It wasn't to rescue me, I don't believe. She probably wanted to know if there was a government payout if I kicked the bucket in India."

"Oh, stop it." Maureen chided me.

"Okay, she was worried. But I doubt I look much like that guy anymore. Maybe it's the extra hundred pounds, maybe it is misplacing my hair somewhere, or maybe I should look for another pair of cool Buddy Holly specs. As our first reunion approached, I showed around a group picture taken during our India training days. You guys from B might remember the one where we were standing at the edge of a field and an ag instructor was trying to educate us. Talk about a hopeless task. I asked a few of my university colleagues and friends to pick me out. Only one or two did so successfully. Often, when I pointed out the correct choice, my guinea pig would be incredulous. *'That's not you, no way,'* they would exclaim in shock. What really hurt was my wife guessed wrong, and then muttered for weeks afterward something about how cute I was back then and asking what happened."

"Your wife thought you were cute once?" Dee asked as if the very thought was beyond comprehension. "Does she have eyesight problems?"

"And for the record, my wife had perfect eyesight. On the other hand, I once suggested that she had a problem with her hearing."

"Idiot?" Paul levied at me. "You never suggest that your spouse has a shortcoming of any kind." He then cast a quick glance at his wife. "Which you don't my dear, not a single one."

I laughed as Connie elbowed him once again. "Back to my wife. Thing is, she never seemed to hear a word I said. At my strong urging, off she went to get her hearing tested. At the end, the audiologist asked why she thought she had a problem. She went through the story of how her dear spouse, me that is, raised the issue and blah, blah, blah. The technician laughed, telling her she had a common ailment, one they see all the time. This dreaded condition is called *selective spousal hearing*. She heard everyone and everything perfectly except anything said by her husband. We had a good laugh on that one until she wacked me upside the head for sending her on this wild goose chase."

Connie took a break from whacking her husband. "Well, maybe people would listen to you if you said something interesting every once in a while."

—

"Moving on!" I said quickly. "India also involved colorful festivals and sights you would never experience again. Even the weddings and wakes were events. Old pictures reminded me of such memories. Some of it was sad. Poor farmers would be expected to put on lavish ceremonies that cost a fortune for them. To cover the cost, they would borrow from a local money lender at usurious rates. Then they were trapped. I vaguely recall one of these events in Rooknot's family. I asked him why they had to do it. *'We have no choice,'* he responded. Some things were culturally expected. All so sad. There is a photo of a band that visited our house and pictures of many government officials with whom we worked, some who were appreciative of our presence and others who tolerated us."

"I think we were a pain in the ass to most of them" Harry said.

"Speak for yourself." Paul tried.

"We would head out in scorching heat day after day. The farms were in tiny villages outside of Salumbar. To get to them, it was a matter of hoofing it over the countryside in temps that routinely were on the north side of 100. Or you could try those useless Superman bikes that were designed to be death machines. You only worked with a few locals who seemed promising and their farms might be scattered. I might put on a dozen or more miles in an average day just to exchange a few words. It was not like I was bringing crop saving advice or anything like that to them. But I had this drive to appear useful, to keep occupied. And damn, it could be hot. Ever see a movie of some guy, lost in the Sahara Desert, parched and dying of thirst?"

"Sure." Someone responded.

"I was that guy. And I still refused to drink the water for fear of guinea worms."

Mel laughed at this point. "Let me add some of my memories to this trip into the past. I remember getting fired up for a second time at one point. I was going to make a difference, goddamn it.

So, I got a list somewhere of the farmers who were experimenting with the new high yielding wheat strains and tearing around to their fields on my bike, picking up soil samples, and connecting or reconnecting with the farmers themselves. It wasn't long, however before the deadening inertia that was rural India once again made itself felt and I suddenly remembered why I fell into such a torpor the year before. The climax came sometime toward the end of the two weeks of my recommitment to the 'green revolution' in Fatehnager."

"Oh good, I love stories about climaxes." I smirked.

Amidst loud groans, Mel fought on. "So, I was on my way to meet with one of the more progressive local farmers and managed to catch up to him while he was out supervising the seasonal planting. During the chat, he told me that he was thinking of diversifying his crops and wondered about experimenting with potatoes. He asked whether I thought that would be a good idea." Mel paused.

"What's wrong with that?" Ben asked. "Isn't that what we were there for."

"Hell, I knew shit about potatoes. I'm not even Irish. All we had for reference was this *Handbook of Agriculture*, which I knew would be both too general and too specific. As we have discussed repeatedly, decisions about whether to experiment in any bold way involved major risks even for wealthier farmers like these. There were huge downsides for anyone naïve enough to accept advice from a novice like me. It was one thing to give general encouragement to those who could afford to take some risks and another to give advice when the stakes were high, particularly when you had no freaking idea what you were talking about."

"We all know what you are saying." Ben nodded his head.

"Even you, Ben." His self-deprecatory comment had struck me as odd since Ben was widely considered one of the most competent volunteers among us.

Mel continued. "Then, as I retreated from his fields, I must have cemented my image of incompetence. Walking through a newly plowed field, with its deep furrows and large clumps of soil was far from a native talent for a city boy. I stumbled several times on the way back to my bike. I can still hear their laughter as the locals contemplated the spectacle of the 'American agricultural expert' trying to stay off his ass as he made his way across a plowed field."

"Hey, we all have bad memories," Bob inserted to console his good friend.

"The thing is," Mel went on. "I'm not even sure which memories are real. From my diaries and letters, I am finding that what I took with me is not always what happened. The emotional things we imprinted deeply often trump what we experienced. For example, from my diaries, I did get a second wind. On October 4th, I made the day trip to Mavli to meet with the Agricultural Extension Officer. I was brimming with energy. Then I waited in his office for four hours before someone on his staff remembered that he was on leave. I returned on October 7th, according to my diary, and this time spent five hours in his office before someone remembered that he was in Udaipur that day. Two days, completely shot, with the bonus of having severe stomach cramps on the bike trip back home where I was extremely fortunate to make it back in time."

"Not to worry, Mel Sahib, *it is just now coming.*" Harry offered to much laughter.

"And it is coming even faster." I injected while hoping to keep the diarrhea allusion going.

"Let's move on." Maureen chided us.

I agreed. "Remember this one character in Catch 22, oh what was his name?" After a pause while I struggled to remember, "Oh yeah, Major Major I think! He would only agree to see his subordinates when he wasn't in. On the other hand, he had an open-door policy when he was out of the office. When he was there, he wouldn't see anyone. India was our Catch 22. The local officials only would agree to see us when they were not there." I snickered at the cleverness of my literary connection.

"Eventually, according to my diary, I stumbled on to the most successful project of my Peace Corps career."

"Losing your virginity." I threw out.

"No, you nimrod." Mel retorted with annoyance. "Potatoes! I'm still talking about spuds. A month after I had complained in Delhi about not enough work to do, a PC official showed up at my site with 25 kilos of wheat and 85 kilos of potato seed. Since one farmer had mentioned an interest, I spent the next several weeks meeting with farmers explaining the advantage of planting potatoes while enticing them to try the seed I had available. According to my records, it was a success. Even after reading those entries, I still have NO memory of that project whatsoever. None, nada, nothing, totally zip!"

"That's not so bad, Mel. I have no memory of India." My witty observation generated appreciative chuckles. "But I have a similar experience. In one of my letters, I talk about these very expansive plans for the second year as if they were going to happen. Did they? My claims in that letter, which I won't pull out, were so ambitious. I had to have made them up to impress the girl back home, not that it did any good. Maybe we only suppressed our successes."

"I like that hypothesis." Harry said enthusiastically.

"You know the historical evidence where India went from an importing foodstuff to exporting it during the period we were in country. I used to joke about taking credit for that. No longer. From now on, I will outright claim to have saved India from starvation. And all on my own since you clowns didn't help! I'll just assume I forgot how I did it."

That brought the house down.

———

"You know," Ben began as the room quieted. We all knew you had to listen when he spoke. "India had so many great moments for us but challenges as well, some trivial and some not so trivial. Once we settled into our villages, many of us discovered needs and addictions that we never knew we had. At home I had loved to buy a different cheese every week, experimenting with it in cooking and for lunch. At the time, there was only one cheese available in my site. Now, it was a nice cheese but for one who so loved the stuff, it got old fast. Back home, I had been addicted to classical music and was constantly borrowing music from the music library. Now, I had to go cold turkey. That all seems trivial now, but it wasn't at the time. These were things missing from our lives that got bigger over the months."

"Yes, the small things. They got to you for sure." Dee said.

"Ralph had brought a cassette tape with the newly released Beatles album, *St. Pepper's Lonely-Hearts Club Band*. Must have heard that album a thousand times. When the Republicans torture me someday for being a socialist, they will play that album over and over and force me to listen."

Ben continued. "Other things were more disconcerting. Poverty was rampant. Of course, so many lived at a substance level that it didn't stand out. But sometimes it did and in ways that you could not ignore. Beggars with hideous deformities populated the city streets, especially in the train and bus stations. Several have mentioned this, but one encounter has plagued me over the years. The first time I went to Udaipur, I was confronted by a boy with a double hare lip and a cleft pallet. He would come up asking for money. If I would not give him any, he would open his mouth and let you see into his head where the roof of his mouth was supposed to be. Horrified, I gave him a few coins and vowed to avoid him at all costs. The next time I came to town, I had arranged to meet with another volunteer at a certain building. While I was waiting, the kid saw me and hurried my way. There was no escape, so I decided it was him or me. If he ruled the town, I would have to give him money every time I went there. So, I did not budge but just sat and waited for him. When he arrived, I gave him a big smile and a greeting. He moaned and groaned while asking for money. I said no and he got up into my face, opened his mouth and made weird sounds in his throat and stuck his tongue into what remained of his sinus cavities."

"My God, this is reminding me of the blinding of the boys in *Slum Dog Millionaire*." Mel said.

"All I did was smile again and apologize for not giving him money. He looked disappointed, probably because he had not been turned down very often before. This was his craft and he didn't accept failure easily. He tried a few more tricks before his mom spotted some rich Indians and sent him after them. They paid willingly, and so did others. He was a cash cow for the family but left me alone after that. Perhaps that is how I adapted to India, one challenge at a time."

A thought struck me. "When we first got there, we were overwhelmed by the need and the extreme suffering around us. I think then we got to a point where we realized we could not respond to it all, we barely had enough to get by ourselves. After a while, we hardly noticed it anymore. Occasionally, that sense of being overly hardened by massive need would nibble at my conscience. Had I become a different person, an uncaring person. I didn't like to even consider that possibility."

Bob spoke up. "Just how did you resolve this negative feeling… the sense that you might be evolving into a person you didn't like. We all dealt with this I fear."

"Hmm, I think I accepted the fact that I was not God, rumors to the contrary notwithstanding. I could not do it all, be all to everyone. I suppose we all get there, to this place where we know we have to take care of ourselves at some level or we might snap from guilt and this overwhelming mass of need that could never be satisfied."

"That is so true." Sherry said somberly. "We needed our private places where we could heal, feel safe. We were hit with so much every day."

Suddenly, an isolated memory came into focus. "I can recall another day watching a discussion in one of the villages outside of my town where I was laboring as a fake ag expert. A group of elders were in a serious discussion, not about some local miscreant this time but someone in need. Sitting there was an old woman who, from her clothes, likely had just been widowed. She was wailing pitifully. The men went back and forth with no resolution. It took me a while to figure things out."

"Which was?"

"She had no one left to take care of her. I guess it was up to the village now and no one wanted the burden. You knew that such scenes played themselves out endlessly all over India but to see it up close. It was gut wrenching. I can't recall the resolution, just the emotions of the moment. Life was so fragile, so precarious there. Some moments have stayed with me."

"How awful." Sherry murmured.

"Then again, that experience gave me one thing I could not have experienced in any other way."

"Which was?" Connie asked while her face betrayed a concern that she might be invoking another of my terrible witticisms.

"It let me live out my sense of history in real time and in a seemingly real way. Priceless!"

Our bleak and desolate world.

That same location now.

CHAPTER 11

Loves Found

"I have a story, and it involves a suit of all things." Paul announced to the obvious satisfaction of those assembled, especially the women. "Unlike Corbett's endless yacking, my tale is uplifting."

"A reprieve." Laura cried.

Paul smiled broadly. "Yes, my dear spouse and I have a real love story to share with you. While the animals in 44-B were besmirching the good name of Peace Corps, I was doing many good works in my village and, at the same time, finding a pure love with this very woman who sits next to me here today."

"Oh God, spare me," uttered one of the volunteers who had served with Paul in India 40. "The chief mutt of the mutts is taking the high road. But go ahead, we are all still very confused as how you got this beautiful and otherwise sensible woman to marry you."

"We sure are." I added. "After all, she passed on a prince like me. That colossal error yet remains to be unraveled in the long and confounding catalogue of romantic miscalculations."

"Hell," Paul smiled, "it is obvious to all and should be clear to you. In fact, Corbett, you helped me out in a major way."

"How's that possible?" I stammered, falling into his trap.

"After you, even I looked like a catch."

I had no comeback for that. It was true.

Mel asked. "You mentioned a suit a few moments ago. Did you seduce Connie with a suit? Hell, if I knew that worked, I could have bought a suit."

Paul smirked. "Yes, my successful courting strategy involved a devastatingly sexy tan suit."

Tim chuckled. "I have a story that involves a suit. Remind me later."

I continued my grump. "Mel has a point. I should have gotten me a tan suit. Then you would have been toast, my friend. Yup, that is all it would have taken. I'm just sure of that."

"Corbett," Connie giggled. "you could have driven up in a Rolls-Royce and plunked a 10-carat diamond on my finger and it wouldn't have helped your cause."

"*Au contraire*, my dear, one look at me in a tan suit and…" But I had nothing and knew it.

Paul saw that I was finished, defeated. He proceeded. "As you all know, my group, the renowned and even historic India 40, was comprised of the best specimens of youthful American manhood that our country could produce." He glared at the guys from India 44, continuing when no challenge was forthcoming other than a few smirks and rolled eyes. "We had all rolled into Mumbai, then Bombay, for our six-month séance at PC HQ. You recall the drill, an exhaustive set of briefings, debriefings, re-briefings, blood checks, teeth checks, stool checks, mental health checks, safety checks and, of course, the usual warnings and the futile spankings for various infractions… actual, imagined, and anticipated."

"Wait," I jutted in, "you didn't pass the mental health checks, did you? How? Bribes, I'm going with bribes."

He just glared at me before returning the extended middle finger I had sent his way earlier. "After a day of putting up with a lot of '*eat your spinach*' talks, and the rah, rah stuff about representing the United States of America, one of the secretaries in the PC office mentioned that a new group of volunteers, something called India-44, had just arrived. With no emails, tweets, Facebook, or linked-in notices back then, we relied on the oral tradition of communication. It was whispered that this was a group of public health volunteers, virtually all female. Clearly, it was party time.

Damn," Nanette exclaimed, "too bad no one warned us. We would have locked the doors."

"Anyway, several of us decided to go and check them out. We were staying at Terry's house over on Peddar Road. In the face of severe Bombay prohibition laws, Terry, our PC boss and the only person who ever paid any attention to our hard-luck group, managed to stock a respectable cooler full of beer. The secret, he told us, was a loophole in the Maharashtra regulatory maze that allowed foreigners to buy thirty beers a month if they registered themselves as foreign alcoholics. We marched right over and signed up... confirming with the authorities that Americans were not only sexual libertines but also total drunks, surely a danger to the high morals of their own civilization. To tide us over, however, we drank a few of Terry's beers before wandering over to check out the new talent in town."

"Talent?" Nanette inquired. "Did you think you were checking out the livestock exhibit at the State Fair?"

"If you had been livestock, never fear, Paul still would have made a pass at you." I said peevishly, still smarting from my recent string of verbal defeats.

"Shush," Paul admonished me, "I've got a touching story to tell which, unlike yours, people want to hear. We arrive and get this, there are twenty lovely ladies assembled along with a couple of guys to be ignored. While there was not enough beer for a party, who cares about that? What could be better after months in the isolated boonies than this newly arrived bevy of American beauties? They introduce themselves but I only catch some of the names... Kay, Dee, Marilyn, Cate, Maureen, Nanette, Susie, Laura, Sherry, Margie, Janice, and this oriental gal sitting on a footlocker whose name I didn't catch. I remember asking: who is going to be stationed down our way in Ratnagari in the Konkan region between Bombay and Goa, maybe near our towns of Ked and Mangaon?"

Connie chimed in at this point. "It was Margie and Paula. Based on the prospect of what they saw they might be stuck with, they both asked to be transferred to other sites later that day?'

"Hah, hah," Paul said to his spouse. "keeping this story manageable, unlike Corbett, telescope yourself forward many months. You all remember that India is a giant petri dish. There are diseases in our villages that haven't been named yet. Many an eight-hour bus ride was made to the big city for medical treatment or other official PC business. At various times we were treated for ear, eye, nose, and throat infections acquired while swimming in the scummy green waters of the river running through Ked, the small town to which we had been exiled by PC."

"Funny, none of us guys in 44-B ever got sick." I smiled. "We must have been the hearty ones."

"Bullshit!" Paul harrumphed. "So, while the doctors had us in their clutches treating us for a wide assortment of worms, germs, and bugs ingested from bus station food and village water, we decide to have three nice suits made at a little tailor shop not far from the PC office. I went for a tan suit. It struck me that tan was something a cynical and world-weary expatriate type like Bogart in Casablanca might wear. So, we get measured and fitted. The suits are then ordered. Mohan, the tailor says. *Come back in a month, white boys. We'll do a last fitting and off you will go looking first class.*"

"That would take a lot more than a freaking suit, and surely longer than a month." One of Paul's colleagues from the India-40 group muttered but I missed who, wishing I had thought of such a clever riposte.

"Then, a bright idea. Why not employ our new finery to dazzle the gals we had met at the party when they had just arrived in Bombay and we were hardened veterans with six-months under our belts? Remember, this was all before cyber-space. It was communication the old-fashion way: handwritten letters delivered by the ever-efficient Indian Postal Service. To baptize our spiffy new suits, three of us decided to arrange civilized dates in Bombay with those nice public health ladies... assuming any of them might put up with us. After all, we were in desperate need of some spiritual comfort... a little TLC for the soul."

"TLC for the soul? Give me a freaking break." I threw out. "And by the way, to have a civilized date, wouldn't you have to find some guys that had already been house-broken."

"Bite me!" Paul offered with hardly a glance in my direction and brazenly stealing my favorite personal insult. "So, I sent a letter to Kay who says she isn't able to be in Bombay. I then asked Kay if she remembers that Chinese girl who was sitting on her footlocker at the party."

"Hah, Connie wasn't even your first choice." I smiled smugly and looked at the lovely Hawaiian woman who was now his spouse. "See, you made a big mistake in picking him."

Connie just shook her head wearily as Paul, ignoring my rude interruption, continued. "I inquired of Kay as to the prospects of getting fixed up with this Chinese chick. Back comes her response letting me know that she's Japanese, buster. Moreover, her name is Connie and she didn't like you or any of the other mutts in your group. Now a string of letters with Connie, pathetic pleas to look kindly on a desperate man. Hell, I had a suit and everything. I pitch a double date with Connie and her roommate going out with Dexter and me. Back came the usual response, not in this lifetime, buster. A bout of amoebic dysentery sounds more appealing!"

"I get that." It was Harry piling on this time. "My thinking is that you 40 guys would have trouble competing favorably with the dreaded guinea worm."

"Well, the guinea worm wouldn't own a tan suit now, would it?" Paul responded quickly. "In any case, I don't accept defeat easily, so more letters go back and forth between Connie and I. Sensing a slight thaw, possibly even a defrosting, I go to my strong suit, no pun intended, obsequious pleading. I write that I'm so sorry for any misunderstanding and I will pay the transportation costs for her and Nanette, and a hotel room, and an unforgettable dinner."

Laura guffawed. "Wow, you were desperate!"

"Absolutely, by this time I was reduced to abject begging or, as a famous economist once said, *'if your horse dies in the middle of the stream, it might be time to remount.'* Now, Connie is a very tough negotiator and an excellent judge of character. Eventually, though, she is worn down. Ultimately, much haggling mixed with tributes offered in response to her complex and persistent efforts at extortion won the day. We make a date. We go out. Flowers are found. Dinner is served. Dancing ensues. We discover that we both like tomato juice with salt, pepper, hot sauce, and lime."

"Damn," I muttered. "If I had only known, I would have offered her some kind of juiced-up tomato concoction."

"As I was saying, the night proceeds. We learn our family histories. I am from Chicago, first son of Jewish immigrants. She is from Hawaii, first daughter of Japanese immigrants. Her father is a doctor, her mother a nurse. My parents are also doctors, a general practitioner and a pediatrician. Her parents met in Tule Lake Relocation Center, mine escaped from the camps in Europe. My fantasies soar. I imagine her amidst sun, seashells, surf, and tall drinks with little umbrellas and fat spears of pineapple. To my eyes, she is gorgeous. She is smart and kind and easy to be with. And she laughs at my jokes, which no one does."

"We never knew you told any." I threw out and then raised my hand to indicate no more was coming from me. It was now obvious the others were enthralled with his story.

"The night is magic, the prom I never went to in high school. Love blossoms. I am delirious with love and lust. So, history unfolds just as it was meant to be. By the end of 1968, all of us in India-40… the hardest of the hard luck groups to come to India, are now wizened in the ways of the world."

"Damn, if I had just gotten that tan suit," I muttered. "all the girls of 44-B would have been throwing themselves at me. I would have been beating them off with a stick."

"More like throwing up on you." Connie said.

"Touché, my dear." I admitted defeat.

—

Connie took a deep breath. "I need to correct my husband's version of history by the way. Let's back up to that first moment I met this prince here." She nodded toward her spouse. "Here's what really happened. We did hear that there were some veteran volunteers in town, and we were interested in hearing from them on our final day together as a group. There was a knock on the door and in swept this bunch of hooligans wanting to know which volunteers were to be stationed in Konkan region. Two of the girls shot up their hands and got the typical male once over: then two of these losers immediately left, leaving the one nice guy among the three to regale us with tales of life in the village. That was Danny. The two losers were Paul here and some other volunteer who lived sixty miles up the road. I remember thinking at the time, how rude and obnoxious these guys are, except for Danny, who charmed us with his Boston accent, courtly manners, and stories of life in the village."

"Wait," I stammered, "I had a Boston accent."

"Yeah, but you were never courtly, or much house trained for that matter. Don't forget, you kept drooling when around us." As I sat there trying in vain to come up with good counter arguments, Connie moved on. "Fast forward some months later. Nanette, my site mate, and I get a letter from Kay stating that the same guys who had all but up their noses at us now wanted to go out on a date since they now had suits and probably were bored. I'm sitting there thinking that you can put a suit on a pig, but it is still a pig. A date with Paul from that pack of animals known as India-40? No way! If I wanted to date a pig, I wouldn't have shot down Corbett over there."

I tried not to look offended as all the other females nodded in agreement. Fortunately, she did not dwell on me any further. "Nanette, however, was going into Bombay around that time to finalize plans for our year-end conference. I told her she should go out with those guys if she was so inclined. As fate would have it, the night before Nanette was to leave for Bombay, a cap on my molar fell out so I accompanied her, still hoping to avoid those India 40 blokes. To my dismay, that hope turned out to be wishful thinking as I ran into Paul at the Peace Corps office. Much to my chagrin, once again an invitation to celebrate the *Festival of the Suits*' was forthcoming."

"But you didn't shoot him down, like you did Corbett." Hank appeared curious. "What was different?"

"Well, Paul was so pathetic, and he begged. You were desperate, Corbett, but didn't beg nearly well enough." Connie said gleefully. "I suppose I took pity on Paul which, in the end, turned out to be a good thing. Go figure! Surprisingly, it was a fun time. I was shocked as my initially hostile feelings toward him dissipated. Who would have guessed?"

"This is beginning to sound like a Hallmark movie." Bob groaned.

"And then, he went and almost blew it all with another SDI…"

"Yup, a perfect Hallmark flic." Mel agreed with his friend.

"What's an SDI?" Harry asked. "Some kind of venereal disease?"

Connie rolled her eyes. "Of course not! An SDI is a Sudden Death Infraction, basically a totally dumb mistake that Paul and his idiot friends were always making. After our year-end conference, several of us decided to take what we called *French Leave*' back then and asked Kay to buy us return tickets so as not to alert PC to our illegal stay in Bombay. She was supposed to leave them at our hotel. We got to the hostel late at night and, to our horror, no tickets."

"Not my fault." Kay piped up. "Just want to make that clear."

"No, it wasn't. You can well imagine who screwed up. We did have a reservation on the train but had to pay for new tickets. Eventually, we heard from Kay that she had given them to Paul and the other hooligans from Konkan with explicit directions to leave them at the front desk. More letters to Paul and crew and soon I get back this totally lame story. They were in his pocket, he pleaded, when they decided to visit another volunteer up country. He stumbled across the tickets too late. Knowing nothing could be done, they made many toasts to the ladies of India and drank themselves into what I assume was a state of oblivion. There followed a slew of letters back and forth asking for the tickets, so they could be refunded. We were told they had been disposed of accidentally. Finally, I squeezed a half-assed reconciliation out of him where he promised to repay an amount that did not come close to the cost of first-class tickets."

"I would have paid everything I owed. Then again, I never would have lost them in the first instance. I am so responsible." I offered expectantly.

"Hah, I didn't fall of the pineapple truck yesterday." Connie dismissed me without even looking in my direction. "In fact, Kay wouldn't have trusted you with the tickets in the first place."

Pineapple truck? I puzzled. That must be a Hawaii saying. Then a thought struck me. "Wait. You took first-class trains. What's with that? We guys in 44-B never saw the inside of a first-class carriage, not sure I ever made it to second-class. Wow, you gals were pampered."

"Corbett, they had standards for 1st class." Nanette effectively shot me down. "No riff-raff."

Connie went on with her story. "During this time, Nanette and I formed a new organization called WOW, or Wipe Out Whites. Finally, several of us agreed to attend some event in Bombay that turned into a Thanksgiving Day event. Paul and Danny had killed all their chickens and roasted them up. Terry and his wife came down with their two boys in a Peace Corps jeep with a couple of turkeys he had found and several coolers of wine and beer. All this evolved into a whirlwind courtship which is still being tested out five decades later. I think Paul's marital contract review comes up again next month. As usual, its touch and go on renewal."

Paul spoke up at this point. "Yes, she reups our marital contract on a yearly basis, along with my six-month performance reviews which are followed by remedial instructions and corporal punishment."

"Get reprimanded often?" Mel asked with a laugh he could not quite suppress.

"Absolutely! The annual recertifications are close-run things despite the fact I am a prince of a husband."

"Wow, Connie must have a high tolerance for pain." One of Paul's India-40 mates proffered. "We had a pool amongst us as to how long she would put up with you. No one wagered on more than 2 years, the median guess was about 7 months."

Paul seemed annoyed and ignored his group mates. "I left India not long after. By this time, I was totally besotted. I spent some time in Israel, bought a VW bug, then drove to Columbia MO and started graduate school in the Department of Community Development. Couldn't wait for her to rejoin me."

Connie picked up her narrative again. "After finishing my tour, I traveled through Europe with Nanette, Paula, and Maureen. As Paul and I had decided in India, we got married in Hawaii that summer. We finished grad school eventually, me on a Kennedy Fellowship, and Paul as a research assistant. After a period in El Salvador and Boston, we realized we missed the Islands. It really was the best place to raise our children."

"Better than Boston? Look how good I turned out!" I tried.

"My point is proven!" Connie responded without losing a beat. "But the best thing is that I almost have this lug trained. It's been a long haul, but he finally is showing considerable promise. It takes a lot to civilize a guy from 40."

"No," Paul said, "that's not the best thing."

"Then what is?" She asked.

"That we are still in love." He took her hand in his.

———

I was smiling at the two of them when Ben spoke up. "Paul and Connie were not the only one to find love."

"Another nice story?" Kay was enthused at the direction of the dialogue.

"Yes, I believe so." Ben said. "As we all know from bitter experience, 44-B was nothing but single men, and we were discouraged from getting married while in service. The feeling at the time was that a new marriage would require as big an adjustment as learning how to survive in a village, and putting the two together could be doubly stressful, often leading to early termination or the breakup of the marriage or both. I had left my girlfriend Diane behind to complete her degree at Berkeley. We had been going together for a year-and-a-half but had no plans to get married. However, after eating a thousand meals alone and after much correspondence, I began to appreciate the possibility that she might not understand me or even recognize me at the end of my tour. Plus, she would miss out on the Peace Corps experience."

"Shit, I was in a similar situation, but mine married a Harvard Post-Doc even after I mentioned marriage in a letter."

Laura jumped in without missing a beat. "We get that. Look at Ben, handsome and mature and nice. Then look at you... all is self-evident."

"Thank you for pointing that out, Laura. Really, as if I had any self-respect left. I'll get back to my own sorry story later."

"So," Ben continued. "Diane had accepted a job offer in Paris. I just needed to convince her that there was nothing in Paris that was not available in an Indian village in the middle of a desert. She somehow bought the wisdom of my arguments, signed up for a health and nutrition program, and trained with single men and married couples under the stipulation that we would get married if she passed the training and selection ordeal. She did and we got married in Delhi after I had been in country for a year."

"Wow," I said, "a Rajasthani village over Paris. She really must have been besotted with you."

"And it was a lovely ceremony." Mel mused. "You two were a perfect couple."

"I don't recall it at all." I scrunched up my face. "Was I not invited… again?"

"Not sure whether you were invited or just crashed the party, but you were there. In fact, some of the guys missed the early morning ceremony, hungover I think, but Corbett somehow made it to the ceremony. That fact is recorded in my journal."

"Really, this is a blank. Then again, marriage ceremonies always made me nervous, maybe I repressed this memory."

Laura smirked. "Or maybe your mind is going. Do you recall us meeting in Mumbai after the ceremony and having that wild, passionate weekend? The sex was awesome."

"Really?" I responded before thinking it through. By this time, she had doubled over in laughter as all the gals of 44-A joined in her hilarity.

Ben saved me from further embarrassment. "I had to extend for one more year, which I did not mind. Everything worked out well, very well indeed, but that is another story. Another love story that worked." He looked at me for some reason.

I gazed at Laura, who was still smiling at her own joke. In that moment, I made another mistake by sticking my tongue out at her. She responded in kind, along with a pretzel or two.

India 40 farewell, 1968?

India 40 farewell in 1968, Connie and Paul (tan suit) in middle.

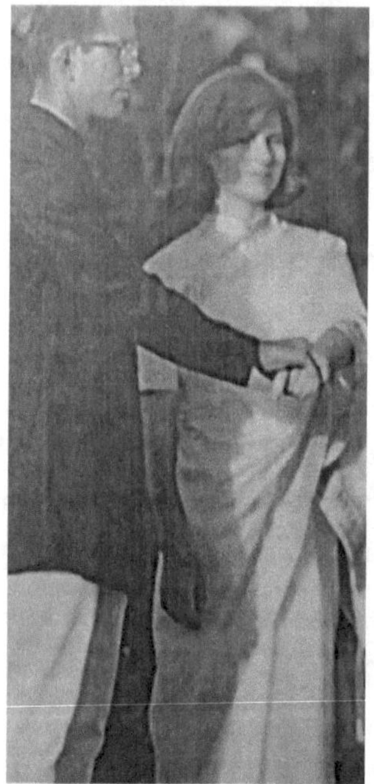

Ben and Diane getting married.

Chapter 12

Intestinal Challenges

"Now those were memories worth sharing." Laura said with meaning. "But Corbett has alluded to a similar story. Maybe we should give him a chance?"

I paused but suddenly felt uneasy. "Uh, I'll share it but maybe later." The others looked surprised at my reticence since I seldom, if ever, pass on an opportunity to hear my own voice. "Hey, Tim mentioned having a suit story. How about we hear that one now. Okay? Go ahead, Tim."

All eyes turned to Tim whose youthful appearance belied his difficult career working for the United Nations in many of the world's more dangerous hot spots over the past four decades. "Okay, but it is not pretty. My suit story involves a disaster that brought me to the point where I wished I might die. Like the stories we just heard, it involves a relationship, though not of the ordinary sort. My tale of woe taps into my intimate and ultimately disappointing relationship with my intestines."

"Ah, from the sublime to the ridiculous" Glen offered.

"I can't believe this." Maureen moaned. "Somehow, when I think things might get civilized, we head back into a downward spiral."

Tim raised a hand indicating his story was about to start. "Please Maureen, this really is a love story. Never forget this, a man's relationship with his evacuation functions is a special bond. That's why we spend so much time in the male throne room, otherwise known as the crapper. Such a profound relationship should not be underestimated and never dismissed out of hand; no pun intended for us India veterans."

As several groaned, I went to his defense. "Women just don't get that, do they?"

Tim looked at me with appreciation. "They don't, you are right. Now, normally, we got along, my intestines and I. We did, however, have some trying times on the subcontinent, as many of us experienced. There were a number of times when we got into, what shall we say, a disagreement where the old internal plumbing acted out in an inappropriate manner."

"No shit?" Someone said without thinking.

"Ah, just the opposite, too much shit!" Tim responded without missing a beat. "Some of our disagreements were on a whole new level of discord. Case in point. I am thinking back to a day when death seemed so desirable. We all had those days in India. They had nothing to do with sex or romance but something more basic, trying to maintain some semblance of dignity when one's insides wanted out, and just wouldn't wait."

"Let me guess." I said. "We're talking about taking a crap in all the wrong places."

"I would have put it more delicately, but you nailed it. We all had our bad days, right?"

"Oh yes," and other affirmations could be heard about the room.

"Likely there were other similar days but this one has remained with me in a vivid manner. To this day, I cannot forget squatting over an open drain along the side of an alley in Benares, talking to my insides as they desperately sought freedom."

"What did you say to your insides?" Paul inquired. "Something profound I hope."

"More importantly, what did they say back" Mel asked.

"Of course, profound! What else would you expect from such a dialogue. I even recorded the moment at the time in writing. Mel had his journals, Corbett his letters, and I also recorded my big moments. I believe I was thinking ahead for when they make a movie of my life."

"Titled what... Death by Dysentery?" I chuckled at my own witticism.

"Corbett, now you are not invited to the opening night." Tim glowered at me before continuing. "I only recorded the highlights, there were times when any real-time recording of history in the making was impractical. Nevertheless, here is what I wrote down about that fateful and unforgettable day.

While you pitilessly empty out your rage along with last night's dinner, people are passing by, walking slowly, and keeping their distance, but also grinning at the sight of my lily-white tail hanging precariously over a ditch in their village. Soon, they will be calling their friends to watch the best show in town, the pucka Sahib crapping his insides out for all to see. Is this to be the highlight of my volunteer experience?

"Well, it was a contribution to India of sorts." Janice weakly offered.

"Yes," Harry added, "you left the best of yourself behind."

Tim ignored them. "Yes, here I was, sick as a dog as I desperately tried to get across town to Banaras University where I was expected. Now, that destination seemed out of reach, sort of like the far side of the moon. I was dehydrated, having nothing left to drink now except for the last few dregs of Paregoric which, at that moment, I was so thankful I brought along. It tastes terrible, but it does pack a kick. And the PC Doc said it would be good for me. How could it not be... tincture of opium? It's the good stuff and powerful... to be used in small doses only. No more than one teaspoon an hour, he said. Yeah, right, except in emergencies and this damn well was an emergency. Okay, so I had gulped down quite a bit in the past hour or so, but I was on freaking death's door here. There is no greater emergency. The stuff did nothing to slow up my raging diarrhea, but it did cast a soothing haze over what might have been a horrific personal experience. Tincture of opium, it would appear, lowers one's inhibitions. And that was exactly what I needed on this day. You see, I was on my way to see my lovely cousin and her husband… a big shot Professor from Princeton."

"Oh shit." Dee let out. "Oops, no pun intended."

"I know," Tim smiled at her. "Didn't this crap always happen at the worst times, pun intended in this case. But yeah, this esteemed academic was on Sabbatical for a year at the University in Benares, in what you might know as Varanasi, the holy city. I was looking forward to meeting him. Perhaps he might get me into a good grad school in the Ivy League. God knows I needed help but the thought of showing up smelling like the latrine eroded any ambition of getting inside his house, never mind into a top shelf school. Worse, I had worn a freaking suit and tie. What was that all about? Did I think this was an interview or something?"

"This really is prime stuff." Paul offered. "Every time I think no one can come up with an even more embarrassing scene, one of you clowns from 44 rises to the occasion."

"Hey," Bob retorted, "it must have worked since Tim did get into Harvard for grad studies. That's not as good as Yale, of course, but not bad either."

"Nor Columbia," piped up Doug, a tall, broad shouldered 44 volunteer who hailed from New York and had graduated from said academic institution.

I recall thinking in that moment that Doug had been quiet that afternoon. In India, it was hard to miss him, he had a large personality back then. Past is not always prologue to one's future apparently.

"So happy to offer up some amusement to you fellow Ivies," Tim grimaced. "So, I make it back to my rickshaw, and the journey continues. My feverish mind wanders back to our earliest days in India. I recall sitting in a PC lecture in Delhi while a doctor started his lecture with something like *'On behalf of the United States Government, the Peace Corps, and the Medical Service, I want to welcome you and your virgin gastro-intestinal tracts to India.'* I sat their thinking that my intestinal track is not 'virgin,' no freaking way. Just think of all the Twinkies, the week-old pizzas, the sloppy joes from the school cafeteria, and all that even weirder stuff of unknown provenance I ingested in my youth. This guy is just trying to scare me, but he has no idea about my history with food."

"Damn," exclaimed Harry, "I remember thinking the same thing. He had no idea what I grew up eating as a poor Black southern kid being raised in a sharecropper's family, basically anything I could get my hands on. Hell, I probably tried roadkill on occasion."

"Yeah, we suffered the arrogant hubris of the innocent for sure." Mel nodded, obviously floating back in time. "We thought we were immortal. Our bodies had other ideas."

Tim sought to regain control. "Then this doctor went on to show us slides of normal intestinal walls of Westerners six months before moving to India and six months after arriving in country. For comparison, he showed us similar intestinal tracks of Indians from six months before to six months after relocating to the West. His point, as I vividly recall, was that the intestinal track wall undergoes a radical transformation in that short period of time. In the West, we have lots of little pockets of bacteria embedded in our intestinal wall that help digest food on its journey through to the colon and beyond. In India, those pockets disappear in a sea of bacteria that often give food stuffs an express ride to the bottom, often with barely a pause along the way. Even a couple of weeks in country demonstrated all too well the fact that food often enjoyed a non-stop excursion to freedom, so to speak. However, so long as there was a toilet somewhere near, we could handle it. True, learning to balance over one of those squat latrine pans was a challenge at first… not falling back on your ass was an acquired and very essential skill not to mention trying to stand up afterwards. These enforced calisthenics did wonders for our thighs. And then there was always the issue of aim, not hitting yourself with a deposit, another skill that demanded both experience and some athletic skill. But we had plenty of water and our handy left hand for cleaning ourselves in the aftermath."

"Just think," I offered. "If civilization collapses, we will have a leg up on most others."

"If society collapses," Dee sniffed, "I am ending it all, buying the farm as they say."

"Me too." Laura added.

"I'll join you," I added to several groans, a response I interpreted as enthusiasm for the notion.

Tim cleared his throat. He was ready to continue. "Back to the past, village life had ended the luxury of latrine pans, at least for me. In my first posting, all I got to use was a communal place to squat and chat with my new neighbors though I must confess that I did not show my best side to the villagers. Then again, hard to find that best side when taking a shit. But I provided a lot of laughs for the locals, with my feeble attempts at Hindi and the chorus of noises that I alone made during my BM performances. My innards sure made a lot of noise as they adjusted to their new reality. Soon, I tried to find a more private time and place for my bouts of self-expression. These moments of evacuation usually are quite special to a man, moments when he can get away from it all and think great thoughts."

"Gross!" Came from a female-sounding voice.

"'*We all seek spiritual meaning in our own way, in our own temples.*' I believe I just paraphrased the great Lebanese poet Kahlil Gibran," My attempt to support Tim fell flat with the women, if their facial expressions were any indication.

Tim carried on. "Things improved after I moved to a real town and rented an upscale place, upscale ONLY by comparison. Then I had a real latrine which, alas, still had its challenges. This was of the famous 'drop and plop' design… a hole in the apartment floor one story above a basket strategically placed in a dark, smelly room below. Some of you might remember the drill. First, remove cover, then hold nose, before squatting to wait for that satisfying plop to tell us whether you had hit the target below. Yup, somewhere down there was a small target, which a sweeper came by to remove once a day. I felt the sting of social injustice in this but who was I to confront the local caste system. He or she was considered an untouchable, destined by karma for this duty. For better or worse, it had been ingrained in their culture long before the first westerners stumbled upon the wonders of the sub-continent. I, on the other hand, was here by choice. I had volunteered to suffer. What was with that?"

I thought out loud. "I wonder if this is what Kennedy had in mind when he proposed what became the Peace Corps."

Bob laughed aloud. "I'm sure it's not what all us kids back in the 60s envisioned as we got excited about saving the world for truth and the American way. Then again, it was a strange decade after all."

———

Tim segued to a vignette recalled by a few. "Early on, you might remember how the Peace Corps doctor in Delhi persuaded us to join his study of steroids? We were easy targets. We thought by volunteering we could get a paid trip to Udaipur once a month, turn in our urine sample and give some blood. It was the prospect of a paid night in Udaipur and not our possible contribution to science that got us to sign on. This was not unlike getting lifers in prison who 'volunteer' for some deadly experiment by offering them a few extra cigarettes. The problem with this plan quickly became apparent. A night in the big city, away from our limited diets and the alcohol-free life of our sites meant making up for lost time. It was always a night of meat eating and beer guzzling, which sent the next day's test results in rather alarming directions. We also discovered that 'giving some blood' involved sitting in an Udaipur hospital while some guy in a dirty white jacket tried to find the veins in our arms, typically using a needle as blunt as an unsharpened pencil. There was more blood on the ground than in the test tube."

"Oh crap, that reminds me," I exclaimed. "I recall Ralph having some infection in his foot I think. So, we decided to go to the local health clinic. I almost passed out when I saw what the technician was going to jab into him, hopefully to inject him with an antibiotic but who the bloody knows? Anyway, this still looked like modern medicine as opposed to killing a chicken and spraying its blood around the room. Then again, maybe Ralph would have preferred the dead chicken remedy since he turned totally white when this technician approached him with what looked like an instrument of torture. That was our only trip to that clinic. We chose death after that but never managed to pull that off. Now, when I look on Google Earth, our old town has more than one building identified as a hospital or medical center. Perhaps things have improved on the medical front at least."

"In what way?" Kay asked.

"Now we might choose their services over death."

Tim struggled on. "The worst, though, was the urine sample. The Doc decided that to avoid the confounding effects of all that beer, perhaps the Kingfisher and Golden Eagle was laced with steroids for all we knew. Now, we were instructed to take a huge lab jar back to the village and fill it for 24 hours before the journey to Udaipur. For me, that meant loading this urine-filled monster of a receptacle on the back of my bicycle and carefully pushing both the vehicle and bottle up the rocky path that led to the nearest town with a bus station, some 10 kilometers away. Then it was all about loading it on the bus for another three-hour journey, bumping our way to the big city. I could see the locals on the bus discussing what the American CIA agent had in the bottle this time. Concerned about potential lethal explosions, several would exit and wait for the next bus which, of course, was *just now coming.*"

"I have no freaking memory of any of this stuff." I threw out.

"They probably took one look at you and decided not to include you in the study." Bob added without the hint of a smile. "I think it was restricted to bona-fide *homo-sapiens*."

"How the frack did Yale even let you in?" I responded before turning to Tim. "Please continue.

"At least we got to go to Udaipur to spend an exciting evening trading latrine and diarrhea stories, each of us trying to outdo the other with the gory details. I always loved the homily about *'you may have remembered to boil the water, but did you remember to boil the cook?'*"

"Forgot that one, thanks." Dan nodded in appreciation.

"Among my favorite stories we shared over time was the one about an earlier PC group. It concerned two guys in the first generation of volunteers who, after a year of insufferable boredom, wanted out. Neither, however, wanted to be the first to send 'that telegram' to Delhi. Instead, they devised a scheme for getting back to Delhi, blowing off steam for a couple of days and then giving PC an ultimatum. Either provide them with something useful to do or send them home. To have an excuse to go to PC headquarters, they decided to use these pre-packaged test kits which were to be employed only in case of an emergency."

"We always had emergencies." Harry belly laughed.

"Exactly! To use these kits, you deposited a stool sample in a container provided and sent it on to Delhi for testing by the powers that be, whomever they were? Fueled by excess alcohol, these clowns came up with a plan.

"Oh, oh, this sounds like a disaster in the making." Paul smiled broadly. "It's hard to believe there were bigger nimrods than you 44 guys?"

"Judge for yourself." Tim directed at Paul. "These guys retrieved some stool samples from a local urchin kid they had seen make a deposit nearby. They used this purloined material to fill the specimen containers, inserting these bogus samples into the kits as instructed. They then left the completed packages in plain sight as they drifted off in an alcohol-infused deep sleep. On awakening, they had second thoughts but their cook, a dutiful servant as they all were, had already mailed the samples off to Delhi. Now they panicked! Going home had its drawbacks… an all-expense paid trip to Vietnam or that girl to whom they had impulsively promised a lifetime of devotion and to whom they might even had given a ring."

"What the hell did they do?" Harry asked.

"They got in touch with headquarters and said they now felt fine. That appeared to work. They were told to sit tight. Disaster averted, they thought, and so they breathed easier. A week or so later, an urgent telegram came ordering them to Delhi ASAP. No one believed their protests or explanations about what they had done. Soon, they were on a plane to a military base in Germany. The PC medical staff had never seen results like this and thought these kids had mere hours to live."

"What happened to the poor bastards" I asked.

"No idea; probably got shipped back stateside. However, PC stopped using those mail-in specimen kits. That's why we were never given them. But I have been rambling on for some time now. I would hate to be compared to Corbett."

"You have absolutely no worries on that score." Paul intoned gravely.

"No, indeed." Laura added. "You are a blessed relief."

—

"Okay then, back to my poop plight that day. My journey to this alley in Benares where I pooped my insides out started off innocently enough. I had gotten two aerograms from my folks back in Pittsburgh, one in which my father suggested I visit a missionary in India to whom he had sent money and one from my mother suggesting a visit to my cousin, whom I never had met. This distant relative was with her Professor husband who was, as I mentioned, a visiting scholar at the University of Benares for a year. Neither quest held much attraction for me. On reflection, though, it seemed like a good excuse to get away for a few days. The trek started off poorly, as getting from Udaipur to Benares via the Indian rail system was torture indeed. After a short stop with the missionary my father suggested visiting, I stayed overnight at the local Catholic school. It was here, I believe, where they attempted to poison me even though I also was Catholic. The next morning, it was off on a long cross-city journey to the campus. For some inexplicable reason, I wore this suit…"

"It wasn't a tan suit, was it?" Paul asked with a smile.

"It was light, I believe." Tim looked quizzical. "Is that important."

"Magical! Have you forgotten already? My tan suit bent Connie to my charms."

To this, his wife groaned.

"No, mine wasn't magical, which seemed increasingly implausible as I bent over this alley latrine crapping my insides out. Besides, by this time my suit looked like I had just finished hand-to-paw combat with a Bengal tiger. And lost. I had barely started out across town when the poison the good Catholic missionaries had laced in my supper the night before finally kicked in. They undoubtedly employed a slow-moving toxin to ensure I was away from their facility when I keeled over and suffered my death throes, less chance my death could be traced back to them. Thus, my public display to the good folk of this most ancient and holy city came to pass."

Dan said with admiration. "You are a credit to us all. Peace Corps should use a pic of Tim crapping in a Benares alley in their marketing ads. They always use a bunch of these smiling idiots surrounded by adoring locals."

"Good point," Bob added, "use something authentic."

"Yeah," Mel groaned, "the only time I was surrounded by adoring locals was when they thought I would build them a freaking new school."

"I'll pass on being a Peace Corps poster boy." Tim protested weakly. "This was not my finest hour. I made it to the university eventually. As promised, the campus was lovely. There were green spaces and lovely buildings. It seemed I was no longer in India. With one final effort, I made it to the front door of the address I had been given and managed to squeak out *'I think I am your cousin.'* At this point I was sure of nothing except my own mortality. They were kind and welcoming, however. They took me in, permitted me a nice shower and rest. Slowly, I came back to life. They were most gracious though I did pass on any food at the dinner party they had in my honor. Interestingly, the conversation among the several Westerners there turned to the general topics of dysentery and intestinal distress. I think Westerners never escape the horrors of the inner truth of the sub-continent… you just never experience the blessing of a normal BM."

"Tru dat." Someone said.

———

Harry spoke next. "Along this theme, Dan and I visiting the home of one of our Stateside Hindi instructors who was from Agra. The evening was lovely but neither of us felt well after. We were on the way to Delhi. By the time we got there, I became deathly sick. I was admitted to the hospital. A nurse came in and took my temperature. On looking at the thermometer, she dropped what she had in her hand and ran from the room. Oh Lord, I thought, I am dying. My temp was 104 degrees and rising. They kept sending blood samples off for testing and shoving antibiotics in me for days. I think they used the same needle on me all that week, just to save money. I had this huge scab where they kept ripping my arm open to get to the vein. Finally, they got my fever under control. I never was told what the problem was but, for once, I was glad to get back to my village."

"We seldom knew what kicked our ass." Ben noted.

"You know, despite all our whining, our villages were somewhat of a sanctuary after a while." I said. "Listening to you weaklings, I was lucky… medically speaking. I had the usual assortment of parasites and stuff, but only had bad diarrhea once. Yeah, it was when I visited Mel and Bob in Sanwar. Did I ever mention to the rest of you that they tried to poison me? I have no definitive proof but am sure of it."

"My theory" Dee offered without a hint of a smile, "is that all those germs hit Corbett's insides and died immediately on contact. His toxic personality is deadly." Murmurs of agreement rose around the room.

"Joke if you must at my near death experience," I tried to dismiss their sarcasm, "all I recall now is that Bob's *hole in the floor* crapper was some distance away from his abode where I was crashing for the night. When the poison they had slipped into my food kicked in, all I could think about was getting to this place where I might empty out all the toxins. Maybe it was sixty or seventy yards and then up a whole lot of stairs."

"Not that bad." Bob protested.

"Whatever, but that night at least it seemed like a marathon and a mountain. Almost made it but not quite."

"We could never take you anywhere, Corbett. And despite your bitchin, you survived, right." Bob looked as if he might say more.

—

"I have another story, more uplifting I think. Perhaps you're tired of hearing from me." Tim appeared apologetic.

"Please Tim, keep going." Laura implored him. "Anything to keep Corbett quiet."

"Despite all the humorous hardships, I managed to contribute something in the end, and I am not talking about parasite-infested stools here." Tim clearly had segued to a different topic. "The early months were tough for me, likely for all of us. My first village was tiny and populated by original tribal people, the Mewari. I could barely communicate with them since my Hindi was useless. There literally was nothing for me to do. What in God's name was PC thinking?"

"How did you cope, even manage to stay?" Maureen asked.

"Luck and a little ingenuity I suppose. Eventually, I got to know an Ag Development guy at the local university who had some students he wanted to put to useful work. Dealing with water issues hit me as a top priority and he put me in touch with an NGO that had well digging equipment. A British Volunteer, a VSO located in Ajmer trained me. They were like the Peace Corps with one huge difference. They had useful skills and knew what they were doing. He showed me the ropes and got me through the credential process so I could legally buy, store, and use explosives. My early vision of merely supervising others who would blast and dig these wells evaporated as I found that Indian students did not do manual labor. Apparently, education in India meant you never had to dirty your hands. Who knew? It would be me risking my fanny blowing up stuff for the most part. But first I had to get this equipment I was loaned to Udaipur."

"I think I remember part of this story. It is great." Harry noted.

"Well, it remains part of Indian folklore for sure. I quickly realized I had no money to pay for a driver. Even if I had, whom could I trust? Sensing adventure, I mounted myself on this tractor, a compressor linked to the back end, then tied my bag onto the back seat. Off I went on the road to Udaipur. Tractors move slowly and Indian truck drivers are not patient men. Nevertheless, the sight of this white guy, a foreigner, driving a tractor down a major highway caused many a driver to slow down. They would look in disbelief… perhaps casting a jibe or two in my direction. Then they might smile and shake their head before moving on. If a man drives a truck in India long enough, he sees everything, even a *Sahib* on a tractor. In any case, the tractor and I were only halfway along the route when evening came. I found a truck stop that offered rooms. Exhausted, I consumed a quick meal and headed for the cabin that was to serve as my sanctuary for the night. Later in the evening, I discovered the real purpose of these rooms, which also explained why the proprietor had been surprised when I insisted on having the room for the entire night. Typically, truck drivers rent these accommodations by the hour. On either side of me, in stereo, the rhythmic bumps and grinds, the wail of feigned passion, went on all night."

"Tim, you should have checked out the other rooms. Perhaps Mel was spending an evening, or a few minutes at least." Bob could not quite get the entire joke out before breaking out in laughter.

"Bob, you're a dead man." Mel shook a fist at him.

"Hah, as if I haven't heard that threat before." The Yale man laughed.

Tim ignored the interruption. "All this was a turning point for me. I had finally found something useful to do as a volunteer. This was good. During my deepest despair, I had gone to Delhi fully intending to pack it in but was convinced to give it another try. Now, I got busy blasting out new wells or deepening existing ones. The list of villages grew and, at each village, a request to go on to the next would arrive. A competition emerged to get me to come and stay in a village, offers of great food and a bed for me and the two part-time students that helped me with some of the work. I had become a rock star."

"You know," Paul announced in his mischievous tone of voice, "I heard rumors even down in Maharashtra that there was competition regarding Corbett among the villagers of Rajasthan."

"To get him to leave and never consider visiting their place again." Bob beat Paul to the punch line but they both roared heartily.

Once again, Tim continued as if no one had spoken. "The village kids would come by to gape at me and even at the students with me, who probably looked foreign to the rural ruffians even though they were not. Being university students, they were from a totally different world. The gap between the educated elite and those struggling to survive is difficult to fathom. Parts of these visits were nice. In the evenings, stories would be told that I could not understand but I would smile, and everyone was happy. The work itself, however, was dirty, hard, and even dangerous. Someone had to go down to the bottom of the well and then drill out shot holes in the rock. Then you inserted the dynamite, along with the fuses and packing, before scrambling back to the surface with the ignition wires. When all was secure, we then would blow it. Most times, it worked fine but there were times when water would seep-in or there was much digging that remained. But it was now much easier since the top layers of the rock had been shattered."

"Wow, you contributed something and developed a skill to use back in the States… Tim's Blasting Company. I can see the motto on billboards now… No Hole We Can't Make Bigger!" Bob laughed as others snickered.

"Why me?" Tim groaned. "I now know how Corbett feels. So, there came a day I found myself down a well. When the students drilled the shot holes at one site, we noticed thin fuses emerging from the rock all around us. I could guess what happened, a farmer had hired a local *wala* to do some blasting, but something had gone wrong and this earlier work had been abandoned. While I had run across this before, this day I was irate that we had not been forewarned and that we had been permitted to enter a well possibly full of live charges. I came out of that well spitting with fury, looking for someone to throttle. Then someone in the crowd called me a *'white monkey'* and I hit my wall. I suppose this happened to all of us at some point. I blew up and was ready to strangle someone. Fortunately, another volunteer was there that day. He grabbed me and said. *'Come on now, just another day in India.'"*

"Oh my God," Harry muttered, "you're right. We all hit that wall. I remember screaming at some kids through a railway window. I completely lost it… became a crazy man.

"Really, Harry, that's when you thought you lost it." I was yet chuckling when a pretzel he threw in my direction plunked me in the nose.

Tim on left, long after surviving his intestinal disaster.

Loves Lost

Harry intervened to take the dialogue in a different direction, "I keep thinking, we did have some great laughs."

"Laughter in the midst of such a disaster." Someone uttered.

Harry was not to be deterred. "Remember the time when we all chipped in to rent this place in Udaipur where we could crash when in town. Then, Peace Corps found out about it and shut it down. Hah, they were kind of pissed at us."

"Oh yeah, our home away from home." Doug threw in.

"What I recall best of that story was a volunteer named Roger. He was from a later group who was stationed in Udaipur, though I can't remember what he was supposed to be doing. Anyway, he was so obnoxious."

Paul looked amazed. "More than Corbett?"

"That's not possible." Dee opined.

"Amazingly, it is, and he was." Harry continued. "I have this great story about Roger and our secret pad."

"Pray tell," Greg encouraged Harry.

"Now, I had made friends with some black marine guards at the U.S. Embassy and could occasionally get top shelf scotch. This Roger character, you might recall, tried to be an expert on everything, including fine liquor. So, one day we got together at our illegal *home away from home.* Anyway, I took an empty bottle of Johnny Walker and put some cheap, local whiskey in it. When we offered this obnoxious know-it-all some he was beside himself with joy. He held the bottle as if it were a newborn babe. With a few sips he was over the moon with praise, saying how great it was to have the authentic stuff at last. The rest of us finally broke down in gales of laughter, confessing what we had done. It shut him up for a while, though not long enough."

Dan, our Wyoming cowboy, smiled broadly as he had a way of doing. "The thing is, we did have a lot of laughs."

"And some tears." Kay added.

"And some unforgettable moments." Tim murmured.

Laura looked from Tim to me, "Corbett, speaking of unforgettable moments, are you ready to tell your romantic story now?"

I sighed. It looked as if they would not let me off the hook. "Well, if it will make you feel better."

"Oh yes, it will." Dee almost clapped her hands in anticipation.

Shit, I said to myself. *How did I get here?* What I said aloud was. "Here's the thing, I was not a happy camper back then… romantically that is."

"Corbett! Tell us something we don't know." Laura sounded frustrated.

"Patience, my dear. I experienced a real disappointment and I'm not talking about getting shot down as I threw around casual passes on the off chance one miraculously would stick." I now paused as I considered if I really wanted to share all this.

"Go on, Tom," Connie urged.

For a moment, I considered substituting a less personal tale for what I was about to reveal, a sort of bait and switch maneuver. No, time to finally share this long held painful memory. In any case, it was too late now to back down. "Okay, here's the thing! I had a real love coming out of college or thought so at the time. It did not end well… sort of karmic justice for Corbett."

"Please tell me it wasn't a debilitating STD or some form of chronic impotence. You are being serious for a change, I hope." Maureen looked at me intently.

"No, nothing like the consequences for sexual excess which, by the way, I managed to totally avoid… both the excess and the diseases. I swear I am being totally serious for a change."

"Okay," Nanette said though she did not look convinced. "I think we should give him the benefit of the doubt."

"What I'm talking about here is emotional pain, not some visitation of cosmic retribution for being a hopeless putz or wannabe libertine. These stories of love found we heard earlier bring back memories of my personal disaster of the heart."

"Meaning?" Janice prompted me.

"We need more," Dee added. "Much more!"

"Getting dumped, and my heart broken, about halfway through my tour." I said flatly.

"While I like the thought of you in pain, this might not make me feel better." Cate said but with only a hint of a smile.

"True," Connie added, "any suffering on Corbett's part might affect how we see him. Of course, to garner any real sympathy for this loser, it would be necessary for some excruciating physical pain to be involved… maybe an appendage turning black or something like that." Her expression was softer than her words. They were listening.

"Damn, this is a tough crowd. Well, I should start by saying that when I came to India, there was the girl I met in college that I left behind. I know, I know, several of us did that. By that I mean we left someone behind with intimations of varying clarity as to how we felt and lots of conflict swelling in our hearts, my heart at least. This one, my relationship, was amazing to me. You might well be wondering how this happened to a non-feeling putz like me?"

"No one asked." Paul offered but was shushed by his spouse.

"No surprise there but I'm telling you anyway. It turns out I was morbidly phobic about intimate relationships in my youth. Intellectually, I considered things like commitment, marriage, and monogamy to be conventional rubbish. I hated the thought of settling down. I suppose fear was involved… the panic associated with vulnerability. But here I had gone and fallen off the emotional deep end. My feelings for her were so deep, remained so deep. Gosh, I hated that feeling. In that state you are so needy and weak… yuck!"

"I can't believe this, real feeling from Corbett of all people! All this time I simply assumed he was not human." Laura opined.

"We all did." Dee added.

"You are right. I have tried to hide my human side, assuming I have one of course." My voice caught a bit to my shame. "Damn, this is hard. Here is an ironic fact. Okay, not a fact but a supposition. Males in general seem to run away from commitment. They are harder to pin down. We all agree on that." I continued quickly to avoid objections. "But, in my experience, I have found that they are more likely to *fall in love* at first sight. Guys who go from female to female will see someone across a room and just know. I've had so many conversations along those lines." I could see doubt in several faces but decided to move on.

Dee spoke with meaning. "All this time I considered you totally beyond redemption. I assumed I'd enjoy your suffering. Now, I'm not so sure."

"I'm also confused." Janice added. "If it hurt so bad, why did you leave her behind?"

"Why did any of us walk away from someone we cared about. For me, I was committed to saving the world. India needed me, right? Anyone buy that? If you did, I have some land in Florida." I looked quickly around to a host of dubious stares that were yet mixed with doubt.

"Corbett, what's the straight story?" Bob asked. "No bullshit."

"Okay, no joking. I was still a kid in many ways. We all were. Besides, my parents had a marriage made in hell, not the best role model for settling down. They had coitus once that we can prove, and thus you are stuck with me. The rest of the time, they fought, but only when they had been drinking which, unfortunately, was most of the time."

"Sorry, I know where you are coming from." Cate said sincerely.

"And then, I had this contrary, rebellious streak in me. I had convinced myself that I wanted nothing to do with conventional society... love, kids, the house with a picket fence, or any of the trappings of an ordinary life. I was going to blaze my own way, carve out a unique path. Bottom line, my feelings for this girl scared the living shit out of me. India seemed just far enough away to avoid, you know, the trap of a normal and conventional life."

"Not to worry, my friend, the prospects of you being normal were never high," Mel offered.

I laughed with a kind of relief. "Thanks, I needed that. But the problem was this. From the from the moment I first saw her, I was in love. I really mean that first moment, before I spoke a word to her or knew her name, or heard her voice, I was smitten. That groundswell of feeling was primordial, and it never diminished one iota after that. After saying goodbye and taking off for India, I was in agony. You all remember the loneliness, the isolation. There is nothing quite like it, to be stuck in an alien culture on the literal edge of society, away from virtually all contact with the world you knew and the culture you at least thought you understood."

"That is the worst part." Kay murmured and then looked surprised that she had said the words out loud.

"I started writing long letters, even mentioning marriage in a round-about way. To be honest, I mentioned the dreaded M word in a letter even before leaving the States. I had suppressed that memory for a long time, thinking I first raised the issue long after getting to India. I could never quite work-up the courage to be totally direct about it, that marriage thing, but my intentions were there. The word was used, that word I never thought I'd use. If she had chosen to respond in kind ... who knows? I might have bailed out and gone home."

"I take it indirection didn't work." Maureen asked when I had paused.

"No shit, sherlock. One day I got *THE* letter from Eleni, maybe half-way through our tenure. Any correspondence excited us, as you all surely recall. Hell, I even loved getting a postcard from my dentist that I was overdue for my checkup and cleaning. I still can remember devouring every issue of Time magazine, several times, within hours after its arrival. For me, any communication from her was beyond special."

"Ah yes," Dee commiserated. "Any morsel of contact from the real world was gold. The weather is good here. Is it hot in India? That post card would be read a dozen times. We all loved even those."

"Well, a letter from Leni arrived one day. I lived for those more than anything else though I feared them as well."

"Fear?" Connie looked puzzled.

"Yes, afraid of what they might contain as you will see. So, Ralph was going on about something or other as I tore it open and started in on it. Alas, this was it… what I dreaded even though I totally knew it was coming. It was *THE* letter, the Dear Tom letter."

"Ouch!" Mel commiserated.

"No surprise of course. To be honest, all the signs had been there. Even a nimrod like me could not miss them. And yet, it was a shock, my whole body reacted. I was stunned. Funny how you can be surprised by getting the most expected news in the world. You just know when horrendous things are about to happen, know it in your heart if not your head, especially if you're Irish. We just know that happiness is not our lot in life. I remember that moment as if it happened earlier today. I raised a hand to stop Ralph from going on about whatever he was babbling about. He probably could tell from my face that something was terribly amiss. Then I informed him that we needed to get drunk, which we proceeded to do."

"Oh my God," Dee murmured, "I'm feeling bad for Corbett, I didn't think that possible."

"Oh, give it a minute." Maureen counselled. "I'm sure any feeling of sympathy will pass, like an attack of gas."

"Or maybe a kidney stone." Laura added.

"No, this is so sad," Dee continued. "Was that it, all over?"

"Well, yes but there is more to the story. She had gotten engaged to marry a post-doc that she met while working at Harvard. He surely had to look more promising than me. I was little more than this piece of damaged goods who had run off to the other side of the world, had no observable skills, and zero prospects in the eyes of any objective female observer. However, we continued to write to one another until I finished my tour. This correspondence after her marriage, oddly enough, struck me as way more intimate than our earlier exchanges, certainly on her end. It was like she was finally talking directly to me. Still, when I left India for home, I told myself to let it go. I forced myself to put an end to it… or so I thought."

"Ah, there is a *but'* coming?" Connie said expectantly.

"Peace Corps didn't select you guys for nothing, a bright bunch indeed. Sure enough, decades went by. Despite my anti-commitment vow, I found a wonderful woman who was silly enough to accept me. See, you can fool some people, even the smart ones. She and I have now been together since God was a little girl, it has been that long. By the way, never believe guys who wax eloquent about never getting hitched though I totally was into that at the time. Others apparently believed my BS since there was widespread shock when I went down for the marital count."

"We are far more shocked that any woman would take you." Paul inserted and then yelped in pain as his spouse whacked him on the arm.

"Good one, asshole." I chuckled. "The wife of my best friend as a young man told me decades later that I tried to talk her out of marrying Ron, that's his name. I told her she should explore the world first and delay tying the knot a decade or so before taking any plunge. Apparently, this was my advice to all females dumb enough to listen to me. Of course, I have zero memory of this, but she is adamant about it. Good thing she ignored me, they had a great marriage… some women really are perfect for motherhood and stuff. She was one of them."

"Are you really worried about people believing what you say?" Bob deadpanned. "Don't be, Corbett. Truth is, no one listens to you."

"Good point, asshole, but that's a relief in a way. Another part of my theory about relationships is that those who protest the most make the best husbands. Why, you ask?" I continued though no one indicated the slightest interest in my theory. "I'll tell you why. They get hitched believing they will be miserable and then it turns out better than they thought. Initial expectations are key, which is why women are more dissatisfied with their couplings than men. They expect too much and are bound to get so little. Think about that. Most women are bound to be disappointed given how excited they are at the initial prospect of matrimony."

There was silence as the females considered my obvious wisdom while the males picked their noses and otherwise kept occupied. I was a bit surprised when no pretzels were launched in my direction. Then Maureen spoke. "Why are men so childish about marriage. It is a fact that married men live the longest of any group and are the happiest. Your average life-expectancy would be at least ten years lower without us."

"Compared to whom," I shot back, "men on death row. Forget that… old habit. Thing is, I never forgot Leni, she remained somewhere inside. I suspect that first passionate love interest is special and unrepeatable, or maybe this one was unique in some way. Who knows? I claim no special knowledge in affairs of the heart, just in getting shot down by those women way too smart for me, which is virtually all of them. I can say one thing on which there is little doubt. Back then, my anti-commitment phobia was coupled with great suspicion about this mysterious love thing. I mean, what is love?"

"Oh, no," Connie groaned. "Here it comes."

I ignored her. "Perhaps it was merely infatuation, lust, or some search for acceptance by that alien species called women. Maybe it was merely a front for some complex bartering process, each side looking for a good deal. No matter, how did you know when it was real? Maybe I was just a horny kid who had conflated lust with attraction, a natural enough mistake. Better not to jump into the fire too quickly. Take some time, perhaps a couple of decades at least. By the time you reached the early fifties you had made it to a good age for getting serious. Your testosterone level was sinking rapidly by then so you could be more objective, and maybe even faithful."

"But children, what about them?" Connie started but caught herself. "Oh yeah, what am I saying? You probably don't like them either."

"Quite true. Urchins do seem a bother, and so smelly and noisy. However, I do like other folk's kids, the ones you can give back after a while. That's why grandparents are more excited about family offspring than parents… they can dump the little shits at the end of the day. Besides, mine probably would grow up to be Republicans. I'd shoot myself if that happened. In any case, all that romantic love crap likely was a bait and switch thing. The lure of lust and of possible issues of one's own was a lure into a lifetime of boredom, bitterness, and burdens."

"That's too cynical." Connie stared me down.

I paused. "You are right, it is. The truth is that I was totally awed by the responsibility involved. Parenthood is the toughest job there is in my estimation. I didn't think I was up to it, nor was I sanguine about the future. I have all the respect in the world for you parents. You are better than I am for sure."

"I'm not buying this. For all our grief, you have some great qualities… wit and kindness and intelligence. You would have been a good dad." I looked at Connie, thinking I would detect sarcasm. But she was being serious. That threw me off my game.

"Well, ah… we'll never know. Perhaps watching my own folks warned me away from that disastrous course in life. Not intentionally, of course, just by example. I can still remember phoning them after I had moved on in life. Each one would get on a separate extension line and it wouldn't take more than a minute before they were going at one another. I could leave, make myself a sandwich, and return to see if I might play peacemaker. They would still be going at it."

"You're exaggerating." Connie tried.

"No way! One day, my dad took me aside. He showed me his closet. *Son,* he intoned gravely, *before I got married I had seven new suits hanging in my closet. Now, I have one old and threadbare one.* He said no more at the time. His lesson was clear, or he assumed I was quick enough to get his meaning. But I was slow even then. I still went and fell into this happy marriage… go figure. I did wait, though, and selected well. Damn good thing I don't listen to my own crap. One Corbett insight, for free, never listen to a fool or yourself. They are likely to be the same guy."

"Profundity from the professor." Mel smiled.

I simply smiled back at him. "As I said, good marriages are based on low expectations at the beginning. If you expect a fairy tale, you are finished from the get-go. Expect little and you have a chance. Very Eastern if you think about it. It might work for children but the consequences for being wrong were too big in my view."

Bob threw his head back. "Damn good thing the farmers in your village never listened to your crap, though I suppose it made good fertilizer."

"Good one, Robert," I laughed before continuing, "and may your manhood wither into a useless and corrupted husk."

"Ouch," Bob winced.

"Over time, I recognized that this one college connection was probably the real thing, even if it happened so early. There had been a couple of other early connections but none like this. Listen,

I had married a smart, devoted woman who put up with me. Hardly a fight in over four decades before dementia began to take her away from me. I was a very happy camper. And yet, there was this nagging doubt that never went away from the moment I got that letter in India. You wonder what might have been, the road not taken, the missed opportunity and all that nonsense. I don't normally do that, focus on regrets. I did in this instance though. It remains the one decision, or non-decision, of my early life that I look back upon and ask… *what if?* And, as you might imagine, I've made some bad ones but this one continued to nag at me."

Connie looked puzzled. "I'm not sure I follow. Why did you come to think this one might have been a missed opportunity? Lots of us had early romantic interests, crushes and the like. They generally fade with time."

"Wait," Paul sputtered, "do you think about old boyfriends."

Connie smiled mischievously. "Why never, Tony, I mean Paul." All laughed except Paul. "My thought is that any old boyfriends we haven't seen in years are now likely bald, fat, and doing time in the county jail for failure to pay child support."

"Hah, hah, that's a good one. You would think so but no. I tried the tactic you suggested by imagining that Leni had turned into a toothless and an overweight harpy with a dozen kids, most of whom were doing hard time in public institutions. I found out differently. No luck there."

"Wait!" Maureen interjected. "How?"

"Yes," Dee seemed puzzled. "We are missing something here."

———

"I should have mentioned. We reconnected after four decades, but only in cyberspace. One day I was fooling around on Facebook. I found stuff from my old college and came across her along with a bunch of others from my class. There was a way to send a message. I typed out something neutral, just letting her know I was still alive, and that it might be nice to hear from her. Then I paused forever over the send button. You know, would she laugh at me, fail to recall who I was, take out a restraining order, the usual experiences I've had with old flames."

"We can all understand the restraining orders." Maureen smiled. "So, you apparently sent it?"

"Oh yeah, after much internal debate. Turns out, she was delighted to hear from me. The first couple of messages were the usual stuff but quickly evolved into a retrospective emotional journey. The guy she dumped me for turned out to be not so good. He was a successful academic but cheated on her starting early on. Still, she stuck it out for almost twenty years. She believed in love, commitment, and the ever-after stuff. She had this innocence about her, despite a devastating wit. Oddly enough, when she finally ended it, he was the one that went into a deep depression, suicidal in fact. She had to support him emotionally. By the time I reconnected with her, she was in a great marriage, very happy. That was a blessing, in fact."

"A blessing?" Nanette asked, looking puzzled. "How so?"

"Well, we could explore what happened back in the dark ages without risk of any real entanglement between us now. I could never have been totally open if there was a risk of complications, if I thought she might be in the market, as they say. And we did, open-up to one another that is."

"How did that go?" Janice asked.

"How can I describe it?" I paused a moment. "Think of our first group reunion after several decades. Remember how we bonded immediately. It was as if the intervening decades meant nothing, absolutely nothing. Same with Leni. We were as close as we had been all those decades ago, much closer in many respects. Funny thing, she kept all my letters to her, and a bunch of other stuff. Being the typical male, I kept nothing. This reconnection, though, did bring a sense of closure for me." Then I stopped, lost in memories.

"You're not stopping, are you?" Mel asked.

"Oh, sorry. I found that she did love me back then, at least in her own way. I did not know it at the time, when we were young. Turns out both of us were too uncertain about who we were. We were incapable of being open and honest then. Now we could. One thing sticks with me, something she said after we had gotten to know one another again…"

"Which was…" Mel prompted when I hesitated again.

"Oh, she said that all the things about me that made her fall in love with me back in college were yet evident in me. No, it was more than that. These things she loved about me in the very beginning seemed to have come to fruition. In her mind I turned out to be the guy she saw back then, the man suggested by the boy."

"Putting aside the fact that she saw things in you we obviously don't, I have to ask something," Dee asked tentatively, then said nothing.

"Go ahead." I prompted her.

"Are you ever going to meet her?"

I just looked at her for a long time, not saying anything. "No," I responded while hoping no one would press the point.

"Why not."

"It's complicated." I tried to end the conversation.

"We got time." Dee said. "Besides, this is the first moment I haven't been tempted to kick you in your family jewels."

I looked at Dee but didn't see her. My thoughts kept drifting back to long lost days.

"Tom, you still with us?" Dee asked, worried that I had drifted off to a place that they might not easily reach.

I realized she used my first name, Tom, which they only seemed to use when they weren't pissed off with me. Clearly, they did not use it often. "Sorry, strong memories there. No, we made an agreement never to do anything that might interfere with our prime relationships. We called it our *Do No Harm* rule. It was sacrosanct. In any case, within a couple of years or so it ended…"

"How… damn it?" Dee was clearly frustrated with me.

"Not important. The important thing is that we did have some time to get things right. She sent back all this stuff she had kept from us as a couple back in the 1960s."

Maureen audibly sighed. "What a blessing. I threw everything away that reminded me of my boyfriend after getting dumped."

"It was difficult to sort out our feelings in the beginning, though. We were both damaged in the same ways, that is probably why we could finish each other's thoughts, understood some things about one another except for what counted most. In any case, I dismissed all the clues... the fact that we dated exclusively at the end of our college years, that she brought me to her home to meet her folks, and to family events which was a really big deal in a Greek household. She even gave me her car so I could get back and forth to campus though warned me that I'd be castrated if I used it to pick up other women." I chuckled at that memory. "She would not have done any of that casually. In my own heart, I knew something was there as well as I knew anything. But I could not accept it. I managed to deflect it all, no matter what she was trying to tell me."

Bob shook his head. "I always have called you a nimrod, Corbett. That was just habit, a kind of joke. Now, for the first time, I believe it."

"Well, she never used the word love, and neither did I. We only spent one night together, after she had moved to Boston and started working at Harvard. It was a night of intimacy but no actual sex. That never happened... sex that is. Funny, she recalled that night as magical all these decades later. Come too think on it, so did I. Outside of marriage, it meant more to me than all the sexual encounters I would subsequently enjoy. Before we might have sorted stuff out, I went off to the other side of the world. I ran away from all those feelings. It never occurred to me that she might be as confused as I was. How could that be? I always thought females knew what they wanted and called all the shots. I learned that was not true but too late in life."

"Oh, my." Connie exhaled. More surprisingly, no one threw anything at me.

—

Finally, Kay spoke up to end the uncertainty hanging there. "I left a boyfriend behind. I had every expectation he would wait for me. Perhaps that was part of being one of those nice Catholic girls. We really believed in the fairy tale."

"You still are." I inserted.

"What?'

"A nice Catholic girl."

"Oh," she looked uncertain. "There were a few of us good girls in our small group, weren't there? No matter, waiting for this boy probably was unrealistic, but that was my intention. What was more unrealistic was the belief that he would wait for me. He sent me a picture of himself, an eight-by ten glossy, and some other things that took a while to get to me, like three months. However, his letter dumping me arrived first. I think it took me four hours to get over this loser. I took great pleasure in ripping his picture up into tiny, little pieces."

Janice gave a small gasp. "I remember that. You recovered remarkably well. I think you knew you had escaped a big mistake."

Kay smiled. "I did, that's what made it easy. What was less obvious to me in that moment was that I was starting a journey toward becoming a stronger, more independent woman. It would take a while but I'm there." She stopped there before adding, "I think I am at least."

Nothing for several moments. Then Harry broke the embarrassing silence. "Okay, I have a painful memory."

"Do tell." We were grateful for his diversion.

I do remember wanting to reunite with the girl I had left behind some two years earlier. As it turned out, we did indeed reunite, but not as girlfriend and boyfriend. She had met and fallen in love with someone while I was gallivanting through Europe on my way home. Sometimes I wonder what course my life would have taken had I had come straight back. She had no way of letting me know so I came home to quite a surprise."

Maureen said. "How sad for you. She waited but not quite long enough."

"Well, I was disappointed but not upset. She had done nothing wrong. Falling in love is natural for a man and woman to do. It was not that she had concealed anything from me; she had no way of letting me know. Today, with cell phones, things would have been different. In any case, we remain friends to this day. And she did marry the young man. I went to Cincinnati to attend Graduate School and quickly put that painful turn of events behind me. Besides, there I met and married a wonderful woman who is the mother of our only son and still my wife and best friend after some forty years."

"That woman has to be a saint, to put up with you all these years." I kidded him.

"No freaking doubt about that." He enthused. "Life with her has never been better than it is right now. By the way, how did we get around to talking about lost loves?"

"Who cares?" Mel said. "We can blame Corbett."

Maureen mused in a soft voice. "Then let me share this before the spirit moves us in a new direction. I haven't thought of this in some time, but I left someone behind. He was an engineer who was getting a master's in theology, and we had dated all through my senior year. He was a bit more serious about the relationship than I was because I knew I was going overseas. But I never told him I was going. I just figured he knew because everyone else did. It just didn't enter my mind to mention it. Graduation night, he said something about coming down to LA to see me and I said something like *I'm going to India in the Peace Corps. Didn't you know?*"

"How could you not mention it?" Kay was shocked.

"Seems fantastic now that I'm talking about it. I'm not sure we had it together at that age, at least I didn't. In any case, he wrote to me in India for several months. They were the most beautiful letters! He was a marvelous photographer and he would tell me about the new places and things he had found to shoot. His verbal descriptions were just as beautiful as the photographs, and I could see every one of them in the pages of his letters. At some point, he stopped writing. Eventually a mutual friend wrote to tell me that he had found someone else and was engaged. I wasn't that cut up about his engagement, but I certainly missed those poetic letters."

"Wait," I stammered. "He never told you himself, never even sent a letter?"

"Nope."

"Damnation!" I exhaled. "This guy makes me look good."

"Who would have thunk?" Laura said looking at me.

———

Dee took a deep breath. "Wow, I love these musings. Listening to you guys, I'm thinking that we were growing in all kinds of ways. Some of us went through an awful lot and learned so much about ourselves as a result." Then she looked at me. "I may regret this but what was your big lesson, Tom."

I looked back at Dee for some time though I suppose it was only a moment or two. Then I murmured, "I think I finally began to learn what love was… or is. Funny thing, I never used the word love back in college…"

"Idiot!" This came from a female voice.

"To my everlasting regret, that is true. I never used the word 'love' until I was 12,000 miles away, baking in the freaking desert. No matter what feelings were inside me, I never could really pull the trigger. It was as if my heart had been shut down. Maybe I should have asked her over for a visit, a couple of the other guys did with their loves. I couldn't. Cowardice… thy true name is Corbett. But when we reconnected decades later, both in happy marriages, we easily could talk via cyberspace. I finally found out what she thought of me back then… that I was brilliant, sensitive, witty, kind, committed to justice, and the best kisser she ever experienced." My voice caught and I stopped.

"Ooh, why do I sense that this saga ends badly." Dee added but something about the look on my face suggested it was time to move on. "I can wait but you won't escape without confessing to it eventually. We women have our ways."

"It just will take me some time to work up to it. I will make a small confession here, but later. I'm always joking or so I'm told, but that's not true, not always."

There was awkward silence. Everyone seemed to wait for the inevitable punch line, but none came. No one knew what to do with a serious Corbett.

I made one final point. "In the end, I figured out that I might be lovable. Don't laugh, that was a huge leap forward for me. I even have proof, sort of."

"Proof?" Bob sounded incredulous.

"Listen to this. Leni's own mother came to her the night before she was to be married. She asked her daughter what happened to me, why wasn't I the guy she was going to marry? Apparently, I was the family favorite, and certainly her mother's favorite. They didn't really like the guy she…settled for. Leni told her mother that I hadn't committed to her, or that I wasn't into commitment. That was not true, it turned out, but it must have seemed so. I had talked so much like I would never commit. I must have been very convincing. I was too broken to commit, and she was too broken to see my heart. Funny, as I listen to the other stories of loves lost while in India, one odd thing strikes me."

"What?" Kay asked.

"I was the cold guy who would never love. And yet, I suffered the loss most of all. Ironic."

"But she did love you?" Connie's words came out as half statement, half question.

I paused, not sure how to respond to a simple question. After a long time came, "Yes, she did. But it was too late."

"Are you sure it was?" Janice asked.

"Oh yes. After all, I had run off to the other side of the world."

Eleni on graduation day.

CHAPTER 14

Roundball

We needed another change of topic, and fast. I could not quite figure out how I had slid so deeply into my pathetic love life. Such a downer topic. Inside, though, I knew I had to talk about it since Leni was such a part of my India experience. Now I reached for something light and, hopefully, safe for me. Any more about my troubles with females and I feared being done in by those same females sporting pretzels as deadly weapons.

"Okay, then, I think we Americans can be proud of one contribution we made."

"Which was?" Janice eyed me cautiously.

"Some of us guys managed to bring some good old Americana to the land of the Hind, something that we Americans developed from scratch and spread around the globe."

"That poor country, our poor globe, but what the hell are you talking about?" Paul asked.

"What is America's singular contribution to the world?"

"STDs?" Mel cracked.

All I got back was more blank stares. "Oh, I'm surrounded by cretins… the game of roundball of course!"

"Okay, Corbett, did you teach the local farmers to plant and grow basketballs?" Paul laughed.

I pointed toward Paul "There you go, you see before you a man who thinks he is a stand-up comedian. He doesn't realize that I'm the funny man around here."

"I yield the floor to the joke from Wisconsin." Paul rolled his eyes in amusement.

"Okay then. Basketball is an American invention, that is clear. Football may have evolved from rugby and soccer, baseball from cricket, golf came from Scotland, the Olympics from ancient Greece, hockey from Canada or some other frozen hell hole like Finland, but basketball is purely American. Yes indeed, James Naismith, a man of many hats such as educator and chaplain and physician and so much more, invented the game at Springfield College in Massachusetts in 1891. He put a peach basket at each end of a gymnasium and wrote out some simple rules to keep the young men under his care physically fit during the harsh New England winters. At some point, he had the brainstorm of cutting the bottoms out of these baskets and later went on to create a college basketball program at the University of Kansas, where he turned out to be the only losing coach in the school's history. From such humble beginnings we now have a sport played around the world."

"Including India, thanks to you?" Mel looked skeptical.

"Please, save the sarcasm for someone who cares. But yes, at least in Udaipur. After all, I am humble in my claims."

"And totally psychotic." Tim rolled his eyes.

"No," Laura interceded, "let him ramble. At least he's off that depressing topic."

Thus, my rambling began in earnest. "It all started innocently enough. I do remember getting to the physical prep part of PC training in a bad way shape-wise. My shape was more round than lean. For some unknown reason, several years of drinking beer and of sitting around planning a leftist revolution did little to keep my once Adonis-like body in shape. No, that's not quite right, I had a shape, but it was not one you would find on the cover of a romance novel."

"More like the before shot for an ad on lipo-suction." Harry belly laughed at his own witticism.

"Anyway," I tried sounding annoyed, "I thought our physical training might be like Marine Corps boot camp, but they merely sent us over to the college PE guy who had us run around the track or something. How can I ever forget that attractive gal I managed to run alongside that first day? I thought to myself… smooth move, Corbett. I could chat her up as we jogged and, you know, seduce her with my wit and charm. Not a well-considered plan. Soon, I was gasping for breath as she pulled smoothly away from me and disappeared down the track? That was just as I lost my final hold on consciousness. Still, I thought, this is a fine way to buy the farm."

"Corbett!" Connie squealed. "You mean you let another one get away. You really were hopeless."

"Oh, for Christ's sake, I was too slow to catch any of you lovely specimens. You all escaped my evil clutches, a good thing really."

"Good thing?" Mel was perplexed.

"I would probably have expired from cardiac arrest had I had caught one of them. The shock, you know."

"Ah, good point." Mel nodded his head.

—

"My real basketball story starts when we got to Cherry Creek South Dakota. This was to be some form of cultural immersion experience. Cherry Creek was a Native American reservation located in the middle of nowhere along the banks of the lovely Cheyenne River. If you stuck a foot in that flowing ribbon of water, you pulled out a stump coated with two inches of silt. Yuck. It was blazing hot when we arrived on the reservation. We applied our usual cleverness by erecting the tents in an overlapping configuration so that it could serve as a kind of communal shelter. Frank Lloyd Wright would have been jealous. Once finished, everyone else went off to a swimming hole, or to get away from me. I'm not sure which, come to think on it. All I recall for sure is that the heat was oppressive that day. I stayed back to keep an eye on things and do what I do best, take a nap. I have always been strong at napping. I keep hoping that they make it an Olympic event someday. The gods, however, once again conspired against me."

"This sounds promising." Laura grinned. "But what happened next?"

"Well, as I was drifting off into slumber land, a storm blew up, and so did our tents. For five minutes or so, I ran around holding on to tent posts while looking in the direction of the swimming hole for reinforcements to arrive. Nothing, no sign of the cavalry whatsoever. Once again I had been abandoned by that bunch of assholes otherwise known as 44-B. So, I just said the hell with it and went back to my nap."

Bob smiled. "We were just helping out, Corbett. "You need all the training you can get for the highly competitive Olympic event of 'napping under stress.'"

"And once again, Bob, bite me. I can't quite recall who was with me there in that hellhole, we were scattered across more than one reservation for this part of our training. I am sure, though, that you Bob were one of those reprobates who failed me that day." I tried to scowl but it came out as a crooked smile.

"Yes! I was." Bob said.

"I knew you had to be." I smiled.

Bob returned my smile as he scolded me. "Hey, you're wandering again. I thought this was about basketball."

"Oh yeah, so the biggest edifice in the town was a kind of community center and church erected, if I recall correctly, by some Mormons. At some point the local boys challenged us to a basketball game at this center. Foolishly, we accepted. What else could we do. After three minutes, however, it was clear we were going to get our asses whipped, which is the equivalent of losing badly, very badly. The big difference was that they could run, and we couldn't. I had not made much progress in the stamina department since my aborted run around the UW-M track. So, I would huff and puff my way to one end of the court while the flow of the game would be going in the other direction. This was getting serious; a fatal cardiac event was likely only moments away for me."

Connie sighed loud enough to stop me. "God missed yet another opportunity to spare us from Corbett."

"And once again, thank you for the heartfelt concern for my well-being."

"Your welcome," she smiled back.

"In any case, my face was red, my lungs screamed for relief, I was now hanging on to consciousness by a mere thread. Death literally stared me in the face as I sought yet again to recover the first line or two of that revered Catholic prayer, the *Perfect Act of Contrition*. You see, I should explain for you non-believers in the true faith. I was instructed as a kid that reciting this prayer would get you into heaven no matter what kind of shitty life you had led up to that point. Saying that prayer was my only hope, given my depraved lifestyle. Okay, it was more like the depraved lifestyle to which I aspired. That prayer was my 'get out of jail' card, like the indulgences the medieval Popes sold to finance their wars, mistresses, and such. Unfortunately, my oxygen-deprived brain was on its very last legs, no way was I going to remember the whole prayer, not even close. Hell, and damnation, here I come! I prayed for a miracle."

"No fear, you'll get to the brimstone yet." Paul threw in. "That's a lock."

I gave Paul the finger. "Not being quite ready for a toe tag yet, I tackled one of the Indian kids as he raced up the court just to get a foul called and the action stopped. But that was not enough. What I needed was an EMT squad, an oxygen mask, and a gorgeous nurse to do mouth to mouth. At my last moment of consciousness, Providence intervened to save my sorry ass. Someone rushed into the Center yelling… fire, fire."

"Maybe someone saw the brimstone you were to be pitched into upon expiring." Mel deadpanned.

"Funny, but this was real. That's right! There was a fire out there in the village. I was saved from sure death by a direct act of the same deity I had discarded so casually in college. Go figure!"

"Perhaps the locals were building a pyramid of wood on which to offer the Gods a human sacrifice or a bunch of human sacrifices, not that any self-respecting God would want any of you guys." Janice added. "Besides, who would have missed you guys if you had never returned?"

"No human sacrifice was attempted though that option might well have been discussed by the locals. Who knows? If we had been sacrificed, I am confident my folks would have realized I had gone missing… perhaps after a year or two. Surely my draft board would have, they were really after my ass. And Peace Corps, they did occasional head counts after all."

"Wandering again, Corbett" Bob again tried.

"Yes! Back to the fire! The alarm being raised, we rushed out to see a brush fire heading toward our tents. We were about to become homeless. I am sure those conspiracy theorists who argued that it was set deliberately to hasten our departure were wrong. After all, we had to be great entertainment for the locals. I still recall attacking this raging conflagration as it spread through the tinder-dry underbrush. We used blankets to beat down the flames which, without question, involved acts of great personal heroism on our part. I am yet stunned Peace Corps never gave us medals. After bravely putting out this raging inferno and dire threat to our abodes, if not our lives, I was much relieved to discover that the game had been cancelled. We readily admitted defeat, at least I did. Hell, I would have forfeited Harry's right arm to escape any return to that torture masquerading as a basketball game."

"Thanks." Harry laughed with his infectious smile.

"So, we returned to camp where we were congratulating one another on surviving the inferno. I was thanking God, privately of course, for surviving the agony of the roundball contest. As it turned out, this was not my only brush with immortality on the reservation. Peace Corps had insisted I get two impacted wisdom teeth removed before I returned to our training before heading out to India."

"Wisdom teeth? Wisdom? You?" Connie looked gave me a perplexed look.

"Ha. Ha! I suspect Peace Corps did not want to get stuck with any bill if these hidden chunks of enamel erupted in India. A difficult dental procedure was necessary to extract these embedded molars which proved to be this horrific ordeal. My only memory of it was blood spattering up on the dentist's glasses as he went after these things. Perhaps I should have employed an orthodontist who, in fact, had both attended and managed to graduate from a certified dental school. I recall my mouth kept bleeding even after I returned home from the dental office."

"Oh, yuck." Someone said.

"Yuck is right. The whole episode really went south when, on the reservation in South Dakota, one side of my face blew up with a hideous infection. Soon, I was carted off to the local medical facility, a kind of National Health Service for indigenous peoples. They got it under control, anti-biotics are miracle drugs which is good. Several of my friends suggested they amputate my face, but I thought that a bit extreme and, fortunately, the docs agreed that was unnecessary."

"Oh yeah," Bob laughed. "I think I first mentioned that, but I had suggested taking off the whole head. The voice vote for approval was unanimous."

I glared at him. "You're in my book, Robert... again! But no matter, the consequences will be manifest in time."

"Consequences?" Bob looked puzzled.

"Yes, of being recorded in my book. Now, though, back to our heroic fire-fighting exploits. Our self-congratulatory session of our firefighting feats was cut short when we noticed another brush fire up on a nearby hill. It looked to us as if it were threatening a house. Off we raced to play the hero one more time. As we were crushing out the last embers, a woman came out of her house looking both puzzled and frustrated. She quietly asked why we had put out the fire she had set herself, as I recall, to keep the snakes away. We apologized profusely, gave her a match, and sheepishly wound our way back to the camp. As I think back on those moments, it struck me that this was a great portent of our coming futility in India… where we were destined to look like idiots repeatedly. We managed this easily since we were, in fact, idiots. For the remainder of the day, though, I worried a lot about what was keeping the snakes away from *our* tents."

Harry piped up. "I believe somebody in our group made it back there in the last few years. I'm sure they said that a plaque had been erected commemorating that basketball game."

"Nice try. But if they had, I am sure it would have read… *'on this spot, we original inhabitants of this land came close to knocking off the descendants of those Western barbarians who stole our heritage, killed most of our people, and kept the rest of us in bondage on this godforsaken hellhole of a reservation. Oh, we came so close that day. Maybe next time.'*

"Look at us now! It would be damn easy to bump us off today." Harry grimaced as he patted his ample tummy.

"We did make quite an impression though. When the bus arrived to get us out of there, the whole village turned out for the send-off. They did seem rather eager to get rid of us. It was a rainy day, so the dirt roads were mighty slick. As the bus started off, a great cheer went up from the assembled throng, which was followed by a groan as we slid off the road into a shallow ditch. Those assembled surged forward to surround the bus and started pushing. They did appear desperate to get rid of us, I wonder why? Once back on the road, that damn bus had to negotiate a muddy switchback road out of the valley, a very precarious journey given the conditions. For not the first time, and certainly not the last, I had visions of headlines reporting the demise of these brave young people who sacrificed their lives for a greater cause. In the end, we made it. There would be no martyrdom for us."

———

"Corbett, you've been rambling on for days and not a peep about basketball in India." It was Tim complaining this time.

"You are plebeians for sure, mere Philistines, why do I continue trying to educate you? A good story must be developed slowly… the audience brought along. These things just cannot be rushed."

Bob finished Tim's complaint. "I agree, a good story does need to be developed with care, but you don't tell any good ones. Listen, you need to get to the damn point before we all expire of freaking old age."

"Sigh, damn good thing I have no ego, and the patience of Job. Eventually, we get to India where our training continues. Plenty of stories there but what I most remember about those final training days again were some more basketball games. Somehow, the American Peace Corps all-stars wound up playing a brief series of games against the local boys from the college in Udaipur. Again, I cannot recall how it all started but somehow all this came to pass. By this time, we were no longer the totally out-of-shape sad sacks that got whipped by the reservation boys. We now were a well-tooled team of superb athletes, not physical derelicts who had spent their college years drinking beer and plotting revolutions while sitting on our ample derrieres. By the end of our school days, I had even given up chasing the young women. They were too fast and, at some point, you understand the futility of any endeavor in which the chance of success is prohibitively, if not impossibly, long. Facing reality, I became a devotee of the God of Sloth."

"Perhaps YOU gave up…" Harry stopped there.

"Now, in Udaipur, we all were back in shape and had our full complement of roundball stars together again. We had been scattered across more than one reservation back in our stateside training days but now were together for our final in-country training. There are pictures of the two teams somewhere. I can remember Bob, Harry, Tim, Sonny, Mack, and several others from those pics. We would be unstoppable, a roundball juggernaut."

Paul guffawed. "Are their drugs around here that I don't know about? Corbett's delusional again."

I instantly sent him another extended middle finger, that universally recognized sign of affection. "These contests quickly became a popular event with local Indian spectators supporting the home team and the PC family cheering for the stalwart Americans. Hah, Naismith (if he were able to look down upon our performances), would have been proud of the way we demonstrated the superiority of U.S. round ball skills. Then again, showing up the local youth may not have been our smartest move."

"What do you mean?" Laura asked.

"I'll get to that in a minute. As I said, it was us against a team from the local college in Udaipur. To say they were a team, and that we played basketball, perhaps overstated the case. They did have a regulation basketball court but I'm not sure we played the first game with a real basketball; it might have been a soccer ball. Either that or it was not inflated properly since I recall some difficulty dribbling the damn thing. We made do, though."

"I am damn sure it was not the ball's fault." Paul snuck in his jibe.

"No matter," I gave Paul my best withering look, "we went at it with vigor and dominated the game. It was a matter of pride. A crowd of local onlookers and everyone from Peace Corps quickly assembled to watch this athletic exhibition. I must say, a good time was had by all as we maintained our American can-do spirit. Hell, we would have been mortified to lose to these guys. I mean, we may have known shit about agriculture, but we did know roundball."

"So, you won the game." Kay asked the bottom-line question.

"Of course! Details now escape me, but it was clear that we enjoyed the advantages of experience and height. At six-foot-one, I think I might have been the tallest player on the floor, clearly taller than any of the Indian kids. Having thrashed them in game one, we were challenged to a rematch on a subsequent day with the same results. This time the crowd had swelled to a considerable size. Word had spread, along with a growing desire to see the arrogant Americans cut down to size. Could the goliaths from the old U.S. of A. be toppled? We swaggered with the confidence of the unbeatable. In retrospect, that might have been a case of pride going before the fall."

"What does that mean?" Maureen said before amending her question. "Okay, I know what it means in general, but what about this instance."

"While there was good camaraderie evidenced by both teams, perhaps local pride had been hurt a bit. After a second, or was it the third, thrashing we arrived for another scheduled match. But, to our dismay, the opposing team had been switched. In place of the local college kids was a military team, or so we were told. Perhaps they were the police or, as I think about it, they might have been lifers from the local prison. You know, guys in the slammer for manslaughter or felonious assault and such. They had the look of serial killers. No matter, they were muscled, and tough, and several of them could have played linebacker for the Packers. It was never clear to us whether they just happened to be there that day or whether they had been specifically recruited to avenge our earlier embarrassments of their locals. Clearly, a sentiment existed to wreak revenge on the hated foreigners. I suppose motives don't matter. The results, however, were undeniable. They inflicted extensive corporal punishment on us, and then beat us in the game as well."

Laura laughed with too much glee. "Karma really is a bitch."

"She sure is. While I don't know how the rest of our team fared, every time I moved to the basket, tried a jump shot, or leapt for a rebound, my midsection would be rearranged by an opponent's fist or sharp elbow. I tried not to be intimidated but, after a while, I was content to throw up hopeless forty-foot jump shots. The locals in the crowd enjoyed the mauling, perhaps our one contribution to improving US-Indian relations. I can still recall our mild-mannered agriculture instructor from some Western state screaming at the officials to call a foul on the other team just once as our esteemed opponents went about the business of beating us senseless. This poor man lost it. Visions of the headline *'Peace Corps group ejected from country after basketball brawl'* danced in my head.

"Getting thrown out would have saved everyone a lot of trouble." Paul observed dryly. "And you even lost the game, right?"

"Frankly, I don't really remember the score but I'm sure we did. Winning or losing was no longer the point. It was mere survival. We were to be put in our place and we were. In retrospect, that was probably a good thing. Their national pride was preserved."

"Ah, a dirty job," Paul wagged his head, "but someone had to do it."

—

"Yet, the adventure continues. Our local university opponents must have forgiven us since they asked three of us to join the regional team that was selected to represent Udaipur at some all-India tournament in Jaipur. We eagerly accepted. After all, how many points would we score for Peace Corps and America if we brought basketball glory back to our home area of southern Rajasthan? I doubt we practiced very much as a team since, by this time, we were scattered in our actual sites. Still, Harry, Bob, and me boarded a train for Jaipur full of confidence that we would acquit ourselves well in the contests before us. Let me just say, hubris is a fickle and heartless bitch."

"What?" Nanette said laughing since she knew another humiliation of her male counterparts was about to be shared. "Are we about to see even more karmic justice here?"

I emitted a low groan. "You might say that. You see, there was one problem with our plan, which quickly became obvious once the tournament games started. Udaipur was a basketball backwater.

They had never gone to this competition before. They now assumed, laughingly it turned out, that the addition of the American ringers would make them a real team. There was one flaw in this perfect plan. Most of the other teams participating in the tournament could play the game. They had real athletes who came from all over the country, including places where the game was popular. I swear, some of these guys were good enough to compete at the collegiate level in the U.S. While my conditioning had vastly improved since our debacle on the South Dakota reservation and my aborted marathon around the track during training, none of us could play at this level. We were soundly defeated in our first game."

"At least you guys are consistent." Laura chuckled.

"Very funny. Being able to run up and down the court was not enough. You needed talent to compete here. I wish someone had warned us of that fact. The contest wasn't even close. We played one more game against some other losers. I think they were from a school for the blind. I believe we may even have won by a basket or two, though no discoverable record of our overall performance remains. Our days of athletic glory were over. The trip, however, was great fun. We got to know the college kids well, and soon got over our humiliation on the courts. One lesson became clear. Just because a sport was invented in your country does not mean you know how to play the damn game."

———

"Well, I must say Laura is spot on." Paul smiled, "you guys from 44-B are consistent. You sucked at being Ag experts and you sucked at being athletic stars. And you, Corbett, suck at being a would-be lover."

"Point made, Paul. That, however, is not quite the end of the b-ball saga. I managed to bring the game to my village, town really, in a small way at least. In the beginning, I spent some time refereeing games at the local high school and, to my chagrin, trying to teach the game to the local urchins."

"That's nice." Maureen was sincere. "But why to your chagrin?"

"It was a bit like herding cats. These were young kids and I probably was the biggest attraction to participating. There were problems though."

"Like what?" Harry asked.

"Well, their English was primitive, if it existed at all. Their understanding of the rules was beyond primitive. Worse, they had little concept of teamwork. I tried to both referee and teach some basics like it was a good thing to pass the ball to a teammate, even if he came from a different caste. When one teammate did pass the ball to a second mate, that one often just stood there gawking at me… undoubtedly the strangest sight he had seen in his life. Too often, the ball would bounce off the kid's head which hardly shook him out of his hypnotic fascination with this alien creature that had dropped mysteriously into his world… me. I didn't stick with it very long, especially after my novelty wore off. Not continuing to work with the kids, in hindsight, disappoints me greatly."

"Why, exactly."

"Oh, I had this excuse that it wasn't my real job there and that it was too hard to make it work but those kinds of excuses seem like shit now. With time, they could have learned a few new words like 'foul' and 'charge' and 'blocking out,' the basic lingo of the game. After I ceased to be a novelty, perhaps I could have given English lessons or worked more closely with some of the kids, been a mentor of sorts. Just exposing them to the wider world would have been a gift. It would have been more useful than whatever I was trying to do as a fake farmer."

"Wait!" Maureen seemed dubious. "Are you saying there would be something positive about teaching a bunch of small-town Indian urchins some basketball skills?"

"No, no, that would be missing the point. Basketball would just be an entrée. It would be a vehicle for capturing the attention of the kids. Here's the thing. I had sensed this enormous change across the generations in this backwater area. It wasn't exactly a generational-based shift toward a more expansive and exclusive understanding of the world but close enough. Each succeeding generation was being exposed to a broader world in small but significant ways. Who knows, perhaps I could have pushed this change along by using basketball to work with kids on their primitive English. Most just knew a few words. At the same time, there was a prospect of opening their minds to greater possibilities. Just a thought."

"I get that," Maureen observed.

"You know, I suddenly recall this vignette from that American Indian reservation where the kids kicked our collective asses on the roundball court. I recall one youth who listened to us talk about college and our dreams. At some point, he was asked by one of us what his future might look like. He confidently said he was sure to go to college now, after hearing us talk. You need to realize that this reservation was at the end of the civilized world. You cannot imagine a more desolate, isolated hell and still be within the borders of the continental United States. There was no freaking way he had thought about college until he heard our stories. He likely had never considered leaving the reservation."

"Wow, touching." Dee murmured.

"You never know what fires up the imagination in another, what touches off dreams and visions where none had existed before. I sensed that when I taught at the university. Even small asides can change the life of a student. This will surprise you but even I transformed the lives of students, not that I'm extra smart or visionary. Perhaps you simply find yourself infused with authority, if not wisdom, just by your status and position… whether as a college professor or as an American on the other side of the world."

"Oh yes," Dee jumped in, "I can recall hanging on the words of my profs at Berkeley."

"Hell, I also can remember being a college student myself, back before the dawn of writing. I ran into my English Lit professor in a lunch line and casually mentioned my dream of being a writer one day. He didn't laugh at me, didn't even smile. He just asked me if I could tell a good story. I did not have an answer that day, just stood there mute. Still, his question stayed with me for the remainder of my life. Amazing, I never forgot it. Just a throwaway line for him to get rid of a pesky student but for me… something more. After all these years, I think I finally have an answer his query."

"Yeah," Bob chuckled, "the answer is *not in your freaking dreams.*".

Maureen cocked her head and brought us back on point. "Clearly, this was about a lot more than basketball."

"Yeah, it would have been a lot more than just basketball." I said while still focusing on my long-ago encounter in the college lunch line.

"Tell us more." She followed up.

I snapped back to my main narrative. "Here is one thing I learned, maybe in India, that I brought forward in life. If you want to reach people, you need to develop a personal relationship. What does that mean? Perhaps an example. A lot of the academics I work with want to influence public policy. However, they are naïve enough to believe that all they need to do is send policymakers a copy of some freaking journal article that is indecipherable beyond the confines of the academy. They believe they can persuade the world by pointing out the statistical significance of their results, and then wow the audience with their impressive academic credentials. They really believe that's all it takes to be heard, especially by policy audiences they feel are not as smart as they."

"Big mistake." Bob supported me. "I worked in Washington."

"You bet, my friend who yet remains in my book despite agreeing with me. Then, they are outraged when ignored, blaming the cretins in the audience while seeing no fault in themselves. I learned early that you need to approach folk on their terms, develop a relationship first, then try to impart new things or even change their minds. I likely sensed that before India, but that lesson was driven into me there. There is an old aphorism in the policy arena that *the best story wins the day,*' but only if related by someone the audience already trusts. Even while I was ostensibly an academic, though a questionable one at best, I spent a lot of time working with policymakers at the local, state, and federal levels. They accepted me, listened to me. Believe me, a lot of my colleagues were shut out, never got to first base."

"And your secret was... drugs? You drugged them into submission, right?" Paul was enjoying our contest of insults way too much.

"I will let that slide, my friend. After all, I assume that Connie punishes you enough daily."

"Hey," his wife protested and then smiled. "All kidding aside, I bet you were good with people, with students. You do make people laugh, and not just at you."

"Here is the thing. Whenever you communicate with people from a different sphere, like academics talking with policy types or political types, you are bridging cultures. It is like crossing into a different realm where they have their own language, reward systems, norms, and so forth. Unless you take some time to learn that world, you will be communicating with yourself. Most of my colleagues never got that. As I keep saying, they think that a peer reviewed journal article is enough to convince the world of their brilliance and correctness. After all, that is what was most critical in their culture. But the whole world doesn't see things that way. Your culture is your culture, period. Another way of putting it is that when you finally understand a culture, that is all you really know... one other culture. Each is unique. You always need to understand the rules of the other person's world. Perhaps that is what we learned in India, to really see cultural relativity, to understand and appreciate its power. The thing is, once people on the other side of any divide trust you, you can talk about more serious stuff. With those young people in India, basketball was a way of breaking down barriers, even if a brawl almost broke out at one of our games. Those Udaipur college kids wanted us to get to know them as equals. Then they could accept us, would listen. That was something, something indeed."

"Damn," Bob sighed. "Corbett is right."

"Too late." I beamed. "You already have been recorded in the book."

"What book is that again?" Mel asked.

"The only one that counts." I smiled. "My book."

Post game group shot: I'm lower left, then
Bob, and Harry is 4th from left:
the three 'ringers' who played for Udaipur in the big tournament.

CHAPTER 15

A 'Time Out Of Time'

"Something's a bit off here." Maureen exclaimed.

"Besides the fact that we are stuck listening to the guys whine about stuff?" Cate, her site mate in India asked.

"No, we're used to that by now. Not exactly off really, but something is bothering me. It seems like we're always looking at the dark side of things when we gather. I mean, we share a few successes and much humor but even the funny stuff tends to fall into this pattern of disaster stories or failures."

Cate was nodding her head. "I think you are right. Why is that?"

Janice chimed in. "I suppose it's our selective memories. The hard things stayed with us, but there was a lot of good stuff as well. India was tough for me, as it was for most of us. Still, there were good things we did and which we all took away."

"Absolutely," Cate picked up the thread of the dialogue. "In the end, it changed my life. It gave me purpose and pointed me in a new direction."

Connie seemed to agree. "Yes, if we thought about it seriously, we would see how our time there changed us in so many ways. I mean, we had loves lost and loves found but Peace Corps was way more than that."

A question I had noodled earlier popped back into my head. "Here's something that I've been wanting to ask."

"No, we won't go to bed with you." Laura responded without missing a beat.

"Funny lady, but you just mean not tonight, right?" When she scowled I quickly moved on. "I was thinking of a serious question. How many of you would do it all over again?"

The women eyed me suspiciously, then determined I was being serious for a change. Most hands slowly went up. "Not unanimous I see, but a majority. Most in fact." I was curious and asked. "What about those with reservations. What are your thoughts?"

Dee spoke uncertainly. "Peace Corps yes, for sure. But maybe a different country or a program where I knew what I was doing."

Dee's comment resonated with me. "I get it. Not rejecting Peace Corps but perhaps looking for situations that make more sense." Several affirmations could be heard. "Let me suggest this, then. How many of you women would do it again if the experience could be tweaked to improve it a bit?" Now almost all the hands from 44-A went up in the air.

"Tweaked how?" Maureen asked suspiciously.

"For example, if you could have been stationed with me for two years." I deadpanned.

"Oh my god!" and other oaths could be heard as all the hands fell again.

"Well, I think we have a consensus here. I was going to going to suggest a recruiting idea to Peace Corps, at least to attract younger women. Envision a picture of me with the slogan… *'spend two years in the desert with this virile example of pure manhood, 180 pounds of twisted steel and sex appeal.'*"

"Shit, Corbett" Paul guffawed, "you passed 180 pounds decades ago and never looked back."

"Alright, point made. Let me also make a point here." I tried to maintain my dignity but that was a lost cause. "Now listen. We all tend to forget this over time but, despite the daily struggle and the dull sameness that eroded early idealism, we must have found reasons to remain positive and upbeat. We could not have endured our trial otherwise. Listen to these words from long ago in another passage from a letter I sent to Leni."

It is another typical Rajasthani day here. The temperature under the aegis of a bitterly hot sun is creeping over the 110-degree mark and the sucking dry wind is blowing off the hills and sweeping along the brittle, cracked earth. Like most of the other living creatures here, we simply crawl into some hole for protection until the sun sinks into a bloody demise toward the west. Life is frustrating, but it is exactly what I expected. It may very well be the difficulty of the experience that gives it value that makes us aware of both our limitations and strengths.

In many ways, though, life is quite satisfying here. There is a great deal of satisfaction in the relationships, the small successes in agriculture, and the increasing awareness of self and other people. And there is progress. Despite some late damage, farmers are impressed and much more of the new wheat will be planted next year along with newer and better seed varieties. A variety of maize (corn) which was used by 30 farmers this year will be sown by many more in the next season. I even heard that some farmers might try a new variety of rice we have brought in. Things are moving, and I am basically satisfied.

"Amazing, really, when you think about it. Despite the hardships, the heat, the boredom, the loneliness, and some late crisis that I thought might have undermined our outreach efforts, I apparently remained upbeat. Either that, or I was lying to this girl I feared losing in some futile attempt to keep her interest. This estimate of what we would have called target group penetration amazes me all these years later, particularly the comments on maize and rice. Hell, they were not grown in my area to any extent as I recall. But, then again, so much has been lost to memory after four-plus decades. Without these letters, I never would have recalled many good things. It would be just the loneliness, the frustrations, the heat, the dangers, and the pervasive sense of futility and failure that would have stuck with me. There were others like this, amidst some depressive ones, that struck the same upbeat theme about the people and the work. Damn, we do mostly recall the bad stuff."

"No shit." Mel intervened. "I kept detailed diaries and, when I look back on them, am amazed at how badly I recall things, and how negatively. From my notes, I did much better than I recall."

I chuckled. "Mel, you did just fine, no better or worse than the rest of us. But you make a good point, my man. After all, what was success for us. Really! Was it about crops? Perhaps not! For me, the firmest memories are not about events or crop yields but something less tangible. It is more about the feel of the place and how that affected us. I think India taught us a lot about life, but about those dimensions of life not easily captured in a vignette or a neat lesson and certainly not in any standard metric of success."

"Not sure I follow." Kay said but was now paying attention, as were the others. She was letting hope overtake experience that I might be serious for once.

"For example, we became much more sensitive to the rhythms of existence, the cycles of the moon, repeated patterns of daily lives. Here and now, I never pay attention to things like full moons. There and then, a full moon was a blessing. At a minimum, it was easier finding the outhouse after a night of local brew if the moon were full and the sky cloudless. More importantly, these were the essential rhythms of existence."

"Yes, I remember!" Someone uttered.

"Calming patterns were everywhere. They slowed us down, reset our inner clocks. I remember watching water buffalo wander down the highway. They seldom hurried. Okay, a bus would roar by and then we would begin to count… one, two, three. Around six or seven, the buffalo would suddenly react, long after the bus had moved on. Apparently, it took that long for its brain to be engaged. That was the only time they reacted to anything. I recall thinking, *Gee, I have a lot more in common with these creatures than I would have imagined.*"

"Damn, I have to up my game," Paul complained. "You beat me to that one."

I smiled. "Some of us kept engaged by writing… journals or letters or even short stories and books. Who writes in today's rushed world, other than emails and Facebook posts? I suppose I do but what sane person does. I wrote one book in India and I know Ralph started one. And reading became an obsession. We devoured every piece of literature we could find and desperately savaged every letter and magazine from home. We all read more, and thought more, and became much more introspective. I think that was a critical time out of time for each of us, perhaps in different ways."

As I smiled at my own reflections, I heard someone say. "Damn, Corbett is making sense again. I hate that." I was more into my own thoughts to identify the speaker.

I merely smiled in response. "For me, India felt like you were enjoying a pulp-fiction Western thriller, living it in some real way. I have always liked history, visiting famous sites, reading historical books, and the like. You might have seen historian Doris Goodwin on television, she was always brought in to give a big picture perspective on current events. Well, as a little girl growing up in Brooklyn, she often talked about imagining what it was like living in far gone times. I have always felt a similar pull of the imagination. Walking through parts of Salumbar, I would envision I was in Dodge City, circa 1880. I recall a herd of water buffalo kicking up dirt as they were driven through town by tough looking men riding camels with carbines slung over their shoulders. One could easily see Matt Dillon (Gunsmoke) drawing against some desperado or Wyatt Earp waiting to confront the Dalton gang. So much of what we saw and felt would fit nicely into a time capsule… the women beating clothes by the lake bordering the town, the simple farming tools and techniques used for generations upon generations, the feudal customs that shaped interpersonal interactions for good and bad."

"You are right." Glen agreed.

"Yet, if you looked closer, change was palpable, subtle transformations both deep and profound. This is something I mentioned earlier when talking about the village kids."

"Go on with that thought. I was intrigued when you brought this up earlier." Bob asked with a sincerity that almost threw me off my game, but I recovered.

"Well, I would look at the generation of elders. They typically spoke Mewari (the local dialect), had grown up during the British Raj and thus were governed for all practical purposes by local nobility, and had a world view that seldom looked beyond their immediate experience. Their children, the adults of that period, typically spoke Hindi, read newspapers, and had a world view that stretched to Delhi and beyond. The young, for the most part, were in school, learning elementary English, and soon would likely have access to technologies that would broaden their world view significantly. If you looked closely, one's sense of the world, and the individual's place in it, was evolving across generations in dramatic ways."

"Not sure I follow you there." Someone asked.

"Let me give this a shot. You could sense that so many in that land were trapped in more traditional ways of understanding their world. I would look at these farmers with tiny holdings who had far more children than they could support on their meager assets. Siring fewer children risked not having anyone to care for them in a society where no public safety net existed. While many more of their children were surviving and reaching adulthood, it was hard to take that risk. India would have to make a profound leap forward if it was to absorb all the kids who would be pushed off the land in the coming decades. It struck me at the time as a Malthusian apocalypse waiting to unfold."

"An apocalypse that never happened." Bob interjected.

"No indeed, though population density remains an issue. Rather, India would become part of BRIC, a group of developing countries that amazed the economic world at times with their rates of growth. Despite our, or I should say, my pessimism, the decades after our service proved that the improbable was possible though not easy. Perhaps we should not have been shocked since the horrors envisioned by Malthus never came to pass. Of course, our pessimism might have arisen from the fact that we saw only a part of the country, not the whole thing. We lived in a backward area where most were yet trapped in the past. Thus, our presence among them was more of a shock to them, and shocked us more, than might have been the case elsewhere."

"No doubt." Greg affirmed.

"I recall a conversation with a black fellow student during graduate studies back in the States. I mentioned this one thing about our common experience… the sense of being the total outsider in India, our total lack of anonymity. Wherever you went, particularly in rural Rajasthan, you were an object of curiosity, a freak. Children would stare and follow you. You were subject to endless and repetitive questions. Sometimes you were made fun of, not surprising given how many mistakes we made, but sometimes you were treated with a deference and respect you did not deserve. But the inescapable reality was that you were always center stage."

"For sure." Mel affirmed.

"Like I said, I was going on about this one day shortly after returning to the States in a chat with this student back in Milwaukee, this African-American. He looked at me with a smile and said, *then you do know what it is like being me.* He was dead serious. And he was right. Our cultural cocoon was shattered. I keep saying this in different ways, but you cannot appreciate the fishbowl in which you are swimming if you never get outside it. You need to be an outlier for a while. Where else in the world could I have gotten that experience, could we have gotten it."

"Yes, yes, yes!" Mel said excitedly. "When you are a white American in your own land, all is simple. You may screw up but that is unlikely due to skin color or some cultural difference. But when you are the outsider, the visible outsider, that can be tough. I lost it one day when one beggar too many harassed me on the streets of Bombay. Why I snapped that time, of all the many encounters with all the many beggars… who knows? I hit some invisible limit."

"Oh yeah." Harry exclaimed but did not expand on his comment. "Lots of times, I battled my emotions when I was called Muhammad Ali over and over. It was a struggle."

Bob spoke up. "I recall that, Harry. During our basketball games with the university kids, the locals in the crowd kept calling you Ali. I was so impressed with you. You remained so composed. I might have lost it."

Harry shook his head. "I tried my best but sometimes I hit my limit as well. We all have them. Think about it, Ali was the only American black man they knew. I'm not sure anyone was trying to be mean, not like what I faced in the States. Hell, it might have been a compliment of sorts though it didn't always feel like it. I was just so different to them. In the end, it all made me a better man, a tougher man."

Greg snickered. "Yup, I look at Harry's body now and I see Muhammed Ali in his prime."

Harry gave Greg a demonstrative finger.

"Harry, you nailed it." I raised my voice to be heard over the ensuing laughter. "The thing is that we experienced things in that time and place that we would never have elsewhere. We absorbed lessons and insights that we took with us and which colored and informed our view of society and ourselves. You cannot buy such things at a local store, nor can you glean them from a textbook. We were exposed to things that were priceless."

"And for which we paid a big price." Janice added thoughtfully.

"Let me finish this thought before I blow my temporary stay of execution and say something stupid again. I doubt very much I'll survive the next pretzel attack." Seeing I had the floor I continued. "In India, it seemed you had this major role in a continuing play that used a set of complex characters and a convoluted plot. As we touched on earlier, that really wears you out. In our ordinary lives, you basically function on this automatic pilot thing someone mentioned."

"You brought it up." Bob nodded toward me.

"Probably! In India, you realize at some point that everything requires thought. It was all improv on the go. Everyone else had a script except you. You are immersed in a society that is an incredibly complex and chaotic canvass of caste, color, class, religion, language, history, ethnic identity, political disposition, and on and on. You had to continuously calculate with whom you were interacting and what rules and conventions governed those specific interactions. Virtually every social interaction contained at least the possibility of misunderstanding and hurt feelings."

"That is so true," Dee exhaled. "I think someone else mentioned this, but I was exhausted at the end of each day, even when nothing was going on. That puzzled me for a long time."

"It simply is hard to think about what you are doing all the time. Often, even the simplest interactions demanded thought and care. Our embedded scripts no longer worked. Obviously, social mistakes were all too frequent and sensitivities hurt more than we liked. Over time, that effort to negotiate the labyrinths of this social web wore you down. But it was more than that. There was nowhere to go to "blow off steam," to just relax. You couldn't go drinking with the boys because the boys didn't drink, at least in public. That was even more so for the gals. For us guys, we could not consort with comforting women to soothe the weary spirit since the potential cost was a lot more than a few Rupees; it was the loss of respect along with any effectiveness in your site. You probably could do drugs, but your ticket home would be punched early if caught. Consequently, you stuffed it in, plodded on, and did your best not to leave with the local's perception of America worse than when you arrived.

"I really do wonder what our record is on that score?" Ben mused.

"You mean what the locals thought of us in the end? Me too, I have no freaking idea." I looked at him, then away.

"I believe it was positive on balance. I went back, it was a good experience," Tim observed. "Like all things, there is a balance of good and bad, but my sense is that the scale in our case leaned positive. At least they talked well of the crazy Americans in their midst for a time."

"No matter, though, we were learning things and experiencing things that we never would have otherwise. I had a conversation with a neighbor not long ago. He and his wife served in the Philippines, not long after our service in fact. He remembers the shock of coming home and not feeling the same about things. Peace Corps spent all this time preparing you for the culture shock of where you were going and little to nothing respecting the return trip home. Yet, we were quite different when we came back. We were no longer the same. I bet no one can point to any specific moment when that change occurred. We only sensed it in retrospect."

Several affirmations came from different directions.

I paused, trying to think through my own experiences so long ago. "We changed by a thousand small moments and experiences, few that stand out. Still, each is unique, things we would never have encountered in our ordinary lives. I remember so many the small things, everyday images that somehow stuck. These insignificant memories sparkle momentarily and then are replaced by others so quickly you wonder which were real and which somehow have been fabricated. Ever wake up and wonder if something in your head was real or a dream. It's like that."

"How about a couple of examples?" Connie asked.

I thought for a moment. "Oh, let me see. Well, I have this image of a group of farmers encouraging me to go ahead and pet that cute baby camel and then laughing themselves silly as the mother charged while I ran for my worthless life. They knew this would happen. Fortunately, I could run with considerable celerity by this time. In another, I recall being offered sugar cane juice squeezed fresh at harvest time. Nothing is sweeter, trust me, sitting at the side of a field as the farmer was running sugar cane stalks through his grinding device and offering you the product of his labors. I recall our Superman bicycles with unbridled hatred. Month after month I cycled over paths that would suddenly turn to sand. That would send me flying over the handlebars into a heap of hurt on the ground as the damn bike landed on top of me. I was spared even more accidents by the fact that the piece of crap was broken half the time. Years later, my wife could not understand why I did not share her romantic vision of us riding our bicycles at sunset. Personally, I would prefer drinking crushed glass to getting on one of those things again."

"Infernal machines!" someone muttered.

"I can yet almost feel the streets of Salumbar where, over time, our presence evoked less and less curiosity. I had some local friends with whom I would sit and pass the time of day. It was a good way to get a sense of local life. After the fact, I realized I spent about equal time with a Hindu merchant and a Muslim merchant, instinctively seeking cultural and political balance. Still, as eager as each apparently was to have my company, neither ever invited me into their homes or for dinner. Some degrees of separation were hard to overcome. I recall doing some fun things, attending local celebrations, one that stayed with me was the celebration of Independence Day, when the British finally called it quits in 1947."

"Now that I think on it," Mel noted, "we were there only two decades after they won independence. It was still a fresh memory for them."

"Absolutely! During a ceremony at the local school, I remember thinking how much of that celebration focused on forging a national identity. They had been a patchwork of separate political, religious, ethnic, and tribal identities prior to independence. It would take a massive effort to weave a common culture from that chaos. If we thought about that hard, we might be reminded of our own early efforts to forge a common American identity from separate colonies that were growing their individual cultures."

"I'm not sure they have made it yet." Greg observed.

"I'm not sure we have either." Glen added.

"And there are small things that I retrieved from my letters to Leni. We played card games with some locals through which I contributed financially to their economy. My recollection of such events is vague, but so it is written. On days I tried real work, I used to travel to smaller villages outside my town, the names of which I no longer recall. There, I would chat with farmers as I walked around with a local development officer. It was never totally clear what my role was, but no one seemed to mind my presence."

"Hey, you provided comic relief." Paul said.

"And without even trying. The hilarious part came when we filled out some government forms for our BDO outlining all that we had done and all that we intended to do. Ah, if only intentions were reality, Salumbar would have become a beacon to the free world."

"Hell, India would have shot past us to start sending volunteers to help America out." Greg offered with a chuckle.

"No doubt. I especially recall losing copious amounts of weight, this miracle having been captured on film. I looked like an escapee from a Nazi death camp even though my appetite for food and drink never slacked in the least. In fact, I grew to love Indian food, even okra, a love that remains with me today. My vision of heaven has evolved over time. Forget about those seventy-seven virgins who theoretically would find me irresistible in the afterlife. My new vision of heaven consists of an unlimited access to a variety of curries containing absolutely no calories whatsoever. During my tour, my weight bottomed out somewhere in the upper 140s, not very substantial given my 6'1" frame."

Harry grunted, "Shit, some of us can't even recall how skinny we were then. I was able to dunk a basketball when I played on my high school team."

Bob chortled. "Now, you couldn't dunk a basketball with the help of a freaking ten-foot ladder."

"Oh yeah, I could still take you in a one-on-one game, white boy."

I intervened to get things back on track. "Now, gentleman, enough trash talk! Our athletic days are long over. Besides, we would need an EMT team on alert if you guys got back out on the court. Time to move on to challenges more appropriate to our current ages... like trying to remember where we put our hearing aid."

"Point well taken." Bob smiled. "Or remembering to take my Ensure today."

"That reminds me" Mel chuckled. "I better order some more Depends."

With order almost restored, I continued. "The sad truth is that none of us are what we once were. I was lean and mean back in the day. The real culprits responsible for my weight loss in India, once that hard work hypothesis initially proffered by the PC doctor had been discredited, turned out to be an assortment of intestinal bugs with whom I shared my daily sustenance. I doubt I look much like that guy anymore."

Connie chuckled. "No shit. Oops, that wasn't nice of me."

"But spot on, I fear."

Maureen spoke up. "We've all aged over the years and put on a few pounds. The changes wrought by our Peace Corps experience, though, were much more profound. They went way beyond any physical changes. I've thought about this a lot as well. We were isolated in the village even more so than you guys. As women we couldn't go out and about the village in the evening, so we spent a lot of time reading, writing letters, and talking about life. I remember some very deep discussions of life's mysteries in letters to some of the guys, especially Mel. One of the books in the PC book locker that Cate and I inherited from the guys of I-39 in Karad was the *Harrad Experiment* about a college where so-called free love was licit, and even encouraged as a means of finding oneself. Boy, was that a new concept for me. I was one of those good Catholic girls that Corbett despised. I did go to school two blocks from Haight-Ashbury but somehow never absorbed much of that liberated culture. Not only did we discuss the meaning of love, life, and existence, we learned what it was like to be the 'other.'"

"The other?" Connie asked even though she thought she knew.

Maureen continued. "Yeah, as Corbett emphasized, we were always on display. Back home, we were the mainstream color, most of us that is. In India, we all were the outsiders. That was a shock. The villagers were always amazed and amused by us and fascinated about every aspect of our lives. The adults were slightly more subtle in their curiosity but not much. We were plagued by juvenile 'peeping toms' who thought nothing of peering into our windows at all hours or clambering up to watch us over the walls. It got to the point that we kept our window shutters closed, forgoing any slight breeze that might have cooled the house. We also developed the habit of moving about the courtyard quietly, particularly when headed to the latrine in the back corner, just to avoid the wall climbers."

"So," I deadpanned, "my disguise as a village urchin worked. You never caught on."

"Hah, hah!" Maureen responded. "The most common question asked by adults was *'how much money do you make?'* Our answer of $75 dollars per month, when translated into Rupees seemed like a fortune to them. The other common question was *'when will you get married?'"* We saw ourselves as kids while they saw us as way beyond the normal marital age. They worried that our parents probably would have a difficult time marrying us off when we got home."

"A reasonable concern," I noted. "You were getting long in the tooth."

"Corbett!" Connie sent a glare in my direction. "Just how did you find anyone to marry you?"

I suppressed the response that came to mind which involved several salacious references to the family jewels. Going there would have resulted in that toe tag for sure.

Maureen continued. "The bigger problem was that, not being married at this advanced age, we must be *promiscuous.* This was what they picked up from their distorted sense of Western culture and our independent lifestyles. And yet, I was impressed by their tolerance of our cultural differences. When we said or did something unusual, like drawing our own water from the well, usually when our cook was busy, they just billed it as 'another crazy American habit.' Another of our oddities that flummoxed them was when we washed the windows in the health center, which were too filthy to see out of. Pukka Sahibs did not do manual labor. Their preference would have been to whitewash them so the dirt wouldn't show any more, but then why have windows. Similarly, they never could understand why we brought our own water when we were invited to dinner in someone's home. Despite our explanation about the effects of changes in water (we gave up on the notion of explaining germ theory) on our G-I tracks, they never got it, but they accepted it, and us, anyway."

"Hmm, the trajectories of our individual lives accelerated and changed direction from that experience. It was a 'time out of time' when we got outside of ourselves and saw things more deeply, and in new ways. If we simply had continued as we were, there would have been nothing to force us to consider who we were and what we wanted from life. Perhaps that would have been fine, maybe our lives would not have been all that different. Counterfactuals are wonderful to consider but often they cannot be confirmed. And yet...."

"Yet what...?"

"We wouldn't be the same." I whispered as I looked around the room. "I'm sure of that."

"I need more." Bob looked at me.

"For better or worse, we wouldn't be the same without India. Sure, we all struggled, we had numerous failures but, in the end, we came out the other end better than when we started, even if it were not obvious at the time." A thought hit. "Remember the movie A League of their Own?"

"Oh yeah," Janice said. "That was about the women's professional baseball league during World War II."

"Right. One scene has always stayed with me. The husband of the team's star come home from the war and she decides to leave with him just before the playoffs. The manager, played by Tom Hank's confronts her, asks her why she's quitting. *It's just too hard,* she says. His response is classic."

"Oh, yes!" Mel said with excitement. "I love that scene."

"Remember, he next says, *'It's baseball. It is supposed to be hard. If it wasn't hard, everyone would do it.'* You can tell that professional baseball changed the lives of all those women players coming of age in the 1940s. That's what Peace Corps did for us. It changed our lives."

"It was hard. Then again, as someone said earlier, we remember the bad stuff. I sure did, probably part of who I am. India was tough, so remembering the bad stuff was not hard. It was not only the isolation and the futility. It was this culture that was unforgiving. The rules seemed so rigid and so terribly complex. You could never relax, and you had to think all the time. How would I offend the people around me today? There seemed an infinite number of ways to do just that. Here, we go through life unconsciously, at least I do. There, a careless word or deed could, and often would, spell disaster."

"Oh my God," Maureen intoned. "We've all been there."

"No shit." Bob affirmed with more graphic language.

"Of course, there's tons in my letters to Leni about positive things, friendships and projects that worked and experiences never to be forgotten. Great now to have that stuff. I really seemed insightful back then, and so eloquent. Just how could I have deteriorated so much over the years?"

"A mystery for sure," Mel grinned.

"In my words to her, I could see epiphanies going off all the time, about myself and about understanding human nature and what cultural identity means. I wound up focusing on culture, various forms of it, later in my so-called academic career. These were lessons I would take with me through my life. Priceless, really."

"Yes," Bob mused cautiously. "I suspect that we all became aware of what culture really meant. That was something you never understood until you got out of your own world."

"Exactly," I enthused. "One point I was trying to make earlier is that you inevitably were singled out, for good or bad, in India. You could never escape being on display. It was like being an exhibit in the zoo."

"No shit." Tim exclaimed. "Remember that tractor I drove from Jaipur to Udaipur along the major road. "Can you imagine what an exhibit I turned out to be? It was worth the price of admission."

"Well, I would have paid a rupee for the privilege, though probably not much more than that." Mel said with a smile.

"Here's the thing," I added. "All of our experiences, even the worst ones, somehow made us better. Perhaps the painful ones were the most important of all. They made us more aware of who we were. If we are the sum of our experiences in some essential way, India completed us. Can any here say that they experienced anything more intense than Peace Corps?"

"Maybe Stan in Nam." Bob looked at our quiet peer.

Stan thought for a moment. "They were both intense. But the thing is, I made it through Nam. India was a different story."

I thought about pushing him on that comment but saw something in his expression. It was a place he wished not to go, at least in the moment.

The evening water buffalo drive, aka Dodge city circa 1880.

CHAPTER 16

A Celtic Curse

There is a natural rhythm to these confessional sessions. You only can absorb so much seriousness before seeking something lighter as a respite. Then, perhaps, you might return to issues of deeper substance. Life is rather like that, or even a good novel. You search for the balance between competing themes and emotional pitches. Substance must be balanced with the trivial, darkness with humor, insight with nonsense. Otherwise, one becomes bored, even distracted, by a perpetual emotional monotone. I humor myself that I know, rather intuitively, when a dialogue might profit from a new direction. That may just be my one meager talent among so many faults, yet one essential to sustaining an emotional harmony among complex sentiments.

There was a pregnant pause as I thought about where we might drift next. "We have gotten too philosophical. I believe it is time for me to share an inspiring story of male success or, depending upon your perspective, a most disgusting tale of male depravity."

Dee tried to look repulsed, but it came out as a look of interest. "I can see it in his eyes. Ever notice that they grow beady when he's thinking salacious thoughts."

"They're always beady." Laura offered.

"True enough," Maureen agreed.

"What does that tell us." Dee offered to a generous round of hilarity.

"All we need to know about him." Maureen retorted with a stern grimace.

I stepped in to slow up the pace of verbal assaults upon my person. "By the way, Dee, I just love the word *'salacious.'* For some reason, it turns me on."

"Oh my God," Dee half squealed, "everything does."

Laura chuckled. "Pathetic, Corbett. Come on, come on, let's hear your disgusting story."

I gave them my best effort at a salacious grin. "Nothing brings me greater pleasure than affirming every bad thought you females had about us brave young men who ventured abroad to save the world a half-century ago."

"You mean the wonderful guys from India-40?" Paul said chuckling.

"That's so preposterous I'll just ignore it. So, here's the thing. We were all up in Delhi for Christmas. There was this gal who worked for Peace Corps. I should mention that she was an Anglo, of British heritage but born and raised in India and thus an Indian citizen. I wish I had asked more about her life living between two cultures but there were other things on my mind. In any case, we somehow hooked up though I cannot for the life of me recall how. Apparently, even a first-class schmuck gets lucky on occasion. Now, I do remember going with her to the Christmas Party at the American Embassy. We doubled with the Peace Corps Doctor whose date was the nurse who assisted him at the central office, an attractive Asian woman who shared a living arrangement with my date. I recall thinking this was a coup, getting to crash the Embassy party where there would be great food and drink. And I was with a live woman, the best kind."

"And so unlike his usual dates." Paul threw out.

"You are one lucky SOB, Corbett," Mel added.

"Seems that way, Mel, doesn't it? Let me straighten you out on one thing, though. Being a sex object is not all fun and games. It may look like it to all of you gals in 44-A who have never been cursed with this affliction, but let me tell you…"

"Forget the barf bag," Laura cried out.

"A gun! A gun! Did anyone find a gun?" Dee added.

"I'm just saying, being a stud is harder than it looks." I tried to look stricken. "I mean you have all these women throwing themselves at you." I saw a couple of hands being raised, primed with pretzels as missiles. I spoke quickly to forestall any imminent launch.

"All we need is a sharp knife," Nanette asserted. "Surely we have some of those."

———

"Alright! Calm down. Let me start at the beginning. I remember what may well have been my first date with this gal, which was kind of a double date with the other couple being her apartment mate and some other PC guy though not from our group. He and I were invited over to their place for dinner. For the life of me, I cannot recall how I even got this far. She must have taken the initiative. I was like I am now… terribly shy."

"Really, no one has found that gun yet." Surprisingly, this came from Maureen, who typically remained circumspect.

"Is anyone looking?" Nanette asked. "Someone check in the kitchen for rat poison."

"I'm serious about that. Guys that look together on the outside can be crippled inside. That was me, though I cannot imagine I ever looked very together at any time."

Several of the women from 44-A looked at me intently, assessing whether this was more BS. Finally, Connie said, "Go ahead."

"Thanks. Damn, I wish I had kept journals like Mel, just to verify some of the details."

"You mean evidence of your delusions," a female voice uttered quickly.

"Seriously, I am trying to recall things accurately. No matter, that evening turned out nice, great in fact, at least in memory. After dinner, this other guy left, either voluntarily or not. Never could figure out what he was thinking. I never would have left his date, she was hot."

"If she was that hot, you wouldn't have had a shot with her." Bob tried.

"Good point, Robert. Time for another entry in my book." I stared at him with what I hoped was a menacing look, but he appeared unaffected. Go figure! "Anyway, my date, it should be pointed out, was attractive as well. Make no mistake on that score. Her roommate was simply more, how should I put it, exotic. In any case, despite my history of failure with women I remained hopeful that I might get lucky this night. Hope over experience and all that. Really, how many times in a row can a guy get shot down? This must have been just before the Embassy holiday party, maybe she was just looking for a date for that event and that's why she was being nice. That would explain a lot. Oh shoot, I should have taken notes."

"Oh Tom, nothing can explain a girl being nice to you." Connie shook her head. "Just think about it. Why wouldn't she go for some guy who would not be required to wear a bag over his head in public. You know, for the sake of public decency and the good of society. After all, this event was at the Embassy, they must have standards there."

I pointed toward my latest nemeses. "Excellent point, Connie, and remind me later to send a sympathy card to your long-suffering spouse. He must endure a lot from a woman who has delusions of such wit. Whatever the reason for her lack of judgment on this occasion, I was most appreciative of her solicitous attitude toward me. I was always grateful for any crumb thrown my way by those of the female persuasion. Ever notice those guys when we were young who would finally score and then belittle the gal who had been kind to them. That infuriated me, I wanted to slap those morons upside the head. Don't do things that reduce the already sparse supply of sexual favors. What idiots these guys were."

Bob now growled menacingly. "Corbett, your wandering again."

"Oops, my bad! So, by this time in our enforced celibacy, a coatrack standing in the corner would look extremely sexy to me. Still, I was cautious, not being sure of her intentions or interests. At some point, I suggestively told her that she struck me as being rather shy and reserved. Did she want me to leave? I was not about to take any unwanted liberties and I was having my usual doubts that an evening of carnal excess might materialize. They seldom did and why would this night be different? But then she whispered in my ear words that all men want to hear..." I paused for effect.

"What words, you asshole?" Harry made a fist toward me.

"In a sexy voice she whispered in my ear *just wait until we are alone, you won't be disappointed.*' To this day, I have no idea how I didn't collapse with cardiac arrest on the spot, or at least wet myself."

"So, what happened?" Harry asked impatiently.

"Harry, no drooling now. I am permitted to drool but not you. In any case, after this other clown left, her roommate disappeared whereupon we retreated to her bedroom where the night of carnal delights began."

"Hmm, I wonder how she would describe that night?" Cate murmured skeptically.

"Shush and listen. You begged me to tell the story after all."

"Who begged? I don't remember any begging." Cate tried. "Anyone remember any begging?"

"Just shush. Well, I stayed with her during that holiday season. She would go off to work in the morning after which their help, domestic assistance was cheap after all, would make me breakfast. I remember some other volunteers coming around to get me for a pick-up football game, a bunch were in town for Christmas. I tried not to gloat about my good fortune, but inside I was thinking something like... *that's right losers, I got lucky and you didn't.* I know that sounds cruel, but it so seldom happened to me. I deserved a victory dance in the end zone. The Germans call it *schadenfreude*."

"Victory dance? I'm going to puke." Janice even looked ill.

"Wait," Laura asked. "I thought this was a bad story in some way. Aside from what this poor gal endured by being stuck with you, where is the pain? It sounds like heaven for you, much better than you deserve."

"True enough, true enough, except that I am Irish."

"So?" Mel inquired.

"You surely don't understand if you have to ask. We suffer from a well-known *'Celtic curse.'* It is a black cloud that follows us around."

"So, just how does this curse work?" Ben asked.

"Good question. It goes like this. For every little bit of good fortune or happiness that comes our way, we just know we must pay a price. There is a scale of justice hovering over each Irish man's life, I can't speak about the women, a species that continues to baffle me. However, if an Irish man stumbles on to some pleasure, he knows there is a price to be paid. The pendulum must be balanced in the end even if it swings hard in one direction on occasion. No net happiness for Tom. Shit, I think the freaking Irish invented the very concept of Hell."

"Glad to hear it." Maureen said.

"Hear what, exactly" I asked.

"Oh, not that thing about the Irish inventing Hell… more that you realize you must pay for the terrible life you have led." Then she asked. "And just what was your karmic penalty to be paid in this instance?"

"Oh, I think I knew right from the start. Even a nimrod like me could figure out what my attraction to this female was. It wasn't my charm and sex appeal though now I can look back and see that I was not the ugliest cuss on the block." I was shocked that none of the females present guffawed at my modest boast. "However, it is totally true that I didn't see that at the time. I was convinced I was unappealing physically. I mean, you gals all ignored me."

"Yes," Janice spoke up while grinning broadly, "we voted on this. Should we all avoid Corbett? It was unanimous, one voice vote."

Then Dee added, "Didn't even require a discussion as I recall."

"Yeah, I get it. Corbett is a pariah. As if I didn't know that. So, given that universally recognized fact, any woman that didn't shoot me down upon first contact, like Connie did, must have an ulterior motive that I hadn't figured out yet. I just needed to figure out what her angle was."

At that moment, Kay came to my defense, likely out of Christian values. I believe she had mentioned at one point that several of her relatives had become priests and nuns. "Despite all the ribbing we give you, Tom, you were quite handsome."

"Kay!" Laura gasped, throwing a pretzel at her sister-in-arms. "We need a united front here." Then Laura turned to me. "So, what was this woman's ulterior motive? Did she demand money from you? That doesn't seem likely. None of us had money back then."

"Hah, hah, not in the short term of course but you are on the right track." I again paused for effect, making them wait for the denouement of my ambiguous comment. This time everyone waited. "Simple, really, she wanted to snag an American and get to America. Here we were, a parade of likely schmucks flowing through Delhi before her and all she had to do was pick out the biggest PC volunteer schmuck of them all. And guess who shows up? You got it, the biggest-looking schmuck of all time... clueless Corbett. Here was a doofus even dumber than the India-40 mutts. Ta-da!"

"Why, you must have been a perfect schmuck." Connie squealed, doubling over in laughter.

"Yup. Into her life comes Corbett, horny and not the brightest bulb on the marquee. Surely not the swiftest arrow in the quiver, not the sharpest knife in the drawer. Definitely not the..."

"We got it, we got it. You were an idiot… are an idiot." Paul added. "But even you were smart enough to figure out her game. You have many faults, but you were never totally brain dead."

"True enough, her motives would have been difficult to miss. Really, why else would she be interested? It wasn't my six-feet-one, one hundred and seventy pounds of twisted steel and sex appeal. No female ever seemed interested in that."

"I don't know." Cate suddenly looked guilty, as if about to commit a sin. "I agree with Kay. You weren't disgusting back then, not like now."

———

It struck me that this dialogue was beginning to explore the mysterious male psyche. This was a topic that, while primitive and more suited to survival in a Neanderthal tribal context, women yet found fascinating. I thought males simple… eat, sex, drink, sleep, and then repeat. But those of the female persuasion kept looking for deeper meanings in us guys. How futile! As I looked about the room at the women of 44-A, I nevertheless wondered what prompted females to agree to share the planet with us? Did they believe we could be domesticated at long last? These were ancient questions that women probably pondered when they went off to public rest rooms in pairs. Men seldom considered similar questions about females. We are too simple and shallow, focusing mostly on sating our own immediate physical needs. I recalled Maslow's famous hierarchy of human needs, a pyramid shaped representation that starts with the basic ones at the bottom and moves up to higher order dimensions. That works for females. For males, there is only the bottom layer… the primitive animal needs.

"After this exquisite enjoyment of carnal delights, I am back in my village, thinking myself safe. No foolish promises made, several hundred miles between us, just wonderful memories of these erotic evenings to keep me comfort in my lonely and desolate situation. Oh, there were letters from her to which I responded with oh, so careful language. This is always a delicate operation, feeding a female on the prowl just enough positives to keep her pride intact without betraying one's future independence. And if one were talented enough, future erotic evenings might come to pass while maintaining expedient avenues of escape."

"Escape? Escape from what?" Maureen blurted out.

"From what? From paying the ultimate price of course."

"He means marriage." Connie shook her head.

"Yes, of course marriage. Though I was clueless about women, I had been a psych major in college. I absorbed something about the complexities of the human animal. Also, I liked women, a lot, and not just sexually. I'm being honest here. My best friends in college were women, very smart women. They were more interesting than the guys, deeper in their thoughts. The trick was to keep it asexual which was not hard in my case. Sex just complicated things. Okay, it could be sexual if you could keep it non-romantic. I had the gift of doing that, being quick witted. Just born with that talent I suppose."

"Quick witted, my ass. More like being a plug-ugly moron helped you keep things asexual." Bob said to general laughter.

"Bite me, asshole. I was just kinda ugly. And by the way, I've made an appointment to redo my will next week. I had considered leaving some of my vast fortune to some old mates, so maybe you want to be nice to me for a change."

"Well, I agree with those who thought you cute back then." Dee realized her slip. "Oops, didn't mean to say that."

"Dee! What are you thinking? She's probably had too much to drink, shut her off." Laura seemed concerned for her sister volunteer.

Dee dug in. "Oh, come on girls, he did have that sexy Kennedy accent. We all thought so. And he had all his hair back then."

"No matter the truth of the situation," I sighed with emphasis. "I was attractive enough, or more likely clueless-looking enough, for her to give me a shot. I must have been vague in any subsequent correspondence with her. My thought was how to keep her sufficiently interested to invite future carnal adventures without giving away the store."

"Typical pig." Laura summarized to murmurs of assent from the females present.

"No, desperate male. Thing is, I thought I was doing a decent job of it until one day…" My voice trailed off.

"One day…what?" Harry prompted.

"One day, someone showed up at our door in Salumbar. They said I had a phone call in town, at the post office. It was one of the few phones around and neither Ralph nor I had ever gotten a call there or anywhere. They didn't know who was calling so my mind raced as I jumped on my Superman bike and raced the mile or two to where the mystery might be resolved. I was sure that one of my parents had died or some similar tragedy had occurred. Maybe my last medical checks came back, and I had a week to live. Or, more likely, Delhi was calling to tell me to pack my bags and get out, just for being a hopeless putz. What else would prompt such a call?"

"It was her, wasn't it? She really was that desperate? Oh, the poor girl." Nanette sounded as if she was sharing a universal female tragedy.

"Yup, the dreaded Celtic curse had struck. She was in Udaipur. She had taken the time and effort to come there in the hope I might join her. Oh my god, this was horrific."

"Maybe she was just horny." Harry tried.

"Oh, for Christ sakes, be serious my friend. She was moving in for the kill. I remember listening to my heart sink as I frantically thought through various responses. You know, would she buy some story about there being a crop emergency? Could I feign death, right there on the phone. I mean, I really did feel like dying in that moment."

"I would have lent you a hand at that." Laura added without a hint of a smile.

"What did you do?" Connie asked.

"What I did was get on a bus and travel the 60 or 70 so kilometers to Udaipur. Yup, that Irish black cloud had arrived as scheduled to bite me in the ass. That was the longest trip to Udaipur ever, and I needed every kilometer. By the time I arrived, I had convinced myself to be strong. No sex, no physical contact even. I would just explain that, while I liked her a lot, I was not ready for a commitment. But we would always have those special moments… blah, blah, blah! Maybe she would take Ralph. He was a nice guy, and funny. She should move on in any case. If not Ralph, there were many fish in the sea, all far better than me, an argument that had the advantage of being true. Yes, I had a wonderful line worked out, to let her down with grace and sensitivity. The words were plausible and soothing, if totally disingenuous. And if that didn't work, there was crying and begging to be employed. I'm good at weeping copious tears."

"Why do I suspect you screwed things up… no pun intended. Okay, intended." Mel had a satisfied look on his face.

"Wait, you think I am so shallow and weak? Do you really think so little of me that I would immediately cave to my base carnal desires? You actually believe I am that craven?"

"Yes." Several said at the same time.

"You're right. Once we were alone in her room, I must have held out for three to five seconds before we were tearing each other's clothes off. If it is any consolation to you gals, I hated myself as I was doing it. Do you have any idea of the internal conflict when pleasure and guilt are maximized? Yikes… just put a bullet into my head. I wanted to at that moment… use a gun on myself that is. How could I be so weak, so lacking in discipline. But, alas, I was."

"Wait," Nanette raised her hand, "you continued to lead her on, use her? You really are a pig."

"Of course I'm a pig. Hey, I'm a guy after all. Isn't that the very definition of an oinker, look it up in Webster's dictionary. But, I also am honest, especially when it counts. Must be that Catholic thing.

You can leave the Church, but the guilt remains, and certainly the Celtic curse.”

“So true.” Kay agreed.

“When reason finally returned to my so-called brain, I did get around to suggesting that she could do much better than me. Any female could. That had the virtue of being beyond dispute. Hell, that was no stretch at all. In the male talent pool, I was hardly the cream that rises to the top… more like the crap that curdles into a putrid offal which settles to the bottom. There is no way now that I can recall how I told her or what I said exactly. The brain is a very protective organ. It conveniently buries traumatic moments somewhere they cannot be retrieved. Well, at some point she gave up. It was tough, though I don’t recall many tears, if any. Perhaps she knew it had been a long shot or had been through this before. Still, I looked about for sharp objects and was careful never to turn my back on her. Before it was over, she inserted one more virtual knife into my raw conscience just to heighten my guilt and pain.”

“Good!” Came from several women.

“Glad to see that the sisterhood remains united. Yeah, at some point she suggested that she had become pregnant but used a ‘morning after’ pill to deal with this unwanted consequence of lust… mine that is. My recall of this is sketchy, probably repressed. I sense more than remember this. I was taken aback that she was not on the pill and, at the same time, dumb enough to be surprised that there was such a remedy. I had no concept as to how it might work. Therefore, I never knew what to make of her comments. This was a long time ago, not all that long after the pill became generally available which, by the way, was developed in my hometown.”

“Really?” Someone expressed mild surprise.

“Oh yes, another contribution from Worcester.”

“What was the first?” Mel asked.

“Isn’t it obvious,? Me, of course. Anyway, researchers from my college were involved in developing the birth control pill but the work was done in some non-descript building outside of town.

I think the University, or at least those working on this, feared enraged Catholics would storm the campus if such news leaked. By the way, I note all this since Worcester is located smack in the middle of Catholic orthodoxy. How ironic is that? And the trials were done in Puerto Rico, even more Catholic but away from immediate political danger."

"Corbett…" Bob continued to keep me on track.

"Ah, yes, back to my dilemma. I assumed she would have access to medical supplies through her nurse roommate. And yet, I cannot wonder if this was one final push to snag me, it is hard not to be cynical in these matters. Besides, I knew I was destined never to have children."

"You did? At that age?" Maureen queried. "Were you sterile? If so, then she lied about the pregnancy?"

"No, no, I wasn't medically sterile, as far as I knew at least. Still, I had scientific evidence of the best kind that I would remain without issue."

"Oh God, I'm afraid to ask." Maureen moaned.

"I'll bite," Dee jumped in. "What kind of evidence?"

"An incontrovertible method indeed. You see, early in my teens I underwent this test to predict how many children I would have later in life… quite an objective test indeed. Several of the local girls used it."

"The local girls used it?" Cate looked at me dubiously. "I take it no trip to a doctor was involved nor science of any kind."

"No, no, just listen." I scoffed. "A girl would tie a needle to the piece of thread. They would place the thread against a carefully selected finger on a young man's hand and raise it slowly. For every time it swung in a circle clockwise, you were destined to have one boy, counterclockwise one girl. Some poor bastards were destined to have a dozen or more. My needle never swung, never moved. It always remained immobile, much to the dismay of the young ladies dreaming of motherhood one day, and most were in the pre-feminist days of the late 50s. This was back in prehistoric times when motherhood was the dominant avocation for young persons of the female persuasion. Don't forget, this was before Betty Friedan established that all males were irredeemable pigs."

"You probably inspired Betty to write her damn book." Laura was pleased with her witticism.

"Nope, I was too young. Back to science. No matter how often they tried… they got nothing. My needle never moved even after working as intended on the other poor schmucks on my street. I was ecstatic. Siring a future Tommy Corbett never struck me as a good idea. All who knew me heartily agreed. Unfortunately, this foolproof test couldn't tell me whether I would impregnate a woman where the pregnancy never came to term. Not much longer after returning to the States, I affirmed this prediction by getting a vasectomy, thus guaranteeing the accuracy of this teen-girl test."

"Probably an excellent decision on your part, for the wellbeing of society that is." Paul nodded.

"No shit, can you even imagine more guys from my gene pool running around. Lock up your daughters and wives. The way I handled all this probably could have been better." I ignored the guffaws about me. "I can well imagine this woman and her roommate ripping apart this total wanker named Corbett, a name taken in vain by legions of women throughout the world. One thing was certain, my personal mountain of guilt grew a little higher, as if that were possible. Isn't there a song that goes on about *there ain't no mountain high enough?*' I think that song must be about the Catholic boys of my generation. All I know is that I wake up each day and the first thing I do is apologize."

Connie didn't look convinced. "Wait, did you get a vasectomy because of this affair? That sounds extreme."

"My formal reasons were born in my logical mind. I told myself things like the world was a harsh place and I was reluctant to bring another child into it. More to the point, I felt totally unequipped to be a parent, and related things along those lines. Really, parenting struck me as so damn hard. But this incident brought one thing into focus. My logical self would always battle against my hormones. I could never be assured that logic would win; hormones are damn powerful. Mistakes do happen. Since I cannot be guaranteed that rationality would always prevail, better to take the possible mistakes of the table. See what I mean?"

No one responded but I was sure they saw my point. It was obvious to me.

—

"And that was the end?" Mel asked. "The end of your liaison that is."

"Pretty much, though I do have a recollection of getting together again, but that is vague. Then, I remember one more evening toward the end of our stay in India, some PC party in Delhi. Her apartment mate, that Asian looking nurse I mentioned, was there and very friendly that evening. I must admit she had made a couple of suggestive comments to me over time. And yes, I did find her quite attractive, striking even. She was more along the physical type that attracted me… black hair and olive or ebony colored skin. I remember thinking in the moment that it was too bad I hadn't hooked up with her as opposed to her flat mate. Should I give her a shot now?"

"Corbett, you're a pig!" Laura groaned.

"Oh, I did nothing. First, how would I manage that given my past with her roommate? More to the point, there was no way I was risking another broken promise or, worse, taking a wife home with me. That was never going to happen unless I found she could support me in the manner that I fantasized about. However, if she could do that, what in God's name would she want with me?"

"At least you were sensitive enough to feel guilty about what you did." Dee smiled sympathetically.

Bob shook his head as he added. "Sensitive? Really Dee. He was a real shit."

"*Et tu*, Robert? As if you were any different."

"Hey, you were getting some while the rest of us weren't." he smiled grimly. "Talk about freaking *schadenfreude.*"

"I suppose. I will tell you what bothered me in the end. If I had been no more than a calculated move to improve her life, my guilt would be less. If that was true, I was merely her meal-ticket to a better life. She took her best shot and failed. I assumed there would be other opportunities for her, other horny Peace Corps schmucks coming down the road. One of them would work out for her, at least I hoped that at the time, for her sake."

"That's something" Cate agreed.

"I figured there are guys who want to get married, for real. I've met a couple. I have no idea why, but they exist. On the other hand, what if she had fallen for me, really? That would be hard to take. Fortunately, that never seemed possible in my world. A lifetime of unsettling experiences with the fair sex had left my self-esteem somewhat below that of the common anteater, likely the grossest animal around whose daily diet yet was an improvement over mine. It did seem highly unlikely that anyone could love a schmuck like me?"

"Excellent point" Paul chimed in. "My wife saw right through you."

"See, exhibit number one, and look who she settled for. I was ranked below a mutt from India-40 of all things. It doesn't get worse than that. Agreed?"

"Well, good point there." Nanette agreed.

"I mean, whenever a girl expressed interest, I was always suspicious. What are they after, really after? In this case, the reason was obvious… economic security. But think about it. How would I support any spouse? My prospects at the time seemed dim indeed. Who would hire a nimrod like me? The only freaking skill I had was debeaking a chicken. I would think about my affair with this gal and conclude she was damn lucky in the end. She could have been stuck supporting this loser… not a pretty fate."

"Wait," Maureen protested. "You wound up with a great job at a major university."

"True, but there was no prospect of that back then. I mean, I still have no freaking idea how I wound up at the University of Wisconsin, as a Senior Scientist who helped run a major research unit no less. No, I was a bad choice for any female then. I mean, my college love saw that. I would like to think this gal did much better in the future. She did have quite a bit going for her."

"Oh please," Maureen scoffed. "She slept with you."

"And for free." Mel added.

"Exactly," Laura chimed in. "So how much could she have had going for her."

"Excellent point." I sighed heavily. "So, back to that party in Delhi toward the end of our days. She and I talked at length. I was most gratified that she conveyed no lingering hostility. I must admit, for a moment or two I hoped she might take pity on me that night. At the same time, I desperately hoped she would not. How pathetic was I? There, in a nutshell, is the classic male dilemma… hormones versus common sense. My memory was that she was interested but kept me at arm's length. I was so relieved. Maybe that's what the Celtic curse is all about. It keeps us from swinging too far from the straight and narrow. Perhaps we sons of Eire do have a shot at heaven after all."

"Really? You think so?" One of the gals from 44-A murmured. "I doubt that."

I ignored the jibe. "What bothered me that night was a thought. She probably realized that she only had so much time to catch one of these schmucks and she wasted some of her allotted time on me. Suddenly, I felt quite sad, and even more guilty. Then again, I often felt that way, being Irish and all."

"Gee, Tom, you really were damaged goods." Cate said.

"No shit, Sherlock."

Cate continued. "Perhaps we gals from 44-A should have taken more pity on you?"

"Noooo!" Came the chorus of cries once again.

"Just remember, it is never too late." I said with my most salacious smile.

Apparently, it was too late. Pretzels rained down on me. The pile at me feet was now above my ankles. I picked a few up and started munching.

Perhaps my feeling of relief had been unwarranted. I concluded, though, that I was not in real danger as my internal clock told me it was time to shift gears. After all, our male erotic struggles had to be shared sparingly, if for no other reason than to prevent an uprising among those of the female orientation in our Peace Corps family. In truth, we guys were mostly past caring about matters like romance and sex. I would guess our tanks of testosterone were heading toward empty. Our youthful sensual exploits, and their inevitable futility, always were good for a few chuckles. Only in measured doses though, even as I rather enjoyed getting attacked by the distaff side of our group. It was like elementary school all over again when we would tease the girls to get a response even though we weren't sure why at the time.

Now, where should we go next?

Laura and I… one of my prime antagonists in our virtual dialogue.

*From left to right: Cate, Dee, and Connie…
more antagonists enduring my tedious stories.*

CHAPTER 17

Chick Stories

Once the most recent attack on my person had abated, I felt around but sensed no blood nor any open wounds on my person. Another dastardly attack on my person had been weathered without my premature demise.

"Personally, I am outraged at these attacks on my person." I tried to sound indignant.

"Really?" Nanette grinned.

"Yes, after all my bravery in India, I'm deserving of some respect."

"I think we need waders… the BS is rising to dangerous levels." Mel tried.

"I know! Time for one of our conventional Peace Corps triumphs." I said over the groans.

"What? We had some of those?" Harry seemed skeptical.

I sifted through some of my papers before pulling one out. "I think this one is from right around the time that I got that dear Tom letter I mentioned earlier. It has a lot of personal stuff that I am not going to share with you reprobates but there is a passage here that captures that unique Peace Corps spirit. Even better, it captures the real me back then and one of my many acts of bravery. Had Eleni not kept my notes, this moment would have been lost to history." They were hooked, I knew it.

"This ought to be priceless." Mel encouraged me.

"Damn, I only wish Ralph were here to share in this moment. We were true Peace Corps heroes. Oh good, here is one… a passage which captures the bravery and the resolve of the men of 44-B. I just might tear up. Gals, prepare yourself to be impressed by those gallant lads you worshipped from afar. Where does it start? Oh yeah, here."

Randall and I have been enduring the boredom of these last days of April until we are able to take off for the Himalayas on the 1st. today the temp was 120 degrees, a couple degrees higher than normal. But there are diversions to keep our corrupted minds occupied. For example, we just decided to finish off our favorite rat through the discriminate employment of our rational faculties. We have decided, after much thought, on the following plan.

"Oh my god, I knew it," Maureen groaned.
"Shush, all of you," I admonished. "This is a solemn moment."
I continued reading.

When the rat enters our combined living room, study, and dining room, we would: a) close the door; b) position Randall on the cot within easy striking distance of our intended victim; c) I would flush the rat from behind the combination desk and dining room table (the usual habitat of our prey); d) as the rat scurried to the safety of the other room but now finding himself trapped by the closed door, Randall would take careful aim and let fly his sneaker (especially secured for this task) and would do so with precision and accuracy, a shot which would most likely plunk me on the noggin and miss the rat entirely; e) Randall would then fall off the cot in a drunken stupor: and finally f) we would swear a lot and go back to drinking.

"Apparently, there was a pause in the letter-writing to execute this well-considered plan, since it next goes on as follows."

We just blew it. we had the rat trapped in our combination entrance hall and work room. Randall was poised as usual with sneaker while I braved risks far beyond the call of duty to flush out the bastard (the rat, not Randall) from his hiding place. But at the critical moment, my drunken site mate decided to relight his half-smoked cigarette (I think he doused it when he took a sip of his drink while forgetting to remove the cigarette from his mouth). In his rather uncoordinated state, he only succeeded in burning the tip of his nose, which sent him into some ridiculously grotesque dance of pain. As he hopped around the room, the rat took advantage of the situation to scurry to the safety of our kitchen. Well, you may have just witnessed (in a way), one of the great moments in Peace Corps history. Perhaps it is time for plan B, get a cat.

I looked up and smiled to those about me. "There you have it, what my life became after getting dumped by a woman once again, this time my college sweetheart and not the lovely Connie. I was reduced to titanic battles with your common rodent. And by the way, I believe that Ralph became a renowned exterminator of rodents after Peace Corps."

The room now filled with groans. Time to get serious.

———

"I have a legitimate chick story," I declared.

"You are a dead man." Laura warned.

"Just hang in there on this one, okay?"

The women looked deeply suspicious, but Kay came to my recue. "Let's give him a chance."

"Thanks, just trust me on this one." I tried my sincerity look. "For sure, there were moments of triumph amidst the typical routine of heat and boredom and navel gazing. We did more than just look inward by keeping ourselves somewhat occupied with a bunch of useful projects. A few of these efforts even resulted in something being accomplished. Most of all, for me at least, these projects were things I would never have done otherwise. This was a time out of time for me."

"For all of us I believe." Connie cocked her head in my direction.

"I take it you are about to regale us with an apocryphal tale of some successful endeavor," Bob said with a touch of sarcasm.

"Yes, indeed, let me focus on one such project which involved erecting a chicken coop and starting a poultry project."

"Ah, so this is the chick story. You mean real chickens." Laura laughed. "You were this close to death but managed to save yourself… again."

I just smiled. "I assume others in 44-B might have tried this since Ralph and I were not the only adventurous entrepreneurs in our group. Yes, we built our monument to egg production on the top of our government housing, so it would be visible to any who passed by. And up there, the birds would be safe from predators, which were everywhere. Our enterprise was supposed to be a beacon of hope, an inspiration to all who wanted to rise to new heights in life.

"Did it work?" Dee asked.

I looked at her blankly. "Well, I cannot recall anyone actually jumping on the chicken bandwagon. But that's not the point. The thing is, we built this edifice devoted to Peace Corps ingenuity with our own hands. Oh, a few onlookers watched in bemused wonder while chuckling at the crazy Americans. Still, I did it, we did it. Those who knew me in my youth would surely have succumbed to uncontrollable laughter at the very sight. Changing a lightbulb typically is a major achievement for a klutz like me. Building a chicken coop, on the other hand, is beyond the pale and a testament to how Peace Corps stretched me."

Mel suddenly became excited. "Yes! Bob and I tried the same thing though my effort was a disaster if the truth be told."

"Just like your efforts to lose your virginity." Dan, our soft-spoken cowboy originally from Wyoming accompanied his private aside with an audible chuckle though his allusion was not clear to most of the group.

"You guys are terrible." Maureen tried to intervene on Mel's behalf.

"No, no," I gently instructed Maureen, "this is how guys show affection for one another. Go ahead Mel. We want to hear about your stupid project, really we do. And don't mind my snoring."

"Thank you, I think." He looked at me dubiously. "I remember at some point deciding to build a chicken coop on top of my place. Like Corbett realized, security for the hens was a high priority, I was determined to do something right. But my Jain landlord objected. Eating eggs was the equivalent to murder in their view of the world. I tried to convince him of the fact that without a rooster present, there was no life to be destroyed. Alas, my biology lesson fell on deaf ears. In fact, most locals remained perplexed at the fact that eggs were forthcoming absent the presence of a rooster. Their knowledge of biology was rather primitive."

"I was only one step ahead of them." I added.

"So, no chicken coop?" Nanette asked.

Mel nodded sadly before continuing. "With my own hopes of becoming the poultry king of India dashed, Bob here went ahead and built a coop when he was in Sanwar. He was quite successful for a while. From my notes, he had some twenty-nine hens, after one became a meal I believe. As the local egg entrepreneur, he enjoyed a daily production of close to two dozen eggs at the peak of his endeavors. You can well imagine that this became our main source of protein. I mean, some eggs were sold locally, but there was a problem marketing the damn things."

Bob chimed in at this point. "It was always something in India. You might recall that foods were divided into 'hot' and 'cold' categories. The local belief was that you were to stay away from so-called hot foods during the summer, and my eggs were classified as such though only God knows why. So, the demand for my product dropped as the temps went up. Prices quickly followed. An egg went from 50NP to less than 10NP in a matter of days it seemed. My get-rich quick scheme went bust and I liquidated the business. Really, I couldn't eat that many eggs and they kept coming, day after day. Unlike sex, you can have too much of some good things."

Mel then grunted in response to another memory. "We did get a few good stories out of it though. There was this local agricultural officer who wanted to try an egg but was afraid of getting caught. They violated his cultural rules. I think we used the cook as a go between and did the exchange in the middle of the night. It was like a drug drop. Bob, remember that?"

Bob paused before responding. "Not really, but I do recall this college boy stopping by and asking if he could try one. You might have thought we were dealing crack cocaine with all the hush-hush, secrecy stuff. All went well until I made him two eggs over easy. When the yolk ran as he poked it with a fork, he bolted from the room and never returned."

"Perhaps he thought it was blood." Maureen observed.

A buried recollection then occurred to me. "Funny, I thought these cultural prescriptions provincial, old world. Yet, I recall a time when I was a kid, listening to a Jewish neighbor confess to my mother that she had cooked up bacon in her house, which was taboo apparently. She had been curious but was afraid her Jewish neighbors would smell the prohibited contraband. She sealed off her apartment before starting. She would have been subject to cultural opprobrium if found out, surely not by her Catholic neighbors but by her own tribe. We were not so different."

Mel agreed. "Good point!"

Bob picked up his story again. "I kept the egg production thing going for a long time even though few locals would eat my eggs. They were twice the size of the local variety, since I fed them the good feed imported from Udaipur. However, my eggs lacked the pungent taste of those from local hens who feasted of grubs and scraps from the ground. The lack of a rooster also put them off. They were confused as to how there could be eggs and no rooster. Perhaps they feared I was practicing Voodoo."

"You always were our spiritual guru." I threw in his direction. "Never considered you would become a Voodoo Priest though. Interesting choice."

Bob ignored me. "In any case, I decided to take the chickens and sell them in Udaipur as my days in India grew short. Since the train would not accept live cargo, I decided to use the bus. With effort, I hoisted a basket of chickens to the top of the vehicle. The bus driver then asked me to pay full fare for each chicken. *What?* I blustered, *They're all in one basket on the roof. I'm not putting each one in their own seat.* My argument fell on deaf ears, apparently, each chicken was a living being. But I did negotiate him down to half a fare for each. Any attraction to eastern spirituality had long disappeared for me by this time."

"I'm so happy to hear this," I laughed out loud. "I wasn't the only doofus trying a chicken project. I don't recall the origins of our egg industry other than it seemed like something to do when we were not trying to hunt down and kill rodents in our living quarters. We could only tramp around the fields so many times dispensing our useless advice. I know, I know, I am being too hard on myself. Nevertheless, we needed to find more things to occupy ourselves other than reading everything we could get our hands on and writing novels, which both Ralph and I did. Well, he started one and I finished mine. And don't forget, we had all that poultry training before it was decided that India didn't need our expert help in this area any longer."

"You became an author? I didn't know that. And here I've been wasting my time reading Grisham, King, and Patterson." Laura said.

"I wonder how good it was. I did get some good feedback from the couple of folk whom I bribed to look at it. I recall convincing one of the Peace Corps secretaries in the Delhi office to type up my scribbles in her spare time. Unbelievably, she did it. God, perhaps I really was charming back then. And she was cute as the dickens as I think on it. I've always wondered what she thought about it.

After all, she was Indian, and parts of my work-in-progress were racy indeed. She never commented on the sexy parts, but I feared she thought of me as a typically debauched American pervert. She always pulled out a can of mace when I approached."

"Everyone did." Laura deadpanned. "And no one read your book."

As I smiled at Laura, I toyed with going more deeply into how much developing that manuscript meant to me. It would not be until late in life that I rediscovered my love of writing outside the rigid, ritualistic prose imposed within the academy. While I generated tons of academic and policy papers and chapters, personal writing is something special and became critical to who I was late in my life. Instead, all I said was, "If I ever find that manuscript, you can try plodding through it."

"I'd love to see it, seriously." Cate added with no hint of sarcasm showing.

"So would I… see it again that is. I'm afraid it might have been discarded at some point with a pile of used boxer shorts. But I'm working on new stuff in retirement." I looked at Cate for another moment before deciding to get back on track. I'm always surprised when women are nice to me.

"Let me know when you have stuff to share." She added.

———

I turned back to my storytelling. "The only writing I have from that era is the letters to Leni. In addition to being a reminder of lost love, they are my only link to what I was experiencing back then. As we all know, the physical hardships were real enough. After a comparatively pleasant winter, the temperatures would rise day after day, week after week. By April, the heat was overwhelming, surrounding us with a debilitating torpor that sapped our energy. Well, listen to this next passage from one letter to her. It brings that reality back in a visceral way."

"Welcome from the world's original blast furnace. Summer is here and the Loo, the hot, dry summer winds have begun to sweep across our developing desert. The temperature averages about 110 degrees now, but fortunately it is a dry, more tolerable kind of heat. The only difficulty here is that as soon as you step out into the intense sunlight, the moisture is literally sucked right out of you, leaving your skin with the texture of a dried prune.

As you would imagine, we are not getting out very often. Since the harvests are in there really isn't much to do. As an index of our paucity of work, I've devoured four books and started a fifth (Ulysses) in the past five days. This is the worst time of year. Beyond the heat and the boredom, the incidence of diarrhea and dysentery rises sharply. And a host of unsavory beasts (cobras and scorpions) begin to appear. It is truly the time that tries men's souls, both Indian and American alike."

I looked up from the pages in my lap. Boredom was the enemy. We needed something to do other than our so-called official jobs, which simply would not keep us occupied. Over time we engaged in several misadventures but becoming poultry experts was a popular diversion. If only Peace Corps had not dashed my hopes of working in public health. After all, I had cut my teeth on ministering to the sick and dying during my labors on the 11-7 hospital shift during my college years. I enjoyed the work or was it the nurses I favored. Okay, now I'm not sure which. But PC was a bit like the army as I understand the military. If you don't know a thing about tools, you are likely to wind up in the motor pool. Can't cook worth a damn, you'll end up making meals for hundreds of hungry soldiers."

"Good point." Stan offered, our one member with military experience.

"When we started training, we thought that you would be punished if you didn't obey. You would be deselected. I think back to that day when I was told I would be a chicken farmer. That sounded about as exciting as being told I would spend the next two years doing rectal exams. But I was too insecure to plead my case. Perhaps if I had, I would have been reassigned to 44-A. Wouldn't that have been simply great." I looked at the women in the room with this huge smile.

"Oh god. We were spared." Came from one gal.

"Thank you, Lord," from another.

"I would have slit my wrists," sighed a third.

"I knew you would be excited." I raised my hand to forestall further sentiments by women expressing a desire for suicide over the prospect of any time at all with Corbett.

"I wonder if there had ever been a group with a 100 percent self-deselection rate?" Laura asked.

"No matter, I went along meekly with the damn chicken assignment and soon I was engrossed in learning the intricacies of this poultry thing. I just knew I was absorbing skills that I would use the rest of my life. Come on, guys, admit it. What would we have done in life had we not learned how to debeak a chicken or learned the seven deadly diseases that impair egg production? Really, didn't you guys find it a great pick-up line? Hey babe, why don't you come up to my place and I'll de-beak a chicken for you."

"You would have had me for sure with that one." Dee squealed with laughter.

"Do you remember that we had this chicken coop somewhere in the recesses of the Milwaukee campus where we honed our skills. I don't recall much of what we learned though I have a vivid memory of having to kill a chicken at one point. We had other such tests, like giving each other injections. Back to the chickens, I believe we were supposed to axe the bird's head off without upchucking. At the time, I thought puking one's guts out would get you sent home. There was this one trainee, Dick, from Kansas who had been raised on a farm of all things. He knew all kinds of useful stuff. He said there was an easier way to do this, then picked up a chicken and twirled it in such a way that its neck broke. Unfortunately, he left our group after getting to India but before being assigned to a site. His departure had nothing to do with chicken killing as I recall. I think he got word that his stateside girlfriend was pregnant. Hmm, I wonder if he made the right choice in returning home."

"What?" Connie eyed me with that special form of female opprobrium that all males recognized.

I saw yet another uprising possibly brewing and quickly moved on. "Back to chickens, just think about this. You're driving down a country road and see a family pulled over and in distress. You stop to help. They are about to have lunch, like a picnic, but only have a live chicken for food. No one in the family knows what to do. You smile, take the squawking bird, and fling it about as you saw Dick do so many years before. You present them with one dead bird, ready for plucking. A hungry family is forever grateful. These are the moments we former volunteers live for."

"Corbett, is there no end to your BS?" Paul shook his head.

"True, I am a gift to humanity."

"Any other skills, oh wise one." Dee asked sarcastically.

"Let me think. Oh yeah, we learned how to hypnotize a chicken? Yes!" That thought suddenly begged to be shared. "We did, I'm sure. You place the bird's head on the ground and then draw a line in the dirt away from its gaze. You can release the head and the bird just lies there in a trance. She is putty in your hands. It is an amazing and potentially useful technique. I assume it still is, by that I mean that it still works."

"I hesitate to ask," Cate said, "but just how did you use this skill in later life? You might remember that I did some training in poultry with you guys and I don't remember this."

"Gee, I don't know about the rest of the guys, but I knew very well that this skill was transferrable to more practical contexts and, in the right situation, absolutely essential."

"What do you mean?" Cate persisted, then immediately regretted her curiosity when she saw my devious smile appear.

"Well, I would be in a bar with a young lady. As usual, I could tell she was not being bowled over by my charms. Really, how did they resist? So, I would ask her to place her head on the surface of the bar, usually after several beers. Then I would spill a bit of beer on the surface in front of her vertical eyes and draw a line in the liquid just like that line in the sand for a chicken."

"Oh, for god's sake." Maureen sniffed.

"Did it ever work?" Harry asked, looking interested.

"Are you nuts, of course not. I always had to buy them several more beers."

"How about we move back to India, before the gals resort to human sacrifice." Mel suggested just in time. "I believe Laura is in the kitchen looking for some extra-sharp, serrated knives."

"Of course," I said, appreciating his insight into my precarious position. "so, after Ralph and I decided to build a coop on our roof, probably after a night of heavy drinking, we got the bricks and wire netting and tiles for a roof and went for it. I had zero manual labor skills, while my site mate was only marginally better. Now, my father had many practical skills. Unfortunately, I inherited none...not even one. Once, he built a birdhouse which I entered in some contest as mine. I was just a kid at the time. It won a prize, just a silly ribbon, but I felt guilty as hell. Obviously, that guilt is still with me."

"You really are Catholic." Dan observed.

"No shit... a cultural one at least," I nodded toward him. "Maybe this coop thing was an attempt to redeem myself. I recall we were working away, building this monument to Peace Corps ingenuity on the roof of our government housing. Several locals came by to watch including several government officials. There were the usual jokes made at our expense, a few chuckles, but at least one of the officials came to our defense. He chided the others to lay off and give us a break, we were trying to learn something. Yup, his defense of us was like our efforts to be ag experts, we were there to learn how to raise chicken for when we would return to the States. And yet, we carried on and built one damn fine-looking chicken coop."

"Good for you." Maureen said without a hint of sarcasm. "And you got eggs I assume."

"Oh yes, the high moment of the chicken coop project is described below in another letter to Leni." Again, I rustled through my file and pulled out a letter.

Well, the miracle of miracles has just occurred. No, it is not the second coming. The fact is that we are now the proud owners of egg laying chickens. That's right! Ralph has just suffered a case of apoplexy screaming for me to come up to the roof. There, praise to God, was an egg which one of our chickens had the audacity to lay. You may say that that I am perhaps exaggerating the importance of this event. Well, perhaps it is true that we do so little right here that we are grasping at straws. Besides, our veracity and claims to expertise had come under question. We had stated on numerous occasions that chickens were capable of laying eggs without cohabitating with their male counterparts (our course in poultry raising was complete with appropriate references to analogous human female functions). This now vindicates our righteousness and enhances our claims to omniscience.

"See, our early training did not go to waste in the least. Unlike Bob or Mel, I did not keep track of egg production or prices, but we had a going concern for quite a while until disaster struck."

"Should I ask?" someone said.

"Simple enough ending. During the summer months, we went on vacation to escape the deadly heat and left our crack staff in charge. The hens were dead on our return. I guess the heat really was deadly, though we probably would have kept them sufficiently hydrated had we remained in town. In any case, we certainly did not repeat the experiment. Like Bob, what do you do with so many eggs day after day? I can't recall for sure, but I believe we experienced similar marketing challenges."

"Still," Maureen tried to support me. "You learn something even in failure. Right?"

I laughed. "You might be correct. I learned I should never start my own business later in life. Either that or perhaps this was the perfect metaphor for our time in India. I should think on that."

—

Kay usually was quiet. When she cleared her throat, everyone looked at her expectantly. "Strangely enough, I have a chicken story."

"Thank God." Maureen, said. "These men are wearisome."

Kay started her story. "Janice and I were stationed together until she went off and got married to another volunteer."

"Hey, there is a thought. I could have traded Ralph for one of you lucky gals." I was silenced by several cold stares that said, in effect, *'one more word and you'll be singing in the Vienna boys' choir, got that nimrod.'* Why was I such a slow learner?

"Before Janice left, we had an adventure on our cook's day off. Bored with our vegetarian meals and hungry for fried chicken, we decided to kill one of the chickens we had, the one that was not producing very many eggs. Although the 44-B group had poultry training, we had none."

"Like any of us could have helped." One of the guys said.

"In any case, Janice recalled that her grandmother used to wring the chicken's neck, so she took on that task. She says that I kept grimacing and saying *'ooh, Janice, ooh,'* but I have no memory of that. I probably repressed that part. My chore was to pluck the feathers as the chicken looked at me with one pleading eye. Janice cut up the chicken as we pumped up the kerosene stove and heated the peanut oil. We set the table with a tablecloth, played a Simon and Garfunkle tape, and sat down to eat. This was intended to be a feast for a queen. I don't recall who took the first bite, but we chewed and chewed until we gave up, realizing that it was inedible.

Before we could cry after all that work and still no fried chicken, we had to bury the feathers and the debris so that Banabai, our domestic help, would not figure out that we had slaughtered the chicken and consumed the meat, or tried to at least. She was Hindu, a vegetarian, and we tried to respect local customs. Much later, after I was back in the States and married, I received a book on how to kill and prepare a chicken."

"Someone gave you that?" Dee looked shocked.

"I know, really, but I found it useful in that I realized our mistakes in the chicken meal fiasco. We had neglected to drain the blood, we should have dipped the chicken in hot, boiling water to loosen the feathers and, most critical of all, we should not have started with a diseased chicken. There was a reason it was a poor egg producer."

"How did we not all perish." Nanette said with a chuckle.

I shook my head. "I agree. How in God's name did we not all die? I remember Ralph and I asking Rooknot to get us chickens, dead and plucked ones that is. This was done on extremely rare occasions. It never, ever tasted as we imagined it would. I fact, I'm having trouble recalling what the experience was like. In any case, we mostly stayed vegetarian or with mutton."

Ben nodded his head. "If we wanted chicken, we all went to Udaipur, to Berry's Restaurant. That was decent." Several heads from the B-gang could be seen nodding approval.

"Yeah," I exclaimed with enthusiasm, "but there is a bright side Kay."

"What's that?" She looked at me questioningly.

"Well, now you can prepare and cook a chicken from scratch if society ever collapses."

She looked at me sadly. "No, I'd probably just starve to death."

"No, the bright side is," I gave her my best smile, "that we would go together."

"Oy Vey" she said. Apparently, that was not the bright side for her.

Our chicken coop project.

CHAPTER 18

Exotic India

I brokered a momentary lull in the conversation by cleverly shifting topics once again. "You know, women aren't the only mystery in life, though I admit to being utterly baffled by them."

"How so?" Dee queried and immediately regretted her rashness.

"For one thing, it is a complete mystery how you manage to keep your hands off me." Several pretzels arced in my direction, but I deftly evaded them all. "Speaking of actual mysteries, though, let us consider some of the strange things we stumbled across in India. I'll bet we all brought away with us a sense of awe about the place. We all must have stories.

"Good topic!" Tim suggested. "You raised it so why don't you start us off."

"Fair enough." I paused to run through the catalogue of vignettes that cluttered my mind to the exclusion of useful information. "Okay, I recall this legend involving a former local Raj in Salumbar. A long time ago, he was called to battle against some invaders by the big man in Udaipur or perhaps by the even bigger man in Jaipur. Just think of Europe when it had a society structured around a hierarchical set of mutual obligations governing the land. Salumbar, though a small and remote place, was large enough to have its own Prince, with a modest palace and everything. As in any such feudal society, it was his duty to go to war when demanded of him by someone further up the power food chain."

Mel enjoyed military history and got into the swing of the new topic. "Just like our European medieval period, when the lower

Princes paid homage to the more powerful ones all the way up the ladder to the king."

"Exactly! But there was a problem in this instance. The local Prince had just married and could not make himself leave his beautiful new bride. Several times he started out, only to return to ask for another remembrance of her. She would dutifully hand over some article of clothing or perhaps another personal item that he might remember her by. It was all to no avail since he kept returning for one more remembrance. She begged him to go on and meet his obligations, or shame would befall them. He then solemnly promised her that he would fulfill his feudal obligations. Alas, he was utterly besotted and returned to her once more. She now panicked. Fearing total shame, and in despair, she now provided him with the ultimate remembrance of her. He now would have to fulfill his duty." Once again, I paused for effect.

"And it was…" Dee asked impatiently.

"Sorry, did you want to know?" I smiled.

"Yes, you dipstick." Harry sputtered.

"Her servant brought her severed head out to her warrior prince."

"Eew, gruesome!" Connie said.

"I'm sure you would have done the same for Paul."

"No way." Her face scrunched up in an expression of disgust.

"In any case, there would be no more excuses for this prince to shirk his sacred duty. Personal honor was a big deal in those days. By the way, I saw this apocryphal tale portrayed in a Bollywood movie once and only later discovered that it allegedly took place in my very own town of Salumbar where the remnants of that Raj palace yet remained."

"No way!" Paul was incredulous. "Are you making that up?"

"I did see it in a movie, I'm sure about that. And I believe I was told it happened in my site but who knows how many places laid claim to that legend, which I believe was well known throughout the country? I won't bet the mortgage on the veracity of the claim, okay?"

"Hmmm." Paul grunted which I took as a sign he was satisfied.

"Still, I was reminded of how closely life in Rajasthan resembled the way Europe in the middle ages had been organized with the minor princes owing fealty to the major princes and ultimately on up to the king. There still were these Princely States that had survived as semi-autonomous jurisdictions all the way to independence from Britain in 1947, just one short generation before we arrived. The wealth of those Princes had been legendary in the past. Anyway, stories like that reminded me of how lucky I was to be born in a time where personal honor is a bit less exacting, like not cheating on your golf score. There was so much history all about us. I now wish I learned more about the place in which I spent two years of my life. Too busy surviving perhaps."

"I have the same regret." Mel added.

Several others agreed.

I rustled through my papers and pulled another Eleni letter out. "I don't know about the rest of you, but what I did see and hear struck me as romantic and inexplicable at times. What remained beyond our easy understanding might be attributed to the fact that remote areas, at least, had not yet transitioned into a fully rational society. Here is a segment from a letter to Leni that strikes me as interesting and on topic. You guys start thinking about stories you may want to share as I read."

As I write this letter, it is about 10 PM. The world is silent except for the pained groan of the wind. And I am alone. Ralph has gone to Delhi. He has had some form of physical breakdown. To be brief, he has worms, an infected foot, dental problems, nausea spells, general weakness, lesions on his arms, and several other indefinable aches and pains. However, chances are he'll survive. We are a hardy lot. Not too bright but tough to kill.

The nights can be somewhat spooky since we are rather isolated. To compound the feeling, I've run across some interesting tales concerning spirits, holy men, and general extrasensory phenomena from rather reliable sources (university- educated men).

One story is about the former princely ruler of a neighboring district. Since this man was educated at Oxford in England, he often entertained foreign friends, mostly from the U.K., in a palace built expressly for that purpose, at least until one of his visiting friends died in it. After that, no one could spend the night, not even the prince. It was reported that anyone who attempts to sleep in the palace will be physically ejected by the spirit of the dead guest. Stories of communications with dead relatives, physical cures by holy men, and possession of bodies by spirits are legion. After a while, it makes one wonder.

"Religion and spirituality liberally mixed with town life to provide entertainment for the locals and a respite from the tedium of everyday life. It provided us with welcome distractions as well. India also involved colorful festivals and sights you would never experience again. A sect of holy men visited the town for a few days. I watched one of them literally rip all his hair out as an exercise in self-mortification. I am well on my way in achieving the same hairless state on top of my head, but in a more natural way, absent the physical pain at least. This colorful, religiously inspired event is described next . . ."

Another aspect of Indian culture has been brought to light this week. It seems that a group of naked Sadhus (sort of like Saints to those of the Catholic persuasion) have come to town for a while. When they arrived, the whole town, it appeared, turned out to greet them. Even Cutchroo, our 16-year-old cook, took part. Dressed in an oversized white uniform and wearing a hat which hung down over his ears, he produced a cacophony on a drum which some naïve soul had given him under the ridiculous impression that somehow music would be forthcoming.

Well, anyways, amid the heavenly strains (?) of the band, the choking dust, and the milling crowds, these skinny naked men arrived. I must admit, despite that, the town never looked better. Decorations were abundant. Across every street hung banners, streamers, pictures, and other assorted paraphernalia of assorted colors and shapes.

Another interesting point is their culinary habits. When it is time to eat, they proceed from their temporary local temple while thinking of some sign or signal such as a man holding a coconut under his left armpit or something. If they see that sign, they will eat at the nearest house. If they don't, they will fast for another day (they eat only once a day). It really does seem like a tough way to make a living.

"On at least one other occasion, I managed to trade words of wisdom with some visiting holy men, or so I claimed in another letter to Leni. I have no doubt the event happened though, in truth, I can no longer summon a specific recollection of it. The holy men I remember well. I recollect watching these men walking through the streets to the acclaim of the town folk. The residents competed to get them to stop for their one permitted daily meal at their personal residence, a high honor indeed. One thing I can say for sure, Ralph and I did not compete for this honor. We wouldn't know what to do if selected. I'm looking at another passage but don't recall the interchange noted. Our memories are so frustratingly fickle."

Have just returned from Salumbar where I had the opportunity to visit and talk with the visiting Jain holy men. These meetings are, I suspect, the very kind of cross-cultural contrasts which Peace Corps is famous for brokering . . . east and west, mysticism and rationalism, aestheticism, and materialism. These confrontations are more awkward than enlightening. Yet, it is probably true that my somewhat affected interest in the Eastern world does create a modicum of good feeling.

"One of my memories from this visit is that one of these saints took ill and sought medical treatment. I was told of this by a local friend who was upset, not with the affliction but that the holy man sought help. Apparently, this just was not done. India seemed to surprise us at every turn. It nibbled at our comfortable, Western mind-sets. It helped us place all our rational understandings of stuff in a more nuanced and flexible framework. No question, we were opened to new experiences. It was not for the faint of heart or those of a rigid mindset."

"No doubt! You had to be open to grand adventures." Ben added.

"Definitely," I added with enthusiasm bubbling up from another memory. "Once, we were in a boat on Lake Pichola, the big lake in Udaipur. I assume we were going to or coming from the Lake Palace, an iconic site. What I recall was the boat taking a circuitous route, no longer sure why, so that we came near a small island. Were we on a tour? Oh well, this was nothing more than a rock sticking out of the water festooned with trees and bushes. This flora seemed to heave and sway in unnatural ways, as if they were living organisms. For the life of me, I could not figure out what the hell was going on, or what I was looking at. Once we got close enough, all was revealed. Every branch of each tree and bush was filled with colorful parrots. It was a riot of color and movement and sound. More amazingly, all the birds were making a similar, but indistinct sound. It was surreal. We had to get closer before we could make it out what was happening, what message they were conveying to us." Then I stopped.

"So, what sound were they making, or saying?" Kay asked.

"Shivers run down my spine as I think back on that moment. It was magical. It took some moments to sort it out, but they were all saying... *Polly wants a cracker.*"

"Oh my God. Why do we keep listening to him?"

"Because I'm cute?" I tried.

"One last time, I'm begging." Laura now sounded desperate. "A gun, my kingdom for a gun."

"Okay, there was nothing about Polly and crackers. The rest of the story is true, about the tiny island and the thousands of parrots. I have no idea what brought them all to this spot or even whether this was something unusual. It was just India, you marveled and moved on."

"No shit." Paul said. "Right now, I am marveling how your group never voted you off that island known as India-44. Think about it. All those good trainees that were deselected and they somehow kept Corbett in the program."

"Isn't it apparent? I am lovable. Oh, one more flying creature story, plural really... more than one creature involved but only one story. There was this tree between our government housing and the town, but only if we took a back route over the hill and along the lake, not the main road that was paved. The town women tended to do their laundry there as well as bathe. It was always a bit disconcerting when I walked past and they would be staring at me, naked to the waist. They seemed not to care when I stared at their breasts, but I certainly was thrown off my game. After all, some of them were young and well..." I paused not knowing how to finish that thought. "More than once I tripped over my own feet, not watching where I was going, falling flat on my puss to the amusement of the crowd. I actually wasn't bad looking until all those falls."

"Some karma at last." Laura sighed with exasperation. "Now finish your disgusting story."

"Right! This tree, particularly in the evening would hang very low. Why, you ask?

"No one asked." Paul muttered once again to no avail.

"No matter, I will tell you anyways. Hundreds of bats would congregate there. Yikes, passing by as they hung upside down was an adventure. If one or more of those ugly creatures flew over my head, it would give me the willies. Sometimes, something would disturb them, and a flock would flutter about as we passed by. I dreaded that some of them would land on my head. I had hair back then which they might grab onto. Also kept waiting for one of them to transform into Christopher Lee… he played Dracula in a lot of vampire movies, though I prefer the monster's historical name… Vlad the Impaler. Yeah, I always had this fear that I would be the inspiration for the next Alfred Hitchcock's flic, *The Bats.* Fortunately, nary a one ever attacked me. Just as I do with women, I had this way of repelling them."

Laura looked pensive. "By the way, has any volunteer ever died from a bat attack?"

"Rabies?" Maureen said. "In truth, the likelihood of getting rabies from a bat are way overstated."

—

Bob half raised his hand as if seeking permission to speak. "You know, I went to India in part to seek greater spiritual understanding, and to save the world, but mostly for that spiritual thing. I guess it started back in college. One day at school I remember pushing through a crowd desperate to reach this dark man in flowing white robes before he left the lecture hall. He had just given a talk to those students interested in Eastern philosophy, and it was big back then. One part of his lecture bothered me, about the hard road to enlightenment. I had to ask him, *Swami, Swami, why do we have to go through this intellectual phase before attaining self-realization?*"

"Looking for a shortcut were you?" I chuckled.

"Probably. In any case, the Swami Chinmayananda turned, gazed deeply for a moment into my eyes, and placed a gentle hand on my wrist. He whispered. *Just as the plant must flower before the fruit appears.* Then he was gone. That summer, I became a Hindu. If I had been wealthy, I would have left right away to seek self-realization in India. However, I was a scholarship student, the first of my family to attend college, a role model for six younger siblings. I felt some responsibility so returned for my junior year. To get to India, I signed up for early admission in the Peace Corps."

"Jesus, Bob," I marveled, "I went to college, after studying for the Priesthood in a seminary. In just weeks, maybe days, I lost all religious sentiments. You went and got all spiritual, at Yale of all the freaking places."

Bob nodded toward me. "Weird, no? Peace Corps training turned out to be a bit of a shock for me. We were to become *agents of change.*' We had all these social activists in our midst, burning with righteous causes… civil rights and the anti-war movement. What was I to make of all that? All I wanted was to become one with God. At that time, I was into Siddartha, who chose life in the world rather than the path of a monk. Perhaps Peace Corps was a way. Eventually, I arrived in India as a volunteer. Was I an agent of change? I surely was changing, sleeping under a mosquito net, squatting over holes in the floor, wiping my butt with water, and drinking paregoric and gin when I had the runs."

"No shit." Harry threw in, "we all were changing in those ways."

"On our first two-hour train ride to the villages where Mel and I would live for the next two years, I wrote down a list of questions to ask the local leaders. What were the needs of the people, the key institutions and character of the local power structure, and the resources needed to bring about change? I was primed to be this 'change agent' I had been told I would be. The first hint of reality came when no one met us at the train station. I did notice some kids playing soccer, or football as they would say. Having learned that you could reach the adults through the children, I dashed off to show them that Americans can play this game, I had played intramural soccer in college. I assumed that I had no time to lose in changing the world, what I would do next week remained to be seen. By the end of that afternoon, I was sick as a dog with sun stroke. From that moment on, survival became the main goal. To hell with changing the world. Come to think of it, I never did ask those questions about the power structure."

"It was quite a challenge keeping Bob alive." His buddy Mel added with a smirk.

Bob did not respond verbally to Mel's jibe but did give his life-long friend the universal finger before continuing. That symbolic gesture was extended quite often that afternoon. "My village was Sanwar, about two miles away from Mel. As I entered for the first time, a bunch of kids started the chant *'ghora, ghora, ghora'* or white, white, white. As many have noted, we had been dropped into a world where suddenly you are curiosity number one. I was renting some rooms in the old Rajput castle, not as impressive as it sounded. I had no electricity, no running water, no screens on the windows, and no convenient toilet. To relieve myself, I had to cross the main courtyard walk up a set of stone steps to the second floor, and then turn a few corners to a small room with a hole in the floor between two stone footpads, expertly positioned to assist in the proper aiming of your deposit. In fact, this was the sprint Corbett made during a visit when he had the shits. He didn't make it."

"We thank you, Bob." Janice offered.

"For what?' he asked.

"For assuring us that karma does exist in the world." She responded while looking at me.

Bob chuckled. "To set the record straight, we did not intentionally poison Corbett, though Mel and I discussed such a plan. Unfortunately, we abandoned that thought when we concluded that there was no convenient way to rid ourselves of the body."

"Hah, hah!" I uttered amidst the laughter.

Bob smiled broadly. "Back to my crapper, however. Now, if you did make it to the throne, there was no door to close. I looked down through the hole in the floor to realize that the room was perched beyond the edge of the lower wall of the castle. Directly below was a farmer's field so this would constitute at least one contribution I might make to my village… fertilizer. The actual village began just beyond the field so that toilet paper, if available and unwisely employed, might well be carried away by the wind and simply float through the village. I can just hear the village gossip now, *'there goes the pucka sahib's shit again.'* Of course, I had to remember to carry a flask of water with me, for the after-poop cleansing procedure according to accepted local protocol."

"Damn," I said. "you do realize that this was my one and only case of the shits in two years. I swear you and Mel poisoned me. If not for that, I might have gotten a medal from Peace Corps, the only India volunteer not to be laid low by dysentery. And not one fever, I amazed even myself. Then I blew it by visiting you guys. What was I thinking? I can still see myself dashing across that courtyard and up those damn stairs to your luxury commode. I think I was only feet away from the finish line when disaster struck."

Mel spoke at this point, a sheepish grin spread over his face. "I'll confess. I did try to poison you, at the request of the women of 44-A. I never told Bob. But you were a hardy guy, so damn hard to knock off."

"I am a bit like Rasputin." I explained. "Hell, he drank all this poison, was shot several times, and was still alive when his Russian aristocratic assassins pushed him under the winter ice in that river. Bet you used all your poison on me and all I did was crap the rest of the day."

Bob looked annoyed. "Past is past, let us move on. My other big disappointments, besides failing to knock off Corbett and not becoming one with God, were all my failures at giving agriculture advice to the locals. I rode my bicycle alongside an Indian extension worker who began each day by ingesting some snuff-like material from a bowl in his living room. I always wondered why he always seemed to be in a good mood, though less talkative than I would have expected. At first, I thought it might be due to some meditation technique he used or insights into Indian spirituality. Eventually, I learned his 'snuff bowl' was filled with marijuana laced with sugar. So much for Eastern mysticism. He was just your garden variety pothead. Worse, he never offered me any."

"Damn him," uttered Mel.

"Sometimes, I carried sacks of fertilizer on my bike and loaned them to farmers. A few of these loans were paid back. But it was a hazardous undertaking. Many stiffed me and at least one came to me after the growing season and bitterly complained that the fertilizer had ruined his crop. He had no irrigation system, and the rains were sparse that year. The fertilizer drew out the remaining moisture leaving the crops to wither. My sense of mission was flagging along with my search for the meaning of life. I had gone there for a spiritual connection and reality was wearing me down."

"Reality does suck the big one." Greg said and Bob nodded agreement.

"Once I sent away for some films on improved agricultural techniques. The district ag officer drove me in his jeep to several villages to show these flics. He always asked me to say a few words in Hindi first. However, he had this custom of getting the crowd relaxed by showing an exciting historical film of the massacre of Indians by the British at Amritsar. Then he would nod to me to make my remarks. His choice of kick off film and its timing always made me wonder… was he hoping the crowd would attack the only white face in the crowd. That would rid him of this irritating American."

"And serve as a karmic justice for trying to kill me off." I added.

"Hah," Mel responded. "If we had succeeded, we would have gotten those 77 virgins in paradise. Allah would surely have been pleased with our work that day."

"Now, now, children, let me continue." Bob tried playing the adult. "Mel and I did some good, but boredom and survival dominated all else. I thought less and less of the higher purposes that brought me to this mystical land of my dreams. Reality erodes ideals for sure. After a year, I moved to Fahtenager, closer to Mel, where I could have electricity and a convenient poop pot. It was far from paradise, however. One night I was woken in the night by a rat running alongside of my rope bed. After realizing it was not Mel, I was grateful that the mosquito netting had provided some level of protection. The next morning, I noticed gnaw marks in the grease my cook had left in a pan he used. I put out rat poison but then wound up smelling dead rodents decomposing in the walls of my apartment."

"Eew," Connie once again expressed her disgust.

"You said it. Eventually, I developed a better system for coping with the rats. I kept a flashlight and two sticks beside my bed. When a rat woke me up by running across my bed, I would turn on the flashlight, then walk over to turn on the overhead light. With one stick, I would flush out the rat from behind the bookcase where they always seemed to seek sanctuary. Perhaps they thought great literature could save them? As my nemesis dashed out, I would kill it with the other stick."

"You are a true Peace Corps hero. I stand in awe." I uttered with insincere admiration. "Ralph and I got a cat, as I mentioned, which we got after the two of us failed to dispatch a single rat through sheer brutality. Of course, we were drunk when we tried, or maybe just incompetent. Both hypotheses work. Then there was this other time when we lived for some weeks in some school dormitory in Udaipur, during our in-country training. We would return to our room to find the biggest rats I had ever encountered. The smaller of us, like Mel, might have lost a one-on-one contest with the larger of those suckers. When we would turn on the lights, they would scatter, taking refuge in these drainpipes that led to the outside. If we knelt on the floor, we could see them hiding within these ducts through which water would flow, just biding their time until they could return to feast on us. I mean these monsters were hard to miss, being several feet in length. At least several feet! We would boil some water and pour it down the pipes. If it didn't kill them, we at least hoped it would be a form of aversive training. I had this image then that we were the defenders of a town under siege. As the invaders kept trying to scale the walls of our citadel, we kept pouring boiling oil over the side to discourage them. At night, I would have this dream where we would run out of oil, or boiling water in our case, and the rats poured over the wall to devour us alive. Hard to seek spiritual enlightenment or nirvana when survival was the order of the day."

"Might we change topics?" Someone asked to no avail.

Bob continued. "Corbett's comment on large rats reminds me."

"I guess not," the same disgruntled person said.

"Some of them were worthy opponents. Once, a very large rat eluded me. I kept chasing it through my kitchen, living room, and front veranda, whacking away with my stick, but missing every time. By the time we reached the front of the apartment, the neighborhood dogs had been alerted, these stray mutts ruled the streets of Fatehnager after dark. I had a screen around my veranda and the dogs were gathered there, barking and snarling. The rat was climbing on the inside of that screen and I was smashing away with my killer baton. Suddenly, the rat dashed to one side of the veranda, found a hole at the top of the screen where it jumped through and down to the street below. Before the dogs could react, it dashed into a masonry hole in the neighboring apartment. A lot might be learned about survival from a rat."

It was time to give Bob some grief. After all, he tried to kill me when I visited his village all those years ago. "Some seeker of Indian spirituality you turned out to be. You do know there is a temple somewhere in the north where Indians venerate rats. They put out food for them every day. You walk in and thousands of rodents will swarm about you. It would be an unforgivable sin to harm one."

"Did you go there?" Maureen asked.

"Hell no, I would have upchucked at the sight of thousands of hairy rats. But I assumed that Bob would have gone. He had such an intimate connection with them. Besides, he must have run into them at Yale all the time."

"Very funny, Corbett. Mel and I should have poisoned you when we had you at our mercy. Your chopped-up carcass would have made great fertilizer for our villagers."

"And how would you explain my absence? I would have been missed." I tried.

"You! Missed?" Bob retorted incredulously. "We would have just claimed you never made it to our site. '*Oh yeah, he said he was coming for a visit, but he never showed. Missing? How sad.*' At least then we could argue that you contributed something to our mission… your worthless carcass."

"You guys are so full of it." I tried.

Mel and Bob just exchanged nods of agreement as the rat stories came to a merciful end.

——

I noticed Ben clearing his throat. He was very reserved and seldom moved to words, so I was curious. "Ben, do you have something to add?"

"Well," he started slowly, "I was near the end of my three year stay as a volunteer when the '*Day of the Dead*' occurred. On this night, somewhat like our Halloween, ghosts were supposed to come out. These were not kids dressed like ghosts but purportedly the real thing. Not far from where I was staying, two watchmen were guarding some cows in a corral. One of them came to me and asked me to check it out. When I got to the cattle pen with my flashlight, the first watchman had this look of pure terror on his face. He suddenly jumped into the air and fell to the ground, thrashing about in the dirt as if wrestling with an invisible opponent. I aimed my flashlight through the rising cloud of dust mixed with the pungent, acrid smell of dried cow manure. I was looking for signs of a seizure and whether I needed to protect his teeth and tongue. After a brief period, the man settled down, got up and shook himself off. When I asked if the ghost had gone, he said yes and that there was nothing I could do for him."

"They were pulling your leg, I bet." Bob hypothesized.

"That was my initial guess. This was just a prank, a way to get a few laughs at my expense. Perhaps it was an attention-getting display. Or maybe it was a form of hysteria brought on by the power of suggestion. Their emotions, however, appeared so genuine, it didn't seem fake to me. And they asked for nothing. I could not figure out why they might be faking this. Perhaps this was merely an aspect of traditional folk culture which westerners could not understand, or maybe it was far more. That was the beauty and mystery of India. You got peeks behind the curtain but never saw enough to fully understand."

"A magical place for sure." Someone commented.

"The natives thought so," Ben continued. "Indians often commented that westerners were not only war mongers but materialistic while they considered themselves to be a spiritual people. I heard this over and over and, in fact there is some substantiation for this assertion. There is a lot of religion in India… Hinduism, Islam, Christianity, Buddhism, Jainism, Sikhism, and a bunch of smaller sects. Many are vegetarian out of principle while the extreme Jains would sweep the path in front of them to keep from stepping on a bug. Gandhi, of course, was the ultimate symbol of non-violence and the use of moral force to effect political and social change. On the other hand, there was much that confounded Westerners. Newspapers reported that some untouchables had been murdered simply because they turned their moustaches up in the fashion of the higher castes. Parents murdered infant girls since boys were preferred. Suttee was a practice yet remembered by many and still approved of by some. Not long before I arrived, the penalty for getting a girl pregnant was to cut off the man's nose."

"Not a severe enough penalty." One of the gals said so quickly she remained unidentified.

"Better than cutting off something else." I grimaced.

"At least that penalty would have been effective." Laura huffed.

Ben raised his voice to keep control of things. "One day, after having been in the village for about four months, I climbed the highest hill in the area on a beautiful mild day. I got my first overhead view of the plains and farms spreading out as far as the eye could see. I experienced this ecstatic moment, it proved unforgettable for some reason. I felt the scope of wonder that is India. You never forget such transcendent moments. India is an illusion. It can be profane. It can be magical. It can be frustrating. It can be illuminating. I suppose, in the end, it is what you bring to it."

"How odd you should mention that." I mused. "I vividly recall a hill just outside Salumbar. I would tell myself that I should climb it and look out over the countryside. But every time I had that thought I would say something like there is always tomorrow. I'll do it then. Time for a nap now. I never made that climb. I never saw the Taj Mahal because it was always there, and I could go another time. Hell, I never saw all the historic sites of Boston until I got married and brought my wife to see them. She was more curious than I. There is a lesson there, I think."

—

Cate made a muffled sound and we all looked in her direction. "I didn't mean to interrupt."

"Go on," several said simultaneously to Cate who obviously had something to share.

"Well, I recall this old *baba sadhu*, or holy man, appearing at our front door appealing for arms. When I answered the door, I saw this apparition with a drawn and sweet betel stained full-tooth smile. His turban and dhoti were dusted red with saffron. It struck me as I sat with him on our stoop that we now seemed to be in a world without our familiar boundaries. It was probably only a few moments, I really don't know, but I was lost in my exchange with him. Somehow, in those few moments I came to appreciate way more fully another concept… brotherhood. I gave him bananas and a few rupees, and he disappeared. But he left me with something precious."

"How sweet." Maureen murmured.

"And then there was still another shocker when I was visiting *Andra Pradesh*. I was talking out loud about wishing I knew the origins and history of certain historical ruins. There, sitting lotus-like on a ruin was a sadhu-appearing man. He looked at me directly, not a side glance, and then started instructing me about the history and meaning of the place in excellent English. I recall being so taken aback and now can barely remember what he said. It all seemed so unreal. Here we were in this strange time warp, almost like a science fiction novel in which I was a lucky participant. It was like seeing the movie 2001 at the only theater in Poona, then walking outside to 1960s India with the sound of bullock hoofs plodding off in the distance and catching the faint sound of chanting. Funny what sticks with you."

"Indeed!" Bob interjected. "One last thing for me on this topic. Toward the end of my stay in India, I ran into Swami Chinmayananda once again, the same guru who had converted me to Hindu philosophy four years earlier. He was giving a talk in Mumbai, not far from where he had an ashram. After having lived for almost two years in rural India, the Swami seemed so westernized to me. He had lost his exotic allure while I had lost my aspiration for spiritual realization. I had come to accept my identity as an individual. In India, I had learned that I was an American. Being a spark of the divine didn't seem so meaningful anymore. I now wanted to make the trains run on time. I was headed back to business school in the States."

"Funny," I added, "the lessons we brought back with us were not always the ones we anticipated."

"You can say that again." Harry added.

A snake charmer in mysterious India.

Cutchroo (on right) playing drums for arrival of Jain Saints.

CHAPTER 19

Mel's Grand Adventure

I grinned. "Speaking of the mysteries of life, I have a story that perfectly captures that theme. Well, sort of."

"Do we have enough missiles to finish him off?" Nanette picked up one of the pretzel bowls and looked in, apparently unsatisfied with what she saw. "Darn. We need more ammunition."

I tried to sound calm even as I realized the women were primed to strike. "Here's the thing! I was told about this gathering of guys in Bombay, from both India 40 and 44. It must have been at an inter-group wedding since that would explain why they were together. In any case, there was a poker game. It soon was apparent that a lot of tension existed between the groups. The guys from 44 were pissed that their peers from 40 were stationed with *'their'* women while they endured lonely, read horny, lives with only distant memories from their long-ago training days to keep them company."

"That's silly." Maureen announced. "We weren't wasting our time playing footsies with the guys from 40. We were too busy doing our jobs."

"And what's this about being someone's women. We weren't anyone's women." Nanette growled.

I held up a hand. "Listen, I'm just relaying what I heard. Don't kill the messenger here. And I guarantee, you will thank me later, when I get to this story. It is priceless!" Despite the groans of resistance, I continued fearlessly. While I'm not the dullest knife among the household cutlery, there is strong evidence that I court a secret death wish.

"Priceless, you say," Janice huffed. "In your dreams."

"Apparently, more than one of my brethren from 44-B remembered getting mail from the gals of 44-A saying how great the guys from 40 were. That was just what us lonely guys wanted to hear. Now, I never got correspondence from any of you gals." I paused. "Why was that by the way."

"Tom, do you really have to ask?" Dee rolled her eyes.

"No, of course not. Sheesh, what was I thinking? Anyway, I have no dog in this fight. However, several other gentlemen from my hardy band of suffering brothers felt that the good women of 44-A were out to make them jealous."

"What?" Laura was flummoxed. "Who?"

"Jealous… how?" Maureen sputtered.

"Isn't it obvious? You were flaunting the availability of the India-40 gang, pathetic mutts that they were. You were making sure we knew you had romantic alternatives, you know, just to make us jealous. This did not include me by the way. After all, the whole lot of you ignored me from the get-go. But my brothers here were deeply offended and, frankly, hurt." I heard rumblings from both the male and female members of our gathering. Had I pushed this too far? "Now, don't object until I finish." I looked around meaningfully and, to my surprise, not a single missile came in my direction and all quieted down.

"Go on," Paul intoned cautiously. "We 40 guys won't attack until we see where you are going. You are, however, treading on thin ice."

"That's comforting," my sarcasm unmistakable. "At some point, this poker session of which I speak degenerated into harsh words. Excessive liquor likely contributed to this deterioration but who knows. For a while, the verbal hostilities ostensibly focused on the card game but clearly something else was afoot. You can often tell when the real source of any conflict is *sub-rosa*. One of the guys from our side finally drilled down to the bed rock of the underlying issue. It was, no surprise, the old fashion green-eyed monster. '*How do you think we feel? We can't get to first base with our gals because they are saving themselves for you guys. They keep talking about how great you guys are, those wonderful guys from India-40. Enough to make me puke."*

"We never…" one of the women tried to say but I silenced her with a sharp look.

"Again, this is what I was told. I am just the innocent messenger here. At that moment in this potential dispute, a flash of understanding spontaneously spread through both groups of testosterone-driven males playing cards that evening. They realized they had been falling for the oldest tactic in the gender-war playbook. A common refrain arose from both groups of suffering males that night. *'What idiots we are. None of us are getting any.'* Men from each group began to commiserate with members of the other tribe as understanding filled their hearts, the bonds of brotherhood forged in shared travails commonly experienced with their traditional foe, that is treacherous females, had been reestablished. To wit, the women of 44-A had been playing one group of guys off against the other."

"Oh, for heaven's sake…" a female voice uttered.

I continued. "Soon, a smile of comprehension and acceptance spread among all in the card game and they continued playing amicably, now cemented in that brotherhood born of a shared agony that is the universal male condition. Funny, is it not. You can so easily bond with others who might be in another camp when there is a shared suffering and a common enemy… those of the female persuasion in this case." I prepared myself for incoming missiles, but I think the women were too infuriated to launch them. However, if looks could kill.

"That is the biggest crock…" Connie started. "Besides, I don't see the point of this story. Was there one?"

"Ah," I stalled for time, trying to come up with something profound but my nimble mind for once failed me. The problem was there was no point, other than I thought the story hilarious.

"We're waiting…" Connie persisted.

"Ah…" was all I could manage.

Mel bailed me out at this moment by sighing in such a way that everyone looked in his direction. "Sorry," he said quickly. "I do have something to share. If I don't spill the beans, Corbett surely will. I think he was working his way toward it. Damn, should have knocked him off when I had the chance."

"Yes, please, Mel has a story to share." I grabbed frantically at the lifeline he had thrown to me. "Let's listen to Mel.

"Oh yes, please Mel. Anything to shut Corbett up." Laura pleaded.

Mel took a deep breath. "I'm worried that if Corbett keeps talking, he won't last the afternoon and I rather like him, despite everything. By the way, has anyone ever been killed in a pretzel attack before? I'd love to see that police report. Murder weapon… pretzels. Persons of interest… a gaggle of irate female senior citizens." Mel chuckled at his own wit. "Seriously, he's the only guy who can enrage more women, more effectively, and more often than I."

"So wrong, Mel," I interjected, "it is not a gaggle. That term is for geese. The term for a collection of females is *'biddies'* and for senior citizen females, *'old biddies.'* A hailstorm of pretzels descended upon me as I encouraged him with some urgency. "Get on with your story, please. NOW!"

"Okay, then! This is about my own personal odyssey to the erotic promised land, something for which I suppose I can thank Peace Corps. I might as well tell it since I have a strong feeling this is what Corbett was leading us toward… in his usual round about way. Am I right?"

"Oh, could just be." I smiled broadly.

"Thought so." Mel took another big breath. "Let me make it clear that I was a late developer when it came to relations with the opposite sex. I also was aware that India was not the most logical choice if I wanted to develop that part of my life, but I had made the decision to come anyway. In fact, and this is hilarious, I chose Peace Corps-India because I thought it might be a great place to meet exotic women. They were exotic, alright, but I couldn't get near them."

"Mel," Bob intervened disapprovingly. "You're pulling a Corbett, your wandering."

"Oh, sorry. We all know that India is a very conservative culture when it comes to sex. The family is all important, as is its honor and reputation. So, sex outside of marriage is not only frowned upon, but can result in the ultimate punishment of death, at least if the offender is a woman and the family members feel dishonored. It was just not a promising environment for making any progress in my underdeveloped love life."

Tim let out a cynical chuckle. "Mel, you're not the only one who was suffering from an underdeveloped sex life."

"I suppose, but we didn't brag about that to one another." He paused as if thinking about that before continuing. "While I have said that the Indian culture was sexually conservative, that doesn't mean that they didn't appreciate the wonders, or for that matter, the necessity of sex. The villagers tended to marry very young, and sex was a normal part of their lives. They often commented about the fact that we volunteers were too old to be single. Apparently, they wondered how we dealt with the frustrations of not having regular marital sex, especially given their understanding of our wildly libertine culture."

"I wonder if we changed any views on American promiscuity." Bob pondered.

"Likely made things worse." Paul observed.

Mel continued. "Not sure we changed anything there, but Indians did see Americans as being sexually liberated, and more than a little dangerous. Most of their information came from the cinema, and even the poorest villagers had either seen or heard about American films. Movies were wildly popular in India, even at that time. The Indian movie industry was, and still is, the largest in the world, with most films being Bollywood spectaculars. These were usually lavish productions with much singing and dancing to make up for the fact that no kissing was allowed on screen, and anything approaching actual eroticism was strictly forbidden. For a nominal price, all but the very poorest could spend at least a couple of hours escaping into a world far removed from the frustrations of their daily lives. The theater in Udaipur showed American movies on Sunday morning, for the same low price, and they were quite popular with the locals. Occasionally these films were even shown with the reels in the right order. It was a little shocking to realize that this was the only exposure to American culture that most Indians had, but that was the reality of the situation. No wonder they thought we were all perverts or worse."

"I recall a group of us including two of our Indian language instructors seeing the movie *In the Heat of the Night* in Delhi. Great flic but not exactly designed to put America's best foot forward." I added. "America came across in that flic as being populated by redneck bubbas."

"Well?" Bob retorted.

"Pretty accurate," I agreed.

"Continuing on," Mel said emphatically. "The impact of this unfortunate situation was brought home to me once when Bob and I joined a group of local farmers sitting around a campfire outside our training village. They were delighted to hear that we were Americans because they thought we might be able to settle a debate they were having. *In America, does a man have to buy a woman dinner before she will sleep with him? Or is it that sometimes you can get a woman to have sex without the dinner?* The speaker was convinced that his understanding of American culture was that a dinner was required, but one of this group insisted he had seen a movie where the woman had cheerfully gone to bed without demanding to be fed first. The consensus, however, seemed to be that even in America only an absolute slut would surrender her body without first demanding the ceremonial dinner that was her due. Bob and I tried, with our then limited Hindi, to convince them that the situation was a great deal more complicated than it appeared in the movies. But they knew what they had seen and dismissed our explanations as a kind of cultural defensiveness."

"More complicated hardly captures the complexity of male-female interactions." Paul muttered and then looked at his spouse to see if he was about to get wacked.

"Other cultural misunderstandings often played into this image. In Hindi, the crude word for sex is remarkably close to the word for vacation or holiday, like how similar the word 'luck' sounds to any foreign ear to our colloquial word for coitus. For example, it was only through luck that I managed to f…"

"No!" Shouted Connie.

"Okay! Here's a better example, from real life. One afternoon, while talking to a group of Indian high school students, I told them I was going up to Delhi for a week-long *'holiday.'* I immediately saw their jaws drop and their eyes bug out and realized that my pronunciation was a bit off. One of them figured it out and corrected the general misunderstanding. *'Oh, he means 'Holiday,'* and they all collapsed in laughter. For a minute there, I had been their God!"

"You would have been my god." Harry laughed.

"As a matter of fact, many of the people I came to know in the village simply assumed that any time I left to go 'on holiday,' I was actually off in search of the rare American girl in Delhi or Bombay, for whom I could buy a dinner as a prelude to a blissful period in the sack. If not lucky in that pursuit, I could then seek out an Indian prostitute… not that they saw much real difference between those two kinds of females. And on at least one occasion, they were not wrong in their assumption."

"Oh Michael." Nanette said as if disappointed. "You didn't stoop to Corbett's level."

"Hey..." I started to defend myself and then gave up on such an utterly futile endeavor.

—

"Here is my sad tale." Mel sighed deeply and started again. "Bob and I were stationed near one another and spent a lot of time in each other's company. Like me, he had been a late bloomer, having reached the promised land of sexual bliss only in his senior year at Yale. Still, that gave him a big leg up on me, and he seemed to cherish the role of being a sexual guru, explaining all the mysteries to me that he had managed to master in his one exciting relationship. This experience also seemed to endow him with that kind of intoxicating sexual liberation that comes when someone with a strict Catholic upbringing discovers that they are not struck dead by lightening the first time they get into a girl's pants."

"My god, I had no idea so many of us were such a bunch of losers. I thought it was just me." I said with some relief.

Tim smiled broadly. "Yeah, really comforting to know that the fraternity of male losers is endless, perhaps universal."

"Well," Mel ignored both of us. "Bob carried his newly won sexual liberation to India and was determined not to allow himself to be consigned to a two-year sentence of sexual abstinence. A few months after we had settled into life in the village, he managed to find a healthy young prostitute in the nearby city of Udaipur."

Bob coughed, spraying liquid in the general vicinity about him. He had been taking a drink at that moment. "Thanks a lot, Mel. Why don't you post that on Facebook?"

"My pleasure, Bob. Somehow it seemed to him that his role as my guru was not complete if he could not convince me that it was time to lose my virginity and join the neurotic world of fully sexual beings. I was hesitant. I had not come to India to exploit some poor downtrodden Indian woman, but Bob eventually convinced me that this was a lusty wench who would consider me the exploited one, especially given the exorbitant rates we silly westerners were willing to pay for mere sex. After a due period of deliberation, I gave in. We planned to go in for a weekend in Udaipur, where Bob would take care of all the arrangements. I appreciated that, since it was going to take all my energy just to stay focused on my role in this mission."

"You guys really do stick together." Laura did not sound impressed.

"We have to…" Harry shot back.

"It's sick." Laura argued.

"No, it's survival." Harry responded.

For once, I was smart enough to keep my mouth shut.

Mel ended a brewing inter-gender kerfuffle by continuing. "It was November 18, 1967, just a little over a month past my 23rd birthday. On this day, one that will live in infamy, we took the train in from our village to the City of Udaipur. We checked into a room at the Ajanta Hotel. This offered basic accommodations, remarkably like an American motel in that all the rooms opened onto a street. They were sparsely furnished, with just two cots made of twisted rope on a wooden frame, a single wood table and a couple of chairs. Each room did, however, have its own bathroom, even if it did have the typical Indian squatting latrine instead of a western style toilet."

"Wait, I interjected. That might be the same place that the owners of the establishment once banged on our door as they insisted we had women inside. They were apparently concerned about the reputation of this dump. We didn't, of course, but it was nice to know they thought we might have scored. I have no idea what put that ridiculous notion in their head."

"Nice story, Corbett, but shush. Mel's turn." Tim looked annoyed.

"Oops, sorry!" I apologized.

"We ran into several other volunteers who happened to be in town that Saturday and had dinner at Berry's Restaurant, our local favorite. In the evening we went back to our room where we ended up playing poker for a few hours. At some point the game wound down to where it was just me, Bob, Dan and Doug who were still playing, and drinking. You must realize that Dan always struck me as a super nice guy from Wyoming or some godforsaken place in the western wilderness. I was basically shy, and I really appreciated his similar laid-back ways. Doug was more outspoken, shall we say. Tall, with broad shoulders and a shock of brilliant blond hair, he could be aggressive, and carried a personal philosophy based on the notion that confrontation was the way to emotional honesty, or some such nonsense like that. I never understood it, but it did occasionally get on my nerves."

"He has mellowed nicely though." I added.

"Quite true, he's a pleasure to know now. Back then, he was more… assertive. My dear friend Bob here, it turns out, had a Leo streak that could not allow him to concede top dog to anyone else in his peer group. Not surprisingly, he often ending up butting heads with Doug, especially if the drinking started early enough. It was like these two Ivy leaguers, Columbia versus Yale, would circle one another to establish dominance in the herd. Usually Dan and I would just look on in a kind of bemused detachment as the two roosters verbally jousted, but this evening things got a little out of hand. I have no recollection what triggered the confrontation, but Bob said something about being tired of Doug's bullshit. They squared off and told Dan and me to get lost while they settled their dispute. So, we left and wandered about the streets of Udaipur, stopping at a push-cart vendor to buy a bag of roasted peanuts. While enjoying the nuts I told Dan about the purpose of our visit, that Bob was going to arrange for me to get to the erotic mountaintop that very night. Oddly enough, Dan tried to talk me out of it. He said I was the only 23-year-old virgin that he knew, as if that was something in which to take pride. For some unknown reason, he was totally impressed with that fact."

"Mel, that was nothing to be ashamed of." Maureen tried.

"Yes it is. Ask any male." Mel retorted without any hesitation. In any case, Dan's logic backfired. It now seemed even more important that I go through with this plan to shed this albatross weighing me down at long last. I did not want to be the last male of my generation to get laid."

A puzzled look crossed Dan's face. "Wait, did I really try to talk you into keeping your virginity?"

"Yup, you did."

"What the hell was I thinking?" Dan was flustered.

Mel shrugged. "I have no freaking idea what you were thinking. We guys usually encouraged one another to go for it."

Dan considered this for a moment. "I probably didn't want you to catch something awful and have your… Johnson fall off."

"Oh, please!" Kay pleaded. "Keep it somewhat clean."

Several of the other women also expressed surprise at Dan's graphic expression. It was something they expected from me, but he was considered a sweet gentleman while it was universally agreed that I was a depraved lech. Mel hurried on, partly to divert attention from Dan's *faux pas*. "We returned to the room after about an hour, and found the door locked. I banged on it, but there was no answer. Dan went around to the alley behind the hotel to find out if he could see in the back window. Having no luck, he returned. For a bit, we sat outside and talked some more about sex and life. Suddenly, we heard the lock turn on the door. That was it. It didn't open, but someone inside had unlocked it. Entering, we were confronted by a sight I will never forget!"

Again, a pause for dramatic effect which prompted someone to say… "and?"

"The table was on its side. One chair was broken. There was broken glass all over the floor. There was blood on the floor and some splattered on the wall. Bob was stretched out, face down on one of the cots, his bare feet clotted with blood. Doug was nowhere to be seen at first, but then his head popped up briefly from behind the second cot. He looked at us in a daze for a moment, then crumpled back down behind the bed. I was impressed by Dan's quick command of the situation. He immediately realized that all the blood in the room had come from Bob's feet and went to fetch a wet towel from the bathroom. He carefully administered to the injured feet while I cleared the floor of the broken glass. I assumed, of course, that this little explosion had nullified our other plans for the evening. I was wrong. As soon as Bob had regained his senses, he announced that he saw no reason to call off my grand adventure."

"Wait," Bob interjected, "I must set the record straight here. I can believe that is what Mel saw but the truth is there was no fight."

"Really?" Dan added with a skeptical tone. "I was there as well, it looked like there had been a brawl."

"No, neither of you were in the room. Truth is I did take one swing at Doug, but only one."

"Did it land." I asked with a silly grin.

"I have no freaking idea." Bob replied with a decidedly sheepish grin. "In truth, I was pretty much wasted."

⌒

"When do we get to the part about Mel reaching the promised land?" Paul asked as his wife glowered at him.

"Patience, I'm almost there." Mel said and pushed ahead. "So, Bob pulled his sneakers on over his wounded and bloody feet, not realizing until the next day just how damaged they were. He was most committed to ending my long spell of virginity, a true friend indeed. Since he seemed eager to proceed despite his injuries, and so dedicated to my sexual well-being, it seemed odd that I would not follow along. So, we hopped on our bikes and headed up the hills just outside of town, taking Dan along for the ride since he wanted to witness this historic occasion. Well, not exactly witness but… you get the picture."

I was moved. "You are good and faithful friends, Bob and Dan, to your male brother. No man, no matter the pain involved, should ever retreat from helping a fellow male in the pursuit of carnal delights. I bow to your persistence in assisting this poor, desperate soul." I pointed at Mel as I stood to bow toward Bob and Dan.

"Hell, I might have paid for the privilege of being there to share with my fellow male brother this sacred rite of passage. I mean, from a safe distance of course. After all, who wants to see the ugly details?"

"Thank you, I think! In any case, we stopped at a small house at the top of the hill. Bob quickly initiated some negotiations with a group of people gathered around a campfire. Dan and I hung back. After all, Bob was much better with the language than either of us, so I was content to follow his lead. While they were locked in their negotiations, a woman came over and asked Bob which one I was. She was dark, of a small frame and rugged looks with a no-nonsense air. She wore a simple cotton blouse and the colorful skirt of the local tribal people. When Bob pointed me out, she looked me up and down then called back to the group with her price… 15 rupees and not a paisa less! (about $2.00 at that time). This was no cheap whore we were dealing with! Either that, or she doubled her price on seeing what she might have to endure."

"Probably would have been 30 rupees for me." I suggested.

"No less than 60, I would venture," Paul added. "And you would have to throw in a goat to seal the deal."

"Gentlemen, enough squabbling." Mel cut us off and continued as if we had not interrupted. "And now, an unexpected problem. I had forgotten to bring any money with me! Was that a Freudian slip, or what? I told Bob about my situation, but he had not brought any cash as well. In desperation, we turned to Dan. Fortunately, our practical Westerner stepped in to save the day. In the end, it had been a real team effort with Bob negotiating the deal, Dan paying for it, and me doing the work."

"Ah, teamwork, the very essence of the Peace Corps spirit." Tim threw in.

"Disgusting!" Laura added.

Mel quieted the crowd by standing up and walking over to Dan. He pulled out a five-dollar bill and handed it to his friend. "I never paid you back. This should do it, interest and all."

Dan blushed and chuckled. "No, really. It was a gift, just a donation to a man seeking comfort. Any one of us would have done the same for one of our brothers."

"Nope, though I appreciate your sentiment." Mell insisted. "That debt has bothered me all these years. I'm proud of my small band of brothers, always coming through for a fellow volunteer in need. Anyway, this woman led me into the house and to what could only have been the main room, dark now and lit only with a kerosene lantern. She was all business, plopping down on the rope cot, pulling up her skirt and spreading her legs. I'm pretty sure that she did not have an egg timer that she had set, but I've imagined that every time I remember the scene. No doubt I was paying by the minute, If I managed to last that long. In any case, I felt I was on the clock! The act itself was non-descript, surely not the stuff of legends, nor of Hollywood standards. From what I've heard, many first times are somewhat clumsy, and this certainly was. It was mainly a question of figuring out what went where and how to get into the proper position. It was over before I really knew what was happening, and I wasn't all that sad about that. She was up and out of the room before I got my pants back on. When I went out, I saw her at the campfire playfully teasing Bob. He was still too drunk, and too poor, to call her on her offer. Still, it was clear whom she preferred."

"She just didn't get to know all your wonderful qualities, Mel." Dee suggested. At this, several males started to giggle. "Oh, shut up," she added in disgust. "You guys really are pigs."

"On the bike ride back, there was just one thought that completely dominated my mind: *Is that all there is?* Sex is such a big thing in our lives and in our society. What was I missing? Was there something wrong with me? You all know very well that I kept a journal in India, more than one. It's good to go back to it now from time to time see what was going through my head forty years ago. This is what I wrote the next day when I had some time alone in the hotel."

Mel pulled a book out, as if he knew we would head down memory lane. After rustling through the pages, he stopped and read the following:

The room is barren and austere – a call to meditation. I want to be alone, to think and reason out the experience of this weekend. Yet I did not seek this solitude, I simply let it come. Just as I did not seek out any of the experiences of this weekend, I only allowed myself to drift, to be pulled where the current chose to flow without offering any resistance.

Right now, I feel a strain, a strain in trying to write this. Perhaps some resistance coming from something in my own personality, a reluctance at trying to systematize or put into words what I am feeling – and a simple fatigue – too little sleep, too much booze, too little food, too intense an experience.

The experience itself weighs in my consciousness like a lump of undigested food. I can't seem to break it down, to make it a part of me. Maybe I haven't had time yet. Right now, there are only flashes of memory and feeling without any rhyme or organization.

I felt no pleasure. Of all things this is the strangest. I am not being profound or deep or obscure. I am talking about simple physical pleasure. And I cannot remember a single moment of anything like physical passion. Other satisfactions and disappointments but only a few physical sensations, all of which were surprisingly neutral, like washing my hands or putting on my shoes.

I do not feel like I have lost my innocence, but rather that I have regained it. It is not the act, or the mere physical contact that marks the boundary of virgin innocence it is the participation in passion. It was an experiment inspired by curiosity, an exercise in physical powers, completely untouched by the power or the mystery of the Life Force.

I now feel even more intensely the desire to make love to a woman who means something to me. A dubious addition to my 'unfulfillable desires while in India' list.

"This whole experience really bothered me."
"Is that where it ends?" Greg asked. "I hope not."

———

Mel smiled. "No, the saga continues."
Maureen and Kay groaned but most of the guys seemed riveted to his erotic journey.
"After brooding about it for weeks I told Bob that we had to go back. I still needed him to show me the way and do the negotiating, but I would remember to bring some cash this time. I also had a laundry list of things I wanted to try, to see if I could make this experience work more like the way it was in my imagination. Trying to be more in control, this time I told the lady I wanted her to take her top off. I believe that because breast feeding is common in public in India, the female breast has never taken on the full sexual connotations in India that it has in the west. Indian women seem more than a little baffled by how interested western males are in that part of their anatomy. When Corbett mentioned that the women bathing had no problem exposing their breasts to him, I thought about that."
"Huh!" came from me but nothing more. I was fascinated by Mel's story.
He continued. "Since I was the one with the rupees, off comes her top. It was my theory that a little foreplay might add a hint of passion or at least lust to the experience. But even here, the lack of experience tells. My effort was along the lines of what I have heard some women describe as *'tuning a radio.'* Overall it was a

mild improvement, but still nothing to write home about, if I was inclined to write home about such things."

"Hey," I said, "don't be so hard on yourself, at least you were trending up."

"Perhaps, but it had to be better, given how nondescript my first go was." Mel said.

I started in without thinking. "Yes, I was lucky that my first go was rather positive, even romantic, as I recall." Then my words struck me as insensitive. "But there is a downside to that. There really is." I looked at Mel, wanting him to feel better.

"How so? Sounds damn good to me." Mel looked confused.

"Well, my first go left me kicking myself for being so backward during my unfortunate youth. Hell, I even considered suing the church. I was thinking, this is great, I should have started years ago, if I could have, while you were going *'meh, I haven't missed much.'*"

"Good point," Mel offered. "I think that the lady was more than mildly amused by my strange requests, and even stranger execution of them. At the end of this event she turned to me and said: *'You should talk to your friend. He knows what he is doing.'* Now if that wasn't a calculated ego deflator, I don't know what would be. After my semi-traumatic experience with the Indian pro, the rest of my experiences in India were of a different quality. I learned more about romance, and absurdity. I'm not sure that they always go together, but there seemed to be a karmic link between them for me."

"Your right, Mel," Paul asserted confidently, "romance and absurdity are definitely linked."

"What?" His spouse, Connie, sputtered. "Do you want to reconsider that?"

"Oh, sweetheart, I meant for the clowns of 44… B that is. Not us."

"Nice try." Connie said and then hurled a pretzel in the direction of her own husband. She could hardly miss at such close range.

Mel with his cook, grinning after his own 'grand' adventure (I think).

Mel and Bob, still good friends on Mel's 75th birthday.

On the Road Again

"What's next?" Paul asked. "I'm enjoying these tales of woe and misfortune from those losers better known as 44-B. Listening to their whining, I feel better about my group, the stalwart men of India-40."

"Always glad to help the self-described 'mutts' of 40. They sure need it." I thought a moment and exclaimed. "Hey, I've another painful topic we can chat about. Who remembers the third-class trains, particularly during the hot season?" I noticed expressions of painful recollections cross many a face. Apparently, this was a topic that elicited terrible memories for all.

"You got something there." Greg winced. "We've all tried to forget that experience and the freaking busses."

Bob chuckled ruefully. "And the city cabs. One of them blew an engine while Harry, Corbett, and I were trying to get somewhere, in Delhi."

I picked up on the theme. "Remember the sheer joy of traveling by rail during the marriage season which coincided with the hot season. For most of the year there were two kinds of heat, the dry, scorching heat that ran from the beginning of March to sometime in June and the wet, humid heat of the monsoon season. You thought the first version was bad until the second arrived. I vividly recall 3rd class trains when the heat was 112 degrees or higher. Half of India seemingly was on the move, so the trains were packed on the insides, with additional scores perched on top of the cars or hanging off the sides. Remember the movie Dr. Zhivago when the family was fleeing Moscow after the revolution along with thousands of others. The huge crowd rushed to the train as it pulled in, pushing and shoving their way into a car until a soldier started beating them back when the car was full."

"I remember that scene." Laura enthused. "I loved that movie.

"So did I. Anyway, that pretty much captured the Indian train experience during marriage season except there was no soldier to beat back the surging crowd. I recall hurtling through a window to get aboard and enjoy the luxury of riding in a packed train in blistering heat while village women threw up next to me, if not on me. I recall thinking of that scene from *Gone With the Wind* where Scarlett Ohara rips a turnip or something out of the ground and eats it since she is starving Then she utters that memorable line where she *'vowed to God that she would do anything but she was never going to be hungry again.'* After India, I made a similar vow about never going anywhere on a third-class train again."

Janice winced. "God, it was stifling in those carriages, hell on earth. If the windows were open, you ate soot and cinders. We all remember that. Good news for you, Corbett."

"What do you mean?" Harry asked my question for me.

"I think Janice meant that the trains were a good preparation for what Corbett can expect in the afterlife." Dee added to appreciative laughter. "Yup, heat and misery."

Maureen tried to remain serious. "Really, when we travelled, it often was to find an escape from the heat. Unfortunately, we had to endure the most miserable heat to get where we were going."

I pushed this theme along. "I may have mentioned that I never did get to the Taj Mahal. My journeys did, as Janice suggested, prepare me in part for my anticipated afterlife enjoying the comfy warmth of fire and brimstone. I recall our trips to various destinations typically were hot, real scorchers. In summer, we went to a hill station in the foothills of the Himalayas but getting there was torture. In winter, of course, we went to Goa, the former Portuguese colony on the west coast south of Bombay. The hill resort was cool with magnificent views, as you well might imagine. My most persistent memory from that visit was less inspiring."

When I paused to reflect on my memory, Bob played his expected role "Keep going, Corbett."

"Yup, I recall sipping my drink on a veranda looking over a majestic vista before me. My sweet reverie was disturbed, however, by the sight of several Sherpas carrying cases of Coke and other drinks on their backs up the side of this steep mountain. Apparently, human labor was cheaper than trucking the liquid up to us pampered Westerners. Good to support the local economy and all, but my drinks never quite tasted the same after that. I really felt like the ugly American that day."

"Corbett, you are the ugly American… every day." Paul enjoyed the softball I had thrown him, as did the others.

"Goa, on the other hand, was paradise. Back then, the best places in the world had been discovered by the international hippie community… Nepal, Negril Beach in Jamaica, and Goa, just to name a few. My memory was that the beach was perfect, unspoiled except for a couple of small hotels. The landscape was dominated by local fisherman plying their trade, cool evening breezes, and spectacular sunsets. At noon we would amble down to the small restaurant and tell them what we wanted that night for dinner, then dine rapturously on marvelous cuisine to the beat of the surf just yards away. Or, we might have a lobster lunch for what amounted to something like forty cents as I recall, including the tip. That is not all, though. It turned out there was a special viewing at the Cathedral of the uncorrupted body of St. Francis Xavier during our visit. For those not of the One, True, Holy, and Universal faith…"

"What are you babbling about?" Laura looked lost.

"Okay, for those not Catholic, let me explain. There are two famous Saints with the name Francis. There is one who created a monastery and a new religious order in Italy, the Franciscans. The other one did missionary work in India, the Jesuit known as Xavier.

This was the second one of course. Occasionally, they would show his body which they claimed was uncorrupted, a sign of his favor in the eyes of God. The occasion this time was a visit of some papal official. We went of course. How could you pass on this? There was his body, in a glass case. To be honest, I thought he looked a bit worn, but I suppose he was in decent shape considering he died several centuries ago. I should look so good and I am, technically speaking, still alive."

"I would have loved to have seen that." Maureen was serious. "Thing is, we didn't get to travel as much as we would have liked. You felt like you were cheating and there was never enough money."

"Absolutely," I agreed with her. "Mostly, our need for Western contact was satisfied by periodic visits to Udaipur, on weekends or whenever we could drum up an excuse. Other volunteers always seemed to be around. We generally stayed at the Chetna hotel, a dump without any charm but within our price range, or the Ajanta."

Mel then added. "There was this moderately upscale hotel we stayed at if we had some extra money. Can't recall the name but you could get an English meal there, sort of a holdover place from the British Raj."

"Oh yeah, I remember sitting on their veranda, dreaming of being a member of the British Raj and enjoying a life of privilege. It wasn't the Lake Palace, but it was several steps above our usual hovels. One time, Dan unexpectedly approached as I relaxed on this veranda with this awful expression on his face. I knew something was terribly wrong. He told me the news of Martin Luther King being assassinated, or perhaps it was Bobby Kennedy? So many tragedies in that era, our world seemed so fragile in those days, a bit like today."

Dan looked at me. "I remember the place and, unfortunately, the event."

"We would go to this place to order these English dishes for some reason. Then, we would complain that the food was so freaking bland. Little wonder no one goes to England for the cuisine. Mostly, we ate at Berry's restaurant when in Udaipur, which had decent grub, served meat, and looked Western but the cuisine was at least tasty. Occasionally, we saw an English movie that always ran on Sunday mornings. Udaipur was a lovely place with lakes and hills and a rich history. The city stood at the northwest frontier and guarded the country from periodic invasions from the northwest. Traditionally, Rajasthan warriors were known as fierce fighters. As I looked around, what they were fighting for during all those centuries escaped me. It was mostly a bleak desert but their desert I suppose."

At this point, Laura took the floor away from me, which greatly pleased me. I was tired of my own voice and always wanted to hear what the females among us had to say.

"I surely remember my first solo trip within India," she started. "After six months in my hot dusty village, I was READY for a vacation. Coincidentally, a newsletter from PC India arrived with the mention of a ski festival in Gulmarg, Kashmir. Wow, snow, coolness, this Michigan gal would have a chance to ski again. I decided to go. After scrounging appropriate clothes from local missionaries and other volunteers, I made the 24-hour bus and train trip to Bombay and then flew to Delhi. The next morning, I was again at the airport for an early flight to Kashmir. Of course, the India curse decided to strike once again. The flight was to make a stopover in Jammu, below the mountains that enclose Kashmir. The weather was, of course, socked in. Twelve hours after taking off, I was back again in Delhi."

"That could happen anywhere."

"True, but the tortures had just begun. Day two was a repeat of day one. Where was my vacation going… was the dream of snow to remain a mirage? Fortunately, I had found several other volunteers and staff members on the plane all heading to Kashmir to ski. Now on to day three. The flight to Jammu was cancelled again. However, this time we thought we were smart and hopped off the plane and onto a 'luxury' local bus, complete with statues of Hindu saints and tassels. Thus, divinely blessed, we continued our ordeal to get to Kashmir. Plan B worked splendidly for a few hours until the road ended at a landslide and we could go no further. Fortunately, the Hindi speaking volunteers got us into a decent hotel."

"See," I tried. "It is always us Hindi speaking volunteers, those gallant and chivalrous guys, that women come to rely upon."

Laura just looked at me and just shook her head. "Day four was a long wait, and the word was the road would not open; the ski festival now was due to start the very next day! Later, our problem seemed solved as the Indian army was driving a convoy of trucks to test the condition of the road, and we could ride in the back. Off we went on this hair-raising ride over snow covered mountain roads. Just at dusk, we were dropped off at the edge of Srinagar. From there, we caught a taxi to Gulmarg and then completed our marathon journey by pony. By this time, I was so exhausted that I only remember the pony tender running alongside in the snow while I barely clung to the saddle. After a torturous five days on the road we were welcomed into rooms that had fireplaces for warmth."

I tried once again. "If it was warmth you needed, you should have brought along one of the guys from 44-B. I personally would have been most happy to help you out."

"Hah!" she exploded in laughter. "I am positive the fireplace was infinitely better. It wouldn't go out at the critical time."

My so-called brothers in 44-B howled at her well-placed cut. "Touché, my dear. I surrender."

"The festival the next day was a riot as many locals from Srinagar came to participate and bravely strapped on skis to give it a try. They fell everywhere. I managed to come in third in a three-person race but got a prize. The thing was, I was on skis. It was bliss. It turned out to be a very original and yet typical Peace Corps vacation. It was testing, for sure, but very much worth the effort."

"Anyone else?" She asked.

———

Kay took over. "This is less about traveling than about a memorable Christmas story while in India though a trip is involved. From my letters home, I was delighted to come across my description of my first holiday season in country. This would be the first yuletide celebration in my life when I would be separated from my several siblings, my parents, and my extended family. With no cell phones or internet available, six months earlier I booked a trunk call to my family. When the time came, I called them from Terry's place in Mumbai, or Bombay as we knew it then. It was 4:30 in the morning in the states, and mother had everyone around the phone to wish me Merry Christmas. What a wonderful gift."

"Now, with today's communications, it is hard to imagine just how isolated we were." Tim noted gravely. "We were not just on the other side of the world, but also in a very foreign culture where nothing was familiar. Then, we were dumped in remote villages far from any hint of civilization. Nothing can prepare you for that. Any connection with the familiar was priceless." His observation was met with the nodding of heads.

"My Christmas package, which mother had mailed three months earlier to reduce costs, arrived. She sent a tape on which the family recorded Christmas songs while she played the piano. Hearing my family was a real treat. I played that tape endlessly until I needed to record something from the BBC. She never forgave me for that; it was the production of her lifetime and a tribute to me." She stopped for a moment, there was wetness at the corner of her eyes.

"Oh, we all have those sad memories." Dee commiserated.

"Janice and I were to leave for a holiday trip to Bombay and Goa but first we had a party for our friends in the village. She had bought some decorative materials and had Santa and reindeers hanging from a coat hanger in the window. Our tree sat on a poinsettia printed cloth, and Christmas cards hung on the walls in the form of trees. We wore our American frocks, sang Carols, gave small gifts to the children, and served snacks and drinks. After our program was over, Mr. Joshi, a friend of our health officer doctor, made a speech about this being our first holiday away from home and how he hoped we were happy."

"Oh," Maureen exclaimed, "all this sounds very nice."

"It was, it made us feel accepted. Later, we had supper with the Revenue Director… a feast of chicken, fish, and mutton. We had dressed in our best saris, and the villagers stopped in their tracks to gawk as we walked to his house. One of us almost got run over as a bullock cart driver focused on us and not the task at hand. We left the next day for our Christmas Holiday in Goa. In Bombay, we met Dan and someone else, I now forget who, for the trip. Dan and I went to the Elephanta Caves and then took a flight to Goa since we heard the boat was full. For only 100 Rupees, we put our lives at risk on that plane. It was noisy, had no air conditioning, and our landing almost split my eardrums."

"A quick personal note," I interjected before my thought might be lost, "three of us once took a plane, from Bombay to Udaipur I believe. Can't recall the identity of other two but that makes no difference. Just before we were to board, we heard our names called. The local gendarmes insisted on opening our luggage and going through everything with a fine-tooth comb. The guys with me on that trip must have looked like sinister drug dealers because I know I was as innocent as a babe. Unfortunately, since everyone in 44-B looks like an ex-felon, that's no help in recalling who they might have been." I looked about but no one spoke up to admit to being there. "Of course, they found nothing and off we went."

"I would have stripped searched you." Laura said with a broad smile."

"Pervert." I responded.

"Had you stripped searched, I meant to say."

"Nope, too late. We know exactly what you meant." I nodded to Kay to continue with her tale as Laura sought to recover from her *faux pas*.

"In Goa, we stayed at the misnamed Palace Hotel since finding a decent place was impossible. This place was worse than the biblical stable; I was sure that rats were everywhere. On our way to Midnight Mass we heard a group singing lovely Christmas melodies, then Santa came by on a float, adding to the magic of the place. The Mass was at the foot of the stairs of the Cathedral, the altar on the first step facing the congregation. The most beautiful part of the Mass was the Gloria when all the bells were ringing including the huge bell at the top. The choir added much solemnity to the moment. The whole scene was heavenly, and it made me nostalgic for my family."

"Wow," Cate said in a low voice with a tone of regret, "I wasn't sure India was far enough away from my family. Sorry, continue!"

I braved the mobs of people to take communion. Janice had gone back to the hotel, not feeling well. While Dan also was Catholic, he didn't join me for Communion. He had fallen asleep on the steps of the Cathedral."

"Like I usually did during every Mass I attended." Dan added.

Kay smiled before continuing. "The rest of this vacation consisted of riding bikes to the lovely beaches of Goa, meeting other Peace Corps volunteers along with two Australian women who came to our villages. I then traveled to Bangalore, another lovely town, and met some India 30 volunteers who had finished up their training as we were starting our advanced training ordeal in 1966. It was great to hang around with them. I often think of that first Christmas in India as a milestone for my own education in cultural diversity; juxtaposing a treasured festival for us onto a country some 12,000 miles away. I also learned much about Hindu festivals and found their Diwali feast to be like our Christmas. I learned that family celebrations can happen in so many ways, and the flexibility comes from the decades of Christmas celebrations since that first exotic one in India, so many decades ago."

—

"Goa was special." I asserted when it was clear Kay was finished. "I loved the beaches back then. They were so unspoiled. That area had been colonized by De Gama and other Portuguese explorers who found an eastern alternative route to the Indies not long after Columbus went west. The Portuguese clung to this base of operations for about 450 years until the Indian Government finally threw them out only about six or seven years before our arrival. Still, the culture was European. Better yet, commercial development was yet to overrun the beaches. It was paradise. I can still recall this small, white chapel nestled among some palm trees on the edge of the beach. I think it was there that I made my move…"

"Drop it, Corbett" Connie cut me off but laughed at the same time.

"Got it! I do have one more recollection from my trip to the Hill Country, up in the Himalayas. The views were breathtaking. From one vantage point, we were told you could see into China. Others got up early to hike to a place where you could, in theory, see all the way to China. I stayed in bed. Frankly, I figured all the mountains would look the same."

"How could you not go?" Ben seemed disappointed in me.

"That was stupid." Hank chided me more directly.

"For sure, sloth is my favorite sin! To be serious for a moment, going halfway around the word shattered my provinciality and opened the world to me. Over the next several decades, I would visit every US state and perhaps thirty foreign countries. I remember my 55th birthday, when I realized there were three states… Oklahoma, Arkansas, and Kansas that I had not been to and might never visit. I traveled a lot for my work, conferences and talks and consults, but I could never imagine getting to these godforsaken places. I told my wife that I was going on a road trip, jumped in the car, and knocked those three off my list in one swell swoop. When I saw them at last, it was apparent why I had never gotten to them earlier."

"Didn't they have guards posted at the state border to keep you out." Paul quipped.

"Hysterical. What I do remember is that some trips were special for other reasons. We had two language instructors, Amar and Usha. Bob, Harry, and I struck up a friendship with Amar and her family. We visited them in what was called the Radio Colony section of Delhi. I remember Amar talking up her younger sister, how beautiful she was, and how she had won a beauty pageant sponsored by the U.N. as I recall. I had that uneasy feeling she was hoping one of us might be interested, again the ticket to America. What I remember most fondly was that the family invited us to Punjab for the wedding of one of Amar's brothers, an officer in the military. Now that was a lavish affair, it seemed to go on for days, with big tents and neon lights erected just for the event. There were bands and great food and dancing."

"They did know how to throw celebrations." Cate offered.

"Of course, we all know that the purpose of these elaborate and painful wedding fetes is to ingrain into the groom that he is now stuck."

"Corbett!" Connie hissed.

"No, really! You just knew at the end of one of these ceremonies that you were married. No exit now, you poor sap. However, there was one member of Amar's family that did catch my attention. She was the youngest sister, probably just entering college. I think her name was Batchue, just a nickname I believe. I really thought she was cute… very innocent and she had this impish smile that melted my heart. And yes, I do have a heart, no matter what the doctors say."

Harry spoke next. "Peace Corps opened up the world for me as well. I am not entirely sure how much of that thought process I remember today, some four plus decades later. I do know, though, that I did not want to return to the United States and not take the opportunity to see some of the wonderful places the world had to offer a poor tenant farmer from North Carolina."

"You were no tenant farmer, your dad was." Bob reminded Harry.

"Okay, fair enough. Still, it hit me that this might be the last opportunity I would have to visit these wonderful places. No one that I knew from my rural childhood home had ever traveled abroad, other than serving in the military. We were lucky if we got to travel to the big city of Durham occasionally. Let's face it, travel was an unaffordable luxury if you scraped by like we did. Even though I was anxious to get home, I needed to see some of the world first."

"No doubt," Bob observed. "We pretty much all came from families of modest means. I can't recall any of us travelling before Peace Corps. At least no one talked about it."

"So true," Harry pushed on, "Dan and I started out traveling together and went to such places as Istanbul, Belgrade, Rome, Athens, Mykonos, Amsterdam, Copenhagen, Paris, and London. At that juncture, I was really getting homesick and a bit low on cash. I would not see Dan again until we got together again for our 40-year reunion."

"I missed you, buddy." Dan threw out.

"And I missed you. Did we have fun during this trip home? You bet we did. We were able to visit some of the most magnificent wonders of the world. We climbed the Acropolis in Athens and visited the Parthenon along with other iconic monuments of ancient Greece. We saw the Louvre, the Eiffel Tower, and so many other French sites, like Versailles. We drank great wines and room temperature beers in Europe. We attended a Russian circus in Tehran and made it out without incident. You cannot imagine what travel did for a young man from my limited background, how liberating and educational it was. A world was opening to me. Still, home was calling. After London, I flew to Boston and then on to Washington from where I navigated my way to my sister's house. The moment I walked in the door, I found that she had just baked some the best biscuits I ever tasted. I can still see her taking that pan of golden-brown biscuits out of the oven, ones that had been made from scratch. Why is that important you ask? Well, I hadn't had any home cooking in two years. She asked me what I wanted to eat. *Peanut butter and her biscuits with some ice-cold milk,* I told her. That was my first meal back home and it was freaking awesome!"

"Yup," Paul intoned gravely, "there is a God and He is found in freshly baked biscuits and cold milk."

"Of course," Harry added, "a lot of us got to the Taj Mahal, except for Corbett. I must say, it was as advertised."

"That country has sites and sights positioned at both extremes… the sublime and the disgusting. So much to remember. Okay, time for one more travel story." I said. "Nanette, isn't it time to tell us why you pulled the emergency stop cord on a packed Indian train."

She threw a pretzel at me. I guess she wasn't in a sharing mood at that moment.

The Taj Mahal… never got there but I hear it is nice.

Harry, Me, and Bob visiting Amar's family in Delhi (a good family).

Disrupted Dreams

"You know, I felt awkward about coming to this shindig," intoned Stan, a reserved man with a pleasant demeaner and gentle ways. He evidenced a slightly avuncular air about him. When he spoke, people listened closely to what he might share. His prepossessing demeanor helped in that regard. I often talk a lot but soon realize that most stopped listening to my drivel after the first couple of sentences. But I never stopped listening to Stan, nor did the others.

"What are you talking about?" Maureen was genuinely puzzled. "I'm thrilled that you're here."

"Listening to all these stories, I realize how much I missed. As most of you may recall, I didn't stay in India long. I worried that you might not accept me as someone who belonged… in the group that is."

I jumped right in. "Hell, anyone sufficiently lacking in judgment to go to India on our fool's mission is one of us, so forget that awkwardness crap. You made it there, no? Besides, you were one of the few guys who got stuck with the gals of 44-A. Now that's punishment enough. I mean, a couple of weeks with them must have seemed like two years. For that, they should have given you hardship pay, maybe a freaking medal, just for putting up with them." Several pretzels came in my direction, one plunking me squarely in the middle of my forehead. "Damn, I'm going to lose an eye before the day is over."

"You're in extreme danger of losing something else… something lower down and to which you're probably quite attached." Laura said menacingly. "Get my drift?"

"Got it." I said while crossing my legs. "Your drift is unmistakable." I then noticed several of my male peers crossing their legs, the autonomic response to many female threats that is shared by most members of the male tribe.

Stan laughed; his nervousness now dispelled. "Thanks everyone. You're really a great bunch. I do have a few memories I wanted to share about what went wrong for me."

"Good," Greg said. "People disappeared sometimes, and I wondered why, especially after we went our separate ways in country."

—

"Here's my sad story." Stan took a deep breath. "It started with the Peace Corps staff in Milwaukee giving me some bad news about a week before we were to leave for India. I wouldn't be able to go, at least not right away. Thing is, I had a small opening at the base of my spine that hadn't closed properly during my early development. In most people, this defect doesn't cause a problem. Nevertheless, it was a possible entry point for germs and close to my spinal column. Let's face it, germs were India's number one export at the time. I couldn't leave for India until it was surgically corrected."

Bob looked puzzled. "That's odd. Corbett had this huge cavity where his brain was supposed to be, and they let him go to India with us."

"Bite me, Robert. And by the way, Yale is way overrated. I'm surprised it still is in the Ivy League."

"Calm down boys, let Stan talk." Maureen often put us in our places... a good thing since someone needed to be the adult in this group.

"In any case, waiting until the last minute to tell me about my medical condition might well have been a calculated decision on the part of staff. You see, it turns out that I had been assigned an iffy readiness designation by the stateside PC staff. I don't remember the name of my assigned psychologist, though I do recall the little battery-powered fan he had on his desk. He told me I was classified as *'high risk.'* That immediately sounded ominous. As I understand it, they thought there was a decent chance I would be a good volunteer. At the same time, I might just as easily chuck it if my boredom level got high or if I lost interest. I was this high-risk and high-reward candidate as far as Peace Corps was concerned. It struck me at some point that perhaps this medical thing was just a ploy on their part, especially if there were not enough real slots in India and they were getting rid of some excess volunteers. Perhaps if they threw this last-minute curve at me I would select myself out and save them a difficult decision. As it turned out, I really wanted to be with you guys. It took a near-death experience and lots of time to think at a Bombay hospital to get me home early."

"My god," Mel uttered. "That whole selection process was macabre. The psych exams, the self-assessments, the peer group evaluations, the knowledge that the cut could come at any time and for any reason that you could never fathom. It was like this sword hanging over you."

"It did seem arbitrary, sometimes unfair." Maureen affirmed.

"My guess, after the fact, is that Stan hit on the problem." Tim observed. "They didn't have enough confirmed slots on the ground in India. It became a numbers game… too many trainees for too few slots. You must remember, there was this long lead time between our application for service and being sent overseas. A lot could change during this period. As a result, some potentially excellent volunteers were axed."

Harry nodded vigorously. "Until I was in my village, every morning I awoke fearing that I would be sent packing. I had never failed in life, that would have devastated me. I can laugh now, but I felt inferior to a lot of you, given your backgrounds."

Several of us opened our mouths to respond but realized how the world might have looked to him back then. Rather, it was Dexter, one of the self-described mutts from India 40, and Paul's site mate, who broke in at this point. "We all agree on two things.

First, the guys in India 40 are way sexier than you losers in 44, and more worldly and sophisticated. And second, the deselection process was inexplicable. Their selection decisions for our group struck us as utterly bizarre. I always wanted to get Donald, our esteemed leader, cornered somewhere and ask him how they came up with some of them."

While I was tempted to counter Dexter's ridiculous assertion that the guys in his group were sexier than us, I was more interested in Stan's story. "Here's the thing, Stan, I was in Udaipur when you had what sounds like a near-death experience. Fill us in on what happened."

"Well, I'll try not to go on for long." Stan said in an apologetic manner.

"Take your time. Otherwise, we might degenerate into a debate about the relative stud ratings of 40 versus 44. I think the women should be spared that spectacle." I had played nice for a change, to the surprise of all.

Stan looked appreciative. "So, I get this disturbing medical news. However, in college I lived with my best friend's parents. Turns out his dad was a doctor. So, when I got this news about needing this operation before going overseas, I called him and asked if he could arrange an emergency operation. I really wanted to be on that plane with you guys. No problem, he said. I flew home the next day to have a pilonidal cyst removed. Being a dumb kid, I didn't realize that this operation was a serious invasion of the body and leaves a rather large wound that is left open without stitches to heal from the inside out. Clueless about the healing process, I pleaded with the surgeon to let me leave his care early to join you guys in New York. Unfortunately, he listened to my pleas and let me go. This was only two or three days after the surgery."

"Shit," I said, "I worked in a hospital while in college. Back then, you were on your ass for at least a week after that kind of surgery."

"I recall being shocked when you showed up." Maureen affirmed.

"I found that out the hard way. So, after flying all day from Montana, I arrived at the gate on the concourse where you all were waiting to board the first leg of the journey to London. I was ecstatic, watching the boarding of our trunks from the plane window and excited to be on this new adventure. I was tired but probably on an adrenaline high that only youth and the prospects of a grand adventure can produce. Hell, I thought I was healthy, what did I know? One problem, though. There were these large pads to cover my open incision which had to be changed often. I had Darvon for pain, but I couldn't see back there to redo the dressing. Maureen and Jack stepped in to help."

Maureen snickered at this point. "Oh yes, I recall one time when we snuck behind a statue in Westminster Abbey. You lowered your pants and I changed the dressing right there."

"Damn, some women will do anything for a peak at a man's goodies." I foolishly said.

"Corbett!" Maureen said as she launched a pretzel at me for her first and only time.

Stan then continued. "We next landed in Beirut, where the bus taking us to the terminal during the brief layover was escorted by two or three jeeps with mounted machine guns and soldiers at the ready. Of course, it was only weeks after the Israeli Six-Day War. I'm sure I saw 60 to 70 burnt out armored vehicles and tanks in a field as we flew in. Anyone else remember that."

Several yes's and maybes could be heard while I added. "I do remember all these places on the tarmac where it looked like there had been recent explosions."

"Next was Tehran to drop off another group of volunteers. I thought that country looked bleak from the air. Little did I guess what was in our own immediate futures. Then, somewhere over eastern Afghanistan, I saw some flapping of the aluminum skin near the intake on one of the plane's engines. In a second or two, it flipped over on itself and started to peel backward. And then it was gone. I raised the alarm and a stewardess came, looked, and ran back to the cockpit. The plane slowed, dropped in altitude, but we made it to Delhi in one piece to be met by an array of fire equipment."

Mel spoke up. "I never forgot that. The next day I recall touring Old Delhi and seeing a headline in the *Hindustani Times* that read, in bold type, '*Peace Corps Volunteers Narrowly Escape Death.*' Should have grabbed a copy as a souvenir. I am sure, if there is a parallel universe out here where we all perished in a fiery crash, President Johnson himself would have attended our memorial service. It would have been a grand affair, perhaps even a memorial in Washington to the brave volunteers of India 44 who gave their all in the pursuit of better agriculture and health."

"As I was saying, at least I was in India. I had made it, or so I thought." Stan said to regain control, "By now, my lower back was starting to ache, and my thinking became a bit fuzzy. However, I wanted to tough it out, not show any weakness. We soon arrived in Bombay after a grueling 3rd class train ride with soot coming in the window. This was not the kind of sterile environment my doctors would have wished on me. But I made it, barely, and we soon met the PC Staff at headquarters. There was this nurse who had helped with stateside training, I believe she had been an early volunteer. She took one look at me, visibly blanched, and soon I found my ass in Breach Candy Hospital, a very *pukka* British style institution of healing. By now, I had a massive deep infection at the site of my operation which was overpowering my immune system. I have this vague recall of hearing a conversation about medivacking me to a military hospital in Germany, but they would give it one more day."

"But that never happened, right?" Dee asked knowing the answer.

"No, they never did, send me to Germany that is. Clearly, I had more guts than brains."

"Ah, yes." Mel added, I do fondly recall my being medically evacuated to the American military hospital in Germany, an experience never to be forgotten."

"It wasn't a vacation in the Bombay hospital either. I was there for several weeks. I only recall Jack coming to see me, when he could sneak away. We were supposed to be site mates. I was alone, and bored, and slowly I began to lose my motivation. I can't recall any staff visits to pump me up. Maybe this was another of their tests to see if I had the 'right stuff.' I did get to my village, Poona located on the Arabian sea, but I never recovered, not on the inside. I do recall a couple of things. The first night, we had a chat with a couple of old men sitting in front of a hut. The only light was from a candle or oil lamp, very orange and dim… eerie really. I asked Jack why one of the men was laughing so loud at something I said to his question about how long my family had lived in their village. Apparently, my Marathi came out as *my grandmother is thirteen years old and which way is the train station.*"

"I said dumber things." I tried to cheer him up.

"And Corbett screwed up while speaking in English." Paul added.

"Things never got better though it was not any one thing. The village was on the Arabian sea and one day we went walking out onto this this long expanse of relatively flat beach which was not the normal color. Rather than being light tan or white, it was very dark. Still, we took our sandals off to walk barefoot until we were told we had wandered into the area that was part of the village latrine. Not long after, I just decided I wanted out. Peace Corps had been right, I was a high-reward, high-risk volunteer. My final Indian legacy was a case of *giardiasis,* a protozoon that attacked the small intestine. Wow, I had a helluva time kicking that sucker back in Billings."

"Damn," Maureen exclaimed with language we did not expect from her, "we should have done more to keep you in country. I think we were all working so hard to adjust to our own sites. I feel so guilty now. I mean, you would have been a great volunteer."

"A better one than I." I added.

"Corbett, the lamp on that end table over there would have been better than you." Paul smiled.

Stan seemed not to notice the interruption. "As you can imagine, my draft board was eçstatic to see me back in the States. It didn't take long. I was inducted into the Army in August of 1968. I was assigned to the 199th Light Infantry Brigade, 3rd Battalion, 7th Infantry, as a combat medic based just outside Saigon, now known as Ho Chi Minh City. In the end, it turned out that I did get to be a healer. And I was back in a climate like that of Bombay with the same smells and visuals, so my adaptation was quicker than most of the other grunts. I was the only medic in a platoon of 30 men, a job that had its perks. As the guy with the drip IV, morphine, and lifesaving first aid essentials, I got a certain amount of deference. No one wanted to piss off 'Doc.' It turns out that I found the same satisfaction and fulfillment as an Army medic as I had imagined I would experience helping the people of India. I didn't have to be a 'fighting' soldier or kill anyone. My job was to tend to the wounded, friend and foe."

"How odd," Paul observed. "Peace Corps helped you be a better soldier."

"Well, a better medic at least and maybe a better grunt, never thought about that. Peace Corps had prepared me for a radically different culture. Lots of young kids were lost when they got to Nam, it blew their minds. It's always a shock going from one setting to another, different rules and expectations. I think we underestimate the challenges. I remember Maureen telling us that she stood on a street corner upon first arriving in Boston after India. She mentioned this at the dinner we had our first night here in Oakland. She felt lost, bewildered, and frightened, broke out crying for no apparent reason. Her words made me think. You can get very emotional remembering your return from doing something so challenging, something that changed your life. Then you get back and realize no one gives a damn."

"Returning from war must have been worse, I would think" Connie asked.

"They were both hard. I had this sense of failure after India, that I had not measured up, wasn't tough enough. And after Nam, I could sense the ambivalence people felt about our role in that forsaken place. No one wanted to be reminded of what we were doing over there."

"But we have each other. Each of us knows what India was like. That's one small thing, maybe why we keep getting together." I said quietly, deciding to forego any of my wit, such as it is. "In the end, we are a band of brothers and sisters and you, Stan, are one of us. Anyone that survived that training to make it to the subcontinent is one of us. Anyone motivated to make this world a better place, put it on the line so to speak, is one of us."

I was not sure, but I thought he teared up. "Thanks. You know, I am grateful for one thing. I have this unique perspective that few other Americans have: an intimate knowledge of two different groups, Peace Corps Volunteers and Army grunts. The thing is, they have more in common than you might imagine. Both of my groups had about two-dozen members, each were assigned to carry out just about the most difficult tasks in their organizations. Think about it. If you were a front-line Army grunt in Vietnam, you had drawn the toughest slot possible. And if you were in India, and assigned to rural India, you had gotten one of the toughest roles Peace Corps offered."

"Hah, good point." Bob murmured thoughtfully.

"Moreover, both groups were thinking of a bigger picture and not just of themselves. That bigger picture might differ across groups but that's the beauty of America, it takes a host of different folk, each with their own view, to make our country stronger and better than the sum of its parts. In the end, members of both groups watched each other closely in training and in the field. Whether or not you liked a given individual, you respected them because you knew they would deliver and had been through exactly what you had experienced. And both groups witnessed those who wanted to be included but were turned away. In the Army, the best grunts were not the 'gung-ho' types because their aggressive thinking would get you into trouble. You needed soldiers who were not prejudiced and could get along with others. In the Peace Corps you had to have an innate sense of compassion and tolerance. You had to be quite intelligent, could not harbor prejudices, and certainly had to play well with others."

Paul laughed. "Again, I ask, how the hell did Corbett make it?" I threw a pretzel at him, retrieved from the substantial pile around me that had been sent in my direction during earlier assaults.

Stan sighed. He was coming to an end of his story. "I am so grateful for these experiences. We were a special group of young men and women. Unfortunately, there are not enough people like us in the world."

There were several moments of silence as we embraced what Stan had shared.

—

Then Glen spoke up for the first time, having joined us late. He was a string of a man whom had looked awkward in his youth but now seemed perfect for the slightly bohemian elder he had become. "Stan decided for himself to go back home. Not all of us had that choice. Some of us made it to India only to be sent home involuntarily."

"What happened at the end, Glen?" Janice asked. "We already were separated from you guys when this happened. I always wondered about what was behind the fact that some of you just disappeared."

"Hard to say. Probably, in the end, I didn't quite fit the image of a clean cut, well-scrubbed volunteer. My father was a conscientious objector in WWII, so I was raised in an unconventional family. In that last year of college, between the first and second summers of training, I befriended Mel and transferred from UCLA to San

Francisco State College. We had an apartment close to the Haight-Ashbury District just as the *'Summer of Love'* became a glimmer in many a young person's heart. I attended the *Human Be-In* in Golden State Park on January 14th, 1967, when Timothy Leary famously declared, *'Tune-in, Turn-on, and DROP OUT!'* The Grateful Dead played. Janis Joplin and the Jefferson Airplane wowed the crowd at the Fillmore. At the time, I played a gigantic 12-string guitar with a deep sound, wrote many songs, and performed them in coffee houses on Haight Street and around the Bay area. Mel turned me on to KPFK, the pioneer Berkeley public radio station that was the mouthpiece of the nearby Berkeley counterculture. As the anti-war fever grew, I attended all the sit-ins and protests but remained committed to the Peace Corps ideals of volunteering to build a better world. On the long flight to India, I wrote a poem, maybe more than one, but I still have this one."

IN TRANSIT [7-29-1967]:
Then the sun did its morning thing
With the colors spread out,
Together with the brown earth
Curving of so slightly under the weight.
When the sun rises, as it did
It sets for all my life so far lived.
A light cloud layer
Like the surface of a lake;
As though to see its bottom
I looked downwards.
The clouds came up to greet me,
Or am I descending?

"Quite lovely." Cate said.

"All my lovely sentiments were immediately confronted by the reality of India. An abrasive brick wall of hot sun and humid air hit me without a hint of mercy as we stepped off the airplane. The foreign nature of everything fascinated and repelled me. Bazaars were filled with people in bright costumes and headdresses. Three wheeled scooters careened down streets filled with dogs and cows and endless people. The locals stopped in their tracks, slack jawed, to stare at us as if we were aliens from space. Beggars flaunted the fetid diseases rotting their flesh for spare change. Parentless children roamed the streets in gangs. I saw beautiful temples, awe-inspiring countryside, and sensed the ancient past as very much a part of the present."

"One thing is clear." I thought out loud. "You can be told what to expect from here to Sunday, but you are never, ever ready for the reality of the place."

"Amen." Piped up Harry.

"When I got to Udaipur, I met Tim Peters who helped us get settled as he finished up his two-year stint. He was really connected locally and introduced me to the music culture in the area. I started making tapes of local musicians, met Sri Dagar who owned and taught at the local music school. I started becoming familiar with new musical instruments I had never seen before. I loved it. I was in my element."

"I can just imagine." Janice concurred.

"However, the pinnacle of my brief Peace Corps experiences soon followed. The mayor of Udaipur threw a festival to mark the arrival of our group. There were speeches and then local musicians did their thing. Then it came time for us, at least those of us with musical talent. Milt played a Bach *partita* on his violin and Dick sang *'The Hills Are Alive with the Sound of Music'* from the *Sound of Music* with my accompaniment. Now, I had a recording of a Sanskrit song Pete Seeger had done at Carnegie Hall in the 1950s. I learned it just for such an occasion. I stood up at the microphone and began to sing:"

Raghupati raghav rajaram

Patit pavan sitaram

"I sensed the crowd stirring. They looked from one to another with startled expressions, then back up at me. Then, they all began to sing along. All of them! Sensing their excitement, I played on with ever more energy. They responded by clapping along, some rising to their feet and dancing. I finished the song with a flourish."

"I remember that. It was amazing." Ben murmured. "I wish Milt were still with us. He was so gifted but so troubled."

Mel mused out loud. "Dick soon went back home, to Kansas I believe, something about a pregnant girlfriend if I recall. Too bad, he was the only one of us who knew anything about farming. It would have been great if at least one of us had one freaking idea about what we were supposed to do there."

I laughed abruptly as people looked in my direction. "Sorry, funny recollection! I remember Dick in training one day, when we were on that farm in Waunakee. The family dog, a big dog, tried to mate with him, pushed him over and mounted him from behind. Dick could not shake this amorous canine. At the time, we told him to relax and go with the flow, it was probably the best offer he was likely to get for the next two years." Before I could be assaulted with more pretzels, I changed topics. "Tell us, did you ever figure out the response to your song."

"Yes! Peters explained to me that the song, *Raghupati Raga*, was considered the unofficial national anthem of India. Their beloved Gandhi-Ji had penned a new verse to this ancient song, one that I had sung that day. The verse Gandhi wrote went like this.

Ishvar Allah tero nam,

Sabko samadhi de bhagavan.

This was a message to his brethren. It said that Ishvar and Allah are simply two names for God, we all worship the same thing. He always felt his inability to stop the religious strife between Hindus and Muslims to be his greatest personal failure."

"But then what happened? Why did you leave?" Maureen persisted.

"To make a long story short," Glen breathed hard, "I was deselected on the day when training was at an end and the others were getting their assignments. It happened as we were being turned over to the local Peace Corps officials, a group headed by a dour, Midwestern couple. I have no sensible explanation for why, after fourteen months of training and passing all the earlier tests, I was now being kicked to the curb. The next day, I was struck down with diarrhea and a raging fever that reached over 105 degrees. I was flown to Delhi where I spent a week in the hospital with bacillary dysentery, amoebic dysentery, and possibly hepatitis. Still, I didn't want to go back, and they talked about another possible assignment in India. Unlike many volunteers, I was discovering a cultural home, an affinity for all about me, but that was snatched away from me. I am not sure they even tried to find me another site. I simply was not wanted. Peace Corps told me that they would pay my flight home but only if I left right after recovery. Apparently, they really wanted me out."

"Bastards." Harry mumbled.

I could feel my Irish temper rising. "If they had any brains, they would have found a way to use your musical gifts and cultural connections. You could have been a huge asset, better than the rest of us clowns stumbling around these fields with our fingers stuck up where the sun doesn't shine." My Irish was now at a boil. "All these years later, I'm still incensed at what seemed to be so many arbitrary deselection decisions and the rigidity with which the program was run. They could have been a bit adaptive, flexible. You know, I understand that they now permit trainees to participate in developing a work plan and goals before the final site selection.

That strikes me as a more reasoned, ground up approach. In our day, it was a one size fits all, top down operating style. So primitive."

Tim shook his head in agreement. "I came so close to baling out. I stayed because I found something useful to do, blasting and deepening wells, which had little to do with our formal role."

Mel joined in. "And several of us built schools, no way that was in our job description."

Glen, looking wistful, went on. "Then, to make matters worse, I get a letter from my draft board telling me to report for my induction. That turned out to be a mistake, but it was yet another blow. It reminded me of the fact that I would have a long battle with the Selective Service System upon my return, which I did. I remember the night after being cut, before getting sick, I penned a poem. I can still recall it."

Catharsis
Glen, I think it's about your mind we are talking
Sitting here on the riverbank
That runs so deeply.
Is this you're river?
It isn't, is it?
A bubble, deep under the surface
Races and fights its way
Desperately to the surface:
"Now!" It shouts, as it breaks away.
And the gravel of a thousand roads
Rushes up at my feet.

We looked at him in silence. Each of us knew how easy that could have been any one of us, told to go home after investing so much of ourselves in getting ready. And then, for reasons never clear, we would be turned away as we sought to bring our idealism and energy to this harsh land.

"It was the beginning of a long struggle with my draft board and with myself. But I emerged whole in the end, and never had to fight in a war I despised. After all my battles, I eventually got a Doctorate from Stanford, became a very early employee of Apple Computer, wrote a two-volume work on the mathematical foundations of music and, best of all, became a happy semi-professional musician."

"Semi-professional?" Maureen asked.

"Yes, I played a lot of venues, wrote a lot of songs, but never was successful enough to give up my day job." His ending smile let us know he was finished.

———

After a brief pause, Kay cleared her throat, indicating she had something to say. "You know, after Janice moved to her new husband's village, I was alone and missed her companionship. I continued my medical center work, attended deliveries, taught some English at the high school, worked with women's groups, prepared posters, created kitchen gardens, and worked on nutrition programs. My biggest project was enlisting the help of the rotary club in the district town to cosponsor a triple antigen vaccination program for diphtheria, tetanus, and whooping cough for children in the village. Despite all this, I was very lonely and struggled quite a bit."

"That was unfair." Maureen asserted. "They never should have left you alone like that."

"I have this letter to my folks dated March 19, 1969. Apparently, a lot of us brought stuff along that would help us remember. This one says a lot.

I was just in Bombay for a week. Our director, Terry, called me in and wanted to know if I wanted to terminate early, that he was worried about me. He came in February to visit our sites and said mine was the worst of any in our group. Last July, when I asked for a transfer, Terry was not our director at the time or else he would have immediately done so. They have had three cases of volunteers in this area having nervous breakdowns, so he wanted to avoid that. I am tired tonight and thinking that it's been a good two years. I've grown in so many ways, only to find that there is always room for self-improvement. Being alone and living with one's faults is not easy, and I have this inferiority complex. I can get unbelievably tense at times which is due to suppressed emotions. There are moments when you really want to blow up at the doctor or shopkeeper cheating you or the drunk Indian man who grabbed me last week…"

"That's enough, you get the drift. This remains painful all this time later."

"I'm so sorry." Janice offered with obvious sincerity.

"It's okay, not your fault. The end of my time in India was a blur. The date of my last letter saved by my mother is April 4, 1969. From the time Janice left for Rajasthan to be with her new husband, I had requested a transfer. There was talk in one of my letters of assigning me to the village where Maureen and Cate lived so that I might work with them until our time in India was up. I so wanted to complete my tour. What I recall is that there was some glitch, the nature of which I do not remember. And so, I was sent home early, just weeks from the end of my tour. I missed the termination conference and the travel through Europe which I was planning to do with friends. Maybe Peace Corps was right, but it didn't have to end that way. It didn't."

———

"No, it didn't. You were so close to finishing." I said, feeling a flash of the old anger I had felt on our last train to Delhi in 1969 as we were about to muster out. "On our final trip to Delhi, I recall chatting with several others in 44-B about the mistakes that PC management was making. I tried drumming up support for confronting the brass about how bad things were in the field. It all seemed Kafkaesque, from changing our technical focus halfway through training to sites that seemed to have no idea we were coming to grudgingly providing resources and help once we were in our sites. Of course, the prime sin was selecting college kids who had no aptitude for their assigned roles. Then, the moment of truth came when we were being debriefed. I now recall being alone in my complaints, no one backed me. Perhaps that is not true, but that is how I remember it."

"No," Ben said. "I was there. You were at least the most outspoken critic for sure, probably the only one."

My Irish once again was a bit up. "Well, just think about it. They dumped us in these remote areas with only couple of us knowing what the hell we were doing. Okay, mistakes are made. It's not a perfect world and they had a tough job. But then they dug in. They really could have been flexible. Think for a moment, they could have used Glen's talents in a different, more culturally focused way. They could have paid some attention to Stan when he was so ill, just to keep him motivated. For God's sake, they could have moved Kay to be with other volunteers to finish out her tour. Oops, I better stop. You don't want me to get on a rant. I start to froth."

Connie looked at me closely. "Wow, I've never seen that temper, just the jokes."

"It's there, I just don't bring it out very often." Then I smiled. "You should see what happens when that bastard Trump comes on TV?"

"Shit! None of us can stand that asshole" Connie spit out between clenched teeth. We all looked at her in amazement since we never had heard such colorful language from her before.

"Wait," I chuckled. "Did that come from sweet Connie."

"Sweet?" Paul laughed. "You should see her when I don't do my assigned chores. The woman is relentless, utterly merciless." At that point, Connie elbowed her spouse in the tummy.

"It just burns me." Connie went on. "We had problems in this country when we were young, big ones for sure. But we had someone like JFK in the White House to motivate and inspire us. What do kids have today?"

"I'm not sure," I mused. "We had external enemies back as well as the usual array of internal whack jobs. Still there was a consensus about wanting to preserve our democracy. Today, the American experiment is hanging on by a thread. We seem on the verge of succumbing to a theocracy or white nationalist autocracy. At a minimum, it is government to the highest bidder. Really, why would kids today go overseas to save democracy or extend our values. They are now needed at home just to keep our own democracy from perishing. I keep thinking of Ben Franklin's words at the end of the Constitutional Convention when someone asked what kind of government the attendees had delivered to this young nation. Allegedly, his response was… *'a Republic, if you can keep it.'*"

"He said that, really?" Mel asked.

"Something like that," I shrugged. "After all, I wasn't there."

Stan in Vietnam as a medic after leaving India early.

Leaving for India, Glen with his guitar. PC screwed this one up.

CHAPTER 22

The Promised Land

Mel's brow furrowed. "Corbett, you said something a while back that intrigued me… something about your love life."

"Nooo." Came from several women. Their wail was becoming a familiar cry of desperation.

"Sorry ladies, but I'm curious," the man was not to be dissuaded. "When you mentioned that your claim of two years of celibacy was not quite true, I had this feeling that you were talking about more than your pursuit of guilty pleasure with the Anglo-PC staffer in Delhi? Did you have other successes? Could that possibly be! If true, that would put you in the India Peace Corps *Hall of Fame,*' or at least make you an iconic hero among the poor schlepps of India 44-B. Even the mutts of India 40 would bow to your mastery of the female seduction arts."

"Hall of shame you mean." Maureen uttered disdainfully.

"Mel, you know a gentleman never tells," I tried. "Perhaps the high road is appropriate here."

"Corbett!" Paul sputtered disdainfully. "You are no gentleman, and you couldn't find the freaking high road with GPS and a guide dog."

I smiled at Paul's good-natured jibe, then paused as if deciding where to go next. Quickly I concluded that the women already hated me with a passion, so why not. How much worse could their vitriol get? "Fair enough, I'll fess up. After all, I suspect the statute of limitations has expired on egregious acts of bad judgment."

"Oh, great," Maureen groaned loudly, "yet another story of depravity from our very own debauched pervert."

I smiled broadly. "I just love an eager audience, don't you guys? Surprisingly, Mel, you are right. My two years of involuntary celibacy were exaggerated. Perhaps not by that much but I did get to the promised land more than once." I paused with second thoughts. "Maybe I shouldn't, this really is embarrassing."

"You're in too deep now," Mel encouraged me.

"My God, you're not talking about one of us?" Nanette exclaimed with great concern.

"No, no! Even if I had enjoyed the fulness of your favors, from even one of you, I would not say a word. I may be stupid but I'm not suicidal."

"Good," she yet eyed me warily, "because I know where the knives are kept."

—

"Alright then, let's do this. Hell, I'm through the looking glass already. There is this one night I cannot forget. It's both memorable and, in a way, so very revealing. It is a kind of confession, like Mel's."

"Yes, do confess…" Paul enthused with a sinister smirk, then his face turned to concern. "Wait, not a night in Goa I hope."

"No, you moron! And yes, that WAS embarrassing but I was often embarrassed in my romantic misadventures, too often to keep count. If I had a dime for every time I flamed out, I would not have to rely on my favorite charity to survive… YRA.

"YRA?" What the hell is that?" Bob asked.

"Yachts for Retired Academics. Hell, if I had a buck for every time I've been shot down by a woman, I now could afford that private Lear Jet I've always coveted. No, this is a special story, a tale about that moment when I first climbed to the mountain top." I hesitated a moment for effect. "Here's another hint. I beat Mel to the mountain top but not by that much. What does that tell you?"

Bob laughed aloud. "Oh my God, this is about Corbett losing his… never mind. Is someone recording this?"

"Hey, no more interruptions please. No laughing! And no freaking audio or video recordings! This is like going to confession as a teenager and I don't want to see it on YouTube. But yes, a horrific admission… I was virtually in my dotage before I finally lost my virginity though, as it turns out, some of you characters didn't beat me by all that much. We all were so pathetic, the Catholics amongst us anyways. It was a different time for sure."

"True enough, but you just might have raised the futility bar here, Corbett. A new level of pathetic behavior." Paul looked pleased.

"Paul," Connie admonished her spouse, "let the poor man speak."

"Thanks. Some of you likely believe that I was a pillow-to-post guy, that I had a whole bunch of notches on my gun or wherever studs note their victories indicating female conquests. But such was not the case for me, just the opposite. Yup, it was a long and frustrating road before lust overcame virtue, or should I say guilt. Hell, I grew up as a classic basket case of enforced Catholic virtue despite myself, or at least despite my fondest hopes. There had been opportunities, of course, quite a few in fact. Alas, I remained a total numb nut for a long time. Let me define a numb nut for you, a man without any redeeming qualities, and certainly no common sense. The best thing to do when you run across such a numb nut is to take him out to the back-forty and put him out of his misery, like you do with a diseased cow."

"Volunteers, please! Looking for volunteers to take him out to the back-forty." Laura chortled at her small quip. Several hands shot up, all female.

"Yeh, yeah, big talk. Now, it is very difficult for me to admit that I was such a loser when it came to women. Sitting here, uttering these words, I writhe in disbelief that I might have turned women away, even females who indicated an obvious interest in some form of erotic congress. What kind of total moron was I?"

"I know, I know," Bob volunteered. "Call on me!"

"We all know, asshole. I was a total and complete moron. Truly, God cannot forgive a man who denies a woman in need since it so rarely happens… stumbling across a woman in need that is." I paused to look about and check if the guys were laughing at my confession of being such a late starter in the sack. To my relief, they weren't. Perhaps they had their own admissions waiting to be revealed. Perhaps they shared a similar shame of youthful romantic failure. Among members of the brotherhood, these were private failings seldom to be acknowledged before the world.

"Go ahead, Corbett, clearly you are not the only loser among us." Mel said as a kind of reaching out, commiserating with a fellow male sufferer.

With my toe already in the water, and sensing I was not alone in my personal suffering and private embarrassment, I permitted my tale of woe and then triumph to unfold. "I have a whole bunch of what I call *'ouch'* recollections, inevitably painful when brought to the surface. These recollections are among the most disquieting still retrievable from a largely misspent youth. They invariably involve failures in athletics, or in my scholarly pursuits, or in my early money-making ventures, and especially my numerous travails with those mysterious creatures of the female persuasion. These were areas of life, especially the last, where males were supposed to dominate back then, and where I didn't. I never came close and assumed I was alone in this."

"You weren't, of course." I missed who said that.

"Not by a long shot, a truth learned too late to help. Sometimes, though, I would hear stories." I paused, not sure I wanted to continue but then did. "I recall Ralph mentioning some of the women in training, none in this room by the way. He would casually note sleeping with someone. When I looked surprised, he would just as casually say *'you didn't? But everyone did.'* I knew that was crap, or thought it was. Still, it made me feel like a young teen again where all the guys knew more than me, and enjoyed more. It is a terrible feeling to sense you are behind in this race so essential to reaching manhood. Oh, and there was this language instructor that they brought in to upgrade our language skills in country. She was Christian, and married, and maybe fifteen years older than us. I mean, she seemed middle age to our young eyes. After the fact, I found out she had slept with half the guys in our group. Again, that feeling of being left out."

"Oh yeah," Harry had a huge smile. "I know who you're talking about, but I doubt it was half."

Mel groaned. "Guess I missed out again as well."

I wanted to get back on track, perhaps to get my confessional over with. "Now, admittedly, the number of females pursuing me was never overwhelming but the number was greater than one, perhaps measurably greater. Funny how different the male and female world views are. I recall women lamenting the fact that they had been loose earlier in their life, typically a confession made with copious amounts of self-loathing and guilt. When pushed for specifics, however, their alleged promiscuity never amounted to much. Their number of lovers over the course of years would be the same as claimed by some of my normal male buddies on a decent weekend. Males, of course, exaggerate here. They tend to reflect on their sexual conquests with pride and a sense of honor. I realized at some point that I had no honor… none. I was a loser who needed many more erotic memories for my future nursing home days. You know, for those days when I'm too old to chase the female nurses since I'll be using a walker to stay upright."

"Who knows?" Laura laughed. "Maybe then the gals will let you catch them, take pity on you. After all, what could you actually do after you managed to run them down?" Several women laughed. I tried to ignore them but found myself suppressing a giggle. The image of me chasing caregivers with my walker indeed was hilarious.

"Whatever! I suppose I can claim that my big moment arrived in a rather unexpected and memorable manner, or at least in an exotic location. It occurred early in our India adventure. We had just been officially sworn in as volunteers at the end of our long, arduous training period. It felt good to have survived this marathon process of preparation and testing. So, I was feeling a bit of pride and more than a touch of apprehension. The real test was ahead. Never thought about this possibility before but my self-confidence likely was up a notch or two for having made it through training and the selection process. That was a victory of sorts. My self-image typically wasn't high back then, to say the least, so anything positive was a marked improvement."

"Right," Janice affirmed, "the swearing in ceremony was a significant moment after all we had been through up to then."

"It was," I seconded her comment. "In any case, the next day we were to be sent off to our sites for two years of what, in our mind, surely would be enforced celibacy. On that long-ago day, I would have bet the mortgage that I would hit senility before reaching the promised land of sexual bliss or, failing that, just getting laid period like hapless Mel here. No offense, my friend." I looked in his direction.

"None taken, asshole." Mel smiled. "Now, excuse me a moment while I check to see whether they have any extra rat poison under the sink."

I looked around once again to see if anyone were laughing, or even smirking. I was most relieved to see that no one had descended into an uncontrollable bout of hilarity. In fact, they were listening respectfully.

"Don't stop now." Dee said. "This might be interesting."

"Really, Dee?" Paul smirked. "I think you might need to get a life."

After hurling a well-aimed pretzel at Paul, Dee said, "No, no, I'm hooked which, given the source, shocks the you know what out of me, probably because he is about to admit to a human frailty. Who knew he even had a heart?"

"Thanks Dee, I think. Now, before my fellow PCers and I descended into two years of Hell in our newly assigned villages, there was to be one last fete at the Lake Palace in Udaipur. Think about this as the last meal for the condemned man… a bit of pleasure before descending into Hades. This palace was an iconic site belonging to what had been the royalty that reigned over the local Mewar kingdom for several centuries. After independence, it had been converted into a glamorous hotel. As you can infer from its name, it is situated in the middle of a lake and is only accessible by boat. Jackie Kennedy, among other celebrities, had stayed there and the James Bond movie *Octopussy* used it as a prime shooting location for that epic flic. I would often see it pictured in tourist advertisements put out internationally by the Indian government. I read somewhere recently that it is now considered one of the most luxurious, and romantic, hotels in the world… probably because the site is unique and unparalleled. Here we were… for one night we embraced the kind of opulence reserved for a Maharaja. You are surrounded by water and the magic of the ancient Rajput city of Udaipur as it glistens on the far side of the water's edge, and all within sight of the Aravalli mountain range."

"It does sound romantic." Janice observed.

"In fact, two of my close colleagues from the University stayed there at my suggestion during a recent trip to India. They raved about it. Good thing, I believe they went out of their way on my word alone. Of course, none of us volunteers ever stayed there, way out of our price range. The bar would be as close as we ever got, and only because Peace Corps hosted this shindig before sending us into exile for two long years. In fact, back then I think only foreigners were permitted to take the boat to the hotel since liquor was illegal to Indian nationals. I believe you had to show your passport to even get on board the boat taking you over. Surely, this night was like the last wish to be granted before the guilty miscreant is executed for his dastardly crimes. Did I use that line already?"

"Not a problem." Laura said. "At your advanced age, repetition is to be expected."

"I would argue with you Laura, but when you are right, you are right. In any case, it turns out that one of the Peace Corp staff members was tall, slender, attractive, and smart. Indian herself, she graduated from the prestigious Smith College located in western Massachusetts. She was, as the saying goes, a stone-cold fox though considered to be off-limits since she was way too sophisticated for us Philistines. Besides, she was engaged to be married to another volunteer who would soon be finishing up his tour of duty. So, there were two strikes against us mortals. She was way out of my league and already taken."

"Corbett," Bob smirked, "any female with the requisite number of limbs still attached was out of your league."

"I gave Bob an appropriate response using my now well used and fatigued middle finger before continuing. "My prior in those days was that any female who had already scored a schmuck for herself, gotten a marriage commitment that is, would have little carnal interest in any other schmuck. And let's face it, on the pyramid of schmuckdom I was positioned at the pinnacle or is it the bottom. No matter, I was an outlier. I had neither wealth nor fame nor position going for me and what else was there to attract any female's attentions. My sparkling wit and continental charms were not worth bull crap. I mean, women couldn't turn those attributes into cash."

"Your Boston accent! You had that." Dee offered.

"Good point, but still not worth anything of value to a woman. No way to turn a cute accent into hard currency." I lamented.

"In case you hadn't noticed, you're being terribly sexist here." Maureen observed.

"Ah, the truth is never pleasant. It typically is painful in fact. Bravely, I shall shoulder on if you will permit me."

"Go ahead." Maureen sighed with a hint of resignation.

"Normally, I would think my odds of scoring with such a woman to be somewhat lower than winning the Nobel Prize in physics. Somewhat lower? Let me be honest here. I would have put my chances here at well below zero, a mathematical impossibility yet still the closest accurate estimation of my true odds at the time. Hell, I think the last time I had employed my patented seduction move, a coat rack shot me down. In my defense on that occasion, the lighting was poor. Wait, that's usually a point in my favor, never mind."

"Corbett, your wandering again, not that anyone is listening." Once again it was Bob who was proving to be the good taskmaster. "By the way, everyone agrees that poor lighting would be essential to any success you might have… even with a coat rack?"

I didn't even bother with my usual response. "Yes, in truth I am digressing once again. Thanks Bob. You are an ass, but a necessary ass. Thinking back, I don't recall spending much time with her that night. In a picture surviving from that glorious evening I am chatting with my two favorite language instructors, Amar and Usha. I loved Amar's personality and thought Usha way too cute. But I never even considered either in a romantic way. I would not risk two good friendships. Indian gals could be friendly, but you just knew they would knee you in the nuts if you got frisky. Well, probably not, but I have always been attached to the family jewels and prefer not to put them in harm's way. Still these Indian women have some fine qualities, like being oriented toward serving their men, attributes long lost among American broads."

"Oh, bite me." Connie said. "I knew my instincts about you back then were right on."

"Damn it, Corbett, when does the good part start?" Harry was impatient.

—

"I'm there, ready!

"We were ready four hours ago." Bob was impatient now.

"Right, here we go! At the end of this last evening before heading to our sites the next morning, we were in a good mood and well lubricated with Taj Mahal beer. This was very potent stuff by the way, stronger than American brew. In any case, we left the hotel to journey back to our quarters. First, we waited for the boats to take us back across the lake to where several taxis would then make their way back to where we were staying. As we waited, the woman in question and I started chatting, about nothing of consequence. Then, we were crowded next to each other in one of the taxis taking us back to the training facilities. I thought this positioning totally random, at least on my part. In hindsight, I wondered if she could have been making a move… on me! Still, the thought I might get lucky with this goddess was simply ridiculous. I never got lucky. Any such fantastical hope never even crossed my mind."

"Finally, the story is getting good. I was almost asleep here." Mel whispered to no one in particular.

"The intervening decades mute surviving memories but there must have been some electricity between us. I do recall that our hands met in the dark safety of the crowded taxi. She must have sought out my hand since the reverse seems highly unlikely. Could she have been lusting after me all these past weeks? Doubtful, but I was terrible at reading women. As the old saying goes, I would have trouble getting laid in a woman's prison with a fistful of pardons. In any case, upon arriving at our destination we hung back as the others drifted off to their rooms. Without words between us, the two of us wandered off to a secluded spot where some privacy could be secured. There, just like in any classic male fantasy, we tore each other's clothes off before sinking into the lush grass, limbs intertwined and, as they say, need finding its ultimate expression."

"Oh, my word! Who the hell ever uses that kind of flowery language?" One of the gals muttered.

I paused, suddenly embarrassed at my choice of such words. "Sorry, I'll try to keep this clean and simple. If I had had a chance to think, I undoubtedly would have talked my way out of yet another opportunity to score, simpleton that I was back then. But maybe it was in the stars. After all, it was a typical lush, Indian night and there was that canopy of those very stars looking down upon us from above. The night sky in many parts of India, by the way, seems brilliant if not breathtaking. Here you might see a sprinkling of stars. There, you often saw dense fields of prickly lights, especially in rural areas."

"That's true, it could be romantic." Dee offered and then blushed.

I smiled and continued. "I had grown totally weary of being the last virginal numb nut of my generation. I did not know about Mel's struggles at the time so considered my virginal state a singular failure. Yes, I am sure it was the romance of a warm Indian night, and desperation at the thought of two more years of celibacy, that pushed me to the top of that carnal mountaintop. Finally, I had reached that promised land."

"Hear, hear!" a male voice uttered.

"A capital moment in every man's life." Dexter from India 40 added.

"Come to think on it, I recall so many nights where we sat on top of our government housing appreciating the night sky, perhaps for the first time in my life. I yet miss that experience… of the night sky, not the sex. Too old now to care about that sex stuff." I noticed Bob eying me. "Oops, I'm wandering again. In any case, we dressed after a bit and snuck off to her room where the lovemaking could continue in more comfort. My most vivid memory from that night, one of them at least, was her exclamation that I was *a real man.*"

"Now you're making crap up. No way!" Paul chortled.

"I swear. But I do understand your reaction. That was my reaction as well. Like, excuse me! Was she kidding? Just how did that happen? She must have been fantasizing about someone else at that moment, maybe her betrothed. How could I be a 'real' man, whatever the hell that was, since I was freaking clueless! How could someone oppressed by many years of Catholic guilt do so well the first time sliding into home base? I could hardly figure out where freaking home base was, the thought of crossing it successfully was on par with discovering a cure for cancer or coming up with a general theory that explained all the forces of nature. That goal, by the way, eluded Einstein during his lifetime though, if the reports are true, that man was quite the hound dog with the ladies. In any case, she must have been dynamite at faking orgasms and in jacking up male egos. Perhaps that is how she snagged this other schmuck. No, what am I thinking? She really was a catch."

"No doubt about that." Harry threw-out in the direction of several male heads that were nodding in agreement. "We all remember her very, very well. Sonny was totally smitten with her."

"I recall thinking at the time. It was not like I had not been drunk with other women who seemed willing in the moment, though the Catholic girls of my acquaintance universally had been ambivalent on the topic of sex. By ambivalent, I mean they were either dead set against it under any circumstances or they were desperately dead set against it just with me. On the other hand, perhaps Catholic girls already knew that three-fourths of women would never achieve orgasm through intercourse alone. Males, they intuited, were far less essential than a well-charged vibrator. In any case, it was a bleak era indeed in which to grow up. Let me be more accurate here. It was a bleak period to grow up if you were a Catholic boy, ridden with guilt, and too stupid to breathe on your own."

"Amen!" Tim issued and then blushed.

—

"Now, finally, I had reached the mountain top. The dirty deed was done. I was shocked to discover that I was not struck down by God. The earth did not open, my family jewels were not suddenly covered with hideous warts, nor was I caste into a bottomless pit of hellfire."

"Still might happen." Maureen smirked. "We gals have hope."

"I'm voting for the warts." Laura added.

"So appreciative of all the support." I chuckled. "What did happen that night was that I had a great time. Hmm, I promptly concluded that this sex stuff was worth pursuing with greater purpose. And I did, though India is not fertile ground, no pun intended, for uncovering many new sensual opportunities. That ancient culture may have given us the *Kama Sutra* but that is where their generosity in this matter ends. I must say that, once I started, I did make up for lost time. If the better survey data is to be believed, I wound up enjoying more sexual partners than the typical male, though I am always shocked at how low that median number is. In any case, I will have some explaining to do for St. Peter when the time comes."

"That was it?" Laura asked. "Wham, bam, thank you ma'am."

"Now wait. You make it sound as if I tricked her into sex. She seduced me."

I looked about at a host of skeptical female expressions. They could not believe that any woman had such low standards. "It's true, goddamn it. Impossible to believe but true."

"If you say so, stud." Dee smiled.

"Oh, come on! Surely, she was bombed out of her skull." Even Paul looked skeptical.

"True, the evidence would suggest that, but she seemed totally sober at the time and quite sincere when she called me *a real man.* I mean, why should she lie? It wasn't like she wanted to snag me, she was already set in the husband department, an American catch who would take her back to the promised land where she had been educated. Hell, she was more Americanized than half of us. There really was no explanation in my confused, but sexually sated, brain."

"Did you continue seeing each other after that?" Laura asked with a note of derision in her voice. "Don't tell me it was just another typical male quickie. God, you men all the same."

"See, always thinking the worst of guys. That was, in truth, our only real carnal experience, though I would have been most happy to, what shall we say, service her again."

"Oh, puke!" Cate groaned reaching for another pretzel to launch in his direction.

"To me, she was the perfect woman, engaged to some other Peace Corps schmuck. This is what all guys seek, an attractive female with nonexistent standards who will not go all commitment-phobic on you."

"Commitment phobic?" One of the gals sneered contemptuously.

"You know," I said, scanning the audience for signs of hostility or, worse, an immediate physical attack. Thankfully, all seemed calm. "Commitment-phobic… that's where mere kisses become emotional contracts that are way too difficult to break. One night in the sack and suddenly you're picking out linen patterns at *Bed, Bath, and Beyond.* In truth, I did see her once or twice after that but there were few opportunities other than stolen moments for some brief, light petting. As I recall, she soon married this guy when his tour was up and lived happily ever after."

Laura groaned. "And men wonder why we ignore them."

"That really is a mystery. After all, we are such prizes." I argued, trying to sound sincerely perplexed.

"Let me return to Laura's question about what happened after that night. One subsequent connection deserves comment. One of her duties was to visit the volunteers in their sites. I assume we needed to be checked on after all the antics from the mutts of India-40, the group that set the bar exceptionally low for all future male volunteers. In fact, they set it below zero."

"We were only paving the way for you losers." Paul agreed. "You can thank us later."

"It would have been better had they sent a male official since being visited by an attractive female raised eyebrows among the locals but there you have it. I recall a local man of some import asking me where she was staying, and I had no good answer. In fact, I had no idea at all. He looked at me with obvious disapproval. Peace Corps brass strikes again."

"Where did she sleep?" someone asked.

"As I recall, she just rolled out a sleeping bag and slept on our floor in a different room."

"That definitely was not well considered by central office." Connie noted.

"Understand! Ralph was around so nothing much was going to happen in any case. But she and I did find ourselves alone at one point. We kissed, and I touched her breast. I could feel her shiver. I remember thinking that I did turn her on, or everyone turned her on. I cannot say for sure which. No, for once I'll go with the interpretation that puts me in a good light. She was responsive to me, end of story. Ah, self-delusion really is a wonderful thing. I have no idea why it is considered a mental problem. I love my delusions. They are quite comforting."

"And what makes it all so wonderful is that you have so many of them." Connie smiled.

"However, since you women love it when we males suffer from our obsession with sex, I will make your day."

"How's that?" Connie said with an even broader smile.

"My guilt. Hey, I slept with an engaged woman before my college girlfriend got around to dumping me which I guess is a form of cheating. On the other hand, I was not actually engaged to my girlfriend back home, though I had tried, sort of. I had raised the issue of marriage in a letter, more than one I believe, which she studiously ignored."

"So, you had proposed to the girl left behind."

I demurred. "Yes! But as I said, my timid offerings of some form of commitment were met with general silence, on that issue at least."

"So," Cate pronounced, "it is apparent that your college sweetheart was a very bright woman. I mean, she was smart enough to identify a loser."

"She was, both quick and astute. In fact, all my real girlfriends early in life were exceptionally smart. All the serious ones, as far back as high school, went on to earn doctorates. The bottom line is that while I am a pig, I am not a complete idiot. Sex is a rather small part of any significant relationship. You need to connect on many levels, with intellectual compatibility being one of the most important."

"Well, Corbett, whatever you feel about things, she was a fox." Harry exulted. "You are one lucky SOB, and so freaking undeserving."

"Harry! Don't encourage him." Nanette said in a scolding tone.

"And I forgot my ear plugs this time." Kay said but smiled.

"Really, no applause is necessary. I will be signing autographs later, though."

"Oh damn," Dee snickered, "I forgot my autograph book, thankfully. I can just imagine what she thought after sobering up and realizing that she had slept with you? That must have shocked her, and surely caused a bout of nausea."

Despite the insults, I continued undaunted. "Maybe she really liked me or maybe I was a diversion. After, in my village, I wondered what might have happened if we had met and she was not already taken, so to speak. She had all the right qualities… intelligence, education, wit, looks. Most amazingly of all, she responded to me sensually. It was the trifecta. However, a guy always calculates the price he must pay for sex. I knew the price would be high in this case. After all, she had been born to affluence and status, I think her mother was a well-known author. What hope would I have had to meet her expectations?"

"But Tom," Dee said with excessive affectation, "you always meet ours." She fluttered her eyes in an exaggerated fashion.

"All I am saying is that there is nothing worse than an asymmetrical relationship where some equity of talent and circumstances is missing. I never start out to be a bastard, not every time at least. Really, I'm not as evil as I sound. I think about the long haul."

"Yeah, right!" Someone said.

I decided that defending my sorry ass was doomed to abject failure. "Let me just say, I have paid a price on the scale of justice where the gender wars are measured. At the risk of getting voted out of India 44…"

"Didn't we do that already. I am sure we did. I remember distinctly since I voted him out at least seven times."

"Hah. Hah. What I was going to say is that we guys do have it rough."

"Oh please!" Laura sniffed. "Anyone have one of those little violins on them?"

"My God, I certainly hope you are not up for canonization as a saint." Dee joined Laura, who had simulated a gun with her hand that was aimed at me.

"In fact, the canonization process is moving along well. Right now, they are looking for two miracles that I performed, one of the criteria that must be met. Surviving India was one."

"And the other?"

I'm hoping that surviving this session will count."

"You better not pin your hopes on that one." Laura smirked.

The Lake Palace, where my journey to the 'promised land' started.

Chatting with Amar and Usha before my big moment.

CHAPTER 23

A Petri Dish

I looked about me. The situation seemed perilous as I saw several females picking up pretzels. They were not looking for salty snacks. No, their intent clearly was to cause me bodily harm. For a moment, I thought one started playing with a knife that had been laid out to cut the cheese. I next considered that a considerable collection of these offensive missiles, normally known as pretzels, already had accumulated around me. More likely would soon find their way in my direction. Yes, it was clear that several excursions into the labyrinths of my erotic past had elicited the expected response… disgust and something akin to homicidal retribution.

"Wait, I apologize for taking us so deeply into the depths of my love life, a tragedy for sure."

"You're the one that keeps talking about it. You make it sound as if your romantic escapades were all you brought back from our Indian experience." Laura observed.

"Oh my God, that is so not true." I tried to protest. "There are many other scars, some of them that I realized even as we made our way back home."

"Like what?" Maureen asked to encourage me away from those erotic debacles on which we had been stuck. She put down her pretzel but kept it within easy reaching distance.

"Okay, I remember getting to Athens. What struck me, at least, is that we could walk about the streets without anyone paying attention. Simply amazing, we could walk the streets in anonymity. After two years of standing out, being treated differently, this was like a total release. Does anyone else get what I'm saying?"

Various affirmative responses came in his direction. "But go on. We want to hear your take, heaven forbid." Connie looked uncertain even as she said the words.

"Well, it was several things but let me see if I can sort them out." I paused to figure out how to find safety in some serious topic. I find it easier to joke about my sexual mishaps and escapades, topics that are humorous by nature. Serious issues demand more thought and consideration, always a challenge. "Okay, invisibility can be a good thing. How is that you ask?"

"No one asked," Paul shot out.

I ignored him. "Think about this. As we have discussed, we go through life with these hard-wired ways of dealing with the ordinary events and interactions. For example, I know that Paul will try to insult me, as many of the mutts from India-40 are disposed to do. Then, I will come right back at him. Of course, I will get the best of the exchange since he labors under an intellectual disadvantage."

"Hysterical, Corbett!" He huffed but with a smile.

"And, of course, he will continue to grind endlessly on the fact that I tried to hit on his future wife, even though unsuccessfully, and this happened some five decades ago. That's like another life. But we do this dance effortlessly, without thinking, and certainly without animosity."

"No animosity? You think so?" Paul said continuing to smile.

I smiled back. "But think about this, and now I'm totally serious. While we were in India, remember that everything was a conscious act, everything in public that is. I joked about debating with our domestic staff about sneaking women into our home. Sure, it was a funny anecdote but also deadly serious. Prostitution may be illegal in the U.S., but it is so common that no real censure attaches to it. The authorities merely go through the motions trying to outlaw the practice. In India, by engaging in that same act we likely would have been ostracized in our site. Essentially, we would have been rendered ineffective, even more useless than we already were. Likely, we would have been sent home if not careful. Bob and Mel scampered off to Udaipur to do the dirty deed where there was little chance of getting caught. Using working women, though they supply a desperately needed service, is taboo there, a much greater cultural violation there than here."

"No shit!" Nanette exclaimed. "Being a poor woman in India was worse than being a black female in the United States."

"I agree with you. A young Indian woman losing her virginity back in the 1960s would have been a catastrophe for most families. Honor killings were real. But thinking hard about stuff, what we experienced, extended to all phases of life and not just the big stuff. Hell, India has as many rules as it has gods. I think I read somewhere that over 30,000 deities, major and minor, have been identified in the Hindu pantheon. No matter the real number, the fracture lines dividing people are endless and everywhere. In every conversation, no matter how casual. You need to be aware with whom you are interacting including what specific configuration of cross-cutting roles and identities they represent. There really are few casual conversations. It is just so easy to make a mistake and some mistakes are difficult to overcome."

"Like what?" someone asked.

"Well, I recall early on, as we ended our training in country. I was being asked endless questions by students from the local school. They were asking about life in America. One of them inquired about what we ate on a typical day. I struggled through several food items when I started running out of items for which I knew the Hindi equivalent. Without thinking, I threw out beef as an example. I knew it was a huge mistake the moment the word was gone. Alas, there was no taking it back and nuanced discussions of cultural relativity in a language over which you had elementary fluency was out of the question. Try discussing cultural preferences with a primitive command of Hindi, especially with those who have an absolutist view of things. Multiply such incidents exponentially and you get the idea. After two years of thinking, and screwing up, you are exhausted. Moreover, you are not aware of how tired you are until you escape the fishbowl."

Maureen spoke thoughtfully. "It was hard. You are right. At the same time, being in a new environment, a new culture, helps you see yourself. It gives you a chance to look at your own culture from outside that fishbowl you keep referencing."

"Yes, absolutely. There were moments of clarity where how we personally had changed became clear. I recall going to the Oberoi Hotel in Delhi once. It was a hotel that catered to Westerners. Of course, I could not afford to stay there, I was just splurging on a breakfast, an American breakfast, while dreaming about the day when such a thing would be normal, not the highlight of the month, probably the year. Nearby, I could hear an American guest complaining loudly about his orange juice not being fresh. Not fresh enough! Really? That's what was bothering this nimrod? I had spent several months crapping in a hole and sweltering in 115-degree heat and worrying that I might be screwing up the lives of local farmers with my ill-conceived advice and all this clown could do was complain about his goddamn morning libation. He was lucky I didn't pour my coffee over his head. Talk about ugly Americans. Okay, I was an ugly American, no doubt about that. But he was even uglier."

"Good point, Tom. We were ugly but there were worse. We tried at least." Tim offered in his quiet way.

"We did. Now I know that all of us felt deeply guilty about bringing so few skills to our villages. We all can think of things we might have done better or with more energy or imagination. But past is past. We tried our best and probably did some good. Hell, the Indian Embassy in D.C. even had a fete for the volunteers who were in town for the 50th anniversary of the creation of Peace Corps. They couldn't have been that pissed off at us for mucking around their country a half century earlier. Time heals all wounds I suppose, or some at least."

"That was a lovely evening." Connie said. "Corbett even gave a copy of our first India 44 edited volume to the Embassy officials during the ceremony. "We were rather proud."

"That was Harry's idea. Fortunately, we had brought a copy to show others. He and I scrambled to find it after he came up with this notion. I wonder if any of the Embassy staff read it?"

Mel chuckled. "Hope not."

"Probably not. There was no ensuing international kerfuffle." Bob added.

"In any case, here was my take-away that slowly dawned on me as I made my way through Europe. I realized that I had a deeper appreciation of my own culture, of the very importance of culture in our lives. If you live in the same fishbowl all the time, you have no freaking idea where you are. You must spend time outside that bowl to fully appreciate the reality of life on the inside. Most people never get that opportunity. They go to a default position, assuming their cultural milieu is all that exists and then walk about confused as to why the whole world does not see things from their perspective. Look at the Trump phenomenon, his cultish devotees are hyper-tribal people, incapable of appreciating anything outside their own small fishbowls."

"Toilet bowls, you mean." Greg laughed grimly.

"Very clever... and spot on! Beyond the jokes, I think we learned something irreplaceable, even if we could not articulate it. Let me try a simple example. Take how we view time, for example. This was a jarring and universal experience that we all ran up against. Hard not to. Time for westerners had an almost concrete feel to it. The word had substance, a tangible meaning. If the bus was just *now* coming, that meant in a few minutes and, if it didn't, we would expect an explanation. In our minds, our anger was justified. We normally did not see that among rural residents of the subcontinent. They accepted inconvenience passively. My guess, the difference is based on a culture that had been static for centuries. They have developed a different appreciation of concepts like time. Our bodies evolved within an upbeat time schedule. That accelerated pace is the same for most westerners around us, surely for those with whom we interacted. Naturally, there is heterogeneity within the western world. The pace in New York is faster than Podunk Iowa. So, I suppose Dan had no problem in India, being from Wyoming or some god forsaken backwater hell hole."

"Hey!" Dan objected.

"And I'm from Montana." Stan noted.

"Oh Stan, I would never admit to that, not in public at least." I smiled at him. "Listen, we all know this classic example far too well. You would ask, when will the bus be here, the common response is that it was *just now coming,* expressed with that little shake of the head. So, dutifully trained in the western concept of time, we would move from the shade to the sun-bleached spot where the bus was supposed to be just now arriving. After all, we wanted an advantage in finding a seat on what would be a jampacked bus. Next, we craned our head in anticipation of it coming around the corner. An hour later, now tottering from sunstroke, we would return to ask the same question. When will the bus arrive? *Oh Sahib, no problem*, the same informant would respond, *it is just now coming.* Thanking our helper once again, we would return to our sun-drenched position to keep expectant watch. It never seemed to occur to us that no one else ever joined us in our faithful watch for the arrival of the bus. Of course, the bus eventually did arrive, some two hours after we had been carted off to the hospital with a severe case of sunstroke. In the West, now means now or soon at the worst. In India, back then, the same word meant sometime in the indefinite future but before the end of time if you were lucky. A subtle difference, yet critical to those whose internal wiring is configured so differently. The concept of 'now' might mean five seconds, five minutes, five hours, five days, or five months but it is coming, *just be patient Sahib.*"

"Yes, yes, and it took us so long to get it no matter how many times we were told during training." Harry moaned. "There are some things that don't come easily, they have to be experienced."

"For sure, conceptually understanding something is one thing, emotionally getting it is quite another. We have India to thank for teaching us this simple, yet invaluable, lesson. Here is another example, one that we took away from the place. Remember how we interacted with all the vendors we dealt with, though perhaps I shouldn't speak for us as a group. I don't know about you guys, but I usually counted my change carefully in normal transactions. You assumed that the natives, those who did not know you personally, thought you were rich and thus ripe for the plucking. They also assumed you might be ignorant of the local currency and prices. So, you assumed that you might be an easy mark, especially since you were not experienced at bargaining nor highly fluent in the language. Your white skin, except for Harry and Nanette and maybe Connie, set you apart, sometimes for good and sometimes in not such a good way. In retrospect, the vendors there were no different than elsewhere where bargaining still happened. It is just that presumptions were made about us based on superficial attributes."

"No shit!" Harry groaned. "I got so tired of being called Muhammad Ali."

"Yeah, too bad you couldn't fight like him." I laughed.

"Probably could still whip your ass." Harry quipped with a chuckle.

"Hell, Nanette could whip Corbett's ass." Glen said as Nanette and the others howled with laughter.

I smiled. "True enough. I always was a make love, not war, kind of guy. We came away with some scars based on experience. An example... in Greece, Bob and I went out to one of the Islands for a day. Toward late afternoon, we realized we had to get back to catch the last boat or be stuck on the island overnight. We found a cab and off we went, so far so good. Then the cabbie stopped to pick up his friend, and we saw the fare continuing to mount. He dropped off his friend somewhere and we now assumed we were going in some circuitous route as the fare continued to climb. Bob and I were fuming in the back seat. Based on two years in India, we presumed the driver saw us as easy targets to be cheated. By the time we got to where the boat fortunately yet awaited, our adrenaline was pumping. We jumped out of the cab ready for a battle royal. The cabbie calmly asked for less than half of what was on the meter. Bob and I were stunned into silence and meekly handed over the money. We were not prepared for honesty. I mean, he still might have cheated us but not by nearly as much as we originally thought."

"Funny, I don't recall the cab drive." Bob observed. "I remember the island though."

"I remember the silliest stuff. Hmm, do you remember the time Hank, you and I saw two American girls on a beach in Greece? We thought our prayers had been answered at long last. They weren't, of course, but I do remember we struck up a conversation. One was a decent-looking young woman, nothing special though. The other one was a total stunner who, if she had been a couple inches taller, could be mistaken for a model right out of Vogue. Immediately, we found that the average looking gal was quite interesting while the ravishing beauty had the IQ of a tadpole. So freaking disappointing. She could only respond monosyllabically, not due to lack of interest but from her lack of vocabulary and of anything remotely interesting to say."

"Been there!" Harry shook his head.

"That story reminds me of the Rauschkolb principle, which was self-named after an old friend of mine from graduate school. He insists that he first articulated this universal principle. According to this deep thinker, there were three essential dimensions that males look for in women… looks, intelligence, and personality. If you were lucky, you could find two of these in any given female. However, you could never find all three. He considered this fact some form of divine law. Anyway, I immediately lost all interest in this goddess, not that I had a chance to begin with. She would have been perfect for Trump, though, brainless and beautiful. Remember that, Bob?"

"Sort of," he shrugged his shoulders, "but I definitely recall Greece."

"Clever lad. Apparently, it is the way my brain works. I remember vignettes, small events that mean something to me and nothing to a normal person. Ask me about something useful, like how to charge a car battery and I can never recall which connector goes where. The stupid things I do remember usually are small in themselves but carry something of significance only to me, an insight to be stored for future use. For example, I recall a picture I took of you pushing one of the fallen columns of the Parthenon as if you might restore it to an upright position."

"Wait," Bob piped up, "what freaking insight did you get from that?"

"No idea," I admitted. "However, I believe they made those columns off limits to tourists the very next day. But what I considered at the end of that near kerfuffle with the island taxi driver is this. Did our India experience harden us in some way? Along with so many good lessons, had we also come to generally expect less of people? My guess is that the lessons we took with us are complex indeed, some good and some not so good."

"So, what did you learn from all your romantic disasters?" Cate asked. "Did those harden you?"

"I learned that I'm a putz. But I knew that going in, so I can't blame India for that. Okay, I'll be half serious for a moment. I learned that it is so difficult to understand others. We cannot presume that others see the world as we do. If male, that is true of women. If white, that is true for non-whites. If Western, that would apply to Indians. Sometimes, the barriers are cultural, or educational, or experiential. In the case of women and men, the barriers emanate from our different wiring. God really is Don Rickles in disguise. Remember him?"

"You mean God?" Tim asked.

"No! Rickles. He was this comedian who specialized in sarcasm. Like Rickles, God loves playing games. He gave us two genders that are close enough to appear to be the same species. We therefore believe that both genders think the same way and feel the same things. And so, we walk around totally confused because we are not operating out of the same hymnal, not even close. Makes for good sport though and plenty of laughs for whomever is in charge."

"My god, I think he's being serious." Laura sounded shocked.

"Rather cynical." Janice added.

"No," Mel said, "I think he's finally on to something."

"Just my observation, who knows the truth. Anyway, when I got back, and was in school, I think I approached people differently. I did not dismiss people based on superficial things. I listened and probed and got to know them. There were some I would have dismissed in my pre-India days based on first impressions. But, upon my return, I was more open to them and we had a greater chance of becoming friends. I found I could learn stuff from those whom I might have dismissed with my pre-India dispositions. We close off so much in ordinary life. There's the Frank Zappa quote I love. *The mind is like a parachute; it only works when it is open.* Peace Corps helped us develop parachute-like minds. It helped me be open to people."

"And yet, Corbett, you still don't have any friends." Bob smiled.

I smiled back. "Not true, my good man, I have this firm called Rent-a-Friend on retainer. I mean, I must pay premium prices to get anyone from there to spend time with me, but still, they deliver on demand."

"Mel," Bob said as if serious, "you should give that firm a call."

I continued as Mel tried in vain to respond. "Moving on. It's just that the cultural mosaic of India is a living lesson in cultural nuance. If you paid attention, you would see just how encompassing one's culture was, how fully it shapes people. Each specific culture imparts its own language, world views, norms, values, expected roles, meanings of life, group aspirations, and so much more. The amazing thing is that, as I noted earlier, the individual member of any group often remains oblivious to how trapped they are by their version of the world. Oh sure, individuals knew they were different, had distinct gods, or marched to their own rules for managing daily life. Still, most fail to appreciate just how much their own cultures inform and dictate everything about them. So much of our cultural baggage is pre-conscious. More deeply than ever before, I began to see how much of what I was had been forged in the petri-dish of my working class, Catholic, ethnic world in Worcester Mass. I never interacted with 'others' until I got to college, and they weren't that different from me."

"Wow, you did have two strikes against you." Cate, from California, offered.

Paul said thoughtfully. "Everyone is vastly different than you, Corbett."

"Spawned by a unique culture for sure." Mel added.

I deadpanned in response. "Of course, I also realized how superior my culture was to most of you barbarians, especially you west-coasters. Then again, we all can't be lucky."

I ducked to miss several pretzels, this time from my west coast male peers who, for some inexplicable reason, took exception to my characterization of their universally recognized cultural backwardness.

At that moment, Connie wound up and threw a perfect strike that hit me in the nose. "Bullseye!" She said with glee.

"Okay, I was just kidding. It's only the *male* west coasters that are backward." I instinctively ducked once more but nothing was thrown. "Seriously, these lessons in the deeper meaning and significance of one's culture were treasures that I kept closely held. In some ways, they shaped how I saw things as an academic and policy wonk later. I don't know where else I could have picked up such insights. Reading about culture in a textbook is sterile, abstract. Watching it in action is profound, sometimes leaving indelible imprints."

"Of course, for you Corbett, textbooks would be useless. You must be able to read above a 5th grade level to profit from them." Paul smiled.

I hurled an available pretzel in Paul's direction. Unfortunately, I hit his spouse on top of the head instead. In response, she shook her fist at me. "Oops, my bad. Really, I never did have good control as a baseball pitcher."

———

I took another stab at being serious. "India was the perfect petri-dish."

"What?" Sherry asked.

"Think about it. Where else can you experience a radically different world, something capable of giving you a unique perspective on life in the West. It had the perfect conditions for developing a new life, at least new ways of looking at stuff. I can remember sitting in our site watching the water buffalo amble by, as if the world had nothing better to do than wait for their journey to be completed. Everything moved with the energy of molasses. And yet, from another perspective, you could see great change which, compared to previous rates of societal change, was approaching warp speed. The juxtaposition of the immediate and the micro with the long-term and the macro was amazing."

"Now you are losing me."

"Let's see if I can articulate what I'm thinking more clearly by returning to an old theme we touched on earlier. Perhaps your villages were like this. If you looked closely, there were these generational levels. In my site there were. First, there were the elders, often still residing on tiny, postage-size farms. They drew water from wells as they had for centuries, plowed their fields and sowed their crops as their ancestors had done since Shiva was a boy. I've touched on this point before, but it bears repeating. Life was endless repetition, no wonder they readily accepted the concept of reincarnation, everything was a repeat of what had come before. That led to a sense of resignation, perhaps acceptance of what life had given them. It looked like passivity to us Westerners. There were many other things. Most of these poor, local farmers spoke the local dialect, Mewari in my area. They had a world view that did not extend beyond their immediate area. And they were least likely to try new things. Let's call them the *traditionalists*."

"That pretty much summarizes everyone in my village." Don, a sweet guy raised in Wyoming, said.

"Mine as well," Hank added.

"I may have been a bit fortunate. Salumbar was a somewhat bigger town, greater heterogeneity. There were merchants and tradesmen and government officials living in the town. They had some education, for the most part, a few were decently educated. They spoke Hindi and some spoke English, a few with fluency. They read newspapers and discussed politics on a broader scale. They certainly were cognizant of what was going on in the wider world, in India and the subcontinent. Still, their lives pretty much centered on Salumbar and Udaipur, the main city in our area. Let's call them the *transitionals*. Obviously, I'm making the labels up as I go."

"Isn't that your strength, making crap up?" Dexter, from India-40, offered this assessment.

"We still can't believe his students didn't ask for refunds." Paul tried his old joke again.

"Ha, ha. I have no idea why some of you guys were not chucked out of India immediately. You are such nimrods. Moving on. Then there were those locals fortunate enough to have attended university. They were the professionals like the lawyers and medical specialists and teachers and higher government officials, though some were merchants or wealthier farmers. They tended to be younger and many oversaw educating the younger generation or helping the locals move beyond the feudal-age technologies and practices that were holding the place back. They spoke English, knew about world affairs, read the Hindi Times, and could debate issues at some level of abstraction. They were the *futurists*, for want of a better term."

"Wouldn't you find these groups anywhere?" Janice asked.

"I think not. Some sites were too small. You'd probably only find traditionalists there. In larger cities, these groups were segregated and hardly interacted. This is like the three bears with the porridge either being too hot or too cold or just right. Salumbar was just the right size, big enough to have all three but of a scale that you could easily observe how each looked upon the world and interacted with one another."

"Interesting point." Bob grudgingly conceded.

"At the end of the day, it was the kids that impressed me the most. They had curiosity. Many were learning English, reading about the broader world, and thinking about things their parents and grandparents could barely appreciate. All three worlds were reflected in the kids for sure, but I sensed things were rapidly moving away from the traditionalist camp to the other groups. It was like, I don't know, that in the space of three generations the culture was moving from medieval times into the modern world. I'm sure this had been going on for some time but not on this scale, nor so quickly."

"Generalizations are tricky." Greg noted.

"I know that full well. But I remember what happened with Japan in the latter half of the 1800s. In a generation or two, they went from a feudal society to a modern nation capable of defeating Russia in a war, which happened in 1906. Never forget, we went to India only one generation after the end of Colonial rule. They were just starting their way forward on their own. Not all that long after we left, communications with the outside world improved. The pace of change must have been very visible after that. On Google Earth, what had been a barren desert outside our front door was now fully developed. There are fertile fields, homes and streets, businesses, a hospital, a government college of some kind, and so much more. The leap forward in other countries from China to South Korea to Abu Dhabi has been just as remarkable. Sophisticated societies dominated by high rises and educated populations erupted in a generation or two."

Ronald, whose home we were using, spoke to us from the doorway. "When I went back to India for a visit, I made it to Salumbar. I had visited you and Ralph as a volunteer and was curious how it might have changed. You are right, it is so different now."

"I do recall you visiting our site. While there I think you read a draft of my literary masterpiece or a bit of it. Anyway, a while back I saw this golf tournament in China being played at a coastal city I had never heard of before. The commentator said that this had been a small fishing village at the beginning of the 1980s when the central government decided to invest in the area and turn it into a commercial giant. Now, little more than one generation later, it was a thriving metropolis of over 13 million people. Freaking amazing! Just a decade before this regional metamorphosis began, China was still backward and going through destructive infighting called the cultural revolution. An objective observer would say they had no future."

Mel cut in. "And there were those scenes in Slumdog millionaire. The protagonists were looking over what had been the slums where they had been raised. Now it was a set of gleaming high rises emblematic of the new, vibrant India."

"Interesting. But what did you take away from all this?" Connie inquired.

I responded to her. "Good question. I think I took away the ability to listen, to observe, to see beyond the obvious. All I can say is that I am convinced it helped me in my career. Most academics are hidebound, narrow specialists, seldom seeing beyond their own intellectual interests. They are products of their own culture even though they feel superior to everyone else. They too often have blinders on and are overly cautious. They see part of reality and conclude they are looking at the whole. Remember the old saying, generalists are those that know less and less about more and more until they know nothing about everything while specialists know more and more about less and less until they know everything about nothing."

"Quite clever," someone muttered.

"From the beginning, I think I saw some things that my academic peers missed, as a professional at least. In my first real adult job, I was in a state agency that had recently been grafted together into something called a super-agency by combining the welfare, health, and the social services systems. I watched the staff from those worlds struggle to communicate and understand each other. The welfare group provided income support to the impoverished while the services side tried to habilitate vulnerable individuals and families. You might think they would have compatible institutional cultures, but they didn't, not by a long shot. Each side sought distinct purposes, to reduce want or to improve personal functioning, that played out within competing ways of organizing their worlds. Those different ends had evolved into their own institutional frameworks and approaches. That proved comical, sometimes disastrous. Few realized what was happening at the time, why this marriage was proving so difficult, but I thought I did. Every day, in every way, there were clashes of norms, understandings, and languages that they drew from their professional and institutional cultures. I'm not sure I would have seen that, or at least seen it so clearly, without India."

"And what did you do with these insights?" Maureen queried.

"Not so much in the beginning. But as my career progressed, I spent a lot of time doing what I called boundary spanning. I would walk between the academy and the real world and among different parts of the real world. I was good at broaching the differences across institutional and disciplinary cultures. More than that, I could walk into new settings and ask the right questions to understand what was going on, get beyond a surface understanding that you might find in an org chart or flow chart. Remember Bob saying that he had these questions to ask when he got to his village, and never did ask. Based on India, and our training for India, I suspect we all embraced this notion of asking the right questions. We explored new ways of looking at the world around us. It probably didn't matter whether we asked them or not."

Maureen had a quizzical look. "This sounds fine, but did it have any practical consequences."

"Well, I am convinced the skills I absorbed in India helped me immensely in putting together one of the first one-stop welfare-workforce development shops in the country. At its core, that proved to be a cross-cultural challenge. It also helped me put together networks of officials that seldom worked together before. And it provided me with a set of intellectual themes on which to focus over the later part of my career. I didn't realize it until much later, but India gave me so much, it helped me understand the world about me in new ways."

"You were lucky," Mel said. "I took away a detached retina and several wonderful cases of dysentery."

I laughed. "Mel, in your heart you know you took away much more. We all did. Well, maybe not Paul."

"Hey," my nemesis responded. "I landed Connie."

"I stand corrected. In any case, none of us guys took away any STD's that I know of," I said lightly, "though I cannot speak for the ladies."

"Corbett…"

My name was on the verge of being taken in vain as I held up my hands in a gesture of submission.

"You better surrender." Laura said.

"My bad. Why I opened myself up to abuse all the time with my damn wit is beyond me. It is a curse. But that was, and is, my weakness. I recall the time, later in my career, I was introducing some high Federal officials to an audience of state officials. I had worked closely with these feds since I spent a lot of time in D.C. Some of them were responsible for providing the fiscal support to the University research entity that I helped manage. So, I went through this cute drill as a way of introducing them. I started by saying something about how so many people have a dim view of the federal government, and of most federal officials. However, I have been so fortunate to work with some of the brightest and most committed people working in Washington. I could have stopped there and just introduced them. That is what a normal person would do. I, however, just couldn't do that… that devil inside wouldn't let me."

"Oh God, what did you do?" Maureen shook her head.

"More like what I said next, not what I did. What next came out of my mouth was *'however, none of those people could be with us today.'*"

"Hysterical!" Bob laughed. "Did they cut off your funding."

"No, fortunately everyone knows I am full of it."

"And there was the time I was sitting in an important meeting in the Old Executive Office building which technically is part of the White House. This was during my one-year stint there when I consulted on Clinton's welfare reform agenda and related matters. The Chief Domestic Policy Advisor to the President was preparing us for a big meeting the next day when we would be briefing some movers and shakers of D.C., mostly on where the President's reform plan was headed. I had never met his Policy advisor before so, in retrospect, my casual wit surprised even me. Perhaps people are right, there is no off switch. I went through my planned talk. She liked it but said it needed to be shortened somewhat. Without batting an eye, I said *'no problem, I'll just cut out every other word.'* The look on her face was priceless. The problem with Washington is that everyone is so serious, they all claim to have just consulted with God."

"You just can't help yourself, can you?" Maureen said with a touch of disapproval.

I smiled at her. "Maureen, there is an old saying. You can't take out what God has put in."

"But you can sure try." Laura said with sly grin.

"I'll tell you one thing, though. India, our experience, it was like living in a petri dish for two years. The environment was right for growth and development even if you didn't know the end result at the start. Even some of the unexpected mistakes turned out okay, like Fleming stumbling on penicillin."

"Good one, Corbett," Mel nodded his approval. "I always wanted to be compared to a wonder drug."

Bob, connecting with a local. All in all, they did like us.

Kay in her strange new world.

CHAPTER 24

Close Calls

"Does anyone mind if I go back to a story I wanted to tell earlier. If I don't get it out now, I'll forget, a familiar failing at my age…" I paused, betraying with my facial expression the fact that I was about to make someone uncomfortable.

"Heaven help us," someone uttered with a hint of resignation.

"Earlier, I was going to tell you a story about Mel until my fond memory of Billie, my India cat, came up. It's a good one, Mel's story that is. Of course, that might not keep the good women assembled here from attacking. I see a future, not far off now, where I am being carried out of here with a tag on my toe… a tragic ending for sure."

"Not for us." Laura chuckled.

"On with it, Corbett." Bob again played his familiar role of timekeeper.

"This tale starts when we were heading to Delhi at the end of our heroic efforts to save India. Our trials were at an end, or so we thought. By the way, this tale is only semi-embarrassing."

"Easy enough for you to say." Mel looked a bit pale at that moment.

"As I said, it all starts on this final train ride to Delhi. Mel casually mentions a problem with his eyesight. Immediately, we jumped all over him to tell the Peace Corps Doc about this before he officially musters out. If there was a problem, they would have to take care of it and pay any medical costs. Sure enough, the PC Doc immediately sent him to a local Indian Ophthalmologist to have things checked out."

"Wait," Tim complained, "I was sure this would be about Mel's sex life."

"I never said anything about sex." I tried.

Tim was too sharp. "Listen, you promised embarrassment and shame and it involves Mel. What else could it be about."

Harry started laughing in anticipation of the witticism he had yet to share. "Let's see. Eye problems and sex. I know, I know. You guys must have heard the one about blindness being caused by masturbation."

I tried looking annoyed, which merely caused more hilarity. "Blindness, indeed! We know that's just stupid. Masturbation only causes your hand to blacken and wither. Why do you think I keep my right hand in my pocket all the time?" I chuckled as several of the gals instinctively checked out my right hand, then quickly pretended indifference.

"Corbett, you've just wasted all the sympathy from your Leni story." Laura sounded miffed.

"Okay... onward! So, when the eye doc finished his exam, he told Mel that *yes, he had a very serious condition indeed. Oh, so very serious.*"

"'*What is it,*' Mel asked with alarm? But the good doctor said he would have to wait until morning when the PC physician could discuss the situation with him more fully. But it was serious, so serious. Poor Mel returned to the hotel where he and I had been assigned to the same room. Now, I had tried to trade him for one of you 44-A gals earlier in the day but there were no takers. To be fair, several of them would take Mel in a heartbeat but none of the gals wanted to be stuck with me. In any case, all of us had gone off to this final blow-out party. In truth, I can't recall if Mel ever showed at the party. In case you have forgotten, this was the event about which Mel had feared competition from this handsome lothario and irresistible stud... me."

"Yeah, but now we know that he was off his game. The poor schmuck thought he was dying." Paul snuck in.

"And losing his eyesight." Connie added.

"Silence, my story now. So, Mel wandered around finding no one with whom to share his misery. Now, amazingly as it may seem, I was having a bit of good fortune with a young lady from 44-A." I saw the women from 44-A look around. "Not to worry, she shall remain nameless to preserve what remains of her reputation. I cannot imagine any female living down the fact that she had stooped low enough to consort with the likes of me. Surely impossible to recover from such a disgrace."

"Is she in this room?" Sherry asked as she looked about her.

"No, no! A gentleman never gropes and tells. God occasionally does smile upon his most worthless creatures, probably just to tease guys like me. Remember Don Rickles, my favorite comedian. I could never shake this image of God as a mischievous Don Rickles, looking down and saying, '*Corbett! I haven't made your life a misery for hours now and I need a diversion.*'"

Harry took a turn at keeping me on task. "Corbett, your drifting again. Get back to the sex."

"Oh yeah, sorry. Apparently, it would appear, excess liquor makes even a total putz like me tolerable on occasion. This gal and I left the party. We jumped in a cab and headed back to the hotel for some privacy. I must admit that we were all over each other in the back seat. I am sure the cab driver was shocked by our amorous antics, but at least he now had incontrovertible proof that Americans were nothing more than sex-starved animals. The motivation of my amorous partner that night remains a total mystery, though she may have been three sheets to the wind."

"There can be no other explanation." Laura quickly inserted.

"Nevertheless, back in my hotel room we continued with our sensuous activities when there was a knock, and then pounding, on the door, which I had bolted from the inside. Irritated, I went to see who had such abominable timing. It was Mel, looking like shit with his face contorted in anxiety. He said he needed to talk. It was important, he claimed. With my customary empathy for my fellow man, I told him to get lost and slammed the door in his face."

"You are terrible, no wonder I shot you down in Goa." Connie threw another pretzel in my general direction.

"Really, are you just now realizing that I'm one step below slime? I thought that fact was universally known."

"Corbett, you are beyond rehabilitation." Maureen said and shook her head.

"To continue, poor Mel next wandered down to Bob's room, his bosom buddy, who was similarly occupied with another young lady. Now Bob, being a sensitive guy just like me, also slammed the door in Mel's face. That was even worse since those two had shared a site for two years. They were best friends, even destined to become brothers-in-law after returning to the States. But, as I said, the male loses all human sensibilities when moving in for the score."

"Just as I always thought, men are uncaring sub-humans for sure." Maureen continued to shake her head with disapproval.

"No wonder Peace Corps placed the guys in a different province." Cate added.

"Hell, I'm surprised they didn't drop them into a different country." Laura added.

"Wait, just wait, redemption is at hand, for me that is." I raised my hand intimating that I might be about to regain the moral high-ground, or at least give it a try. "After Mel wandered a bit more, he returned to my, or I should say, our room. Now, he was anticipating rejection and was not about to go down without a fight. He immediately stuck his foot in the door when I finally opened it in response to the racket he was making in the hallway. There was no keeping him out this time, which I thought was terribly selfish of him. Then again, he now looked totally desperate, not surprising since he thought himself on the verge of death."

"Perhaps a bit overstated, but not much." Mel protested. "I was thinking brain tumor and all kinds of stuff like that. Surely I had just months to live. Why else had the Indian doc refused to reveal my condition? He didn't want to be the one stuck with breaking the bad news about my terminal affliction."

I waved a hand at him. "My story now, rebuttals later. This time poor Mel managed to spit out what was going on just as I was contemplating the physics involved in how far I might throw his body down the hotel corridor. He was, after all, slight of build and I was in decent shape back then. Then, a small miracle took place."

Another pause for dramatic affect.

"Yes!" Harry was irritated again.

"I am still shocked to this day." I paused again for more dramatic effect.

"Corbett…" Bob groaned. "I swear."

"Okay, okay! Apparently, as he later told me later, I did the right thing when he finally managed to get out his tale of woe. Shockingly, I immediately forgot the pursuit of every young man's holy grail… the promised land of erotic bliss. Rather, I started calling everyone I could think of to find out what his medical situation was and whether we would all have to defer our departures to attend his funeral. I have no memory of this but presumably this was the case. It's apparently all in Mel's journal. *Mirabili dictu*, as the Romans would say."

"Mirabi…what?" One of the gals asked. "Is that a Hindi phrase?"

I gave her my best Professorial look of disappointment. "No, the Romans didn't speak Hindi. It is Latin. Basically, it means an amazing sight or event, something hard to believe."

Dee was wagging her head back and forth. "All this sure is hard to believe. However, it is comforting to hear that there is some evidence you have a heart."

"I suppose, though it is not something of which I'm proud. Just the opposite. It demonstrates weakness and lack of purpose. In any case, Mel told me that, while I was on the phone trying to track someone down, he chatted with my female associate that evening…"

"Female associate?"

"What should I have called her?"

"Try victim." Dee laughed.

"Fine… victim. As I was saying. I immersed myself in the task of tracking someone down, any PC official who might relieve Mel's anxiety. According to Mel, who told me this decades later, she told him how sexy she thought I was. That was sure to put this poor schmuck even deeper in the dumps. Apparently, even a schlepp like me had gotten lucky while he was suffering on death's door, or so he thought. And now this vision of loveliness was calling me sexy. This was not Mel's night."

Mel groaned. "I was dying, and she was making me feel more worthless than I normally did. How bad can it get? I couldn't believe this. '*Corbett… sexy?*' Just shoot me! Then I suggested that she also might have an eye issue. But she dug in, doubled down in fact. '*No, no, he sounds just like Jack Kennedy… that Boston accent. It's just so sexy.*'"

"Mel, you've always been nicer than Corbett." Maureen tried, not realizing that being nicer than a sexual pariah was not what any male wanted to hear.

I cut back in at this point, saving my friend from further embarrassment. "Really, If I had figured out that my accent was an aphrodisiac, I would have perfected it even more. Of course, it never worked back in college but then a lot of the guys had Boston accents at Clark, which was located only forty miles west of Beantown. It worked a lot better in India, halfway around the world but I discovered that just a bit too late. Kennedy was still popular in India though this was now a half-dozen years after his passing. Then again, he personally had not sent over all these incompetent volunteers to mess with their country. Johnson was blamed for that."

"Yes," Maureen interjected, "Kennedy remained popular. We saw that in our sites."

"What really shocked me that night was, if Mel's version of events is true, I did the right thing, at least in the end. I dropped all else and searched for someone who might tell us how much longer this poor schlep had among the living. I started thinking of him and not myself. That is so out of character for me. Ordinarily, I never do the right thing, not intentionally at least. What the hell was I thinking? I should have dragged his sorry ass down to Bob's room and dropped him off there. As I said, they supposedly were best friends."

Several women groaned before Maureen asked. "By the way, what was this serious problem?"

"This is the corker." I sniffed. "It was just this detached or detaching retina he alluded to earlier. That's all. He wasn't about to kick the bucket. Not life-threatening at all, though we did not know this in the moment. If I had learned that at the time, he would have experienced something life-threatening for sure. I would have kicked his ass to the curb."

"Well, that explains any remaining mystery about his comment that you looked like some freaking male model." Paul smirked. "The poor guy couldn't see worth a dime."

"Very funny," I shot back trying to look indignant. "Yeah, Poor Mel was soon flown to a military base in Germany where they fixed him up. This was major surgery back then and he was yet convalescing when Bob and I visited him on our tour through Europe on the way home."

Mel spoke up. "I was grateful for the visit. By this time, I had even forgiven Corbett and Bob for being schmucks that night."

"Schmucks! Have you forgotten our situation? You would have done the same thing." Bob said, looking at me for support. I just shrugged back. What Bob had said I thought was self-evident, at least to all males.

Mel ignored our reaction. "It was quite an experience being in a military hospital. I was treated deferentially, at least compared with the enlisted men. There was this orderly, an enlisted guy, who kept making remarks about my facial hair and how he was going to cut it off. Then, the doctor, an officer, stopped by and complimented me on my beard. On a dime, the enlisted man did a 180... *'Listen here, you better not cut off that beard.'* Made me grateful I chose the Peace Corps over the Army Corps."

"When Bob and I got there, they had his head rigid between these two blocks so he could not turn. But they forget to bind up the most critical thing."

"What?" Mel asked innocently and immediately realized his error.

"Your mouth. You were still able to talk." There were several groans. "In any case, by this time, I had forgiven him."

"You forgave *him*? For what?" Laura asked in confusion. "I don't understand."

"Isn't it obvious? I interrupted my carnal activities only for his stupid detached retina. He should have had the courtesy to be on death's door or at least have some form of excruciating flesh-eating bacteria that was consuming him from the inside out. I would understand his rude behavior if he had just hours left to live, like from a virulent Ebola attack. That might, just might I say, have excused his selfish interruption of my chance to get lucky that night. But only a detached retina? Hell, he still would have had one eye left. He could have suffered in silence a few hours more. We were, after all, desperate men."

"You mean pathetic men." Laura said and Dee high-fived her.

The next pretzel plunked me in the middle of my forehead. "Ouch! That hurt."

"Good." Laura said triumphantly.

———

"Speaking of hurt, if it were not for international events and those damn Russian Commies, my site mate Ralph and I would have had a sure thing with the fairer sex on the way home."

"Oh my God!" Connie moaned.

"Really, we almost had a perfect set up. You see, after your future spouse had shot me down in Goa, Ralph and I travelled back to Bombay on the overnight boat. Of course, I had a broken heart at the time."

Connie rolled her eyes. "Spare me, oh Lord. To have a broken one, you have to have a heart in the first place."

I patted my breast and tried making some pathetic sound. I think it came out like the bleating of a sheep being castrated. "Now, we could only afford to travel steerage given our poverty status or perhaps they merely asked us to hang on the side of the vessel... to spare the other passengers. In any case, we went on the cheap. However, being white and Western, we snuck up to first class where no one questioned us. We had no private room of course but slept outside on these comfortable chairs. At least it was away from the *hoi polloi* below."

"That's the Peace Corps spirit." Connie laughed.

"By this time, we had had our fill of crowds. Anyway, we met a Czech official top side who was also working in India, doing what was not clear but probably something useful, unlike us. Either that or he was a spy. Being a good Commie, he had purchased a first-class ticket and was legitimately traveling in style. We joked for a while about which of us were the real spies. But he agreed that American spooks would never have to sneak up to the first-class deck. James Bond we were not. Over drinks we became quite friendly. He would be returning home soon and insisted that we stop in his country on our way back. He promised to show us a great time."

"He probably wanted to recruit you as Commie spies." Glen suggested.

"Very possibly, not that we knew anything that would be of help to them. Still, for a couple of easy women or just a good bottle of scotch, we could have been had. Of that, I am sure. Let me be clear, I could have been had. I cannot speak for Ralph. But, alas, we never got the chance. It looked good for a while. We wrote to each other. At one point he asked some detailed questions that sounded promising. What kind of liquor did we prefer, what kind of car would we like and, most importantly, what were our preferences in women?"

"You're bullshitting us," Harry sneered skeptically.

"No, this is absolutely true. I wrote back to tell him my tastes in women were not strict but that I did prefer that they still be alive, if possible, and that at least three of their limbs still be attached." I smiled and ducked as a pretzel caught my left ear lobe. "Alas, that was the last of it, I am sorry to say."

"What happened?" Mel asked.

"Ralph and I were in Berry's one day, the establishment we often frequented while in Udaipur. As we dined, another of our group came in and asked if we had heard the news. The Soviets had invaded Czechoslovakia to crush the liberalization program of Alexander Dubcek, a thoughtful leader who was not following the Moscow line. His rather short-lived regime was known as the Prague Spring and now it was over. We wrote again to our Commie acquaintance but never heard from him again. So sad."

"Do you think he might have been assassinated." Dee inquired.

"Possibly, but all they did was demote Dubcek to some harmless public post in the boonies, not wanting to make a martyr out of him. I think they made him a forestry inspector of all things. Then again, the less well-known officials might have been eliminated without fear of any international fuss. After all, this guy had been writing letters to some Americans. Maybe he was considered a spy for the west and the letters were a code of some kind. You know, easy women meant nuclear secrets. Sad for me, though."

"For you?" Maureen was incredulous. "How do you figure that?"

"Hey, I would never get to see how cheap it would be for them to get me to sell out my country."

"So," Paul smiled, "you would have sold out your country for a ..."

"An easy woman or two? Do you need to even ask? Like I said... desperation will do a lot to a man." Pretzels and other assorted snack foods pelted me all at once, generally coming from where the female volunteers of India 44-A were congregated. I casually picked the snack food missiles off my body and leaned back a bit in my chair, signaling that story time was not over. I liked telling stories and what else did I have to lose. I already was on the shit-list of the good women of 44-A, so why not.

———

"Ready for some coming home romantic adventures?"

A chorus of *NOs* greeted my innocent query.

"Hah, hah! I'm sure you can't wait to hear of my near romantic misses on the way home. I have similar stories for every stop we made but I'll share just a couple to give you the flavor of my personal agony. You might think that God might favor me after two hard years in India, but my karma must really suck."

"We cannot imagine what you must have been like in a previous life to be reborn like you are in this one." Laura said to general laughter.

"Let's see. Athens was our first real stop after one day in Istanbul. Hank, Bob, and I were travelling together. This pimp approached us on the street, steering the three of us into a store, a cafe of sorts, as I recall. They did sell conventional sweets there, displayed behind the counter. That was for show I think. I'm not certain they were real. They immediately offered us some alternative sweets, attractive females who emerged miraculously from a back room. The bakery clearly was a front employed to cover an offer of more sensuous delicacies for purchase. I've often thought... how did they know we were such likely marks. Were we so desperate looking?"

"Undoubtedly, you were drooling all over the streets of Athens." Laura deadpanned.

"Of course, that's it. I did tend to drool when passing attractive women on the streets. By this point, virtually all females looked good to me, so the drooling probably was pretty much continuous. I think I was the only guy who wore a bib just walking about town."

"Please spare me, oh Lord." One of the 44-A gals sighed.

"In any case, they had brought out these gals who gave us their best come-hither look. The three of us looked over the offerings, then at one another and... "

"And what you dillweed!" Once again, Harry was vexed.

"Nothing. Once again, discretion prevailed. I have no freaking idea how. A coat rack would look damn good to me at this point."

"You guys passed? I'm shocked." Harry did look amazed.

"Yes, we did. Not only that, but that was the last time I seriously considered purchasing a carnal delight in my life, ever. By that I mean using the services of a professional, not trying to seduce a coat rack. To this day, I'm not totally sure why I resisted the services offered by practitioners of the world's oldest profession. Prostitution seems so much better than the usual way we go about this casual mating business. Think about it. When sex is approached as a commodity for purchase, there is no misunderstanding of the nature of the transaction. The price is known going in, there are no false expectations, and the post-coital separation is quick and easy. As the old saying goes, men don't pay to have sex, they pay good money to depart after it's over and absent any complications. Despite all these benefits, I have avoided using civilization's most ancient and still honorable avocation."

"Wait! Post-coital separation? What the hell is that?" Laura said with more than a little annoyance in her voice. "Really, does anyone have that gun? I really need it now."

"Please, don't play naïve. You know what I mean. Okay, I'll skip over Rome with another near miss at the top of the Spanish Steps. How pathetic must one be to not score at that romantic spot? Alas, I was still paralyzed around women. And there was Zurich. We saw 'The Age of Aquarius' in the company of two lovely females. With each stop, erotic possibilities were to be had but, as always, we were going in different directions, I was too reticent, or some other disaster struck. God is a female because she keeps punishing me."

"All of us women thank Her." Dee pronounced.

"However, I cannot pass over Paris. Hap had left us by this point but surely Bob and I, two studs of proven quality, could score here. This was the city of romance after all, the city of lights that was made for lovers."

"I think I'm getting a bout of nausea." Cate feigned a sick look.

"Now, let's review the record to see how I did in the city where all fantasies come true. On cue, Bob and I ran across several cute American gals of college age who were being hustled by some French guys. These gals somehow signaled us that they wanted to be rescued, which we did. Who said chivalry was dead? They were grateful and, as luck would have it, it was Bastille night, very much like our 4th of July. The city was rocking, the streets alive with riotous celebration. For some reason, Bob peeled off before the night was over to return to our hotel. I recall making out in the middle of the sidewalk with one of the gals as her friends pretended not to watch. They might well have been taking notes now that I think on it. Either that, or they were wondering why their otherwise sensible friend had settled on such an obvious schmuck. I had great hopes of an evening of carnal delights."

Paul scoffed aloud. "Poor Corbett, still delusional."

"Well, here's the thing. I thought I had them with my sorrowful story of heartrending sacrifice and personal self-denial. I went on about my two years in India absent sensual comfort. That's right, I used our enforced celibacy to elicit some pity sex. I remember one of them literally screaming *two years, how did you last that long?*"

Maureen scoffed. "So, you lied to these poor girls since you weren't celibate for two years."

I looked at Maureen with uncomprehending eyes. "Of course, I lied. How else is a guy going to get laid? In my mind, it was close enough to the truth. Just a little white lie. Besides, I thought I could appeal to their sense of Christian duty. If they were Catholic, perhaps they could be moved to provide me with a corporal work of mercy or two. Alas, it didn't work though."

"Why not?" Harry asked.

"Turns out they were Jewish. Then things further unraveled as I realized the complications of the three to one ratio. I began to curse the fact that Bob had abandoned me. By the way, why the hell did you do that, go back to the hotel early? It cramped my style. I always meant to ask you that."

"Not sure," he said sheepishly. "I did have this young lady waiting for me back in the States. Maybe I was saving myself."

"Saving yourself?" I intoned with total incredulity.

"Ah," Maureen intoned, "one gentleman in the group."

"Yeah, right! Eventually the three girls and I wound up sitting in a café as the sky to the east was easing into daylight, signaling that dawn was upon us. The café staff finally threw us out and we said our goodbyes. This was a recurring pattern. The females I met on this journey were going in one direction and I in the other. Quite frustrating. At the least, I got a lot of sympathy, more than I ever got from my so-called friends in 44-A."

Laura laughed aloud. "Well, they didn't know you as well as we did."

"I can say one thing for them. They were most concerned about the state of my mental health."

"We all are." Cracked Mel to general laughter.

"One more stop will have to do. Eventually I made it to Dublin after Bob had peeled off for home. Ireland was the old country for me. Back then, though, it yet reminded me of all the frigid Catholic girls of my youth. This was not a place where erotic dreams might be realized. Naturally, my romantic tragedies continued."

"Hey, don't blame an entire country." Someone said.

I raised my hand in surrender. "Shush and commiserate. Dublin was poor and shabby back then, this was long before the economic Celtic tiger emerged, but it seemed very romantic to me in a cultural way. There were plaques and monuments all over the place commemorating this or that event in the cause of Irish freedom. You know, Billy O'Toole fell off a bar stool and broke open his skull on this very spot in 1912 while singing songs of Irish freedom. I must admit, the tug of my Irish roots remained strong, and I had a great time embracing my ethnic origins. I remember one night I was sitting in the hotel bar. I had my eye on an attractive bar maid. She had the classic Irish lass looks, the dark hair and the Devonshire 'peaches and cream' complexion. Worse, she smiled at me. Then again, perhaps my memory might not be accurate or, much more likely, she had hopes for a good tip from this sad-sack of an American. We were always a soft touch. I must admit, my standards were more questionable than usual by this time. I recall examining the coatrack standing in the corner for some time… a little on the skinny side but very doable, I thought."

"Gross." One of the gals erupted, making a face.

"So, I sat at the bar trying to decide if the smiles she cast in my direction were genuine or just a ploy for a tip. Reading women was never my strong suit. My internal debate was interrupted when an Irishman sat next to me and we struck up a conversation. He was killing time before heading off to see his girlfriend and proved quite interesting to chat up. We traded drinks until he said he was late for his date and off he went, not any the worse for wear. On the other hand, I could barely remain vertical. You know, I thought I could hold my liquor, but that Irishman seemed perfectly sober while I desperately tried not to fall off the bar stool. I truly doubt they would have erected a monument to me, as they had for that immortal martyr named Billy O'Toole. Had I cracked my head open while hitting the floor, they probably would have double bagged me and put me out for the morning trash collection. Hell, I didn't know any songs of Irish independence, not by heart. And besides, I could only make sounds like a castrated frog."

"You really are a loser," Bob gratuitously threw in, "a discredit to all males everywhere."

I gave him the finger, and then continued. "By now, though, the bar maid was looking extremely fine to me, much better than the coat rack adjacent to the front door."

"Oh my god," Laura gave a short cry, "she did escape your heinous intentions I hope."

"Of course! We are talking about me, aren't we? In the end, she was saved by my inability to move at the critical moment. I realized that I would not be able to do anything even if she tore off her clothes and begged me to do her right there on the bar. I suppose being blotto spared me from another amorous flame-out, if not a night in the Dublin pokey. That would have been flame out 2,637 in my disastrous love life, at least seven of which had occurred on this trip home. In any case, I had an early morning train reservation which I somehow made. How I managed not to barf my way across the Irish countryside remains a mystery to this day? What a hangover."

"Wait, did you say she was doable? That's disgusting! Has anyone told you that you are a pig?" Cate said at the same time she could not suppress a smile.

"Hold on now, how is doable anything but a compliment for a woman?"

"Corbett, you nimrod, you're supposed to get the girl drunk, not yourself." Bob chuckled.

"Thanks for pointing out the obvious, Bob. Like I didn't know that already. But there was one final erotic disappointment on my way home, make this one flameout 2,638. I made a mental note at the time to check to see if I could get a mention in the Guiness Book of World Records. Most male romantic failures by age 25 or something along those lines."

"No chance for you, Corbett." Mel shook his head sadly. "I got that one sewed up."

"Excellent work, you have always been my hero," I nodded to him. "On another day, while still in Dublin, I was touring Trinity College, Ireland's version of Oxford University. I was most impressed with the architecture and this sense of encrusted intellectual achievement. Their library must be one of the wonders of Western civilization. However, I was even more impressed with this attractive Swedish lass with whom I crossed paths. She was also touring the college on her own. We spent the remainder of the day together before making it back to her hostel where we found a private place to make out. All was going very well until she pulled away a bit and said something like, *'but I will never see you again after tonight.'* I think I stole the Bogart line from *Casablanca,* whispering something like *'but we will always have Dublin.'* Maybe that line would have worked in Paris but not there. As usual, we were going in opposite directions. The litany of my close calls, the unending the story of erotic near misses, continued."

"You really were snake bitten." Mel was shaking his head.

"There is a silver lining, though." I tried to smile.

"You scored with a coat rack." Paul could not resist laughing at his own witticism.

"Connie, stuff a rag in his mouth. No, I had to find my way back to my own hotel which was not easy in the middle of the night when public transportation had shut down and cabs were scarce. Somehow, I did make it back around 3:00 AM. Good thing I wasn't in a big U.S. city. I surely would have been mugged three or four times on such a journey. As I walked through my hotel lobby, there were a few people watching television in the bar which had long closed. What the hell was this, I thought? Dublin was not exactly the Big Apple. Here, everything closed early. Curious, I rambled over to find out what the draw was. Lo and behold, it was Neil Armstrong, about to take the first step from the LEM on to the surface of the moon. Someone brought me a drink, no charge. Rules be damned when history was being made. Our small group stared at a black and white, grainy TV screen in amazement as Armstrong uttered his classic words… *'this is one small step for man, one giant step for mankind.'*"

"Really, that was like Kennedy's death. You never forgot where you were when it happened." Sherry murmured.

"So true. I was proud to be an American that night, sitting among these foreigners. I seldom have felt that way since then."

Mel trying to defend himself from another of my 'tell all' stories.

CHAPTER 25

Choices & Consequences

The afternoon was shifting toward evening and the mood was getting nostalgic. I could see that several had that vacant stare of seeing things not present to the others. They were looking upon ephemeral images from a misty past, reminders suggested by the afternoon's dialogue. I ran with that mood.

"You know, I still occasionally look at old pictures from those days. They evoke such memories, small things that yet bring some joy after all these decades. I guess they also remind me of the choices we all made, some of them so casual."

Maureen joined in. "As do I. The older I get, particularly now in retirement, the more I tend to look backward. We are at that age when our past becomes more vital."

"I bet we all do something like that. It's as if the rearview mirror of life becomes more important than the front windshield. Sometimes, an old mental picture comes to me, something from India. Other times, it might be a real photo I stumble across. It could be of the smallest thing, like one picture that involves Cutchroo, our cook. He was milking a goat in the entrance way to our place. His appropriation of the goat's milk clearly was without the permission of the owner, as could be detected from the mischievous smile on his face. I think we tried to dissuade our staff from their larceny, but they never really listened to us. In the end, Ralph and I never inquired too closely on their shenanigans."

Mel brightened. "Oh, a goat, that reminds me. In a letter home, I told my folks that I bought a goat. Apparently, my cook had convinced me this would be cheaper than buying milk locally. Now, for my life, I cannot remember this goat but thus it was written."

"Is this the goat named Desiree?" I asked.

"Desiree?" Mel wrinkled his nose. "What are you talking about?"

"I never met this Desiree, but you mentioned her often, and always with this smitten look on your face. Oh, my Desiree!" At this point, Bob broke up laughing as Mel sent a pretzel in his direction. "Hey, I understand. A lonely guy in his village can form strange attachments."

For just a moment, I wondered if anyone had eaten any of these salty snacks as opposed to employing them as weapons of mass destruction. "Another small vignette I recall was the time I, perhaps several of us, got a wire from Delhi. That was unusual to say the least. It said that some of us who had been at Peace Corps headquarters in the recent past might have been exposed to a rabid dog. It was just a heads-up as I recall, quite vague and absent any instructions about what to do. Perhaps we were being told so we could say our final prayers or make out a will. I remember walking around for several hours envisioning my end days where I would be frothing at the mouth but too far from help to do anything about it. I'm probably making this way too dramatic, but it struck me as one of my first moments where I considered my mortality. I mean, I almost died at age thirteen when my appendix burst. Only emergency surgery saved my sorry ass. I learned only later how close I came to buying the farm, news that only came after I had survived. I still have no idea why that Peace Corps message about the rabid dog hit me so. But it did. I had this gloomy feeling that I would soon perish in agony."

"I'm tempted to joke once again about all your escapes from death, just to continue haunting us." Paul looked more thoughtful than mischievous. "That theme already has been worked to death."

—

"Our experiences were so profound," I said matter-of-factly. "Who remembers what they were thinking at the beginning, when they made their choice to apply?"

Dan laughed out loud. "I was just thinking about that very thing. Like Stan, I grew up in a rural state, Wyoming. Stumbling into Peace Corps was an odd choice but, like we've been saying, it changed my life. Trying to figure out how it happened isn't easy. Perhaps it was my Catholic school training that suggested a vocation in the missions. Still, from an early age, fourth grade or so, I remember being extolled to admire those who left their homes in our comfortable 'developed' land to live in a 'primitive' culture, These heroes helped the less fortunate acquire some of the skills and comforts we enjoy, as well as avoid the hunger or disease that we do not experience at home. A seed had been planted early."

"With me as well," I supported him. "As a kid, though surrounded by all the prejudices of a working class, ethnic, white neighborhood, I had these liberal impulses. I argued with those that went ballistic after the Supreme Court ended apartheid in our schools. No one in my circle believed as I did. I could not understand why we didn't share our agricultural abundance with the less fortunate around the globe. I even spent over a year in a seminary training to be a Catholic missionary until I figured out I didn't believe in God. In college, I led the leftist group on campus. Yup, I was doomed to Peace Corps and being a wannabe do-gooder from the start. Hard-wired I think."

"Hah," Nanette laughed loudly, she had a raucous, even infectious, laugh which I loved. It was just so genuine. "Corbett as a Priest. I would have paid good money to see that."

"And Nanette, I would pay good money to hear your confession." I smiled.

Nanette rolled her eyes at me before speaking. "I don't remember what prompted me to join Peace Corps. It was not the first choice of those around me. I do know that a recruiter came to my college campus. Somewhat curious, I went to hear what was being said, liked what I heard and the rest, as they say, is history. But it wasn't totally easy for me, a black female. Race and civil rights were very much in the news and on the minds of Americans everywhere, especially my people. I had experienced segregation first-hand and here I was going off to another country with mostly white people. Was this stupid or what? Shouldn't I remain at home and carry on the struggle? But, you know, it proved to be the right decision. Peace Corps proved to be a cultural shock for me, not only to adjust to India, but also learning to live with and among whites. They had been almost as foreign to me as the Indians I was to meet on the other side of the world. In Milwaukee, the world beyond the boundaries of the north side ghetto might as well have been a foreign land to us."

Bob spoke in a serious tone. "For me, as some of you know, I was looking for spiritual fulfillment in India and eventually wound up an economics and business guru. Talk about a transformation, how odd is that? Yet, if I hadn't gone to India, perhaps I never would have wrung out all that misplaced spiritual searching I was into while in college. Perhaps I would never have discovered what I was meant to do."

Glen added. "When I found we were headed to India, I wanted to absorb all I could of the culture and especially their music. Wish they had let me stay. I am confident that India was the right choice for me. For the few weeks I was there, I felt so connected. Yet, even those few weeks stayed with me, in my soul, in my music. The experience was too short, but the effects were permanent."

"I just wanted to help and get much more confident of my nursing skills. Worked like a charm." Maureen said. "I was ready on my return. I've had this amazing career as a nurse and an academic. Would I have achieved as much without India? Possibly, but I'm glad I never had to find that out."

"For me," Kay noted, "part of it was that Catholic sense of guilt and doing good, surely a lot of us were Catholic, weren't we? And I think I wanted to escape my provincial upbringing, experience things outside my cocoon. Perhaps I could have done that somewhere closer to home." She smiled as she said this. "But the more I think about it, the more I listen to the rest of you, I doubt it. Going to India launched me toward being a strong, independent woman who was able to help so many struggling females in Appalachia. And that wasn't always easy."

Harry spoke excitedly. "Me too! Not helping Appalachia women but becoming someone that no one back home ever expected I'd become. Peace Corps exposed me to the fact that there was this bigger world beyond a sharecropper's life in rural North Carolina. And where did I wind up? I found myself in a rural farming community in Rajasthan. How freaking ironic is that? Still, like Nanette, I learned so much from my fellow trainees and volunteers. Until I showed up for training in Milwaukee, I hadn't interacted with whites. You were aliens to me. I was so worried I would fail, that you all were better prepared for life. But everyone was great, and I learned so much about who I was and could be. I can't thank you all enough. After India, it was on to graduate school and eventually all the way to Washington and a top union position. What a fabulous choice."

Mel smiled. "I went for the noblest reason of all... hoping to meet sexy women." We all broke into ribald laughter at his quip. "That's all I'm going to say."

"And you did, Mel. Just look around you at the women in this room." Connie said and continued before Mel could respond. "I, on the other hand, did not join to meet handsome men, now that would have led to disappointment for sure. Rather, I was taken with Kennedy's words, his charisma, and his idealism. I'm not ashamed to admit this but I had to make his senseless death mean something. Remember when our leaders could inspire us?"

"And guess what," Her husband said, "you wound up meeting that sexy man of your dreams." Paul smiled broadly.

"True, my dear, I never would have met Corbett otherwise." Connie gave Paul her devilish smile as she added quickly. "I had to wipe that stupid smile off your face somehow."

"Well, I for one was sure glad that Kennedy inspired you," Nanette said. "You were a great site mate and have been a lifelong friend. You know, back in training it was a revelation to me that that all whites were not segregationists or bigots."

"Nanette," I threw in, "obviously you don't remember that confederate flag I kept waving."

She laughed again. "You are such a funny man. The truth is that I thought you were a genuine Communist at the time. I was a little leery of you."

"My folks felt the same way. They were leery of me as well." I quipped. "Why do you think they stopped at one?"

Nanette continued. "What I really found was that whites were this diverse set of folks with different heritages of which they were proud. Hah, I thought you were all the same. So much was new to me, like my world opened, in big and small ways. I was amused when the white trainees would watch me straighten my hair with a hot straightening comb. I experienced my first plane ride. I recall being hustled out of the Sheraton-Schroeder Hotel in my hometown of Milwaukee as riots broke out on Third and North streets. I can yet remember being called names by two rickshaw drivers because I refused to pay their inflated fares. I can still feel the hustle, bustle, smells, overcrowding, and beggars of India, and its beauty… the Taj Mahal, the Gateway Monument in Bombay, the Vanassi Caves, the colorful people. I learned to wrap a sari and miraculously became quite fluent in Marathi. And I remember being welcomed in my village with curiosity where I had to convince them that I really was from America and not Africa. I fondly recall the village children calling me *Kalichibi*, or black woman, and Connie who was with me *Goribichi*, or yellow woman."

"Did that make you feel awkward at all?" Dee asked.

"Oh no. After all, I am black, and Connie is close to yellow. Besides, their words were not said with malice, more like wonder. And I remember the monsoons and the darn heat, the 3rd class trips on the Howrah Express in the lady's section, always a delightful trip… not! And who can forget just missing the cow dung in the streets or, more memorably, stepping right in it. What about the giggles of my hosts when I was hot but insisted they boil the water before we would drink it? Then the horrendous memories, the assassinations of Bobby Kennedy and Doctor King? I established lasting friendships and became, of all things, a bibliophile, which we all did. I became fond of village life, the Cadbury chocolates, the chai and biscuits, shopping in the bazaar, the many festivals, and being wowed that a mother could give birth and return to work in the fields the next day."

"Yes," I said, "those were real women, not like you soft Americans."

"Just once," Connie said with a smirk, "I would love to see one of you male clowns get pregnant and give birth."

I considered making a stupid comment about trying to get pregnant but, for once, kept my mouth shut.

Nanette paused and then added a final thought. "What I remember the most was something unexpected. As much as Peace Corps wanted us to live like villagers in our site, the locals themselves didn't expect it. Good thing since living exactly like locals proved rather impossible to do. But I believe our neighbors did come to like us and that we bonded very well with them."

"You know, they accepted us much better than if we had been plunked down in rural America. We would have had much more trouble being accepted in parts of our own country." I said.

"For sure!" Mel nodded.

A painful memory popped into my head. "I recall that we stopped to eat in Aberdeen South Dakota. I believe that was the place. We were on the way back from that Indian reservation we stayed for a few weeks in training. Several of us dropped in a local café to no avail. We would not be served."

"Someone of the wrong color was with you I presume?" Glen asked.

"Yup! One of the Indian language instructors was with us. He was too dark for that place. More likely, they thought he was Native American. My blood boiled. It still does when I see those Trumpsters talking about making America great again. Great my ass."

"Oops, Corbett's Irish is rising again. Better cut him off." Janice intoned.

—

"As I think back, we were such a sad experiment."

"What do you mean… a sad experiment?" Janice looked quizzical.

"You know, our old gripe that it was ridiculous for PC to assume that college kids, with a little training, could contribute to technical areas where they had little or no real expertise. Really, what in God's name were they thinking? At best, it was patronizing to the host country. We had been a virtual army of volunteers sent to satisfy a promise that Lyndon Johnson had made to Indira Gandhi… to ship over thousands to help the country on the road to development or at least get it past the current severe drought. By the end of my tour, I wondered if that had been a threat rather than a promise, choose us over the Soviets *or* we will send hordes of incompetent and hapless kids to mess with your minds. It would be better, I thought, to send fewer volunteers but ones that might know what the hell they were doing. And yet, despite these failings, the whole sorry venture might well have been a success."

"Not exactly a linear conclusion there, from obsessing on our mortality to PC screwups," Bob observed. "Just how did you make that leap?"

"Not linear at all but perhaps those images that keep returning have some deeper meaning. Does that make sense?"

Connie cocked her head. "Not yet but keep going."

I considered my thoughts before speaking, something I did not always do given that my mind functioned though these non-linear leaps. "If you think you might die, then you consider your life more carefully. Maybe, just maybe our PC experience had little to do with what we would do for India. Perhaps it was all about what India might do for us. Beyond even my greater appreciation of our personal cultures, that place left me a changed man. It left all of us changed. Speaking for myself, a hopeful, if uncertain, youth joins the Peace Corps with the best of intentions and brimming with ennobling idealism. After two years of unrelenting heat, frustration, cultural friction, disease, loneliness, technical futility, and romantic disappointment, that now young man leaves apparently dispirited and directionless. But is that the truth of it?"

"I hope you are going to answer your own question." Janice noted.

"I am reminded of a fellow student I met in Milwaukee after returning to the States. Great guy, an Irish lad from Boston who played football at Boston College. He also had been in ROTC at BC, went to Nam after graduation, and led a platoon as a newly minted Lieutenant. He was gung-ho when he got there but saw how ridiculous it was within weeks. In his mind, he wound up doing nothing positive for that embattled little country except to try to keep his men alive. Reality had crushed all that early enthusiasm for war. He had only been in Nam for a few months when he was shot up badly and sent home. He will limp the remainder of his life. That experience transformed his whole outlook on life. Now, he was way more against the war even than I was. Last I saw of him he was headed back home to get into politics."

"I know that story." Stan affirmed without elaboration. "Not your story I mean, but that story of the reality of conflict turning someone against war is universal. Not all choices were equal. We made some that turned out great, others were disasters."

Maureen looked to Stan and then me. "Wait! Are you guys saying that you turned against the idea of Peace Corps after spending time in India? You made bad choices?"

I had not been clear. "Heavens no! I guess it sounded that way. No, it is just that the volunteer experience proved more subtle and complicated than expected. On the one hand, I was a bit angry at how we were misused. On the other, it proved such a transformative moment in our lives. I can't speak for the Army which transformed my buddy from a war advocate into a peacenik. Thing is, Peace Corps is one of those sleeper experiences, sometimes painful in the short term and priceless over the long haul. It can transform how you think about the world, and what you do in it. And consider the *cui bono* question."

"What?" Sherry asked.

"Oh, who benefited from our meager efforts? Well, we did. We were the real beneficiaries, not the country to which we were sent. But that's not so bad, not when you think on it. After all, the hard things are what makes each of us great in life, or at least a little better."

Paul cleared his throat. "You might remember that the Indian official made that same point at the 50th anniversary of Peace Corps fete the Embassy in D.C. threw for us. From their perspective, the payoff was that many young people had an opportunity to learn about their country, embrace its lessons both good and not so good. I remember thinking how perceptive his remarks were."

"Good point, Paul. No question that India was hard, extremely hard. It tested us, perhaps in a different sense than training did though both had their challenges. India pushed us to the point where our core character solidified and matured. You either grew or, given the challenges, you would bend or even crack. Some left early. Others stayed but left in not very good shape. And a few may even have felt good about things. But very few of us, if any, came out the other side the same as we went in."

"I bet a lot of us feel like hardened veterans." Dee suggested.

"I guess I'm saying that most things worth doing exact a price. Becoming a world-class athlete or concert pianist demands early sacrifice and endless practice. Want to be a healer, you must put in endless hours as an intern and resident. To become an academic at a top research university demands years of study and competition with others seeking the same end. The peak of any pyramid is narrow and the base, all those who start out on the climb, is wide indeed. Making one's way to the top is challenging but we get better through trials by fire."

"No shit." Ben concurred. "India surely was a trial we all experienced. And the thing is, there aren't that many transformative experiences in life available to any of us."

I chuckled softly.

"What's funny, Corbett?" Mel asked me.

"Nothing, really! I was thinking of a lawyer I met after I had retired from the University. I met him as part of a bunch of retired academics, professionals, and other successful people who met to discuss and influence policies affecting children in Wisconsin. This was your usual bunch of do-gooders looking to keep relevant after their noteworthy careers were over. This lawyer had been a partner in his firm, a mover and shaker in Wisconsin politics, and a highly respected attorney who had been involved in high stakes political and policy battles. He was also a kind and gentle man. As he talked in our sessions, I realized he often went back to his army days in World War II. It was from that experience that he drew his most profound life lessons. I thought that odd, given his stellar career, and the breadth of his professional accomplishments."

"Hey, war is intense." Stan said thoughtfully.

"So true, and you should know my friend. One day, I was in his law office though he was emeritus at his firm by this time. He had as many pictures and awards and other memorabilia from his military days in WWII as he had with all the governors and senators and even Presidents from the next fifty plus years of his career."

"I can see that," Stan offered again.

"It hit me as I gazed at that wall. He had been a tank commander, fighting across France and into Germany. Those days constituted the transformative experiences of his life, not that he had a choice in being there. Still, what he absorbed in those few months shaped the man he was to remain for the remainder of his career. Later, I was reading a book about Wisconsin young men who fought and died in the war, including a couple of Wisconsin football All-Americans from the early 1940s, one of whom died on Iwo Jima. This lawyer was mentioned, he had been one of the Wisconsin soldiers who liberated a couple of the Nazi camps and freed at least one those Badger football heroes who had been a POW. You can just imagine the impact."

Ben looked hard at me. "Are you saying Peace Corps was the equivalent of war for us?"

"Oh, can't say for sure but maybe. I'm just saying each of us likely has very few opportunities in life that fundamentally shape who we are. Anything that is intense and challenging can fit the bill. Peace Corps had to be one of them for us. I've noticed people who think of things like their training to be a doctor or the first year of law school or being part of a team to challenge a mountain or the trials of getting a doctorate. They look back on those seminal experiences, and the people they shared them with, in a different way. Well, for me at least, Peace Corps was far, far more significant in defining me than getting any silly doctorate. Frankly, I don't remember my fellow students from those years."

"Perhaps if you hadn't gotten your degree from a correspondence course." Paul tried but was ignored.

I chuckled at a private memory I thought might lighten the mood just a tad. "I can say one thing with certainty. I kept dreaming about my village in India, about going back. I could never quite recall how the villagers responded to my nocturnal return. That was probably a good thing since their reception of me was not likely positive. The image of an angry mob running me out of town with flaming torches awakened me in a cold sweat. Remember those classic Frankenstein flics. I can almost hear the desperate cry of the mob now, '*My god, the crazy American is back!*'"

"Loved those movies, the one with Gene Wider is a classic." Glen offered.

"Sure is. Did you ever read the original book? It's actually well written and quite sad. You feel bad for the monster." I immediately looked at Bob, assuming he would chide me for wandering again. But he didn't.

"Of course you do! You and the monster look like twin brothers." Nanette smiled.

"Why am I punished so, oh Lord? In any case, over the years my spouse had asked me whether I was interested in returning to India or my village. Curious, yes, but I had never felt compelled to return. Perhaps I never quite got over a lingering sense of guilt. Like the rest of you, I could not shake the feeling that I took far more than I gave. We were young, naive, lacking in appreciable skills. What were we thinking back then? Where did our arrogance and hubris extend that we thought we had something to offer? What would I say to those villagers who might possibly recognize me after all this time? Yes, I was that tall, skinny kid who stumbled around your fields looking totally helpless, hopeless, and surely hapless. But at least I left you with a few laughs."

"I doubt Peace Corps uses that when lobbying Congress for money." Bob suggested.

"Use what exactly?" Maureen asked.

Tim answered her query. "The theme that Peace Corps volunteers left their site hosts doubled over with laughter."

I went on. "I will say one thing. These gatherings have proved so useful in some ways. I had never gone to a reunion before. Well, not quite true, my dear spouse did drag me to her grade school reunion. Yes, that's right, a grade school reunion! I mean, who remembers grade school? I, however, had never been to one of my own, at any level. When I heard about our first Peace Corps get together, though, I just knew it was not to be missed. While there were individuals I might like to see again in class reunions, those particular experiences were never intense."

"Yes," Maureen spike with enthusiasm, "I get what you are saying."

"And when we did first get together, it turned out as worthwhile as I had hoped. As soon as we began sharing with one another, my sense of failure did not seem so personal or so unique. We all harbored a shared sense of limitation, a harsh personal assessment born of unrealistic expectations. In the end, we could have done better but we probably did okay. But beyond that, I've really confronted what that long-ago experience has meant. And that is a good thing."

"Yes, it is." Maureen affirmed.

"I had little contact with you guys over the four decades following our service. Absent any reminders, you stuff things way back in your mind. I recall my wife answered the phone one day. She typically performs that service since I have few friends of my own as you can well imagine by now. She continued chatting, so it wasn't someone marketing steak knives, time shares, or cemetery plots. Suddenly she said, '*Oh, Tom will definitely want to talk to you,*' which surprised me since I never want to talk to anyone."

"And vice-versa" someone quickly noted.

"I suppose. You know, most of us have experienced running into someone out of their usual context and, for this reason, have difficulty recognizing them. That's why I always asked my wife to wear a name tag whenever she wanders into the kitchen by mistake. This is what happened in this instance. Who the hell was on the line? I faked a conversation while my mind raced to figure out the identity of this vaguely familiar voice. About three minutes into the conversation, it finally hit me. It was Doug, the Doug from

India. He talked about a reunion, maybe even in India. That never happened but I was intrigued at the thought of seeing everyone again. On another day I was giving a talk in Milwaukee and a black woman who looked awfully familiar approached me, but I couldn't quite place her. I gave a lot of talks and met a lot of people. Then she asked if I was the Tom Corbett who served in the Peace Corps in India. My first reaction was to say, *'not me, I'm innocent.'* Then I recognized Nanette and we gave each other a big hug."

"I remember that so well." She said. "It was so good to see you. If I remember correctly, you even made sense in your talk."

"Really? I made sense? Whoa, must have been an off day."

"When we did get together that first time in 2009, I was shocked by my reaction. I never thought I might enjoy myself, but the experience proved more moving than I anticipated. Immediately, it felt more like forty hours since our time together on the other side of the world. Toward the end of the second day, as the reunion was winding down, I recall looking around the room as people chatted and shared so much with one another. Sure, body parts dragged and drooped in awkward ways, a few extra pounds could be found on most, and more grey hairs could be detected in what remained to them. But I could easily think back to those bright and shiny faces that gathered some forty-plus years earlier in Milwaukee. Though I am, by nature, a detached guy, someone who skips through life with a joke or two. Suddenly, I couldn't quite ignore the very real emotion that surged through me. I really do love these guys, I thought to myself."

"Wait," Cate asked, "you love us?"

"Despite how you abuse me, yes." I smiled broadly. "Go figure, a moment of weakness. Not to worry, I'll recover in a moment or so."

"That's okay, Corbett, beyond all your BS, we can see that you're human." Maureen opined.

—

Time to shift gears again, I thought. I was revealing too much of myself. "Listen, exiting India in 1969 was an experience in and of itself. The process of returning home was part of the transformative experience."

"It sure was." Harry agreed heartily.

"I mentioned earlier that I started out with Bob and Hank. Quickly, we discovered we were not just traveling across physical distances, we were also journeying across time. Reentering civilization affected each of us in idiosyncratic ways, I suspect. First stop for us was Istanbul, which still felt like Asia. The airline put us up, so we stayed at a fancy hotel overlooking the Bosporus Straights. To this day, I can recall standing on a balcony mesmerized by a romantic vision of this fabled link between Europe and Asia. So much history there, the Byzantine and Ottoman empires. The Western world I grew up in was now so close I could taste it. But I was not there yet. I realized that I did not even own a pair of shoes, just flip-flops, and was refused entrance to the fancy hotel restaurant due to my untidy appearance. Civilization, at least as I understood it, would have to wait a day or two."

"Yes, we were all a bit like Alice in Wonderland" Maureen said.

"Speak for yourself, I felt more like one of the characters in Homer's epic poem, the Odyssey. A plane trip that took just a few hours seemed to transport us over many decades. Athens immediately felt like the modern civilization that was embedded in my memory but had become a lost world. The first thing I did was buy a pair of shoes. Then I recall getting excited by an escalator, feeling the comfort of walking the streets without attracting attention, and gawking at women in Western dress. Feeling freaking invisible for the first time in like forever, was such a liberating feeling. On the other hand, we couldn't have been too anonymous since we were hustled by these guys who introduced us to the charms of several young ladies whose interest in us, shockingly enough, was totally pecuniary."

"But you did the right thing in that instance." Kay said with conviction. "You made the right choice not to exploit those women."

"You think so? I was never sure. Unless they were forced into the life, they were not exploited. It was just a job for them."

"I can't accept that. Few females choose that life." Maureen pushed back.

I decided not to debate the point. "The reentry process was surreal in so many respects. Literally days earlier, we lived in isolation on the margins of a desert. Now, armed with an open ticket, only if we kept going in one direction, we felt like jetsetters. Several times, we got up in the morning and chatted about where we might fly that day. Athens was followed by Rome, and then Geneva, and so on. Wait, it was Zurich, not Geneva. Anyway, we began to experience on a grander scale what we sometimes encountered during brief trips to Delhi or Bombay while in India. The contrasts between modernity and feudal, rural India could be like a slap in the face. Even going from the village to the big city involved culture shock."

"For sure," Dee murmured. "It was disorienting."

"Yes, I recall one day, we were visiting someone in Bombay whose father, I believe, stopped by. He was a native Indian who worked for the Times of India. When he found out we were living in rural villages he began to ask us what life was like there. Turned out he had been educated in the U.K. and spent his life in cities like London, New York, Delhi, and Bombay. He had no freaking idea what his country was like for 90 percent of his fellow Indians. After all this time, I'm still taken with the fact that he looked to us to discover his own country. That was an eye opener. We had experienced more of India, the real India, than many urban natives. Now, though, I realized this transition was permanent. I was leaving the real India behind and I would soon return to my own whining ways absent much guilt."

"Yup, we never totally lose who we are inside." Paul offered. "It does take a while to get back there though, and we do not return fully to what we had been."

"So true." I supported him.

"In any case, my final flight, on *Aer Lingus*, landed at Logan International in Boston. My parents were there, of course. It turns out my father had just been released from the hospital. His lungs were already shot from too many cigarettes and from the foul air of pre-OSHA factory work. My parents kept his condition from me, so I would not worry or cut my travels short. I was taken with that. Both were to pass too early of lung-related diseases among other problems, the consequences of hard lives and hard choices made in a relaxed regulatory environment. Let no one be fooled on this point, we do sanction outright corporate homicide in this country."

"And our health care system is an international embarrassment, so expensive and unfair to far too many." Cate exclaimed with a touch of bitterness.

"I'm so with you on that one. Don't get me started." I paused to keep myself in check. "Anyway, shortly after my arrival back in Worcester, Dan visited me. I thought this an opportunity to recapture one more time those precious memories of India and with someone who would know what it was all about. So, I dragged out my several hundred slides to rev up our trip down memory lane, dimming the lights so as not to lose anything in the moment. All went well for a while. As I approached slide 300, however, I noticed that Dan was no longer responding, not even issuing the occasional grunt that accompanied every tenth slide or so. Turning on the lights revealed Dan in a deep sleep, head plopped on his chest, his face twisted in a look of absolute torture. Since then, I have noticed that I have had that effect on many folks, particularly students. Now that I think on it, perhaps I should have rented those slides to Dick Cheney for interrogation purposes in the war on terror."

Dan laughed. "Now, there is a memory that I repressed. No recollection of that whatsoever."

"How could you remember? You were in a freaking coma for crying out loud."

—

"New topic!" Dan intervened to save the group from one of my rants. "I remember that we ended our summer of training with everyone being given a slip of paper to go to room 101 or another room. Those going to 101 were selected, the others were deselected. Deselection had become a new word in our lexicon, one that had much anxiety and pain attached to it. Really, just how were those decisions made. Who chose which of us would stay or go, and how? I don't remember the numbers exactly, but I recall reading somewhere that back in our day something like six out of 100 applicants were invited to training. From that pool, maybe half got to go overseas. Then an additional twenty percent left on their own or were deselected in-country for one reason or another. Only a small minority of the original pool of applicants finished up two years of service."

"The question is." I posed. "Were we the best, the most talented, or simply the most stubborn."

"My guess," Harry piped up, "is that we were the biggest idiots on the block."

"No, at long last I'm thinking we might have been the luckiest." I added softly.

"Dan continued. "I remember being sent to this training village. We were slowly immersing ourselves into our Peace Corps persona. You must remember that the early programs, like ours, used the *parachute* method. Basically, you dumped kids into these pre-industrial villages and waited to see what would happen. What happened was not pretty… a high rate of early terminations. Our training was different, perhaps unique, in that it was long and strenuous. Toward the end of training, though, we were still dumped into one of those primitive villages to do a job that no amount of short-term training could prepare us for. Drew, Glen, and I were put in Lakavlie, a couple of miles from Udaipur. Here we faced our new reality for the first time. We had to find food and water and all the other necessities easily obtained in the West. We had to squat on the ground to defecate in full view of whomever happened by and cleanse ourselves with our left hand and a little bit of water in a *lota*. You adapt to most of it, but I must admit to never becoming totally comfortable with defecation as a social activity. And besides, I was right-handed damn it."

"Which is exactly why we were to use the left hand; you used your right hand to eat. I wonder if left-handers had a problem?" Bob paused as if this were a momentous question that demanded serious consideration.

Dan's face made an involuntary grimace. "I suppose. Still it was hard getting used to being treated as side-show freaks. I remember one evening, the three of us were lying on the charpoys we used for sleeping. The room we were in had two windows opposite one another. There were bars on the window but otherwise they were open. Each window had four or five boys on the outside shouting at us within. I imagined this was the life that animals had in most zoos before those places became more humane. I think that broke Drew. He called it quits and left. After all we went through in training, you would think we would be ready for the PC experience."

"Another hard lesson," I offered. "You cannot ever appreciate reality until you experience it."

Tim spoke in a voice so soft that I leaned forward to catch the words. "I've wondered whether Drew, and others who chose to leave so close to the goal line, later regretted that decision."

"I suspect most of us teetered on the edge at one time or another." Greg offered.

"Damn right," Dan exclaimed. "After all our training, I was still shocked when Lal, the Peace Corps driver, drove me to Kathar, some twenty miles north of Udaipur in the mountains.

He unloaded my Peace Corps footlocker and a few other items in the middle of the road. Then he said goodbye, shook my hand, and off he drove. I was left standing in the road now surrounded by a crowd of curious villagers who had no idea who I was or why I was there. They mostly spoke Mewari, unintelligible to someone trained in Hindi. And, of course, there were no living quarters as promised, not a comforting situation as the sun disappeared. That moment is frozen in time. It remains indelible to me even today. I can feel it, *'what have I gotten myself into?'"*

"And yet, we survived." Someone murmured.

"Damn" Tim uttered meaningfully. "who would have thought that a throw away comment made during the heat of a campaign so long ago would unleash so much on the world… so much that was crazy, humorous, and great, all at the same time."

"Ever wonder," Bob mused, "what might have happened had Kennedy not chosen to use those words that night? Would there have been a Peace Corps? Would we know each other or be what we became?"

We all sat quietly pondering his counterfactual.

Tim ended our contemplation. "I can't speak for all of you, but I wouldn't have missed it for the world. We survivors were the lucky ones."

Dan (left) listening to the shared memories.

Back to the Dear Tom Letter

Dee pointed at me. "I fear bringing down the wrath of my peers here, but can you go back to that girl you left behind. I'm struck that you have all these letters you sent her from India. I sense there is a story in this we need to hear. Am I wrong?"

"Wait," I said in surprise. "I thought you wanted nothing more about my romantic disasters."

Laura spoke up. "No, I'm with Dee. There is something about the way you've talked about her that gives me hope."

"Hope?" I hesitated. "Really?"

"This story about Leni, that's her name I believe, suggests a real relationship. This might be worth exploring. Who knows, it might show your human side if, of course, you have one." Laura looked about to see if she had generated any wrath among her sisters, but there was nothing. "I'm just curious, that's all. After all, your reputation cannot get any worse."

From the reaction of others, most were curious. Still, I paused while considering whether I might yet circumvent this topic. "You're not setting me up, are you… just to assault me with more pretzels or maybe some bric-a-brac? You actually want me to talk about this."

Paul chuckled. "Oh, don't worry about being done in. Your fate has already decided. Right now, someone is digging the hole where we'll bury you."

"Don't listen to my husband." Connie piped up. "This story promises to be different, not so sordid. Besides, the hole is already dug."

In fact, this story was the one I consciously had avoided to this point. I backed off whenever tempted to share it. Perhaps now, though, I was beginning to feel more grateful than wary about getting it out.

———

I plunged in. "Listen, when I was not out saving India, or at least Salumbar, which was my world then, I kept busy by devouring every piece of English-language literature available to us. We surely savaged every letter and magazine from home. The written word was pure gold. Naturally, some words were more prized than others. Any letter from my college girlfriend, without question, was the most prized of all... though I painfully learned that was not to be the case. One day I ripped open this aerogram from Leni as Ralph was chatting away on some nonsense or other. I soon lost track of what he was saying. In that moment, I found that some written words create wounds not easily repaired."

"Oh, oh." Someone uttered.

"Yup, it was the dreaded Dear Tom letter, the one I mentioned earlier. As you guessed, there is more to that story."

"Of course there is," Dee said, "that's precisely why we are pushing you on it."

"Ach, you are a tough crowd. In the infamous letter, Leni told me that she had met a post-doc while working at a Harvard lab and was getting married. Even though I had always been quite ambivalent about marriage, I had weakened on the topic. India was a lonely experience but, more to the point, my memories of her remained deep and intense. As you know, I had finally screwed up my courage and mentioned the M word in letters I had sent off to her, even the dreaded L word. I never thought I would use either word in my lifetime, at least not when I was sober."

"I assume you mean marriage and love." Kay wanted to be sure.

"Yes! I still hate to use the full words out loud..."

Bob interjected. "Stay on point, Corbett. We are actually listening to you now."

"Got it. Not long ago I discovered that I had mentioned marriage to Leni in a letter sent early on in our training. That shocked me. For decades, I thought two critical missives had crossed paths... my proposal of marriage, such as it was, and her letter dumping me. In my memory, both happened halfway through my service. That would have been a good Hollywood script, but things were not that dramatic. In pre-satellite days, communication was labored and slow. Even air mail took weeks, or so it seemed. For example, someone sent me something via ground mail to save money and I think it arrived in June of 1987. Perhaps it all would have been different if we had today's instant communications."

"Oh my God, yes." Kay said. "Relationships were quite impossible given how isolated we were."

"I was numb at first. Then I thought, she made the rational choice no doubt, all my wit and charm notwithstanding. Well, it was the right choice given our situation at the time. After all, my prospects were dim indeed, as I have repeatedly pointed out."

"Wait, you are being too hard on yourself. Let us do that for you, okay?" Laura smiled as she employed Paul's tired line. She used it, however, with a hint of sympathy that he seldom employed. Was she trying to cheer me up?

"Ah yes, my main role in life... to be the group punching bag." Laura's smile evaporated just a tad. I could see her thinking that she had missed her mark. Was her timing off? Too strong, she feared. I returned her smile to comfort her and plowed on. "The basic pieces are straightforward. After graduating from Clark, Leni went off to Boston and started working at a Harvard lab. I started training for my Peace Corps assignment and finished up my remaining credits at Clark, having lost much of one year in the Seminary after high school. Except for the time I was off in the Midwest becoming a faux farmer, we had plenty of time to date, talk, get to know each other even better, and spend more nights together. But we didn't do much of that, something that remains a mystery to both of us. The immaturity and insecurities of youth seem virtually impossible to comprehend now. What could we have been thinking? How could I not have spent those last days in the U. S. with the person whom I…" I found I couldn't end the sentence.

"Sorry Tom. I shouldn't have asked. Listen, you don't have to…" Dee started.

"No, no, that's okay. Time to get it out, all part of the Peace Corps decision after all. Leni and I forfeited our opportunity to share how we felt about one another before we left. I would never really know whether her occasional remoteness was either an expression of underlying indifference or, ironically, a fear borne of too much attraction. Ironically, when she seemed more available emotionally, I would withdraw. The reasons for my retreats were clear to me… an incapacitating fear of intimacy and commitment. Well, it was clear to me in retrospect at least. I simply could not reach out for what I wanted at the time. In consequence, I would endure a continuing regret for my cowardice. I think, deep down, I assumed rejection was inevitable, so why fight it. After all, it would have been a stunning miracle, and poor judgment on her part, had she waited upon my return."

"Wait," Connie interrupted. "I love insulting you, we all do. But here's the thing. You were kind of a catch back then. You weren't half bad, so don't be so hard on yourself. I'm serious now."

"But I couldn't see it, even if it were true. Her decision to move on made perfect sense to me at the time. She now worked in an invigorating intellectual environment. She met a man who appeared smart, caring, stable, secure, and (importantly) present to her. In any case, he was a Harvard post-doc and had an academic position waiting for him at Georgia Tech, a real career. Beyond that, he probably had a bunch of other qualities that would make me very jealous if I thought on it too much. Contrast that real person who had a future with me, a guy who flew off halfway around the world with no discernible prospects and a tenuous grasp on adulthood. It was no contest. Hell, I certainly would have dumped myself at that time if it were feasible."

"Corbett, you are taking all the fun out of shitting all over you. Stop with the self-deprecation, even if it is accurate." Paul looked serious. "And damn it, my wife is right. You weren't that bad. I know losers. I served with them. You were not as bad as them."

"You really are a rotten friend, Paul. You manage to insult me with faint praise while throwing your own group under the bus." He started to respond but I raised a hand. "Just kidding, my friend, I do appreciate the effort. In any case, while sitting in India I knew the end was coming even before the dear Tom letter arrived. I could feel it coming. You could literally see that creeping awareness reflected in a growing desperation that seeped into my correspondence with her. By then, however, there was little I could do, and what I could have done, I didn't. I could not overcome my insecurities and negative self-image of that time, not even close. Frankly, I did not think I was lovable, and certainly not by someone like her who was so lovable. So, I never fully verbalized a commitment to her, never formally proposed marriage except in round about, obtuse ways. The train, long approaching, ran straight over me. There were not enough body parts left for the toe tag."

I looked through my file. "Here's something. This following passage likely comes from a letter sent around the time of the infamous 'Dear Tom' missive."

I heard the music from Zorba the Greek the other day. As usual, it sparked a flood of memories . . . For one thing, it reminded me of Zorba's recommendation that we all must possess a little bit of madness, madness that has placed me here, madness that may never allow us to see each other again, but more importantly the madness by which we dare to hope. But the ultimate madness of them all is the one by which we desperately yearn to survive and, in the face of all this increasing insanity, seek the kinds of futile happiness that our illusive dreams pretend. Yet, maybe, just maybe, we'll make it.

Still, I want to say something now, not out of fear or lack of trust in you, but simply to clear up any ambiguity. While I love you and do hope the relationship will endure my service here, the reality of the situation is that we will be separated two years, a little over a year more. I also realize that my irascible moodiness, chronic immaturity, and impractical idealism hardly make me an ideal catch. If you have any doubt, or change your mind, please feel completely uninhibited to communicate this to me. Perhaps, given my peculiar Irish pessimism, I anticipate it anyway. And, of course, if you are insane enough to like me, you are also allowed to tell me that as well.

"Her Dear Tom letter soon arrived. At least things were clear then."

"How awful." Cate said with sincerity.

"When she and I finally got around to processing the whole thing several years ago, after decades of no contact, we were dumbfounded at how stupid we had been. We could not understand how we let things happen the way they did."

"You were both kids, for Christ's sake." Bob stated the obvious.

"I suppose," I sounded unconvinced. "Want to hear something hysterical?"

When I remained mute, Mel sputtered, "Of course we do, you moron."

"Sorry, this is embarrassing. It turned out that she remembered me as being this kind of perfect guy. She had me on a pedestal of sorts. She did, Gods truth! Oh, and she loved my self-deprecating style. I think… I think that part of her charm was her innocence and shyness. She probably couldn't open up in college. Wow, it might have helped had she said something positive like that back then, not that I would have believed her. I couldn't hear such things about myself. Besides, if she had told me how she felt, I probably would have run for the hills in total panic. What basket cases we were!"

"And so you were just as bad, right? You never opened up to her." Connie said.

"I was afraid someone might point that out."

"But apparently you had a second chance at communicating." Dee offered tentatively. "Just how did that happen."

"Through the miracle of Facebook, I managed to stumble over her after four decades of no contact whatsoever. She wound up with a Ph.D. in molecular virology, or something that sounds like that. Clearly, it was a real degree in a difficult discipline that involved real courses that I would never be caught taking since I would have flunked out. She wound up doing research and teaching in that field at the university level. Of course, I would be even more impressed with this had I gotten around to reading my biology text in college and knew what the hell molecular virology was, though I think my doctor gave me a shot for it once." I chuckled then stopped. "The thing is that, at the time, her dumping me hit me hard. No, more than that, it devastated me. Something irreplaceable had slipped from my grasp, another road not taken. It gave Ralph and me an excuse to get even more blotto than usual that evening."

Did anyone else know this about Corbett, that he has human feelings?" Laura asked in general.

There were several negative responses from the women.

The guys remained mute until Mel spoke. "We had our suspicions but there was never enough indisputable evidence. In truth, there was no evidence whatsoever."

After displaying my middle finger once again, though to no particular person, I continued. "Beyond Ralph, I never shared my feelings about this with anyone. Not sure anyone knew there was this gal back home. It was my private agony, no need to dump it on others. I did the stiff upper lip thing, just sucked it in except for my site partner. I kept it under control even from him after that first drunk. It helped a lot that I thought this ending was inevitable. Isn't that the essence of a traditional Greek tragedy. You know the denouement, your assigned fate, and you realize there ain't a damn thing you can do about it."

"Damn," Connie said. "I can't imagine if I had gotten a Dear Connie letter from Paul. Everyone would have heard about it as I looked for a hit man to hire."

"Well, the thing is, I blamed myself, not her. Remember, I was not loveable. I had convinced myself of that."

"Must be a male thing." Connie concluded. "But you have these letters you sent her. Surely you did not make photo-copies of them back then in India."

"Good catch! As I suggested, we reconnected after several decades. I remember the reconnect well. I stumbled on to Facebook after getting a smart phone or whatever they are called. While figuring what it was all about I found this connection to many of my college alumnae, something I can no longer find by the way. Curious, I scrolled down our class at Clark and up popped Leni. Oddly enough, I didn't expect to see her. Only a handful of former classmates had put themselves on this site and she seemed an unlikely candidate to do that."

"That must have been a shocker. What did you do?"

"I froze. I never expected to come across her again. It had been so long with no contact whatsoever. Worse, I realized there was an easy way to message her. It was decision time. For a moment, I hesitated. Maybe, just maybe, it would be better to keep on scrolling. A bunch of thoughts crowded my head. Would she remember me? Would she want to remember me? Would her reaction be *'Oh god, I thought the nightmare of Tom Corbett was far, far behind me?'* An even more menacing thought intruded. Would she be the same woman I recalled from college days, or would those fond memories be shattered by peering into the past? Perhaps my recollections were highly idealized, even totally fabricated. Perhaps she had changed, or never was that ideal inside my head."

"We've all changed." Mel pointed out the obvious.

"I was thinking more along the lines of catastrophic change. Rather than the Leni of memory, would I now find a fat, toothless, harpy with body odor and a long prison record. That hesitation really did not last long, though. After all, in one way or another, she had never left me. Our last contact of any kind had been a set of pathetic letters full of self-loathing and narcissistic whining I sent from India in 1969. This was after her marriage and shortly before my return to the States. Letters that tedious and full of self-pity would certainly be a capital crime in most states, or at least should be. By the time we stopped communicating, she had been married for about a year. Now, it was over four decades later, a lifetime. Then I thought, *What the hell!* What's the worst thing that could happen… a restraining order?"

"That's what I would have done to you, at a minimum." Laura said but with a gentle smile, with concern.

"I typed out a simple message. It went something like, *'Hi, this is Tom Corbett, from Clark. Remember me?'* I thought she would need a clue to place me, to dredge up some recognition of who this guy was. I am not sure what my expectations were, maybe a polite reply with *'Oh, are you still alive?'* At best I assumed a few pleasantries, an update on career and family, and that would be that. After hitting the send button, I regretted it instantly. In truth, I had prepared myself for nothing. The Eleni of my stored memory seemed more like a fantasy or dream than a living person, more like a hyperbolic mirage."

Dee seemed captivated. "I can't believe this. Corbett is telling a story and I am not looking for my ear plugs, or that gun. Okay, what happened next?"

"What happened surprised me as much as her agreeing to our first date so long ago, which took me forever to ask. I really was pathetic around women. Anyway, she seemed happy to hear from me. I was shocked. We started off with the expected polite catching-up exchange. These pleasantries quickly morphed into an intimate journey into our past and the meaning of 'us' back in college. What happened, how did it happen, where did we go wrong, and where were we now? What touched me very deeply was that she had saved old pictures of me and us as well as many of the embarrassing letters I had sent from India. She even saved small notes I had left for her in her dorm room and other assorted junk that seemed trivial beyond belief. Somewhere in her stored memories, I still had a place no matter how tenuous. The letters from India she saved, which obviously she returned to me, gave some texture to recollections tarnished by time."

"That's quite a gift!" Mel asserted.

"And so, we plowed on, separated by nine hundred, or was it a thousand, miles. I was in Madison and she in Atlanta as we tried putting together an emotional canvass of what our world looked like so many decades earlier. Our emerging dialogue reminded me of how alcoholism works. Take a drink after a period of sobriety, even a period of forty-plus years, and you immediately find yourself further along in your disease. Very soon, we were way more open with one another than we had ever been in our youth."

"All kidding aside, you had grown up." Connie appeared surprised at her words. "Damn, did I just say that? Corbett had grown up? But I suppose it's true. Miracles do happen."

Dee looked at me. "I'm beginning to think his bad boy thing is an act."

"Oh god, I've been revealed as a fraud. No matter, all this new intimate sharing with her led to the most surprising aspect of this so-called reconnection. What hit me, with stunning force, was that this really *was* Leni on the other end of cyberspace. And apparently I was still me. One of her first observations I recall was a comment that she immediately recognized my self-deprecating style. It was me and she was so glad I had not changed."

"No wonder you loved her, the rest of us were praying desperately that you would change while she liked what you were. There IS no accounting for taste." Laura's quip lacked the usual bite.

"That's it. Yes! What I started to discover, at long last, is that I wasn't all that bad back then. With just a few typing conventions such as underlines, smiley faces, exclamations, assorted emoticons, she managed to convey all the endearing values and mannerisms that drew me to her in the first place. There it was again, the sassiness, wit, intelligence, insight, insecurity, a sense of common history, and a shared perspective on things with enough differences remaining to spar with one another. More than that, I felt I knew the rediscovered Leni with more depth and clarity than at any moment of my youth. I doubt she had changed at all. I think I finally could see things more clearly at long last, with far less personal baggage to get in the way. On the other end of cyberspace, I could 'see' her smiling, glowering at me in mock (or real) frustration, jousting with me with her impish look, pricking my pretensions, and stimulating me with her insights and deep sensitivity. She remained a deep body of water ever undulated and changing color as we peeled back layers of forgotten feelings and memories and began to recall what 'us' had meant. I finally saw why I had such a strong attraction to her in my youth, how she penetrated the defenses of the guy who was *never* going to let girly emotions get the better of him. It was as if we had a mutual resonance on things, a shared cloth from which to weave a common bond."

Cate exhaled. "Corbett the romantic. Who knew?"

"No matter the sarcasm, I am continuing."

"No," Cate hastily added. "No sarcasm."

"Of course, you cannot really go back again. We both were in stable, loving relationships. Neither one of us would ever jeopardize our significant others nor cause any harm or hurt. We were committed that our piecing together the past would never interfere with our current lives. Given this mutual understanding, it would be easy to characterize our reconnection as a soppy chick movie. Two people who had loved one another are then fated to be apart forever because personal frailties and insecurities doomed them from the start. Then they find each other again, at least for a while. We did talk about hearts being absorbent. They could always encompass more love. Maybe this nonsense called love is not a zero-sum game. Maybe we can add to each other's happiness and fulfillment in small ways, simply exchanging thoughts and support and comfort and laughs and memories through this miracle of a cyberspace connection. Is that sufficient? Who knows? As I thought back on things, my closest relationships with women were never sexual. They were about connecting."

"Sorry, I do hope there is an EMT squad nearby when I go into cardiac arrest at all this." Connie said as several colleagues from 44-A nodded.

"Not to worry Connie, I'll give you mouth-to-mouth." I chortled at my words.

"My fault." Connie replied as she instinctively gave me the finger which she then regretted. "I gave him an opening he could not resist."

"Thank you dear. In any case, we speculated on what would have happened had we not acted like childish idiots back them. She first thought that we might have escaped a terrible fate. Were we too similar she wondered? I had long thought that our attraction might have failed given the similar insecurities we would have brought to any longer-term relationship. We were very much alike, almost able to finish each other's thoughts and sentences. It was eerie. We had that same mental quickness, that wit. She was half Irish as well as that Greek part, the later ethnic tradition which dominated her home growing up. Our commonalities might have been impediments, that was possible. If we had made it past those early challenges, I could easily envision a shared life of many laughs and much love. We will never know since that was never to be. If there was any difference that separated us, it rested on her being so nice, and me being… not so nice."

"This is so sad." Dee offered.

Laura cocked her head. "At least you have this second chance. No? Who knows the future or am I missing something here?"

I smiled sadly at her. "No future. Our so-called second chance was short lived. Several months after I found her in cyberspace, Leni fell ill. It was a somewhat slow decline though she was to pass from cancer less than two years after we reconnected. Since it was terminal pretty much from the first diagnosis, we knew what was coming. I recall one phone conversation. I told her that this was like reliving our youthful relationship all over again, the painful part. I had found her back then and, all too quickly, lost her. Now I had found her again, in a different way of course. Once again, I was fated to lose her a second time. She felt that same pain." I stopped, wishing I had not gone there.

Connie seemed upset. "Sorry, I'm having trouble here. Didn't you hate yourself for walking away from her in college?"

"I hate myself for a lot of things but not that. Listen, here's my bottom line. I probably couldn't do both. I was either going to let Peace Corps further develop this guy I was to become or stay at home and pursue this relationship. Listening to her, I guess the basics of who I was already existed. I didn't know that, though. I didn't think I had much to offer her, or any woman for that matter. I had to test myself, prove that I was more than I thought at the time. India was like this furnace that forged the final touches on me. In the end, I lost a lot but gained even more. Probably all for the best but I can never really know that for sure. Those damn counterfactuals are fun to think about, but that's it. They do drive you crazy." I opened my file of papers and looked through for an email message I wanted to share. "Bear with me while I find this one letter. Okay, not a letter but I kept copies of our communications via email. Here is the one she sent me."

To Tom:

You've given me such a great gift in reconnecting and sharing your memories and feelings so openly. I'm very grateful. I had never really understood how you felt. The mystery of "us" has been clarified greatly. There may be strong twinges, but for me, our connection has replaced the question marks with treasured, positive feelings.

How do I really remember you from college? You were kind, sensitive, super smart, passionate about causes, and the best kisser ever. Frankly, I was awed by you.

I am sure that my own insecurity and naiveté fueled your ambivalence. We were both just beginning to evolve. I was afraid to say the words "I love you" because back then I had this dumb idea that saying it was a total commitment. Total, as in body and soul, forever. I was scared.

I must admit. You write beautifully. I was blown away by what I read—from the beginning to the end. I had such a swirl of thoughts and emotions. As I read it, I'm not sure I'll ever get my thoughts together well enough to respond. When I found it almost too painful to continue reading, I reminded myself that pain was my guarantee that I was still alive, that I still cared a lot. That's a good thing, right? Sometimes you remind me of the old lyrics . . . the honesty is too much; I must close my eyes and hide. You do take my breath away.

The emotional dust hasn't settled yet, and the worst thing is that I don't have enough time to do your writing justice. I want to read it again, and probably again, with less emotional white noise next time around. You knock my socks off. Thank you for taking the plunge and hanging in.

So much love to you . . . xoxoxo

"Over the months we had, we exchanged many emails, and talked on the phone, texted just about every day. In the end, I found out the most important thing of all... she did love me. I never knew it back then. She had never expressed it, neither did I until

I did obliquely in my letters and only after I had left town. I can yet recall her voice when I would call her after our reconnect. She would be so excited to hear from me. We both were much more cautious in college, as if we were scared to death of our feelings."

"That strikes me as odd." Dee thought about my words. "I would have guessed both of you would be more emotional as kids. Weren't we all?"

"Leni and I were emotional eunuchs. Both of us held back, neither of us could commit. Besides, we missed all signals which were way too subtle and too frightening I suspect. So, India became a convenient place to run off and hide from all my terrors and fears as an insecure man, I mean boy, in his early 20s. Do I regret going to India? No. Do I regret letting Leni go? Sure, but you make the best decision you can at the time, no matter how pathetic. You can't look back. In any case, I had a good life, found a wonderful wife, and had a superb marriage. Moreover, Leni's second marriage turned out fine, her first, not so good. She had found a man that was good to her. All in all, no complaints on either end."

"Wait, something occurs to me. We give you a lot of grief. It doesn't help you when we always treat you like shit, does it?" Paul sounded concerned.

"Don't worry, it no longer matters. I'm no longer a basket case, at least not a hopeless case. You know, I sent many letters to her from the other side of the world. I'm so glad I kept writing, even after getting dumped. The letters were probably the most meaningful correspondence I ever wrote in my life. They served as a window into me as a young man. Here are some thoughts from a letter I sent even before heading overseas. Reading it now, my sense of fatalism is palpable. Somewhere inside, I just knew that, in leaving for India, I would never see her again."

The course of human involvement typically seems to run from the improbable to the absurd. The grasping, hoping, seeking become inevitable frustrations and unfulfilled anticipations. Today's bliss and ecstasy are tomorrow's despair and emptiness. To maintain your purpose and direction, you must love and believe in it. And out of the deepest despair of its reality evolves the highest respect for its necessity and appreciation of its existence.

Partially, one may say that love is illusion, or some form of selective reality, and further, that distance perpetuates these illusions. But the emotional character of love is only the superficial surface. Its real nature lies in the contract made between two people. It is the arrangement between separate individuals to share common excitement and joys and accept each other's burdens and fears. It is the merger of their identities as well as their bodies, an investment of themselves and their trust in the other. It is perhaps the most incredibly difficult goal to accomplish and yet the easiest thing to convince yourself that you are doing. It is something that cannot be manufactured but rather must simply exist.

Yet, it cannot be taken for granted but rather nurtured and cultivated with all the strength that can be mustered. As you know, this kind of investment has been particularly difficult for me. Both the exposure to and investment of ourselves with other humans is a noble aspiration, perhaps ultimately unrealizable yet seemingly the only reality worth pursuing.

In rereading this letter, I have realized that it is extremely ambiguous and unintelligible. It is just so incredibly difficult to verbalize emotions in general, never mind probing one's own thoughts and feelings. Beyond that, these kinds of thoughts are alien to my analytical, pessimistic nature. Perhaps there is a metamorphosis taking place, a maturing which is taking place, and I am neither able to describe it nor analyze its direction.

There is something I want to say now, that I must say or perhaps forever hesitate. I do want to marry you. This is an incredible confession for me, and I know it will freak you out. Before you retreat into a shell of self-security, let me assure you that I don't believe it will ever happen. Circumstances, two years, and certain common weaknesses will, in all probability, prevent it. But let me also assure you that I mean it and that if you ever, at any time, feel strong enough to make that arrangement, that contract of identities, let me know.

"We both were shocked on reading this, and other letters, after so much time. Could this really be the cynical, detached Tom Corbett of our memories waxing on and on about love and relationships? Could this have come from a wounded guy incapable of expressing the most elemental of human sentiments. If I really did express such thoughts or, more importantly, embrace such sentiments, then surely some kind soul could have been persuaded to put me out of my misery. I would have labelled these as one of those back-forty sentiments I mentioned earlier if expressed by anyone else. What the hell was I thinking?"

"The miracle is that you began to express yourself, perhaps for the first time." Laura said with some surprise. "You really did have another side we didn't see. Hell, maybe you didn't want anyone to see it for a long time. So, you were reluctant to display it. As I recall, you didn't permit many others to see this side of Corbett back at the beginning. I remember you as smart but flip, even shallow. If we avoided you, it was because no one could reach you, or didn't think we could. I mean, okay, you were a bit charming but so… inaccessible."

"Point well taken. I did keep a lot of things hidden. Easier that way. That's how the walking wounded deal with the things that count, things that can hurt. I had few positive role models for marriage or what a loving relationship looked like. I wanted to avoid commitment like the bubonic plague. Yet here I was, in black and white, raising the topic of marriage. Fortunately for her, this woman was smart as a whip, certainly smart enough to ignore my so-called offer and move on when a more promising opportunity presented itself. I think, given how Leni reacted to reading my letters four decades after they were written, that she never processed them back then. She couldn't process them. Now, she could, and was somewhat overwhelmed with regret. Our letters are an instructive lesson in how we can reframe our own histories."

"You can say that again." Mel added. "My journals are a godsend."

"Once I got overseas, one reality set in. I really missed that woman. What in the world had I been thinking (or why had I failed to think at all?). I thought of this when Ben was talking earlier. He and Diane never talked marriage until he had too many solitary meals. I had left without expressing my love in any way that made sense and without making a commitment. Even as I wallowed in loneliness and frustration in the Rajasthan desert, I had a hard time expressing fully what was in my heart. My letters weaved from spasms of self-pity to obtuse, sometimes obsequious, expressions of devotion. Even when the word *marriage* burst forth, I employed it in ways that would put off most women except for those who would marry any male still breathing. I must have come across as this "lunatic" spouting nonsense from the desert. One could see a desperation born from the realization that the train wreck of our relationship was inevitable. I simply waited for this disaster to obliterate me and then journey on to wherever excess human emotions go to die."

"So sad." Laura murmured.

"I suppose. In my heart, though, I knew two years was a long time. It would take a lot from me to keep this wounded relationship alive. Still, I could not pull the emotional trigger with enough clarity to keep her wedded to me. It was merely a matter of time before she was gone and all that would remain would be the caboose of that emotional train receding into the distance. God, enough with the train metaphors already!"

"Yeah, after India, few train fans here." Paul said.

"One of the only things I could recall from the Dear Tom letter to me was an observation that her family would really miss me not being a part of her life, their lives. Here again, my memory played tricks on me. I thought I wrote only one more letter immediately on getting the "Dear Tom" note to say some of the most obvious things . . . you know, the *I understand and don't worry about me and good luck and have a nice life'* kind of sentiments. I am positive I wrote such a letter though it did not appear to survive, which is too bad since I would be most interested in seeing if I was as gracious and noble as my memory suggests. On the other hand, perhaps I never wrote such a letter. No matter the truth here, she shocked me (again with the shock) by continuing to write."

We continued our correspondence for the remainder of my tenure in India. Below is a snippet from one of my post Dear Tom letter missives:

Your ('Dear Tom') letter must have been an unpleasant experience, one which finally having been done would be difficult to repeat. Writing again was a marvelously brave thing for you to do. I'm not sure it was a wise thing, but it did please me, immeasurably. Thanks.

You mentioned that sometimes you burst into tears without reason. Well, I must admit there are times when I become misty-eyed. It is not so much for what might have been but rather for what was. The years that have just passed were, at least for me, extremely pleasant ones. And the time we spent together was perhaps the most rewarding of all. There was a certain warmth and comfortableness there, and a sharing and excitement which now seem unique and may never again be duplicated. The days at Donoghues (our favorite local bar) . . . are past now and they will never return.

But we are in no way to blame, for it had to be that way. The times and the people who fill those times do change, inexorably, and without apparent conscious direction and there is little, so damn pitifully little, we can really do about it. It, us, would have changed no matter whether I left or not. And I suspect that what we still may fondly be attached to is not what we were to each other or what we might have been to each other but rather the simple function of a time and place in our lives which is irreplaceable. In my Irish Catholic pessimism, there is no room for happiness.

"Wow!" Dee said, "I rather like this new Tom Corbett. Who knew?"

Several snappy and sarcastic responses crossed my mind. I remained mute, however. My heart just wasn't in it at that moment.

"Oh my God… how sad!" Cate whispered. "Did you get to see her before she passed?"

"We never met; that wasn't necessary. Besides, her spouse would never understand. Through cyber-space I could see her well enough. She still had that same aura of goodness and optimism I recalled so fondly even as her health ebbed. She experienced a couple of episodes of renal failure, and near death, during early chemo treatments. She always made light of these episodes, saying she was down a quart of oil. Despite this, she kept insisting how blessed she was and how much she treasured the life she had . . . her husband, her family, her friends and even me."

"I'm sorry," Mel seemed confused, "but what did you get from this."

I was shocked by this question. "Why, everything. I got everything. This time I knew I was special to her. That's what I needed to know when I lost her. I finally knew how she felt about me. In a way, the blessing in all this is that the quality of our reconnection will remain as is, undisturbed by reality."

"Oh no!" Maureen protested. "I can't think like that."

"Me neither," Janice added while others nodded in agreement.

I ignored their protests. "One thing, her positive, upbeat view of life still puts me to shame. Hell, I bitch for days about duck hooking a golf shot into the damn pond. Even on her worst days' health-wise, I could tell she was more concerned with making me feel good. I think she was like that with everyone. She was so well loved, spent so much time doing volunteer work. She was the nice person I wanted to be but never was."

"Oh, there's still time, Tom. We have hope for you." Connie chuckled very softly.

"In several e-mails, Leni observed something that's stuck. She said I had become a more complete version of the young man she knew so many years ago and to whom she was so drawn. In her mind, that was a very good thing, all those traits she so admired back then now appeared fully developed and expressed."

Paul opened his mouth but then said nothing. I had given him an opening and he chose not to use it. I'm not sure I would have been as nice.

Instead, Dee filled up the brief void. "How nice of her to share so much, before it was too late."

I thought back and realized that Dee had been very close to another volunteer who had not been located and never came to the reunions. I suspect she was thinking about him. Those early connections are irreplaceable. So, I kept moving, trying for a more universal lesson from private hurts. "In any case, the core of what people are, who they are, the qualities that center them, appear as constants in their makeup. A relationship is interrupted and silenced for over four decades. When it resumes, a lifetime of experiences does little to shake what made each of us unique and even appealing in the beginning. That is somehow quite remarkable and something I learned from a bond that was never to be in any complete sense. Peace Corps taught me a lot about being an independent, self-sufficient adult. But she taught me how to love, something that was not part of me in my youth. Those were invaluable lessons I took forward into adulthood. I am gratified at long last to embrace the reality that Eleni did love that guy from Clark, and she loved the man he became. Such things are good to know, even if too late. I've had a wonderful life, great marriage, unforgettable career, and even a few trappings of success. Still, I wonder what might have happened if I had not gone into Peace Corps or if they had made one of those inexplicable decisions to kick me to the curb and I had returned home early."

"We've all wondered that. What would have happened absent India and Peace Corps?" Bob mused. "What if I had found spiritual fulfillment in India. Would I be a spiritual guru today? Probably not."

"And if I had made different decisions, you would have been denied the pleasure of knowing this delightful and charming rake you see before you today. What a crushing lost that would have been." To my surprise, and disappointment, no pretzels came my way.

She dumped me for a sane guy… she made the right decision.

CHAPTER 27

Home

"Eventually, we all came home. More importantly, we all came home as different people from those who left two short years earlier." I offered this to bring some closure to this long afternoon. Savory Indian cuisine had been promised and the caterer would arrive soon. Besides, the last topic had exhausted me.

Harry immediately picked up on my comment. "Yes, so true. I came home as a different person for sure. Earlier, I mentioned vegging out at my sister's house in D.C., just decompressing and gorging on good food. Eventually, my mother called and said it was time to come all the way home to Durham. And yes, I still did what my mother told me to do. Funny, I don't recall much of that reunion, which is odd since we were so close. My guess is that my mother, in her infinite wisdom, tried to make my homecoming as normal as possible. What I do remember, though, is that the person that returned from India was very different from the person who had left Durham two years earlier."

"How so?" Maureen asked, genuinely interested, and content to move away from the topic of my love life.

"The person who left was largely impulsive, a hothead, somewhat self-centered, perhaps even selfish. And yet, I could be a team player, extremely loyal. I was persistent, somewhat dogmatic, yet still demonstrating some tendencies toward leadership. I also spoke with a southern accent though I don't believe a big one."

"What the hell are you talking about, none of us could understand you." Mel tried. "That's why we liked you so much."

"Wait, that doesn't work." Bob protested. "We couldn't understand Corbett with his Boston accent and we still didn't like him much."

Maureen decided to get us back on track. "In your mind, Harry, what kind of person were you when you returned home?"

"For one thing, I now had a different accent; one that I did not realize I had acquired. It was one that fascinated my family and friends. After all. I had spent the past two years living in a small village where no one spoke very much English. I had to learn Hindi in order to communicate and in ways that the locals could understand. Then there were all the idiosyncrasies and gestures I had picked up that were necessary to survival in rural India but so foreign in rural North Carolina. After much introspection, I labeled myself *The me that nobody knows.*' I had become this stranger who was returning to Durham County… a man of mystery who was returning from the other side of the world."

"Fascinating." Maureen let slip.

"A different accent was just the most obvious change. I was now much more committed to accomplishing both my career and personal goals. I had set goals in both areas, and now I was doggedly determined to achieve them. Having a newfound sense of worth, I was someone to be reckoned with. My new self-esteem was evident in all I did. If I told someone I was going to do something, you could go to the bank on my word. Being less impulsive and more tolerant of others emerged as strong personal traits. I genuinely enjoyed teaching and mentoring others while being out front, providing direction, leading others to desired conclusions. Thank God I could leave for graduate school right away. There, I was in a place where I no longer had to explain who this stranger was."

"That's an interesting observation." Dan added. "We hungered for anonymity in India and that impulse remained, for some of us at least, even after getting back. We no longer wanted to explain ourselves."

Harry was smiling at his memories. "Yeah, it was funny what my mother said one day about a year after getting back. This was after I had come home again after one year of grad school, during the summer between semesters. After some restless days, she approached me and asked if we could talk. *'Sure, what's up,'* I said. *'Son,* she replied, *I love you and I love having you come home to visit but you are miserable. Why don't you go on back to Cincinnati where you are more comfortable?'* Though I now thought of myself as the 'me' that nobody knows, my mother still knew the real 'me.' I could never fool her."

Maureen caught our attention. "Earlier, I talked about our child immunization program, the one that didn't go as planned. Yet, that semi-fiasco taught me a lot about program planning. I didn't fully get that until I was in my community health nursing master's program and used the project as a case study for my program planning class. Until retirement, I taught program planning and evaluation to both undergraduate and doctoral students. Not long ago, I used the immunization project as an example of how NOT to plan a program. I am convinced the students learned as much from a real, but imperfect initiative as they would have from some abstract presentation of perfection in a textbook. After one class, I recall this student telling me how much she enjoyed hearing about our experiences, and that the story brought home the principles I was trying to convey. Maybe we don't think we accomplished much in India, but we learned many things that allowed us to accomplish so much since. Without those lessons, who knows? Maybe we would still be floundering around like we were before PC."

"Before PC? I like that way of referencing things." Ben observed as he took over. "I spent time working in Africa after Peace Corps, Diane and I did, and then climbing mountains and traveling to far off places. I am convinced that my experience in Peace Corps enhanced my desire for risk taking and adventure. I yet remember visiting a friend while traveling. I heard the musical ring of a sledge on a wedge and looked next door to see a scrawny white haired seventy old man in a string shirt splitting wood. I asked my friend about him and he told me that the guy was a Finn, and that they were *Sisu*. That turned out to be a Finnish term loosely translated into English as strength of will and determination. It signified perseverance and acting rationally in the face of adversity. Watching that old man chop away, I made a vow I would be able to do the same at his age."

"Okay Ben," Bob said, "that is a nice story but what does it have to do with us?

"Don't you see?" Ben looked perplexed. "It has everything to do with all of us. We are all *Sisu*." As usual, I had a dozen immediate comebacks, many hysterical. Yet, in this instance, I said nothing. Perhaps he had touched upon a truth.

Janice spoke up once again. "I so remember my transition back. Everything was moving so fast. The commuter bus must have been careening down the highway at seventy miles an hour. The others on the bus seemed unconcerned. They weren't time travelers like I was, having just returned from some past century. I was used to horse carts, bullock carts, antiquated buses overflowing with people and goods, and trains that spewed coal dust and cinders through open windows. But it wasn't just the speed of the vehicles that unbalanced me. Everything was in flux. The ground seemed to have shifted while I was away in India, and I returned to an altered universe. My personal identity had been constantly shifting in India. I was an honored guest one day, a polluting infidel the next, and a strange curiosity the day after."

"Oh my," Kay said. "We all appreciate that."

Janice continued. "You know, my innate pride in America began to get murky almost as soon as we arrived in Washington DC. Heaven forgive me but I was a little like Corbett though likely not quite as angry, or whatever he felt. Having been medically evacuated early from India, I was being put through a round of difficult medical tests in the daytime followed by watching the Democratic National Convention on TV in the hotel at night. I was appalled to see the Chicago police riot and beat up peaceful protestors and anyone else they could get their hands on, as Mayor Richard Daley played the potentate on the convention floor. To me, this was madness. What to do, go back to India to start over? There was no place to run to escape the horrific reality of what was happening. Even before we left India, we had been stunned by the assassination of King and then Bobby Kennedy. The Vietnam War was becoming increasingly unpopular and there was the fear that my new young husband would be drafted to fight there."

"Maybe we all could have migrated to Canada as a group," I suggested absent conviction.

"Maybe," she laughed. "I remember feeling that I had left one culture to go live in another and then returned to a third culture that was totally unfamiliar. My husband and I chose to start our new life in San Francisco, which threw me into a vortex of the changes going on in 1968. The ground continued to shift under me, I was shell-shocked. I mean, there were things I loved, like the intense idealism and the great music, the 'free' universities, the colorful clothes, and the people trying new things in new ways. But there was a great sadness seeing my generation being pulled apart by the war ... those going to Vietnam with so many getting maimed and killed... and those refusing to fight resenting those who seemed to support the war. We were a country at war with one another."

"Just like today." Someone sadly murmured.

I was hit with a somber mood. "Yes, like we are today, so divided. It was sad... is sad. We all remember the hope and sense of commitment inspired by Kennedy's words, his vision, by the principles of Peace Corps itself. Now, it seems somehow to have slipped through some hourglass, nothing has been left to us except bitterness and division."

Janice looked at me. "Tom, you are the political one here. Are things better or worse now compared to the 60's?"

"No way to answer that. We could debate that for days. I suppose I can talk about what I feel. I feel more sadness than resentment or anger right now." I said, thinking I needed to clarify my thoughts. "Think about this. The country we left in 1967 was not united by any means. Apartheid was being dismantled but not willingly and only at the end of guns toted by national guardsmen and even federal troops on occasion. I often think we just didn't look hard enough, didn't want to see all our warts. The country to which we returned had revealed all its wounds. We could no longer ignore them. Would we have been willing to go off and sacrifice for such a flawed nation, had we really seen it for what it was? I don't know. One thing is different in my mind. Then, I still had hope for the future of this country. No matter the problems, I thought we could make things better."

"And now," she asked me.

"Now," I paused to consider what should come next, "that hope is largely gone."

Janice looked at me soulfully. "Let us pray that you are wrong, Tom. I have often asked myself how Peace Corps and India played out in my life. The idealism that led me to India stayed with me as I moved from San Francisco to Berkeley, to Sonoma County. Not only did I choose to work in non-profit agencies for the causes of health, childcare, and affordable housing, volunteerism also became a constant in my life. I learned flexibility living in a village in India that stayed with me. I never lost it. Perhaps it was better to ignore the ugliness around us, perhaps I employed some of my survival skills honed while in India back in the States. Perhaps it is better to focus on the small things we have some chance to change."

—

"One thing about me never changed." I started. "I've been told that I tend to let life come to me, that I never pursued it with any force or sense of direction. I suspect there is a modicum of truth in that. Virtually every major decision in my life was casually made or was something that just fell into my lap. I had heard about this urban affairs master's degree program at the University of Wisconsin–Milwaukee (UW–M) while we trained there for our Peace Corps escapade. Since I kind of knew about it . . . that naturally became the one academic program to which I applied from my exile in the Indian desert. So, in the fall of 1969, it was back to Milwaukee. In retrospect, I should have been more proactive. I thought urban affairs would teach me how to seduce city women, but it was all about politics, economics, and sociology. What a terrible disappointment!"

Mel laughed aloud. "There's a publication for men on *'how-to-pick- up women,'* I have several copies if any of you guys want one. It's a six-volume set though, with a tiny font. The equivalent for women, *'how-to-pick-up men,'* is only a paragraph long, a short paragraph with big font." He smiled as much laughter followed.

"Jest if you must, I always knew you women were undressing me with your eyes." I ducked in anticipation of incoming pretzels but there was nothing. They must have exhausted their throwing arms, or they were out of ammunition. "Okay, then, that Milwaukee program might not have been very rigorous, but I learned a lot and it proved a perfect segue for someone just back from Peace Corps who still wanted to save the world. It was the end of the 1960s and the energy of that period still could be felt even in a backwater place like Milwaukee. In the Urban Affairs Department, we had lots of kids from the east coast, Northern Jersey in fact. It was hard to explain, but there was a pipeline from a couple of colleges there to this program. They brought an eastern edginess to the niceness that was the Midwest which I liked. The program was stimulating for me... flexible, rather unstructured, and dealt with real life problems. You would take a smattering of courses in economics, sociology, political science, and so forth."

"Sounds perfect for a wanna-be revolutionary like you." Bob said.

"Yup, if you were aggressive enough, you could tie into any number of ongoing urban issues at a time when the memories of urban riots and unrest were yet fresh. In Milwaukee, open housing was the issue du jour. It struck me that the city had an Eastern feel in that it was divided up into ethnic and racial enclaves that were defined by rather impermeable boundaries. There was clearly a black ghetto on the north side of town, a Hispanic section on the near south side, a Polish section further south, a smaller Italian area on the near north side, and so on. Led by Father Groppi, one of those liberal Catholic priests that were common to that era, the protesters wanted African Americans to be able to move into Polish and other ethnic white, working-class neighborhoods. The tensions were electric with protests and marches and many shades of fear and hate. The other explosive issue that absorbed my attention during this period was the Vietnam conflict, a holdover issue from the sixties. Many of my urban affairs classmates were left leaning, particularly the ones from the east coast. The faculty also was mostly sympathetic to our leanings, especially the program director. While Milwaukee had been somewhat behind other hotbeds of protest like Madison down the road some eighty miles, it was catching up by this time. We started organizing teach-ins and discussions and other educational and protest actions. Inevitably, we shut down our department and the school, at least temporarily.

"Still the troublemaker, I see." Harry added but with admiration.

"Or just a foolish kid. One of my favorite memories from this period was my roommate at the time named Brad. He was about the most clean-cut kid you could imagine. He had graduated from Holy Cross which was the college I would have attended as a good Catholic boy had not circumstances, my try at becoming a Catholic priest, diverted me to that well-known den of Communists and other troublemakers called Clark University across town. Well, Brad was very reluctant to get involved in this protest stuff but maybe my bad example led him astray. When events were at their height, some of us first organized a vote to shut down the Urban

Affairs Department and then helped shut down normal university operations. That accomplished, the students tried to disrupt traffic on the main street adjacent to the school. Surely, that act would bring the national government to its knees. A host of law enforcement agencies, along with the National Guard, had been assembled to shut the protest down. It was high noon. Then I saw Brad standing above the crowd shouting instructions about how to protect yourself when the tear gas cannisters started to explode about us. What! Here was every mother's favorite son suddenly looking like some wild eyed radical. I belly laughed at the sight."

"I had no idea we were harboring such a dangerous character in our group." Paul said trying to look concerned but failing. "Should someone call the FBI?"

"I suspect the FBI knew about me at the time. I've always had some pretty liberal leanings and early on concluded that our intervention in Vietnam was insane. I first appeared before my draft board before heading to India, they wanted to check me out to see if Peace Corps was a dodge to avoiding military service. These boards were composed of crusty old men who seemed to look through you with unbelieving eyes. They had heard all the excuses from college shits like me. In the end, they let me go to India. Now that I was back in the States, my crusty old men were after me again. I was inching toward my twenty-sixth birthday, which would exempt me from the draft, but I wasn't getting there quickly enough. My notice to take my physical caught up with me in Milwaukee and so off I went."

"Hard to believe a sad sack like you would be acceptable." Paul tried.

"I know, but they were desperate for bodies. In any case, I was preparing some contingency plans in case they found, as you so aptly put it, a sad sack like me fit for service. I contacted an attorney to talk through my situation and started thinking about a conscientious objector plea. Though some elements from my background and past might give me some leverage, it was a long shot at best."

"Oh Tom, I went that route," Glen threw in. "It was not easy, let me tell you. They put me through the ringer, and I had to do alternative service. Still, I stayed true to my principles."

"Good for you. Not easy I suspect. I also began to think about Canada. Sitting here now, almost five decades later and totally disgusted with the Trump dominated drift of American politics, I almost wish I had been forced over the border back then. Today, I belong to a country club and have some good friends from Canada there who recently became American citizens. I keep asking them, *why are you doing this?* All the Americans in my circle are talking about where they will emigrate if Trump gets reelected in the future and the Republicans succeed in dismantling what remains of our democracy. Most want to head north, where sanity yet prevails. How quickly we can go from seeking things out to do for one's country to wanting to get away from it."

"What was their response?" Greg inquired. "I mean when you asked why they decided to become citizens here."

"They just smiled and said that they had not given up their Canadian citizenship. When things go into the crapper here, they can easily leave."

"It would be nice to have an out." Someone murmured but I missed who.

—

"My draft board caught up with me upon my return from India."

"Shit," Bob laughed, "they didn't know you like we did."

"Got that right! Nevertheless, I dutifully showed up for my physical. I never tried to trick out the exam by eating five thousand bananas or something to get my readings out of whack. Others attempted to be disruptive or otherwise display their unfitness for active duty in various ways. I did none of this. I was still the good boy who went off to study for the Priesthood after high school, even if briefly. I might protest, but I did so politely and with respect. I did what I was told during that physical. I used my own pee when asked to whizz in a cup, bent over and spread my cheeks when ordered to do so, answered all questions truthfully."

"Why does that surprise me?" Maureen looked puzzled.

"Just being the good Tom I guess. The fun began when I got to the written exams that tested your cognitive skills and assessed your character. The math and verbal part of the intelligence tests were quite easy. I did wonder if I could fail this miserably but assumed that they would be suspicious that an honors college graduate had an IQ of 45. Today, that might work but back then it would have been a stretch. On the other hand, I did struggle with that part of the test designed to assess your practical knowledge. They had questions like which of the set of tools on the left is most like the tool on the right side of the page. What? I had no idea what was going on there? I bet the farm kids aced that stuff. My IQ on this practical crap must have been 35 but that would not get me out. Hell, they probably would have assigned me to the motor pool."

"Just think, everyone, if they had taken Corbett, we all would be speaking Russian now." Paul noted, rather proud of his quip.

"Truer words were never spoken, which is amazing considering the source. So, they had these questions to smoke out subversives. They presented us with a long list of organizations and asked whether we had belonged to any of them. It looked very outdated to me with most options striking me as holdovers from the 1930s Spanish Civil War, though I might have joined one of these had I been alive then. The Abraham Lincoln Brigade was one of those listed. It was comprised of volunteers from other countries who signed on to defend the duly elected Republican Government in Spain. An armed coup had been mounted by the opposition fascists upset with the election results, an insurrection organized by dissident military groups under Generalissimo Franco and supported by Hitler and Mussolini. Now why would supporting a democratically elected group be on this list of threats to America, especially when the other side had the support of our country's sworn enemies in WWII?"

Sherry suddenly spoke up. "I followed Corbett on Facebook for a while. He had great political posts but then you disappeared. What happened?"

"The geniuses at Facebook disabled my account. I have never seen a more incompetently managed program as their community standards initiative, and I consulted on program design for human service systems across the U.S. and in Canada. When they disabled me, I had some 30,000 friends and followers and was adding something like 100 in a day. By the way, I restarted as Jim Corbett recently and quickly reached the limit of 5,000 friends. I am exceedingly popular with people who only know me from a distance."

Sherry bowed in my direction. "Ah, I did not realize I was in the presence of such a serial felon. Good work"

"Yes, you are indeed honored to know me. All of us who get thrown into the Facebook gulag feel special, it is proof you are doing something right."

"I agree." Sherry added.

"Now, on this list included in my draft exam I noticed that one prominent group from that era, the Students for a Democratic Society (SDS.), was missing. I had long ceased any connection with them as they spun down the toilet bowl of self-destructive nihilism. Still, I had belonged for a while in my college days and I was curious about their absence from a list that had not been updated since the days of Harry Truman. Then I came to an open-ended question that covered all the bases. It asked whether I had belonged to any organizations that advocated for the violent overthrow of the American government or was involved in other equally dastardly things. I assumed this was designed to catch evildoers who had been born after 1920. So, I raised my hand and asked a scowling sergeant, "Does SDS qualify under question Q?" His scowl grew even more menacing. "You bet your ass it does, buddy." That was clear enough I thought. I duly wrote in SDS in the space provided and gave it not another thought."

"Wait," Paul stopped me. "You should have asked if the Peace Corps was considered a subversive organization.

I laughed. "I'm sure it was for some of these military clowns, no discourtesy intended Stan."

"That's okay." I pretty much agree."

"Eventually, I made it to the end of the process where I was to hand in my now completed paperwork. The door to freedom was steps away. The soldier taking my stuff looked at my name, then at a list in front of him, and then up at me. He also had a scowl. The help that day clearly had not taken any Dale Carnegie courses. '*You report to the third floor,*' he barked. Wait, no one else in line had been told to go to the third floor. They were all exiting to freedom. This did not look good. Could they induct me into army on the same day as my physical?"

"Apparently not, since you are here." Tim suggested. "Surely you would have shot yourself in basic training."

"Got a point there, Tim. Obediently, I trudged up to the third floor where I was told to sit and wait. It looked like the high school vice-principal's waiting room where the delinquents were sent to ponder their impending doom. Of course, I surmised this only by rumor, having been a good kid throughout my youthful school days."

"You?" Maureen seemed shocked.

"I went bad later in life. So, after a decent wait, three men marched in and ordered me to follow them into the grilling room. They introduced themselves. Their titles and uniforms seemed different, but the word *intelligence* was involved in each organization they represented. From what transpired next, the word *intelligence,* I feel, had been wildly misappropriated."

"Corbett, please tell me you didn't pull your typical crap." Bob wondered.

"Me… not behave? How could you even think that? I am always a perfect gentleman"

"Yeah, sure." Paul sputtered. "And I'm the heir to the Russian Romanov throne."

I continued. "I will say that their questioning was exhaustive. They went on about where I had lived, who I knew, what nefarious people I hung out with, whether I was up to no good. They seemed to be taking this way too serious. When they asked me to identify all my sexual partners I considered the possibility that they were trying to develop a list of easy women. If any gal had willingly slept with this schmuck, they must have reasoned, she had no standards whatsoever. I should have made up about fifty names just to impress them and keep them running in circles. Damn, I just thought. I could have named you gals from 44-A now that I think about it. That would have been hilarious. A missed opportunity for sure."

"Hey…" Dee started to protest but I raised my hand.

"Still, I gave no names to my inquisitors, though some reference to a 'rack' left over from the Spanish Inquisition was mentioned as an inducement to get me talking. Mostly, though, I was doing my best to be cooperative. After all, I knew I was harmless. Toward the end, though, my instinct to be polite was drowned out by my desire for some fun. I can seldom resist that urge. My playful side really emerged when they zeroed in on the core issues. *'Okay, buddy, would you fight any and all enemies of the United States?'"*

"Oh brother!" Someone sighed aloud.

"You got it… I was in my element now. For such questions I would lean back in my chair and pause as if I were thinking extremely hard. *'Now, first, I think we had better establish what we mean by the word enemy.'* I was Clintonesque long before any of us knew Bill Clinton. They would kind of huff and puff and make comments about dropping assholes like me behind enemy lines. But that did not seem likely in the moment, though I was not as certain of my fate in a month or two. As they finally wound to a close, one of them confirmed my current address. When I responded positively, he noted that he was aware of that place and gratuitously added that *there is a lot of good-looking ass living in that building.'* Yeah, these guys were from some intelligence branch for sure."

"Really? That sounds like a hoot and a half." Mel was laughing.

———

"After, I realized I should have walked out before agreeing to this interrogation. Still, I must admit to having some fun with them. Great laughs. I heard nothing for several months and then got a letter saying that I had been found fit to serve in the U.S. military. Apparently, I was not enough of a terrorist threat to escape the draft. *'Damn,'* I thought, *'I should have made up scary stuff during the interview.'*"

"Didn't you worry about getting in real trouble." Maureen asked.

"Well, that was always a concern, a minor one though. I recall a guy from my old neighborhood. He was a bit older and had become an FBI agent while I was in college doing my anti-war stuff. I can't recall how our paths crossed but he pulled me aside one day and tried to convince me I was threatening my future. Maybe he thought I was becoming a Commie fellow traveler. More likely, he was just trying to help a dumb kid from the old neighborhood whom he thought had lost his way. I considered his remarks, but no way could I just discard my principles."

"Good man." Greg intoned.

"And I think that's another way Peace Corps helped. I was more confident by the time of my draft physical, a bit hardened to stuff. I had seen much more of the world and had looked deeply into who I was. In the desert you have a lot of time to think. Before India, life was a blur with school and work and protests and chasing women. Talk about a waste of time… the chasing women thing. In any case, I was yet feeling my way through life. I never had enough of a chance to reflect on important stuff. India gave me that precious commodity… time. There was plenty of time to think things through. I was more centered upon my return. My norms and values had solidified into a coherent moral compass. We all need that as we confront life."

"You escaped their clutches, I assume." Paul asked.

"Oh yes, otherwise you would be visiting me in Vancouver these days or joining me at one of my prison reunions. If I had looked hard at things, harder than I did, I might have headed north no matter the outcome of my battle with the draft. A gal I knew well as a doctoral student at Wisconsin became a prof at the University of Toronto. She was so happy up there, felt so much more at home than here. I could have had my career up there. Now, when I would really love to bail out on what the country has become, supporting Trump of all things, I must remain to take care of my spouse. As you know, she has dementia and is in a care unit. I do love her dearly and owe her so much. No way I could leave even though she is in good care. But my heart hurts when I look about me."

"A lot of us hurt now for our America."

"We came of age in the Cold War when the Doomsday clock was poised to strike midnight. Yet, I have never been more pessimistic about the future than I am now. Like the cartoon character Pogo once said, *'we have met the enemy and it is us.'*"

Connie spoke up softly. "Despite everything, Corbett, we know you have a good heart. You really do."

"Really? How do you know?"

"It's obvious," Laura responded. "You feel pain."

None of the other women contradicted her. For once, no pretzels came in my direction.

*Corbett, the rebel, a decade after Peace Corps
at the University of Wisconsin.*

CHAPTER 28

Carpe Diem!

The afternoon reluctantly was coming to an end. We had been at it for some time, though it only felt like a few moments inside our heads. As I searched for a topic that might wrap things up, a memory popped into my head. "I want to remind you again about that final train ride to Delhi, nothing to do with Mel and his eyes. We were in a reflective mood; our service was coming to a close. We all agreed, or so I thought, that we would make the PC brass understand the realities on the ground, *you betcha*... as Minnesotans would say. We needed volunteers with real expertise as opposed to kids with good intentions, A day or so later, we did a roundtable debriefing that was part of the normal exit processes. I was flabbergasted. One after another, you shits talked about your India experience in what I recall as overly glowing terms. So much for searing honesty. I struggled to make the points we agreed on. But none of you backed me up... wusses. I came across as a disgruntled whiner and, there I was, ready to throw my cap in the ring for a top PC job in Washington.

"You were?" Maureen looked concerned.

"Don't believe a word he says." Bob cautioned.

I just smiled. "Then again, there is no argument that I am a first-class whiner, a personal attribute my wife claimed for years I had mastered all too well. I recall a neighbor of mine once giving me a tee shirt with the words *'no whining'* on the front. Apparently, it was common knowledge all over Madison, or at least on my street. It was another strength of mine, like napping. If they make either of those Olympic sporting events, I am golden."

"That's okay Tom, we still love you, even if you are a putz." Laura offered without laughing.

"Flattery like that, my dear, will get you into my bed anytime."

"Oh yuck," she responded, but with a smile. "Last time I compliment you."

"Well, after my complaints about our Peace Corps sacrifices, essentially how we had been misused, were summarily disregarded, an Indian official awarded us certificates thanking us for our contributions. Nice gesture! The only problem was the darn thing said poultry! They never caught up with the fact that our program purpose had been changed some 3 years earlier, halfway through our training. I think their expressions of thanks would have looked more sincere had they gotten the damn program right. No one said anything, at least as I recall."

"That must have been awful." Maureen noted.

"Yes, but all was made worthwhile when we received the thanks from a grateful America on a piece of paper signed by President Richard M. Nixon himself. What an honor! This was before we knew what a crook he was but even then most of us had our suspicions. Yes, that accolade found a place on the wall right next to my commode until that fateful day I found I had run out of toilet paper. I was no longer using the *water and lota* method of heinie hygiene. My one official testimonial to good service rendered from a grateful President was put to better use. Perhaps if I had kept my *lota*."

"I kept mine." Mel smirked. "My *lota* that is, not that piece of paper from Nixon."

"Think about it." This came out of me as a sigh. "It was July of 1969. We were going home. But what kind of home would greet us? For two years, we witnessed what looked like, from afar, the dissolution of American society, rather like we are witnessing today. I would get my copy of Time magazine and devour it from front to back. We would listen to the BBC news on a radio we had. Sometimes, there was good news. I learned that the Red Sox won the pennant that first summer we were in service, something that I had waited for all my life. Of course, they blew the series but still. Most of what was happening seemed like a bad dream, one catastrophic event after another, one conflagration of rage and impotence in the face of insanity. From our far-off vantage point, it looked like the world according to E.E. Cummings where *the center cannot hold, and it all flies apart.*' India looked pretty damn good at that moment."

"You are so right. It did seem as if the world, or at least America, had disintegrated in our absence." Mel offered.

I raised my hand in emphasis. "But here's the thing. Seriously, I'm not sure I was right, back then, when I argued that Peace Corps had gotten it all wrong."

Paul looked amazed. "Whoa, a moment of clarity. What do you mean?"

"I mean, the design of our program was totally screwed up but perhaps that does not matter in the end." I looked about thoughtfully.

"I need more, Corbett." Bob pushed me.

"Obviously. What have we been saying all afternoon? We were the beneficiaries. We underwent the greatest change. Just look around this room. Perhaps we were the successes, all of us, India 44 and even the mutts from 40. We came back to a country that was suffering, right? A lot of kids were dropping out, getting high, becoming outcasts, going off to live in communes to exist off the land. Right, I wouldn't have lasted a freaking week trying that."

Several affirmations were heard.

"We came back hardened and, I argue, better able to contribute something positive. Even I did. We went over as young kids and returned as adults seasoned for the future in a special way. India surely wasn't transformed by our presence there, but we had been changed by India."

"Perhaps we were. It's something I've often noodled." Paul responded in little more than a whisper. "Perhaps Corbett is on to something, at long last."

"Well," Bob said slowly, "even a blind pig finds an acorn on occasion."

"I'll pass right over that insult." I rolled my eyes. "At the end of the day, we had become real agents of change. We would go back home and right things. I think back on some of us little more than idealistic kids then and what we later did with our lives. Damn, we misfits did some amazing stuff. Our subsequent lives might be characterized as promises fulfilled. Perhaps India and Peace Corps played a part in all that."

"You believe that?" Janice seemed doubtful.

"Not sure but just maybe. Consider this. Bob went on to get an M.B.A, from the Wharton School, and a Ph.D. in economics from NYU. His career stretched from being a banker in Paris to an economist with the Federal Reserve Board in DC. Tim, after getting a master's from Harvard, went to work at the United Nations with UNICEF. He worked with refugees seemingly in all the hot spots over the course of several decades. Greg went into the Foreign Service at the State Department. He served in several embassies and was transferred out of Tehran not long before the radical Islamic students took the staff as hostages in 1979. Ben stayed an additional year as a Peace Corps volunteer in India and worked in Africa for several years before starting his own business in the Bay Area, while still managing to get a Doctorate in Religious Studies. Harry first used Peace Corps as an inspiration to rise from a sharecropper's son to greater things. He became a high official in a national labor union and earned a Doctor of Divinity from Cambridge Theological Seminary. Doug got a Doctorate from Columbia in Indian Languages and Cultures and eventually became a managing director of business consulting firm. Glen was an excellent musician and artist. He also earned a Doctorate in Musical Arts from Stanford. He later wrote the book on the mathematical foundations of music and was one of the earliest employees of Apple Computer. And Mel eventually became the CEO of a non-profit that worked to bring automation to public libraries in the New England area."

"And you, Corbett, went on to teach at Wisconsin and run a national research thingy." Surprisingly, this came from Paul

"Thingy? But yes, and then consulted on poverty and social welfare issues across the country and in Canada. I know less about the gals, but a few things. Kay got her doctorate and taught at the college level as well as doing community development work in Appalachia. Sally also got her degree, in Social Welfare I think, and taught at a southern college. And Maureen got a doctorate from the University of Texas and, as a nursing professor at the University of San Diego, wrote a text on the topic widely used in nursing schools. Upon returning to the States, Peace Corps motivated Cate to get a nursing degree and only recently retired from the University of California- San Diego Medical Center. Connie earned an MSc. She devoted three decades as a counselor and member of the diagnostic team at the Hawaii School for the Deaf and Blind. Even her worthless husband, Paul, obtained a Ph.D. in Sociology. He then spent his life resolving organizational conflicts and helping people work together. I'm sure I missed people."

Janice sighed. "I almost feel like a failure. No more degrees, just work with non-profits doing work in housing and childcare."

"And I wound up working in the hotel industry, mostly catering." Laura added as if embarrassed.

"Hey," I almost yelled. "That was real work, unlike some of us who never left the academy. As I oft told my students, *the real world is highly overrated*. Besides, Laura, I literally worship the people who feed me."

She smiled.

Paul sighed. "I was going to say something about those poor students of Corbett, but I bet he was one hell of a teacher. Think about it, he is so full of BS."

"You know, you are right for a change. I was a damn good teacher and a better policy wonk. I learned at least one lesson from

Peace Corps that helped throughout life. You never know, you never know at the time what you are absorbing from any of life's experiences or challenges. It's only after the fact that you get it, sometimes long after the fact. So, look upon everything around you as a learning experience. And remember, you are a learning experience for all with whom you interact. We learned that, even if the lesson was painful at times."

"True enough." Harry agreed.

"And perhaps more significantly," I paused for emphasis. "you never know what you are leaving with others at the time. You don't always know how deeply you are impacting the people you touch. We only know what we took away from our experience in Peace Corps after it was all over, and not fully until we began to exchange our reflections and emotions in these reunions. More to the point, we will never know the legacy and lessons we left behind since we cannot see such things, at least not directly."

"Sad, but true." Paul commiserated.

"There is a simple poem that popped into my head one-day decades ago and I've never gotten it out of there no matter how hard I tried. Let's see. How does it go?"

I dropped a pebble in the sea,
and there a ripple came to be.
On some distant shore and bank,
the thirsty sand my ripple drank.

"Just a nonsense rhyme but it spoke to me about never knowing what you bring to things, to people, to life…"

"Corbett the poet," Bob smiled. "Byron, Keats, and Shelley better watch out."

"They are safe for sure, as is Glen, the real poet amongst us. But I am reminded of a conversation I had with a friend who served in South America in the early 1970s. She and her husband were supposed to be doing youth development projects in remote, rural schools. But they found that these schools were virtually non-existent. Teachers would show up occasionally to get their pay but seldom taught anything. For months, my friends didn't know what they should be doing."

"Now that sounds familiar. It wasn't just India then." Mel noted.

"Hell no. India was tough, no doubt. But some of the challenges were universal."

"What happened." Dee asked.

"Eventually, they decided to be proactive. They found some local collaborators and went about creating the very set of educational opportunities that were supposed to have been in place when they arrived. They developed a curriculum, did staff training for teachers, got them motivated, even got some school buildings erected."

"Great story." Mel added.

"The best part is yet to come. They went back several decades later and ran into a woman who thanked them for creating the opportunity for her to get an education. The school building that she had attended was named after the wife of this Peace Corps team though this woman attended this school well after the volunteers had returned to the states. She had just assumed her American benefactor had been old at the time all this good stuff had taken place, and likely had passed on. She was shocked to find out that the school had been named after a young American college graduate back then. This grateful woman told my friends that she never had a chance to go to college herself but, through the improved opportunities she experienced, had embraced the value of education. Each of her children had gone to college. She was so grateful."

"Wonderful." Someone uttered in a low voice.

"See, you never know. You really never know." I repeated the words though it probably wasn't necessary to do so.

"Maybe we weren't so bad for a bunch of total misfits." Connie offered.

"Absolutely!" I said. "If you took any random group of college graduates in 1966, you would not come up with such an interesting, accomplished, and eclectic group. Perhaps we would all have achieved the same successes even if we had not served in the Peace Corps. I suspect not though. Hell, we likely did some good even as we tramped around those fields like the clueless morons we were. As so many volunteers say, you take away far more than you ever contribute."

"Not hard when you contribute so little to begin with." Mel offered to considerable laughter.

I continued. "For the record, I enjoyed so many epiphanies in my Peace Corps experience as I sat on the edge of a desert in Rajasthan. While our ill-fated program was not the best laid plan of the American government, it gave us a lot of time to think about things, put our lives together, dream bigger dreams. I wrote a novel in India. Now, in my twilight, I'm back to writing. Doing it on the edge of the desert sparked a thirst in me that was never quenched, until now. Turning what was in my head into characters, thoughts, and events on a page truly is priceless."

"Despite all our joking around, we soldiered on." Mel smiled. "Or should I have said *plowed* on?" He chuckled at his own pun.

"And in doing so, we learned something priceless." I said distractedly.

"Pray tell, what might that be?" Bob inquired.

"A simple outcome, not a terribly profound insight by itself, yet it altered our lives. I think that Peace Corps got us all out of our provincial upbringings, our small worlds. It likely accelerated a process that started in college. We learned to see things in a different way, to appreciate the ravages of inequality more deeply, to appreciate other people more profoundly, and to seek creative ways to make a difference."

"Wait, how did the Corps thing affect you and your culture?" Tim asked. "Go over that again."

"Well, it was not until college that I first came across the first hints of cultural relativity. Now, I was interacting with kids from New York and other big cities who shared neither my assumptions about the world, my class biases, nor my religious indoctrination. I went through one epiphany after another while losing my simple ethnic, Catholic view of life's meaning (but not the guilt), my simple-minded patriotism, and my equally innocent notion that everyone both looked, and thought, just like me. The fact that not everyone saw the world as I did was a shocking revelation. And most of you talked funny, no accent or the wrong accent. This experience of your personal world view literally shattering and clanking about you in disarray is both frightening and disquieting. No wonder people bottle themselves up in hermetically sealed islands like gated communities or naturally occurring urban ethnic ghettoes."

"How true!" Janice expressed her thought aloud and then quickly signaled an apology.

"Then, from college, we went into training for the Peace Corps. Once again, we were thrown in with a very heterogeneous collection of young people of wildly different colors, classes, and backgrounds. Think about it, we had the kids from Yale, Columbia, and Berkeley along with kids from the smallest historically Black colleges you might imagine. The aspiring volunteers came from all parts of the country, from urban and rural settings, from well off, but no filthy rich, kids to dirt-poor families, and from every skin color and belief systems. Together, we were thrown in an intense environment where each of us competed, or so we thought, for a few spots in a program destined for exotic India. The training itself was designed to get us out of our normal selves. Some spent time on an Indian Reservations in South Dakota or northern Wisconsin, others in an urban ghetto. We were exposed to speakers and participated in exercises that exposed weaknesses in our dominant world view and helped us question that perspective."

"Yes," Harry exclaimed with meaning. "we all went through something like that, to some extent at least."

"Earlier we talked about one of our trainers asking us to consider where the Middle East was? Of course, it was a way of pushing us to ask ourselves *east of what.'* That was his real point, which led us into a long discussion of the notion of an ingrained sense of cultural superiority that none of us had questioned to that point. Perhaps the greatest epiphany was realizing that differences of color and class and cultural background did not fully determine the other. You, Harry, are a great example… a young black man who had grown up in a dirt poor, Baptist, share-cropping family. You went to college at a predominantly black southern institution where the students were far from the glib New York-raised leftists that I had befriended in college. Ordinarily, I never would have gotten to know you. Sure, I had some black friends in college, but they were from backgrounds like mine. In truth, they were way more middle class than I was. I was just this rough working-class kid. In Peace Corps, though, I found you, someone from a radically different culture. Better, I found you to be a kind and intelligent man with a huge heart."

Nanette broke-in. "You think your life was changed. I was a black young woman from the Milwaukee ghetto. That city was, and still is, just about the most segregated urban area in the country. Unbelievable! Remember when I first told you that our Peace Corps training was a revelation to me. Until that experience, like I said, I was totally convinced that all whites were hateful and racist. Then, I meet all of you. You all taught me so much." She said quietly. "Of course, a lot of whites are hateful and racist, just not all. I met some of the best through Peace Corps and it changed my life, made me a far better person."

"And you changed ours." Cate responded.

The doorbell rang at that very moment. It was a caterer bringing a great variety of Indian delicacies for our evenings repast. A few drifted off to help set things up and soon the aromas wafted our way. Most just sat, as if reluctant to let the discussion end.

As we tried to decide how to bring a finish to what had been a special afternoon, Ben spoke. "We are beginning to lose some of our group, really lose them. They are passing on. Others we have not been able to find and who knows what happened to them. We probably should grab on to what we have and treat all our memories as precious."

"Yes, yes!" There was a consensus.

Ben spoke but his voice caught, he was emotional. "Just a word about one of us that passed way too early. Milt was my closest friend in the group. He was such a talent. He was an excellent volunteer who had been permitted to extend a year. He was also a brilliant improvisational musician, linguist, pre-med student, sociologist, and home-grown philosopher. While we were struggling to learn Hindi and mastering simple sentences like *'where is the bathroom'* and *'please give me back my passport,'* he was coming ups with complex phrases like *'I've been doing such and such since coming fresh from the womb.'*"

I spoke up, my own voice catching a bit. "Damn, I loved that guy. He was such an original… such a gentle soul; You could literally feel the goodness in him. I'm sorry for being even more clueless than usual, what happened to him again?" An image of him with his violin popped into my head.

Ben sighed audibly, struggling with his emotions. "He never adjusted stateside. Back in the Bay Area, he became a street musician in San Francisco. He made enough money to get by, along with a small stipend from a trust fund left by his parents. But he had no friends or family connections around him and became increasingly isolated and, in some ways, disturbed. With all that promise, he wound up drifting."

"Goddamn, that's sad." Bob uttered with passion.

"He would visit me. I would encourage him to get help… to no avail. I remember, he stopped one day. I was so busy preparing for important exams. I told him we would have to connect another time. I never saw him again. I found out much later that he jumped off an eight-story building to his death. I've never escaped the guilt."

I suspect all of us wanted to say something banal like *'it wasn't your fault,'* or *'some never fully recovered from their service overseas.'* Such sentiments seemed, in that moment, weak indeed. What I did say was the following. "There was a cost to our long-ago service, no doubt about that, and some portions of that cost took a long time to become visible." I looked at Stan. "Not all the victims of the Nam conflict are on the wall in D.C. Not all the consequences of service in India were positive, nor manifested in the short term."

"The guilt is inescapable." Paul added. "We had guys who struggled. After, you would ask yourself what you might have done. Worse, you blame yourself for not doing it."

I get it," Connie said. "Corbett mentioned that movie with the line *'the hard is what makes it great.'* The whole India and Peace Corps thing never would have such an impact, nor stayed with us so long if it had not been so hard."

Dee sighed. "Your right, of course. The hard got too much, though, way too much on occasion."

"And, at other times, it gave us gifts that were priceless." Harry said softly as if he were talking to himself.

"There are few unambiguous positives in life." I next searched for some way to bring the afternoon to a close. "Whatever we experienced, no matter how we net out the good and bad, I hope that original Peace Corps spirit is never lost. Future generations of kids, and maybe even some older kids like us, need what we had. I want at least some young people today to put aside the usual obsessions like making money. I want them to journey to the ends of the earth in search of adventure and, just perhaps, make a little bit of difference in the lives of others not so fortunate. In the end, the young of today should try to make a ripple or two of our own, even when they cannot see the effects until they are old farts, like us."

"Come and get some food," came a shout from the other room.

I picked up my folder. "Listen, before we end, I have something that Donald, our esteemed training director, wrote in a letter which we put in one of our edited volumes. He thought it important enough to share. Here it is."

The significance of Peace Corps does not lie in large or visible projects with easily measured markers of success. No, the significance of Peace Corps is found elsewhere...in much smaller things like the personal relationships we developed with those we met in our host sites and in the bonds forged with fellow volunteers. It is about modest contributions we might make in villages and city slums largely invisible to the wider world, tiny gifts to others unnoticed at the time. And perhaps most importantly. Peace Corps is about understanding life in some broader sense including how we came to view ourselves and how willingly each of us embraced subtle lessons that we then treasured for the remainder of our lives.

There was a silence where no one said a word.

"Many a time I've thought back to why I chose, why we all chose, the Corps in the first instance. I suspect that we were a bit different from our peers. We wanted change, in ourselves and in the world. I have listened carefully to you all talk and I can see how similar we all were to one another in one respect. Though our individual worlds were distinct in accidental ways, and we all were uniquely shaped by our early cultures, something inside each of us compelled us to seek out things beyond our own boundaries. Each of us thirsted for a different and better world."

Then Harry spoke. "I feel an amazing camaraderie with those who were part of this grand adventure. We shared a common idealism, sense of frustration, similar experiences, and the knowledge that we were fundamentally changed by our time on the other side of the world. That sense of connection will remain a constant for the rest of our lives. It will for me, I can promise you that."

Then Mel spoke, almost as an afterthought. "You know what, it really did seem like a good idea at the time. It was *our grand adventure.*"

Carpe Diem!

Milt… and all those fondly remembered but no longer with us.

All organizations suffer from institutional sclerosis. Peace Corps is no exception. The early *elan* wanes. The initial visionaries pass on, or get bored, or seek new policy mountains to climb. Initiative and risk-taking decline slowly, imperceptibly as the impulse toward growth and change gradually is replaced by concerns about maintenance and turf protection. These are universal trends, found in both the public and private spheres. Even places that pride themselves on being innovative and ahead of the curve are not immune. Ever try to change anything within the dominant culture of the academy, those university shelters where intellectuals hide from the real world. Good luck with that!

A note of concern was raised almost two decades ago when a 2002 report issued by the U.S. General Accountability Office (GAO) contained a scathing review about volunteer safety. Those serving in the field often were assigned blame for instances of physical and sexual abuse, simply to shift culpability from the organization itself for lapses in management and oversight. A few years later, a group of concerned ex-volunteers began arguing that the parent organization had evolved into a top-down, command and control bureaucracy beset with vertical rigidities and overregulation. Innovation and performance had been replaced by an obsessive concern with avoiding any negative publicity. One critic mused that Peace Corps had become a *'Peter Pan'* program which had lost its way, no longer really knowing what it was supposed to be or how to fulfill its mission.

In 2007, U.S. Senator Chris Dodd, a former volunteer himself, introduced the Peace Corps Volunteer Empowerment Act. The core principle of this bill was simple. Reshape the agency from a typical government bureaucracy into what it had first been envisioned to be. Dismantle the hierarchical architecture currently in place and transform the existing Weberian bureaucracy into a flatter, adaptive, and more responsive structure. Essentially, redo the program into a bottoms-up institution where volunteers could participate in those decisions that impact how they function on the ground. Peace Corps brass opposed the Act and it went nowhere at the time.

The debate about whether Peace Corps management has lost its way has a familiar ring to it. What system, public or private, doesn't defend what it sees as its basic functions and core technologies… what it has been doing in the past. Survival, after all, is an ultimate and unquestioned marker of institutional success. For example, petroleum companies fight the overwhelming evidence of global warming, and the human contribution to it, to preserve short-term returns on investments and forestall being stuck with what are called *'stranded assets.'* If humanity must be sacrificed down the road so that the next stockholder report looks good and equity prices are maintained, so be it. Their year-end bonuses are all that matter.

We expect little else from the private sector which is driven by shallow and mundane purposes. But this is Peace Corps. It is supposed to be different. It was not created to be a mini State Department or Foreign Service or the U.S. Aid bureaucracy or any kind of private enterprise initiative whose compelling rationale is to make a buck and appease investors no matter the larger costs. It was not supposed to be just another bureaucracy. Peace Corps was supposed to be an idea, an ideal, and a vision. It was not intended to be a program or an agency. It is supposed to be a place where dreams thrive and where visions of a better world can be nurtured. As Eleanor Roosevelt once said, *'the future belongs to those who believe in the beauty of their dreams.'*

A vision articulated by Sargent Shriver, an early inspirational leader, has echoed through the ages. Peace Corps, he argued, actualizes…

the idea that free and committed men and women can cross, even transcend, boundaries of culture and language, of alien traditions and great disparities of wealth, of old hostilities and new nationalisms, to meet with other men and women on the common ground of service to human welfare and human dignity.

A simple concept; a compelling idea! The world yet needs such a vision. We should never permit it to die. In a recent article, Baktash Ahadi, a combat interpreter for U.S. forces in Afghanistan commented on the collapse of the Western-oriented government in that beleaguered country after some two decades of war. He thought the explanation for the Taliban's swift rise to power simple to understand. The American initiative was misdirected. It was all about power and money. What was missing was a deeper understanding of the country's culture and some appreciation of how ordinary Afghans saw life and what was important to them. The author directed his observations to the Peace Corps community. He understood what Peace Corps was all about, or should be at least, understanding the hearts and minds of others. That was the driving motivation behind the program in 1961 and is just as critical today. Ironically, the Peace Corps is expected to expand into Vietnam in 2022, several decades too late but better late than never.

Confucius is reported to have said that *'Real knowledge is to know the extent of one's ignorance.'* Those of us who shared our memories in this volume were young and naïve as we journeyed overseas, even though we were well-meaning. Radically different cultures, the challenges of village life, and the struggle to contribute in complex technical arenas that remained foreign to us, all served to affirm our shortcomings and highlight our inadequacies. As revealed in our shared stories, we became all too aware of our personal struggles.

We reacted to the pain and uncertainty that we felt in different ways. Some withdrew into our private spaces, sometimes shutting out the people around us. On occasion, tensions surfaced with the people with whom we shared a site as we struggled to negotiate the demands placed upon us. On occasion, we even lashed out at locals who invaded our privacy in public places or in our own homes away from home, or who behaved toward us in ways that suggested contempt or ridicule. Such things did not happen often, yet it would be disingenuous to ignore the reality of our limitations or our essential humanness.

In hindsight, it strikes us as better to face such realities early in life, though that may not always be the case. Assigned to isolated rural sites, there is more time to acknowledge weaknesses or aspects of our personalities that might need just a bit of polishing, along with greater opportunities to do just that. Peace Corps was perfect for such task. There was also time to think through who and what you might become. You were stretched in ways you would never, or not likely, experience in the comfort of your own culture and in a world largely devoted to muting the sharper edges of most hardships. In the crucible of this alien world, on our own, absent the usual supports, we either swam or sank. Perhaps there were other ways to get such an opportunity to evolve and grow but few come to mind.

Hidden amidst this debris of self-doubt and second-guessing, though, might well lie the real reasons we persisted in our mission on the other side of the world. For all our deficiencies and frailties, we showed the people of India a different kind of America and Americans. From movies and the media, they saw an America of violence and exploitation, a people who too often used power and arrogance to get what they wanted no matter the cost to others. In contrast, here were some Americans who lived among them, simply and without much pretense. Here were Americans who shared their lives and difficulties at the rawest levels. Here were Americans who tried to help, without apparent gain or advantage. If we left only a single enduring contribution, it might well have been a more balanced and favorable image of who we were as human beings with the mask of cultural superiority stripped away and discarded.

In doing that, we opened ourselves to new experiences and challenges barely perceived at the beginning of our journey. Our tenure on the other side of the world remained a time out of time in which we experienced humor, doubt, success, embarrassment, loneliness, connection, understanding, and bewilderment. We endured a kaleidoscope of sensory and emotional assaults that it might take others a lifetime to accumulate. But, to a person, no matter how difficult the struggle, we felt we emerged as better human beings, or at least different. Perhaps that was all we could expect. Perhaps that was enough.

As I said at the outset, this is not a memoir as such. It is a set of imperfect recollections of actual events and raw feelings conveyed through semi-fictionalized characters in an imagined communal setting. These shared stories and vignettes, I must remind the reader, are only as authentic as our imperfect memories permit. The hope was that this sharing of recollections and emotions would impart some sense of what it meant to *serve* in those early Peace Corps days, when the program was brash and young, and when we, though largely clueless, were infused with great spirit and motivated by noble sentiments.

I am reminded of a scene from Shakespeare's Henry the 5th. As the much smaller English army prepared to meet a better equipped French force of overwhelming numbers, the Bard put these words into the King's mouth.

> *We few, we happy few, we band of brothers*
> *For he today who sheds his blood with me…*
> *Shall be my brother.*
> Henry V – Eve of St. Crispin's day battle, 1415.

Yup, that was India 44, an optimistic band of brothers and sisters in way over our heads. Underdogs for sure, we shed more emotional trauma than physical blood. Yet, that sense of sacrifice and the bonding that emerges from it is no less real. History records that Henry's forces totally routed the French that day, a quite remarkable victory. I believe our successes in Peace Corps, *our grand adventure*, proved to be far less dramatic in the moment yet far more consequential throughout our lives.

Thomas J. Corbett is emeritus senior scientist and a long-time affiliate of the Institute for Research on Poverty at the University of Wisconsin–Madison, where he served as associate and acting director for a decade before his retirement. He received a doctorate in social welfare from the University of Wisconsin and taught various social policy courses there for many years in the School of Social Work. During his long academic and policy career, he worked with governments at all levels including a stint in Washington, DC, where he helped develop President Clinton's welfare reform legislation. He has written scores of articles and reports on poverty, social policy, and human services issues and given hundreds of talks across the nation on these topics. In addition, Dr. Corbett has consulted with numerous local, state, and federal officials on various poverty, welfare, and human services issues both in the United States and Canada. Among many other things, he has testified before Congress, worked with the Wisconsin and other state legislatures on important social issues, consulted with many local governments, and served on an expert panel for the National Academy of Sciences. His most recent fictional works include ***Palpable Passions, Ordinary Obsessions, and Felicitous Fates.*** In 2022, he reworked and rereleased his first fictional work under the title ***Choices.*** His sole-authored works include several non-fiction books: ***A Clueless Rebel, A Wayward Academic: Reflections from the policy trenches***, and ***Confessions of an Accidental Scholar.*** He has also co-authored several works and written too many book chapters and scholarly pieces to mention. His latest academic work, the 2nd edition of ***Evidence Based Policymaking: Envisioning a new era of theory, research, and practice*** was coauthored with Karen Bogenschneider and released by Routledge Press in early

2021. Now retired, the author resides in Madison, Wisconsin. You can find more information at www.booksbytomcorbett.com

Author and his long-suffering spouse (she is a Saint).